THUNDERLAND

Brandon Massey

THUNDERLAND

DAFINA BOOKS
KENSINGTON PUBLISHING CORP.
http://www.kensingtonbooks.com

DAFINA BOOKS are published by

Kensington Publishing Corp.
850 Third Avenue
New York, NY 10022

All Kensington Titles, Imprints, and Distributed Lines are available at special quantity discounts for bulk purchases for sales promotions, premiums, fund-raising, and educational or institutional use. Special book excerpts or customized printings can also be created to fit specific needs. For details, write or phone the office of the Kensington special sales manager: Kensington Publishing Corp., 850 Third Avenue, New York, NY 10022, attn: Special Sales Department, Phone: 1-800-221-2647.

Dafina and the Dafina logo Reg. U.S. Pat. & TM Off.

First Dafina trade paperback printing: December 2002
First Dafina mass market printing: November 2003

10 9 8 7 6 5 4 3 2 1

Printed in the United States of America

In memory of Chester Massey, my grandfather,
who taught me how to dream.

CHAPTER ONE

Even though Jason Brooks awoke from the most frightening nightmare in his life on that June morning, the real terror began only a few minutes later, when he entered the bathroom for the first time that day.

Curled up in a fetal position, hands fisted, heart pounding, Jason awoke lying in the cool darkness underneath his bed. He blinked, disoriented. Shards of dream images gleamed in his mind like fragments of a shattered mirror. As he blinked several more times, fully regaining consciousness, the images faded, vanished into the blackness that washed away all bad dreams. Gradually, his heartbeat slowed.

He became aware of his throbbing jaws. Rubbing his face with his hand, he opened and closed his mouth, relaxing the tense muscles. His teeth had been clenched, as if to bite back a scream.

Finally, he rested his head on the soft carpet.

It had been the nightmare again.

For the past three months, he'd had the dream at least once a week. Utterly terrifying, it always concluded in the same fashion: he awakened curled in a ball under the bed, heart hammering, hands squeezed into fists, and teeth clamped together. Frightened to the marrow.

He didn't understand the dream. He couldn't figure out whether it was a chilling vision of the future or only a twisted creation of his overactive imagination. He'd never mentioned the dream to anyone. Telling someone about it would make it more real; keeping it private made it easier to ignore. He hoped the series of nightmares ended before someone discovered him cowering under the bed, shaking like a little kid, though he was clueless about exactly *how* he could make the dreams stop.

Resolving to forget about the nightmare and get his day rolling, he began to squirm from underneath the bed. When he was halfway out, the door opened.

Oh, no, he thought. *Busted.*

"Good morning, sleepyhead," Mom said, poking her head inside. "What on earth are you doing under there?"

"Uh, looking for my birthday presents." He pulled his legs out from under the bed and got to his feet. His fourteenth birthday was coming soon, so he used it to create a half-believable story. "But I didn't find any gifts. Where did you hide them, Mom?"

Mom stepped inside, her eyebrows arched questioningly. "You're kidding."

"I'm serious."

"You were really under there looking for gifts?"

"Yeah. Sometimes the best place to hide something is right under a person's nose. Like that old detective story about the letter. What's the name of it?"

" 'The Purloined Letter,' by Edgar Allan Poe." A full-time freelance writer with a bunch of romance novels to her credit, Mom seemed to know the details of every story that had ever been written. She leaned against the doorway, arms crossed, head cocked sideways as she regarded him. Although

Jason felt strange admitting it, he clearly saw why everyone said his mother was beautiful. Linda Brooks was a petite woman, blessed with flawless mahogany skin, dark, curly hair, and large brown eyes. She was dressed for the season in a flower-patterned blouse, matching skirt, and sandals. He supposed he could understand why guys stared at her whenever she walked past, though it felt odd to think about his own mother as being pretty—especially considering all the dirty secrets he knew about her.

"I'm in the mood to do a little detective work myself," Mom said. She tapped her lip. "Hmmm . . . something tells me this has nothing to do with birthday presents. I'm thinking that you were actually sleeping under the bed."

There was no way he was going to tell her about his nightmare. Sitting on the mattress, he scratched his head, acting dumbfounded by her suggestion.

"Why would I do something like that, Mom?"

"I don't know. You tell me."

"I can't tell you anything. Because I didn't do it."

"Okay, I'm a mother, Jason. Ever heard of mother's intuition? I feel as if you're hiding something from me."

"I feel as if you're hiding something from me, too," he said. "My birthday presents."

She shook her head. "You're something else."

"Mom, I don't know what you're talking about. I told you the truth. Why don't you believe me?"

"I'm only concerned about you. Is it wrong for a mom to be worried about her son?"

"It is if she's only faking."

Mom ran her fingers through her hair. She frowned.

"Let's not go down that road, okay? I'm really not in the mood to argue with you."

"Oh, I forgot. You won't be in the mood to argue until you get drunk."

"What are you saying? You know I don't drink anymore."

"Yeah, right."

"I haven't had a drink since March."

"You could change."

"I'm not going to fall back into those old habits. I mean it."

"So? You've meant it before, then went right back to being a drunk."

"Jason, I'm not denying that. I've made those mistakes plenty of times, and I'm ashamed to admit it. But I've changed, honey. I have a new set of priorities."

"You're going to try a new brand of whiskey?"

"Watch it, boy. I'm not going to tolerate much more of that smart mouth of yours."

"Fine." He shrugged. Although he knew it was wrong, he enjoyed talking back to her. She claimed that she was a new Mom, and as part of her revamped attitude she was determined to keep her cool, so he said whatever he wanted to her until she drew the line. Being a smart-ass was payback for the way she'd treated him in the past. His bold, bratty comments even surprised him sometimes. The old Mom would've popped him in the mouth before he completed a sentence.

"Now, my new priorities have nothing to do with drinking," Mom said. She pulled the swivel chair away from Jason's desk and sat in it, rotating so that she faced Jason. *"You're* one of my new priorities. I want to be a good mother to you because you're a good kid, and you deserve the best I can give you. Showing you that I love you is the most important thing in my life. With that as my goal, I can't afford to ever drink again."

"Yeah, yeah," Jason said. "Right. Heard it all before."

"Listen, I don't expect you to believe me overnight," Mom said. "I know you feel a lot of bitterness. But everyone wants to be loved. You might resent me for how I treated you, but I still believe you want me to love you. You're not above those feelings, honey."

Jason looked away from her. He regretted that he'd let her open this subject. For the time being, she was taking this new-Mom act of hers seriously: talking to him as though she were interested in his life, cooking for him, buying him things, and doing a bunch of other crap that would supposedly convince him that she cared about him. She had begun this act that past March, when he had fallen out of the oak tree in the backyard and suffered a serious head injury. Immediately rushed to the hospital, he'd lain totally unconscious for three days.

Mom had been at his side throughout the ordeal. According to her, watching him lie in a coma for three days had awakened her buried motherly instincts. When he returned to consciousness, from the expression on her face, one would think he had been resurrected. Although he had not suffered any brain damage and was as healthy as ever, since the accident Mom had treated him as if his birth had been predicted by prophets and celebrated by the court of heaven.

But she didn't faze him. It was all a bunch of bull and wouldn't last. She was right to think that he wanted love, but she was wrong to assume that he wanted *her* love. She could tell him she loved him until her face turned purple, and she could kiss him on the forehead until her lips rotted off, but his memories of how she had treated him before his accident were so vivid that he wanted nothing from her except food, clothes, and a bed. She could keep all this new-Mom garbage to herself and stop wasting his time.

"Everyone wants to be loved," Mom said. "Even you. Especially you."

Jason looked at the clock above the desk. "Mom, it's nine o'clock. I should be getting dressed. I have a lot of things to do today."

Mom walked to the door. "Okay, I can accept rejection. I'm a big girl."

"Yeah, whatever." Jason rose. "I need to pee."

"Of course," Mom said. "It's time for me to go, anyway. I'm meeting your father at the restaurant."

His dad owned an upscale soul-food restaurant called The House of Soul. It was the only place like it in Spring Harbor. In fact, it was the only good soul-food joint around until one reached Chicago, forty miles south. For that reason, The House of Soul was always packed with customers—and Dad was always there, running the show. Jason usually saw his father only once a week.

"Well, tell him that his son says hello," Jason said. "That is, if he remembers his son."

Mom nodded. She usually declined to discuss his father's constant absence, maybe because it somehow reflected on her. Jason did not know. His parents' relationship puzzled him—mostly because they did not seem to have a relationship.

Mom left the room. He heard the door downstairs slam shut. He stood at the window and watched her roll her blue Nissan Maxima out of the garage, then drive away down the street.

Finally, he was alone.

Needing to empty his full bladder, he hurried to the bathroom. He clicked on the light switch.

When he saw what was in there, he stopped. He gaped at the spectacle in front of him, his heart halting in midbeat, his body as motionless as a mannequin.

Slowly, he shut his eyes. Then he opened them.

It was still there.

The back of his neck grew cold and damp.

A large mirror covered the wall above the sink. Upon the glass surface, a word had been scrawled in red, in huge block letters:

REMEMBER

He stared at the word, breathless.

Remember.

Remember what?

As far as he knew, he had not forgotten anything.

With a trembling hand, he reached toward the mirror. He touched one of the letters, rubbed slightly.

The letter smeared. It had been written with a marker. He had half expected blood.

But who had done this? Mom? The idea that she would do it seemed totally unbelievable. If she had wanted him to remember something, she would have told him, not written the word on a mirror. When she was sober, she was the most practical person he knew. And when she was drunk—and Jason knew that she had not drunk anything recently—she was obsessive about cleaning the house. She would have never done this under any circumstances.

The possibility that his father might have done it was even more remote. Dad lived at his job and rarely came home. Jason did not bother to consider him as a suspect.

So who was left? Who else had access to their bathroom?

No one Jason knew.

Then it must have been a stranger.

At the thought, a chill swept through him, sank into his bones.

The recurring nightmare was weird. But on the scale of strangeness, it was nothing like this. He searched for a logical explanation, and he could not find one. It just did not make sense.

Again, he stared at the mirror.

Remember.

Who had done this? When? And why?

Remember.

What was he being told to remember? Something? Or someone?

He gazed at the message longer.

The longer he looked at those blood-red letters, the less it seemed like a message. Instead, it began to seem like something else entirely. A warning.

CHAPTER TWO

Linda Brooks sat in a corner booth at The House of Soul, waiting for her husband, Thomas, to take a break from his work and speak to her. Since Thomas rarely planned talks, Linda knew it would be about something important. But she didn't know whether to look forward to, or dread, the imminent conversation.

Thomas was busy checking on customers. Linda sipped her coffee and looked around, trying not to dwell on what the next few minutes might bring.

At nine-thirty in the morning, the large dining room teemed with people. Diners were eating sausage, bacon, country ham, buttermilk biscuits, eggs, potatoes, pancakes, rice topped with red-eye gravy, grits, and other delicious-smelling yet fattening foods that Linda had to use all of her willpower to resist. Discussion of the latest political scandal dominated the conversation at many tables. An old Temptations song played on the stereo system, loud enough to be appreciated but low enough not to impede talk. Autographed photos of celebrities adorned the walls, alongside quality pieces of contemporary African-American art.

In the midst of it all stood Thomas, keeping the restaurant as orderly as a five-star luxury resort. Regardless of her feelings about this place, she admired what he had accomplished. He had built this business into a genuine success.

Finally, he settled opposite her at the table. Even after fifteen years of marriage, he remained the most striking man she had ever seen. He stood six-feet-four and weighed about 220 pounds, every ounce of which seemed to be muscle. His smooth chocolate complexion and his chiseled features would have guaranteed a successful career as a fashion model, if he had so desired. He wore a white silk shirt, hand-painted silk tie, dark-blue slacks, and Italian loafers. His goatee was trimmed, his hair was short and wavy, and his fingernails looked as if they had recently been manicured. He smiled; his teeth sparkled.

Sometimes Linda thought that if Thomas put as much effort into their marriage as he put into looking good on the job, she would be the happiest woman alive.

"Sorry to keep you waiting, but we're pretty busy this morning," he said. "If business stays at this pace, in a couple of years, we'll be able to buy your dream house. And if your book does as well as I think it will, we might get it even sooner."

She smiled. Over the past thirteen years, she had published ten paperback romance novels, most of which had sunk so deeply into obscurity they'd be difficult to find in the world's biggest used-book store. Her novel-in-progress, however, was her most ambitious project ever, an intricate family saga with bestseller potential. She bubbled whenever she imagined the possibilities.

But her smile really arose from Thomas's supportive words. She could not remember the last time he had encouraged her. She leaned forward a bit more, playfully tapped his fingers.

"What did you want to talk about, Thomas?"

"Oh, general things." He scribbled on a napkin with his Mont Blanc pen, his eyes lowered. "Us, Jason, the future . . ."

"Well, that's nice," she said, frowning a little. "Can you be more specific?"

He shrugged and kept scribbling.

She leaned back in her seat, shaking her head. If Thomas were a book, his covers would be perpetually cracked wide open.

"What did you mess up?"

He dropped the pen, looked at her. "Who said I messed up anything?"

"Don't play dumb. I know you did something."

"I was only thinking about our dream house. Is it against the law for a man to think?"

"What did you do?"

"I didn't do anything. Damn, why are you always trying to read my mind? You know I can't stand that."

"Look, let's cut the crap. If you don't stop hedging right now, I'm gonna get up and leave."

"All right, all right." He leaned back and gazed at the table. He exhaled deeply.

Her stomach tensed.

"I lost the tickets," he said.

"You what?"

"The tickets to see Luther Vandross next week. Third-row seats, center stage. I lost them."

She knocked over her coffee.

The steaming coffee spread across the table, but she didn't clean it up. She stared at him.

"I don't believe you."

He avoided her gaze, silent.

"As much as I wanted to go . . . I don't believe you."

He still looked away from her. Then, finally, he faced her.

When she saw his brown eyes, she didn't need to hear anything else on this subject. It was the same story. He had lost the tickets because of plain, dumb negligence. He would give a long-winded excuse, then promise that the next time they planned an outing, everything would run perfectly. "Next time, baby"—that was his favorite phrase in these situations. She had been hearing it for ten years, ever since his daddy had given him this restaurant. Next time, baby.

She was tired of waiting for next time.

As a matter of fact, lately, she had been seriously wondering if she wanted to stay around waiting for next time. Their present relationship wasn't what being married was all about—at least, not *happily married*. They didn't kiss each other good morning. They didn't periodically talk on the phone during the day as they worked their jobs. They didn't sit together at dinner and share their daily experiences. They didn't snuggle on the couch in front of the TV. Unless you considered once a month a thrilling sex life, they didn't have much sex, either. About the only thing they did together was argue, and since whatever she told him always went in one ear and out the other, it was almost as if she were arguing with herself anyway.

She admitted that she had not made any major efforts to repair their marriage. Why bother when he lived for his job? He worked from six in the morning until eleven at night, seven days a week, holidays included. How could you get through to someone that fanatically committed to his work?

Answer: You couldn't. It frustrated her endlessly, because she loved Thomas and wanted them to be happy. She had thought the Luther Vandross concert would give them an opportunity to enjoy each other's company for a little while, but look where that idea had gotten her. Nowhere, where she'd been sitting for ten years.

But a woman could only take so much, and she had taken

all she could bear. She was determined not to let him settle this matter with his patented excuses. She was either going to find those tickets herself or discover what the *real* problem was here. Even if the truth was worse than she imagined.

"I'm so sorry." With a napkin, Thomas mopped up the spilled coffee. "I can't figure out what I did with those damned tickets. I'd really wanted to go to that concert, too. I promise, next time—"

"Where did you keep them?" she said.

"The tickets?" He finished cleaning the table. "I kept them in different places—"

"Did you ever keep them in your office here?"

"Yeah, but—"

She got up and marched to the back of the dining room.

Before she opened the office door, he touched her shoulder.

"I've already looked in there. No luck."

"I'll look myself." She shrugged off his hand.

The room was a model of neatness. A highly polished oak desk devoid of clutter. Built-in bookshelves in which the contents stood ruler-straight. A tall file cabinet. Gleaming beige tile. The scent of pine disinfectant.

She tore open a desk drawer and shuffled through papers.

"Why did I trust you with those things?" she said. "You always pull shit like this. I should have known better than to leave them with you. I should have kept them myself."

"Woman, you're making a mess." He shut the door, nudged her aside, and began reorganizing the desk. "I told you they're not in here, and I'm not gonna let you wreck my place."

She spun, yanked open a file cabinet drawer. She burrowed through the contents. Papers spilled out.

He cursed, gripped her arm.

"Get control of yourself. The tickets aren't in here."

"Looking again won't hurt."

"Yes, it will hurt, because you're not really looking. You're just ripping through shit, scattering important information left and right. I can't let you do that. This is a business I'm running here."

She snatched her arm from his grasp.

He grabbed her again.

"Let go of me."

"Get yourself together."

"I am together. Let go of me."

"Not until—"

"What the hell's wrong with you? You let go of me now, or so help me Jesus I'll make a fool of both of us in front of all those people out there."

She pulled her arm.

He held tight.

"Linda, please. Cool off. It's only a concert, not anything worth having a big fight over. We'll do something better next time. Getting mad about this is stupid."

And that was the main problem here, and, by extension, with their marriage: his feelings had died. Concerts aren't big deals, so don't be stupid and get mad if we can't go. I forgot your birthday? Well, sorry, it's just another workday as far as I'm concerned, but if it makes you stop complaining, I'll give you a card, how's that? What, you want to have sex tonight? Woman, who do you think I am, the Six-Million-Dollar Man? I told you I'm tired, I'm going to bed.

The examples went on forever. Try to get him to see the error of his ways, and he'd look at her as if she had spoken her suggestion in Swahili. He was nothing like the Thomas she had married. *That* man had made it possible to believe in every sweet love song that had ever rolled from a smooth balladeer's lips. She had hung on this long because she had hoped that the old Thomas would one day reappear. But maybe she was fooling herself. This man looming over her was a far cry from the man she had fallen in love with. This man was a stranger.

A heartless stranger.

As she gazed into his suddenly unfamiliar eyes, her heart pounded.

"Did you hear me?" he said. "Get yourself together."

He shook her a little.

"Did you hear me?"

He shook her harder.

"Get yourself together."

Her eyes narrowed. The old Thomas would have never done this. And no man was going to beat her.

He reached for her other arm, probably so he could shake her more forcefully.

She bared her teeth and cracked her hand against his face.

He reeled backward, letting go of her arm. He touched his smacked cheek. His lips worked, but no sound came out.

A knot of pressure swelled within her chest. It was the first time she had hit him. He had never struck her.

Her guilty hand throbbed.

Thomas appeared dazed. He took a tentative step forward.

She backpedaled a few feet, then turned and fled. He called after her, but she neither stopped nor glanced back. She ran into the parking lot, got in her car, slammed the door, gunned the engine, and peeled away in a shriek of tires and a plume of dust.

After she had driven a short while, her shaking hands refused to grip the steering wheel, and the knot in her chest made it painful to breathe. She parked on the shoulder of the road, under the boughs of an elm.

Music blasted from the stereo. She hadn't realized it was turned on. It was a Luther Vandross song: "A House Is Not a Home."

She exploded into laughter. The knot in her chest loosened, and as it did, her laughter grew more hysterical, until she was no longer laughing, but crying.

CHAPTER THREE

Around eleven o'clock in the morning, with the hope that getting away from the house would give him the objectivity he needed to understand the strange message in the bathroom, Jason rode his bike downtown.

A northern Chicagoland suburb with a population of only twenty thousand people, Spring Harbor didn't have much of a business district; a single street, Northern Road, was the city's main drag. Stores, taverns, gas stations, restaurants, supermarkets, churches, and small office buildings lined the thoroughfare. In celebration of Independence Day, which arrived that weekend, strings of red, white, and blue plastic pennants had been hung above the roadway. They snapped in the breeze, an accompaniment to the drone of late-morning traffic.

Jason parked his bike in a metal bicycle stall on the sidewalk. He pushed open the glass door of MacGregor's Bike Shop.

"Well, here comes trouble," Mr. MacGregor said. Wearing baggy Levi's spotted with oil, a Chicago Cubs T-shirt soiled with more oil, and beat-up sneakers, Mr. MacGregor looked like the workaholic he was, as if he was too busy repairing bikes to bother staying clean. He turned away from the tire he had been working on and walked toward Jason, wiping his hands on a cloth.

"What's up?" Jason said. "How's business?"

"Business is fantastic!" Mr. MacGregor said. He tapped a stack of racing magazines on the glass counter. "I've sold two of these, a pair of shoelaces, and a can of spray paint, giving me a total take of maybe ten dollars—before taxes. At this rate, I might manage to stay in business until the end of the month."

"It'll pick up soon," Jason said. "Hey, is my baby still here?"

"Unfortunately, it is," Mr. MacGregor said. "I'm serious, kid. You've looked at that thing so much I'm beginning to wonder if you've placed a curse on it. Everyone loves it, but no one buys it."

"Don't worry. I'm gonna buy it."

"I'm praying that you do. I'm sick of seeing you here every day."

Jason smiled. "Thanks a lot. But I'm serious—I'm gonna get it."

"For your sake, I really hope you're right," Mr. MacGregor said. "You are seriously obsessed, my friend. I think you'd suffer a nervous breakdown if you never got the damned thing."

"Come on, I'm not *that* nuts about it," Jason said. He chewed his lip. "Well, maybe I am."

"I love an honest man." Mr. MacGregor laughed. He went back to work behind the counter.

Jason walked around the rows of ten- and twelve-speeds, mountain bikes, and fitness equipment, heading toward the far-left corner of the room. Once there, he stopped.

"Man, I've got to get this."

He touched the handlebars. His heart skipped a beat.

The Randolph Street M9000 was the bike of his dreams. It had everything he could ever want in a serious street bike: a lightweight chrome-moly steel frame, Syntance handlebars, air-cushioned full suspension, dual-disc brakes, a Selle San Marco saddle, and gleaming thirty-six-hole aluminum rims. Striking red highlights on the seat clamp, rims, suspension linkage, stem, and bar ends completed the awesome package.

Unfortunately, the price was as amazing as the bicycle. Fifteen hundred dollars! What an incredible amount of money. Although his fourteenth birthday was less than three weeks away, he had not asked his parents to buy the Randolph. They would never spend that much for a bike. His granddad was wealthy, but Jason didn't have the nerve to ask him for it, either. He could get a job and try to save enough to buy the bike himself, but any work he could get at his age paid so terribly that by the time he'd earned enough money to purchase the Randolph, he'd be licensed to drive.

Sighing, he glided his hand over the smooth black seat.

It seemed hopeless. Nevertheless, he kept believing he would get the M9000. Somehow. Someday.

He climbed onto the bike, which Mr. MacGregor allowed. He grasped the handgrips, planted his shoes on the pedals.

He imagined himself riding. Slashing through wind. Swooping across streets. Fast. Powerful. *Free.*

He suddenly heard himself panting.

Wiping sweat off his face, he got off the bike, embarrassed. Sometimes the intensity of his imagination surprised even him.

Mr. MacGregor watched him. "Jeez, kid. You really want that bike."

Jason nodded.

"Get your folks to drop in," Mr. MacGregor said. "I have a great monthly payment plan, one anybody could handle. Telling them can't hurt. Sometimes dreams do come true."

"I hope so."

Outside the store, Jason checked his wristwatch. It was almost eleven-thirty. He and his friends planned to visit Water World, the new water park, at noon, but before he went anywhere he had to satisfy his sweet tooth. A McDonald's was about a block away, and the thought of sipping a strawberry milkshake made his tongue tingle. He rode over there.

The restaurant was busy. He waited behind a cute mocha-skinned girl wearing a white blouse and denim shorts. He admired her discreetly, wondering what his girlfriend would do if she could see him at that moment. Probably smack him into next week, he thought, smiling.

Once it was his turn to order, he heard a vaguely familiar voice that drew his attention toward the doorway. When he looked, his gut doubled up.

Blake Grant had entered, along with his two pals. The lobby was crowded, and they were talking to one another, so they didn't see Jason. Yet.

In spite of that day's strange events, he had been optimistic. Now he felt as though he had fallen into another nightmare. But unlike his recurring dream, the villain here was real and could not be vanquished by the arrival of dawn.

Jason had not heard the cashier. "Excuse me?"

"Your order," the cashier said. "Please."

At first, he didn't remember why he had come there. Then it hit him. A strawberry milkshake. He no longer had the craving for it, but he bought one anyway. A couple of people had noticed his delay in ordering, and he didn't want to attract further attention.

He paid for the dessert and went to the condiment table. He withdrew a straw from the dispenser. On the right, at the edge of his vision, he saw Blake Grant.

Blake Grant was only sixteen, but he looked as dangerous as a jail-toughened thug. He stood about five-feet-ten, and he bulged with such well-developed muscles that he either must pump iron like a maniac or had access to an unlimited supply of steroids. His streamlined face reminded Jason of an eagle, his aquiline features accentuated by his hair being pulled into a tightly knotted ponytail. He wore a sleeveless black T-shirt, faded jeans, and scuffed combat boots. A patch covered his right eye. Rumor said he had lost that eye in a playful switchblade duel with his older brother.

Blake and his sidekicks—a baby-faced kid named Bryan Green and an overweight one named Travis Young—waited in the line beside the south-side door. There was another exit on the north side, and the bike stalls were east, at the front of the building. If Jason was careful, he could leave undetected.

But part of him wanted to confront Blake. It was time to end this stupid feud, and because Blake didn't believe in talking things out, a fight was the only way to finish it. Jason had never fought anyone, but he wasn't afraid of Blake. It didn't matter to him who won, really, as long as a fight settled matters between them.

But Blake's buddies were there, and they were almost as tough as he was. Better to leave. He might be able to handle Blake, but only a fool would try to beat three guys.

Because the lunch hour was approaching, the lobby grew more congested by the minute. He welcomed the crowd. He needed the cover.

Warily, he slunk through the throng of people. He would have reached the door without being noticed, except for a hyperactive kid.

When he was halfway to the exit, a child darted around

the table nearest the main walkway, screaming about a Happy Meal. Jason sidestepped, but he moved too slowly. The boy crashed into him head-on.

The milkshake tumbled out of Jason's hands and splattered onto the floor.

People turned to look. The noise level fell.

Jason's heart knocked. Now, Blake must see him.

The kid who had smashed into him had dropped onto his butt. Without looking at Jason, he bounded to his feet and took off, still yelling. A blushing young woman dashed around the corner, murmured an apology to Jason, then chased after the boy.

"Brooks!"

Jason froze. That unmistakable voice made spicules of ice spin through his blood.

"Brooks!"

Slowly, Jason turned.

From far across the lobby, Blake stared at him. A humorless grin sliced across his face.

A month ago, during the final exam for their science class, Jason and Blake had been assigned to sit at the same table. Not surprisingly, shortly after the test began, Blake attempted to bully him into letting him copy. Most kids shriveled under Blake, but Jason refused to give in. His grandfather had indoctrinated him in the importance of standing up for himself. Blake was infuriated. Before he handed the teacher the blank test that would result in his being retained in eighth grade for the second time, he promised that when he next met Jason he was going to beat him so brutally that afterward "Not even God'll recognize you." In Blake's warped mind, it was Jason's fault that he had flunked.

"I'm gonna get you, Brooks!"

Jason rushed out of the door.

Blake and his gang hustled out of the door they'd been near, too.

Outside, the temperature felt as if it had escalated ten degrees since Jason had entered the restaurant. The furnacelike heat snatched the air out of his lungs and made him light-headed. As he ran alongside the building, he dragged one hand across the brick wall to keep from falling in a faint.

He had not locked up his bike. Doubting anyone would ever steal such an ugly ride, he never chained it up. He pulled it out of the stall, hopped on it.

Evidently, Blake and his friends had parked their bicycles beside the entrance. They were on them already, motoring around the front of the building, toward Jason.

"Gonna kill you, boy!"

There were several places to which he could flee. He made a decision in an instant.

A used-car lot lay adjacent to the McDonald's. It was one of the biggest in the county, the size of three football fields, every inch consumed by vehicles. A virtual labyrinth that provided countless avenues of evasion.

He weaved around bumpers, aiming to put as much distance as possible between himself and his pursuers. Searing sunshine ricocheted off hundreds of windshields, and the blacktop seemed on the verge of melting under the heat. Rippling mirages glistened on the pavement like pools of molten silver.

Riding hard and fast, Jason felt as though he had stumbled into an action movie. He had only wanted a milkshake, and now he seemed to be fleeing for his life. Adrenaline pumped like hot oil through his veins, his heart pummeled his rib cage, and sweat drenched his shirt. His bike clanked, whined, and clattered, and he prayed under his breath for the bike to stay in one piece.

Finally, seeing no one on his tail, he stopped between two rows of cars. He looked around.

Blake and the others were nowhere in sight.

But they had to be there. Somewhere.

He licked his dry lips, looked around again. No sign of them.

But it was nuts to think they had given up. Blake had a reputation for being as unrelenting as a pit bull. From what Jason had heard about him, the kid even relished a good chase before he kicked someone's ass.

Against Jason's will, his imagination powered up; a river of vivid images flooded into his head. He imagined Blake, Bryan, and Travis having abandoned their bikes; he saw them slithering like serpents alongside, under, and behind cars, quick and stealthy, switchblades bared and gleaming in the sunlight, muscles tense with pent-up violence, minds boiling over with bloodlust, creeping ever closer, closer, closer . . .

Two arms wrapped around his chest.

CHAPTER FOUR

Unable to stop thinking of his terrible fight with Linda, Thomas left the restaurant and drove to Green Meadows Nursing Home.

He rode the elevator to the fourth level of the building, drumming a pocket notebook against his leg as the first three floors beeped past. He was nervous. Under the circumstances, visiting his father might only worsen what was already one of the worst days of his life. But he had been compelled to visit. He nursed a naive yet sincere hope that an earnest, man-to-man talk with his dad would help him solve his problems.

He arrived on the fourth floor, walked slowly to the last room on the south wing. He paused at the threshold, exhaled deeply, then stepped inside and shut the door.

At the *thunk* of the closing door, his father's eyes opened. He spoke in a slightly slurred baritone voice: "What the hell do you want, boy?"

"I came to visit, Dad." He settled into the chair beside his father's bed.

Propped up by pillows, his dad leaned against the head-board, his legs swaddled under sheets. After a major stroke ten years ago, he had been admitted to the nursing home, and the years had been tough on him. He was seventy, yet he looked ninety. His six-feet-four frame was emaciated to scarecrow proportions, his ashen brown skin stretched so tautly over his bones that it seemed one sudden movement might split his flesh open. His long, bony fingers resembled gigantic spider legs. His lips were gray and chapped, and he had lost his teeth years ago. He had lost most of his hair, too. Only a few brittle white strands remained.

His dad's nickname was Big George, but these days, the only thing big about him was his mouth. Easily the most despised resident at Green Meadows in the eyes of both the tenants and the staff, Big George had a reputation for speaking his mind, regardless of the consequences. About two years ago, his penchant for cussing out doctors, making sexual overtures to nurses, and ridiculing fellow residents had got him banished to his room for a week. After the week had passed, he had apparently decided that he enjoyed his own company more than he enjoyed the company of others, because he rarely left his room anymore. But his mouth was as big as ever.

Big George's black eyes penetrated Thomas. "Why ain't you at work? You slacking off, Tommy?"

"No, sir, my assistant's there. He can handle the place as well as I can. I came to see you because . . . I have a problem."

"You have a problem, all right." Big George straightened up in his bed. "After all this time, you still ain't learned that you can't trust another nigger with your job."

"Huh? That's not what I was—"

"That's what *I'm* talking about, boy," Big George said. "Did I work my ass to death so you could let some fool walk in and shit on everything I earned?"

"No, sir, of course not."

"Did I work eighty hours a week, every week of the year, so you could skip out and let some so-called assistant ruin my place's reputation?"

"No, sir, you didn't."

"Damn right, I didn't." He pointed a gnarled finger at Thomas. "I'll tell you what: if I hear about you slacking off again, I'll climb out of this bed and kick your black ass all over this nursing home. That's *my* business putting food on your family's table, and don't you ever forget it. You hear me, Tommy?"

Thomas clenched his fingers into fists. Why had he come here when the same sorry scenario always played out? Did he expect Big George to listen to his problems, to sympathize with the anguish and guilt he felt since he'd grabbed—even shook—his wife? Did he expect Big George to tell him how to apologize to Linda? Did he expect Big George to advise him on how to save his marriage, which suddenly might be on the brink of collapse?

He turned back to the bed.

Big George glared at him.

No fatherly concern sparkled in those eyes. It had never been there. Why did he continue to hope that one day his father would care about him?

"I said, did you hear me, Tommy?" Big George said.

"I heard you, sir. You're right. I should know better than to trust someone to run the restaurant as well as you or I could. It won't happen again, I promise."

The tension seeped out of Big George's face. Thomas had broken his vow numerous times, but his father never seemed to remember.

"Long as you know who's the boss," Big George said, nodding, "we'll be okay. Now open that notebook and tell me what's going on at my place."

Lowering his head, Thomas opened his pocket notebook, found his page for that day, and began to read.

* * *

Two fat arms squeezed around Jason's chest.

"Blake, come on. I got him, I got him!"

It was Travis Young. Jason struggled to escape the kid's bear hug. His bike dropped from under him and smacked the ground. They lurched over the bike and tottered between the cars, Jason thrusting his elbow backward, trying to strike Travis's gut but missing. Travis panted and snorted in Jason's ear, his fetid breath washing over him, making Jason want to faint.

Three rows away, Blake and Bryan emerged from behind a truck.

Fresh adrenaline galvanized Jason. He stabbed Travis's gut with his elbow. Travis grunted, but he held tight. They stumbled over each other's feet and collapsed to the hot blacktop.

Travis flopped onto Jason, as if to pin him under his bulk. Holding Travis off with his forearm, Jason freed a leg—and slammed his knee into the boy's groin.

"Uhh!" Agony twisting his face, Travis rolled off Jason. He curled into a ball and hugged his stomach.

"Brooks!" Blake said, only a few feet away.

No time to get on his bike or run. So he scrambled under the nearest thing, a red sports car.

In spite of the shade there, the heat was unbearable. The pavement scalded his palms and his bare legs, scorched his chest through his shirt. He rose up, minimizing his contact with the baking blacktop.

Blake's dirty combat boots pounded to the car beneath which Jason had crawled. Bryan Green's battered high-tops followed. Travis lay on the ground, his curled back facing Jason.

"Get that asshole!" Blake said.

He couldn't stay there, he had to keep moving, that was his only chance. Silently, Jason rolled into the blinding sunlight, hesitated, then wormed beneath a low-rider pickup in the next row, sucking his teeth as his skin scraped against the hot ground.

Blake peered below the sports car.

Jason's heart galloped. Could Blake see him?

"Shit, I don't see him," Blake said, probing the shadows with his single eye. He pounded his fist on the pavement. "Where the hell did he go?"

Blake's face disappeared as he rose.

Jason chewed his lip. He squirmed underneath a van.

Sweat streamed into his eyes, stinging them and blurring his vision. He wiped away the perspiration with the back of his hand.

He saw the boys' feet pacing around the area.

"Asshole's gotta be here somewhere," Blake said.

"If Trav hadn't lost him, we'd have nailed his ass," Bryan said.

"If you lose him, I'll nail *your* ass."

"We'll catch him, dude. Keep looking."

Jason scampered into the humid, oily darkness beneath another vehicle. He lost sight of their feet, but their voices sounded as though they were several yards away.

He considered keeping up this strategy, scuttling from car to car, always staying just out of sight, until the boys got tired and left, but he nixed that plan. Blake could probably taste impending violence, and he would not give up until he had appeased his sick hunger. Plus, they had a crucial edge: they could check beneath the vehicles about a dozen times faster than he could scramble under them. Regardless of how quickly or frequently he moved, they would soon catch him.

Now was the time to run.

Cautiously, he crept into the daylight.

The aisle in which he lay was empty.

He rose to one knee. He looked across the car's hood.

As though equipped with a radar, Blake spotted him instantly. He was about four rows away, fists on his waist. Bryan and Travis milled around him.

Blake pointed. "There. Get him!"

Jason ducked out of view. He froze, unsure where to go. Then he noticed the tall chain-link fence that abutted the back of the lot, five rows behind him. He ran for it.

The footfalls of the pursuing boys clapped like gunfire. Jason had a big head start, but he kept imagining a hand grabbing his shoulder.

He leaped onto the fence, climbed.

Halfway up, someone grabbed his ankle.

"Got you now!" It was Blake.

Jason's fierce reaction startled even him. He jerked up his snagged leg, then rammed it down, smashing his heel into Blake's nose.

Blake howled and let go.

Jason climbed to the top of the fence, jumped, and landed in the tall weeds on the other side.

Blake cupped his nose, bright blood leaking from between his fingers. Bryan and Travis watched their wounded leader, Travis holding his groin gingerly, wincing as he breathed.

Jason was simultaneously thrilled and sickened by the savagery of their battle.

Blake's busted nose had to hurt like hell. But the crazy kid ordered his friends to keep chasing Jason. Then he joined the hunt himself.

Jason looked around. The weedy, tree-canopied terrain slanted steeply into a narrow ravine, and past the water, dense forest thrived. After a few hundred yards, the woods parted to accommodate a bike trail that Jason had explored often that summer.

Somewhere in there, he needed to find a hiding place. He could not outrun them forever.

He sprinted as fast as he dared down the slope. Hawthorns scratched his arms and legs, and sinewy vines threatened to trip him. Broken beer bottles bristled like fangs from the grass, snapping at his shoes as he flashed past.

Panting, he glanced behind him. The boys tore down the incline at kamikaze speed.

He vaulted the ravine and plunged into the woods.

Thomas slowly read his business update on The House of Soul. He had carefully arranged his notes to elicit the maximum satisfaction from his father. Beginning the practice soon after Big George's stroke, he had developed it into a highly refined skill. When he finally and dramatically told Big George that the net profit for last month was the largest in the restaurant's history, Big George grinned. Thomas grinned, too, but something inside him was repulsed by his expression.

"You doing good, but don't get bigheaded," Big George said. "Pride goes before that hard-assed fall."

"I have everything under control, Dad."

"You better." Big George cocked his head quizzically. "So. How's married life treating you?"

Big George rarely asked about his marriage. "Uh, well . . ."

"Is Linda still so cute niggers get weak when she walks by?"

"What?"

Big George's face grew dreamy. "When I was younger, I used to have women like her. So fine they make a nigger want to drop to his knees and worship! Those kinds of women can pussy-whip a man, but you can't let any woman stop you from being true to your nature. You're like me in a lot of ways, Tommy, so I know you got a girl or two on the side. Ain't you?"

Thomas erupted to his feet. "Don't you ever accuse me of that. I love Linda too much to sleep around."

Big George laughed, a hard bark. "One way we're different: You don't lie as well as I do. Better pray Linda don't pop that subject. She'd see through your shallow ass in a minute."

"But I don't cheat on her."

"Liar."

"I'm not like you."

Big George chuckled.

"I don't treat her the way you treated Mama. Or any of those other women you were with."

Big George wrinkled his nose. "Do you smell bullshit, Tommy? I do."

"The only bullshit I smell is coming from you."

Big George smiled.

Thomas wanted to knock out every one of those false teeth, smash them down his old man's throat, and make him choke on them. Then he rebuked himself for sinking to his father's level.

"Like father, like son," Big George said. "You might deny it, but that doesn't change what's in your blood. Like father, like son."

"I'm out." Thomas stormed to the door. His hand trembled as he reached for the doorknob.

"Hey, you get your ass back to my restaurant!" Big George said, pointing his long finger at Thomas. "I hear about you messing up, and I'll come down there and mop the floor with you. Hear me?"

"Sure, Dad. Good-bye."

Once inside his Buick, Thomas slammed the door hard enough to rock the car.

Like father, like son.

Lord, he hated that man. His father had an uncanny ability to find an exposed emotional nerve and twist it, and he did so with a sickening, perverse enjoyment. Hating his father was terrible, especially considering his pitiable health, but Thomas couldn't help it. Why did he keep visiting him?

He didn't know. There were a lot of things he didn't understand about his relationship with Big George.

Striving to blot all thoughts of his dad out of his mind, he removed his cellular telephone from the glove compartment. He pressed the *On* button.

He thought of calling Linda. They desperately needed to talk about what had happened in his office. But he wasn't sure what to say, and she probably needed to cool off before she'd be ready for a conversation. He would speak to her later.

Meanwhile, he would call someone else.

He punched in a number. A female voice answered on the second ring.

"It's Thomas."

"I was thinking about you," she said. "What's up?"

"Nothing much. Working hard. You know how it is."

"I heard that. Got to make that money, honey."

"Please. I need a vacation."

She laughed.

They talked about inconsequential matters.

"I'll see you tonight?" Thomas said. "Around ten?"

"Just like always, baby."

He clicked off the phone.

He started the car. He looked up and found his father's fourth-floor window. He realized there was only one person he hated more than his father.

Like father, like son.

Himself.

Running through the woods, Jason soon realized that he was lost. The lush undergrowth, which loomed as high as walls in some places, as thick as canvas in others, prevented him from seeing more than a few feet ahead. Worse, all of the foliage looked identical, which made it difficult to distinguish his whereabouts from moment to moment.

Deciding to keep moving forward, he bent down, hoping to conceal himself. He slipped under leaves, brushed away wildflowers and prickly shrubs. He kept his mouth closed, breathing through his nose, not only because it promoted silence, but also because a haze of insects buzzed around his head.

He heard branches break far behind him. Alarmed crows fled their tree perches.

Blake and his friends must be nearby.

He found a potential hideout: a dense ring of shrubs crowded together so that they appeared to be a single large, thorny bush. Red berrylike fruit dangled amid the green needles.

He searched for a gap in the limbs. He located one barely wide enough to wriggle through.

He looked behind him.

He was still alone.

He crept inside the copse. He squeezed into a ball.

He waited, listening.

He heard only the natural sounds of the forest.

Then, the swish of legs marching through weeds.

"Forget it, man. There's too much shit in here to find him."

"I want to go home, Blake. It hurts, it still hurts."

"Shut up, dick-heads. We ain't leaving until I get that bastard."

Jason's clammy hands burned to form fists. Someone needed to give that punk a butt-kicking he'd never forget. But he didn't move. He was pissed, but not stupid enough to fight three guys.

The footsteps came closer. Stopped.

He shut his eyes.

"Man, I can feel that asshole around here," Blake said. "Can't you?"

Another footstep. Closer.

Leave. Turn around and leave.

Silence.

He imagined Blake examining the shrubs in which he hid.

"I swear, I can feel him," Blake said.

Another footstep.

Blake had to be right outside the bushes.

"That dude could run, man," Bryan said. "He might be out of this jungle already. Or maybe he's cutting around us, going back to his bike. Or—"

"Shut up," Blake said. "I'm trying to listen."

Silence.

Jason held his breath.

More silence.

His lungs felt as if they were going to explode.

Blake sighed. "Yeah, you're probably right. He ain't here. Let's go back to the lot. If we beat him to his bike, there're a few things I want to do to it."

"Like what?" Travis said.

"Like shove it down your fat-assed mouth," Blake said. He and Bryan laughed.

The boys' voices gradually faded.

Gratefully Jason exhaled. When he was positive the kids were gone, he crawled out of the bushes.

CHAPTER FIVE

Jason found his bike sprawled at the rear of the car lot. Both tires had been slashed, several spokes were bent, and the chain was tangled around the pedals. Fluid glimmered on the frame, and drops spattered the surrounding blacktop. Understanding—and the sour smell—smacked him in the face. They had pissed on his bike!

"Those assholes," he said. Balling his hands into fists, he marched to the fence. He kicked the fence as hard as he could once, twice, three times, knowing he looked like an idiot but not caring. He was so sick of Blake and his stupid friends; he wished they never existed. Why couldn't they leave him alone?

The chain-link fence vibrated from the force of his kicks. He started to kick it one more time, then dropped his foot to the ground. What was the point? With the way his day had been going, he'd mess around and break his toe. He walked back to his bicycle.

He considered leaving it there to be either thrown away or

picked up by a scavenger, but he had to take it with him, try to repair it. It was the only transportation he had.

With a sigh of resignation, he grasped the handgrips, which seemed to be untouched, and pulled up the bike. He rolled it to the nearby McDonald's. Inside the restaurant, he got a cup of water and a handful of napkins. He cleaned up the bicycle.

When he finished, it was almost noon. He was supposed to meet his friends. He wasn't in the mood to go to the water park, but maybe hanging out with the fellas for a while would draw him out of his funk. He started pushing his bike toward his friend's place.

As he drew closer to the house, he saw Darren Taylor and Mike Johnson—or "Brains" and "Shorty" as they were known among friends—on the veranda, rocking on the bench swing. Jason had become acquainted with Shorty only three months ago, and soon after they met, Shorty introduced him to his cousin, Brains. They were the first real friends he had ever had. Before he had met them, he'd spent all of his time by himself, reading, listening to music, playing video games, and daydreaming. Daydreaming more than anything else. For as long as he could remember, he had been able to get completely immersed in his imaginative adventures, to such an extent that his fantasies sometimes seemed more concrete than the real world. His vivid imagination was perhaps the one thing that had made living at home bearable, because it provided an escape from the hell around him. But now that he hung out with Brains and Shorty, he no longer needed to seek refuge in a fun imaginary life. He finally had the real thing.

As he approached the porch steps, Shorty jumped off the swing.

"Hey, why're you pushing your bike?" Shorty said. "Chain fall off or something?"

Shorty was fourteen years old, and he was dressed, as

usual, as if he were the mascot for a Chicago sports team. That day, he was working for the Chicago Bulls. He wore a red Bulls jersey, matching red shorts, and a Bulls cap. On other days, he represented the White Sox, the Cubs, or the Bears. Jason sometimes wondered if he had any regular clothes.

"I ran into a little trouble," Jason said.

Shorty laughed and came closer. "Man, if you ask me, it looks like you ran *over* a little trouble." He poked his finger inside a gash in one of the bike's mangled tires. "What the hell did you do, try to ride across a bed of nails?"

"It's a long story," Jason said.

Standing on the porch, Brains cleared his throat. He wore wire-rim glasses, pressed jeans, a blue polo shirt, and low-cut athletic shoes. Although Brains was only fourteen, the same age as the rest of them, Jason always thought of him as older, about eighteen or twenty. It wasn't only his conservative clothing that gave Jason that impression: the way he carried himself made him seem much more mature than his age.

Brains pushed his glasses up his nose, viewing Jason's bike with the intensity of a radiologist studying an X-ray. "Let me guess what happened, Jason: You had an encounter with Blake Grant."

"How did you know?" Jason said. "You must be psychic."

"No way, not me," Brains said. Sunlight reflected off his lenses as he spoke. "I remember when you told me that he threatened you at school, and how you said he never forgets anyone he wants to fight. I figured it was only a matter of time before he caught up with you. Spring Harbor's a small city, and from what I hear, all Blake does is ride around town with his pals, cruising for trouble. He probably saw your bike parked somewhere, knew it belonged to you, and decided to make good on his promise to destroy you. Is that close?"

"Close, but not exactly," Jason said. He walked past Brains, sat on the bench, and told them what had happened.

"Man, it's too bad you didn't face that punk alone," Shorty said. "You'd have kicked his ass."

"Maybe," Jason said. "Maybe not. I've never fought anyone."

"Neither has Mike," Brains said. He never referred to Shorty by his nickname. He smiled. "At least, Mike's never *won* a fight."

"Hey!" Shorty said. "I've whipped up dozens of fools, man. What the hell are you talking about?"

Jason rolled his eyes. Brains chuckled.

"At any rate," Brains said, "I'd be careful if I were you, Jason. Mike has told me about Blake, and he sounds dangerous. Watch yourself. You might not slip away next time."

"I'll be careful," Jason said. "But to be honest, Blake isn't the main thing I'm worried about."

"Why?" Shorty said. "What else is up?"

Jason looked from Brains to Shorty. Originally, he had not planned to tell them about the incident in the bathroom that morning, fearful that they would think he was crazy and make fun of him, but he realized that he trusted them as much as he would have trusted blood brothers. He thought there was a good chance they would believe him—after all, they didn't hang out with him because they thought he was a nut. They respected him. They had grown really tight in the few months they had been hanging out, too. Hiding such a bizarre incident from them would almost be an insult to the bond they had developed.

"Well?" Shorty said. "Give it up, man."

"Okay, I saw something this morning," Jason said. "Something scary and weird that's making me wonder if I'm going crazy. . . ."

"Tell me, fellas," Jason said, completing his tale of what he had seen in the bathroom. "Am I going crazy, or what?"

"You're not going crazy," Brains and Shorty said in unison. Shorty and Brains glanced at each other, smiled a little. Jason smiled at both of them. He was so glad they believed him.

Shorty paced the veranda.

"All right, we've heard the story, now we've gotta think hard about this shit," Shorty said. He twisted his Bulls hat backward, as if adjusting his thinking cap. "Who do you think wrote that word on the mirror?"

"I don't know," Jason said. "It couldn't have been Mom or Dad, and we haven't had any visitors lately. I can't think of anyone who might've done it. It was a stranger, I guess."

"Why would a stranger write *remember* on your bathroom mirror?" Brains said.

"I guess he's telling me to remember something," Jason said. "But I don't know what he's telling me to remember, or why he wants me to. I really don't have any answers. It's all crazy."

"Not only crazy, but spooky," Shorty said. He walked back and forth across the porch, knotting his hands. "To know this guy was in your crib, walking around writing shit on mirrors—man, that scares me. Only real psychos do stuff like that. If I were you, I'd be scared to go to sleep at night."

"I am scared," Jason said. "But I have to do something, you know? I need a plan to deal with this. I can't sit around and wait for something else to happen. Can either of you think of anything I can do?"

Neither Shorty nor Brains spoke. Both of them appeared to be pondering possibilities, strategies, answers. Jason had thought of a plan already, but before he presented it, he wanted to see what his friends could come up with. He had doubts about his own idea—and fears.

Brains removed his glasses, pinched the bridge of his nose. "Sorry. My mind is blank, Jason."

Shorty settled beside Jason on the swing. He shrugged. "Sorry, man. Nada."

"Then I have a plan," Jason said. "Does your sister still have the Ouija board, Brains?"

"Yes. Why?"

"I want to use it. To get some answers."

Shorty looked horrified. But Brains only nodded.

"Good idea," Brains said. "I didn't think about that. When do you want to use it?"

"Today. Right now."

"Okay." Brains stood and stretched his tall, burly frame as though they were leaving to play an ordinary game of basketball, not to use a mysterious device that had spawned a dozen horror flicks. "This would be a good time to do it. My folks will be out until this evening, and Tasha's at work all day. We'll have the house to ourselves."

"Cool." Jason wished he were as calm as Brains. Although it was his idea to use the Ouija, butterflies were tearing his stomach apart. He had probably watched too many horror movies himself.

But those horror films he'd seen had given him the idea to use the Ouija board. In movies, people used the Ouija to find answers about strange stuff that couldn't be easily explained. He didn't know if he really believed the Ouija board could tell him the truth behind the message in the bathroom. But the message was weird, and it seemed sensible to seek answers from the Ouija, an equally weird thing. Kind of like asking a biology question of a science teacher—you wouldn't pose such a question to your English instructor. Weird things in life were probably all connected somehow. The idea made an odd kind of sense to him, and it must have made sense to Brains, too.

Anyway, how else could they begin to explore the mystery? He didn't have any other ideas. He doubted that any adults would believe him. Grown-ups always assumed kids were dumb and making up stories to get attention. The Ouija board was a good place to start their search.

"If you're ready, I'm ready, Jason," Brains said. "Let's go."

"Demons," Shorty said. Standing in the center of Brains's bedroom, he crossed his arms over his thin chest. "The Ouija board calls up demons, man. You guys are nuts to mess with that thing."

Brains placed the long cardboard box that contained the Ouija on the bed. He removed the cover and tossed it at Shorty.

"Boo!"

Shorty dodged the flying lid. "That ain't funny. The Ouija is some serious shit. You shouldn't be using it."

"Come on, Shorty," Jason said. "They sell these at Toys R Us. How dangerous can they really be?"

"So what?" Shorty said. "Haven't you heard that they—"

"Listen, Mike," Brains said, "no one is forcing you to participate, so will you please be quiet? Something bizarre happened to Jason—something none of us can explain—and we need to search for answers. The Ouija seems like a good place to start. Unless you have a better idea?"

Shorty said nothing. Sulking, he kicked the board's lid across the floor.

"That's what I figured," Brains said. "Now, are you going to stay in here while we do this, or are you going to leave?"

Shorty sighed. "I'll stay, Brains. Someone with common sense has to watch over you fools."

Jason and Brains had brought two folding chairs into the room and positioned them at the foot of the double bed. On opposite-facing stands beside the chairs, Brains had placed two silver candlesticks from which jutted long white candles. They needed light. The ceiling light was off and the drapes were drawn, enclosing the room in sepulchral shadows.

Brains ignited the wicks with a cigarette lighter. The flames sputtered, created dancing phantoms on the walls, then steadied. Inhaling the pungent odor of hot wax and glancing at the Ouija on the bed, Jason found himself recalling those horror flicks in which evil spirits summoned by the Ouija invaded the world and wreaked terror on people's lives. He told himself to cut it out. He was thinking like Shorty.

But who would they be communicating with via the Ouija? A ghost? Something else?

We only need answers, he thought. It doesn't matter who—or what—gives them to us. We only need the truth.

Shorty sat at Brains's desk, on the other side of the room. Jason and Brains sat on the folding chairs, facing each other, their knees pressed together. Brains put the Ouija and the planchette on their laps. The letters faced Jason.

"Do you know how to use this?" Brains said. "I've seen a ton of movies about it, so I'm pretty familiar with how it works." He shrugged. "I don't know if I really believe in it, but it's a start."

"I'm cool," Jason said. "I've seen a bunch of movies about it, too."

Brains nodded. He placed his fingertips on the planchette. Jason did the same.

Stillness.

The candle flames flickered, causing shadows to flutter like dark wings across the Ouija.

A light sheen of sweat coated Jason's face. The air was warm, thick with tension.

Come on, Jason thought. *Someone answer us. Help us.*

Another bout of silence . . . then the planchette jerked.

"Whoa," Jason said. Wide-eyed, he watched the planchette twitch a few more times, slide haltingly for an inch or two, and then glide around the entire board, sail toward the center, and wind there in slow loops.

It didn't feel as if he and Brains guided the tripod; it seemed to be driven by invisible energy that he could feel tingling like static electricity on his fingertips. No wonder so many people were afraid of this thing.

He glanced at Brains. Of course, Brains appeared calm. He no doubt had a scientific explanation for what they were witnessing. Brains watched the rotating pointer images of candle flames glimmering on his eyeglasses.

"Let's ask some test questions first," Brains said. "Then we can get into the important stuff."

"Sounds good to me," Jason said.

"First question." Brains focused on the planchette. "What is your name?"

The pointer drifted toward the rows of letters, and slowly spelled a name.

JIMMY.

"Okay, Jimmy," Brains said. "Question: How old is Jason?"

13.

"How old am I?" Brains said.

14.

"When is my birthday?" Jason said.

JULY 19.

"When is mine?" Brains said.

MAY 5.

"What's my girlfriend's name?" Jason said.

MICHELLE.

"What does my mother do for a living?" Brains said.

TEACH.

Amazing, Jason thought. All of the answers were correct. What was this thing, really?

"He seems dependable to me," Jason said. "You ready, Brains?"

"Yeah," Brains said. "Let's start asking the *real* questions."

Jason concentrated on the planchette. It revolved in a lulling, hypnotic motion.

"Who wrote *remember* on my bathroom mirror?"

HE DID.

"Who is 'he'?" Brains said.

STRANGER.

"I know he's a stranger," Jason said. "We want to know his name. What is his name?"

REMEMBER.

"Remember?" Jason chewed his lip. "You're telling me to remember his name?"

YES.

"Is that also why he wrote the same word on the mirror? Because he wants me to remember his name?" Jason said.

YES.

"Can you tell us this person's name?" Brains said.

NO.

"Why not?" Jason said.

CANNOT.

"That's crazy." Jason shook his head. "He wants me to remember his name, so he writes it on the mirror. Is this some kind of game to him?"

YES.

"What's the point?" Brains said. "Why does Jason need to remember him?"

HE IS COMING.

Jason's fingers trembled on the planchette. A feeling of unreality gripped him, as though he had been sucked into one of those horror movies that he loved to watch. He wanted to douse his face in cold water to convince himself that this was actually happening, but he didn't dare leave the Ouija. They teetered on the brink of a breakthrough. He could feel it.

"Okay, you say he's coming," Jason said. "Tell us: when?"

SOON.

"Can you give us a time, a day?" Brains said.

SOON.

"All right, I guess you won't tell us," Brains said. "But why is he coming?"

FOR JASON.

"He's coming to do something to me?" Jason said.

YES.

"What?" Jason's heart throbbed.

WILL SEE.

"Can you tell us his plans?" Brains said.

CANNOT.

"Is he going to . . . hurt me?" Jason said.

WILL SEE.

Jason half wished that they had not begun this line of questioning. The Ouija's cryptic responses, far from relaxing him, put him more on edge than ever.

"Is the stranger good or evil?" Brains said.

WILL SEE.

"Come on, can't you tell us anything?" Jason said. "Stop with all these dumb clues. What should we do?"

REMEMBER.

"But I can't remember!" Jason said. "I don't know a thing about him. Why won't you give us some real answers?"

CANNOT.

"You keep repeating that as if he's right there beside you," Brains said. "Is the stranger there, wherever you are?"

No reply.

Brains leaned closer to the board.

"Is he there?" Brains said. "Can we speak to him?"

"Don't ask that!" Jason said. Fresh sweat popped out on his face.

Across the room, Shorty stood.

After a long pause, the planchette moved to answer.

YES.

"We can speak to the stranger?" Brains said. His eyes shone. "Great, let us talk to him. Let us talk to him now. I want to—"

Jason tore his fingers off the pointer. It slid to a halt.

"Are you crazy?" Jason said. "I don't want to speak to him!"

"Why not?" Brains kept his fingertips balanced on the motionless tripod. "You wanted answers. We should go directly to the source. Jimmy couldn't tell us much."

"But I don't want to talk to the stranger. What if he's a ghost or a demon, something like that?"

"Jason, you aren't making any sense," Brains said. "You're beginning to sound like Mike. It's not as though he'll jump out of the Ouija and attack us."

"Hey!" Shorty said. "What the hell have you guys done?"

Jason and Brains turned to look at Shorty.

"What are you talking about?" Brains said.

"Can you feel it?" Shorty said. He hugged himself. "The temperature in here's dropped at least twenty degrees."

Jason suddenly felt it, too. He felt not only a significant temperature plunge, but also an inexplicable change in the air. The air seemed thicker, more liquid, charged with a mysterious force. His breathing grew labored. The hair at the nape of his neck lifted and stood as stiff as cold wire.

The candle flames flickered, sputtered, blew out. Dense shadows sprang up, crowded the room.

"Oh, no. I think I might have made a big mistake," Brains said. He drew back in his seat, his eyes appearing anxious for the first time in Jason's memory. Slowly he took his fingers off the planchette.

It jumped.

Jason's mouth dropped open. Brains and Shorty gasped.

The planchette bucked again, and then it spun furiously in the center of the board, like a wild top. He and Brains leaped out of their chairs. The Ouija board and tripod flipped and landed on the floor, the pointer still spinning, spinning, spinning, grinding a smoking hole in the carpet.

"A demon. I knew it was a demon!" Shorty cowered in the corner.

Jason backpedaled to the wall. He did not know who the stranger was, or how any of this was happening, but he wanted to get out of here. He looked to the door.

Moved by an invisible power, the bureau jerked from its position along the wall and slid in front of the door, trapping them inside.

CHAPTER SIX

Linda had been distraught ever since her fight with Thomas that morning, so later in the afternoon, she met her girl-friend Alice Franklin at her home in Waukegan. Linda hoped talking to Alice would help her relax. More important, she hoped Alice would help her discover how to heal the most damaging wound her marriage had ever suffered.

Alice opened the door. "Girl, since you called me I've been bouncing off the walls. You only told me bits and pieces of what happened, and it made me sick. How're you feeling?"

"The same way I probably look. Like shit."

"Let's talk about it." Alice took her by the arm and brought her inside. "Maybe that'll help both of us feel better."

Although Alice and Linda shared a variety of interests and attitudes, they hardly resembled each other. Linda was five-four and petite; Alice was five-ten and voluptuous. Linda's hair was short and curly; Alice's dark, lustrous braids flowed to her shoulders. Linda wore stylish yet basically conservative clothes; Alice draped herself in flamboyant, ethnic garments that generated stares and compliments everywhere she went.

She and Alice had been best friends for two decades. They went to the same high school, attended the same college—Illinois State—and both began their careers as elementary school teachers. While Linda left the teaching field to become a freelance writer, Alice scooped up two advanced degrees and became a history professor at the College of Lake County. Now Alice was writing a novel of her own during the summer break. It amused Linda how their lives often paralleled each other.

However, their history of relationships with men was vastly different. Thomas and Linda had been high-school sweethearts and had married soon after she graduated from college; she had never truly been with another man. Alice had been through a long series of boyfriends and had only wedded three years ago. Although Linda had been married much longer than Alice, Alice had such wide and varied experience with men that Linda frequently found herself relying on her for advice and support.

Alice went in the kitchen and retrieved a pitcher of iced tea and two glasses. She and Linda sat in wicker chairs on the patio.

Linda sipped the tea as she recounted her story. The drink quenched her thirst, but she really wished she had something stronger.

No, red-flag the thought, she told herself. *Don't even think about it.*

"I can't believe you hit him," Alice said. "Thomas had it coming, but that's not like you at all. You must've been pushed to the edge."

"I was. But I'm not sure that his grabbing me was the main reason I slapped him. It's more like . . . he's a stranger to me."

"What do you mean?" Alice said, her large, black eyes curious.

"We've had arguments in the past about his carelessness, but until today I hadn't seen how much Thomas has really changed over the years; and seeing it scared the shit out of me. Since he seemed so different, I guess I wasn't sure whether I could trust him not to hurt me. So I did the only thing I could to get away. Smacked him."

Alice nodded. She understood. One of her ex-boyfriends had been abusive.

"Now that I've thought about it, I realize he's been acting like a total stranger for a long time." Linda's hands tightened around the cold glass. "But when he shook me like that, it was a rude awakening."

"I bet it was. I can't see Thomas doing something like that to you. What got into him?"

Linda shrugged. "If I knew what had gotten into him, I'd pull it out."

"It could be stress," Alice said. "That's not an excuse, of course, but it could explain a lot. After all, his dad's sick and cooped up in that nursing home. He's working day and night at that restaurant. All of that pressure would make anyone crazy."

"I've talked to him about cutting his hours, but he acts as if the world would stop turning if he came home early one night," Linda said. "Don't even talk about taking a vacation, girl. The word isn't in his vocabulary. We haven't taken a vacation in ten years."

"Let me guess: your last vacation was right before his daddy had the stroke and gave him the job."

Linda nodded. "Everything changed for us when Thomas took over that damned place. *He* changed. He became exactly like his dad, obsessed with work. All he thinks about is The House of Soul. I swear, sometimes I've actually dreamed about bombing that place."

"I can see why. It sounds worse than a mistress." She eyed Linda speculatively. "I hate to bring this up, but have you ever suspected Thomas of . . ."

"Oh, no. Definitely not. If he won't take time out for me, he couldn't take time out for another woman."

"It was only a thought," Alice said. "Some work-obsessed men have girlfriends on the side. They say it relieves stress, which is a bunch of self-serving bullshit, if you ask me. But you're probably right. I hope you're right."

"I'm right. Thomas isn't perfect, but he's not that low-down. He knows I'd kill him if I ever found out he was messing around."

"I heard that. But to be truthful, girl, we ought to stop worrying so much about Thomas and concentrate on you. Sure, Thomas has his faults, but your hands aren't clean either. You cause some of your problems yourself."

"Give me a break, Alice."

"Hell, no. I'm your best friend, I'll give you my honest opinion. Think about it. Do you have a tendency to shoot off at the mouth when you're speaking to Thomas? Have you ever noticed that about yourself?"

"No."

"Be honest, Lin."

Linda twisted her hands in her lap. "Well, sometimes I guess I'm a little sharp-tongued. But I'm only like that when he's screwed up something. Or when I suspect that he's screwed up something." She laughed, self-conscious. "I guess that's most of the time."

"Nothing turns a man off more than a woman with a smart mouth," Alice said. "Nagging drives them nuts. I've seen it. I love my mama to death, but she had the biggest mouth in Chicago, and my daddy stayed in the streets because of it. If you and Thomas are gonna get back on track, you have to learn to shut your ass up."

"Be blunt, why don't you?"

"You get my point. You have to put yourself in check. You have to convince Thomas that you won't be a pain in the neck any longer. What it comes down to is, you have to show him that you love him."

"He should know that I love him."

"Maybe he should. But do you *show* him that you do?"

"Alice, it's not that easy. I can show him how much I love him till kingdom come, but love is a two-way street. He has to do his share."

"He will."

"How do you know?"

"Because, in spite of all the mess he gives you, Thomas loves you. I see it in his eyes when he looks at you, hear it in his voice when he talks to you. The problem is, while you love each other, neither of you openly expresses your feelings. When you start to communicate your genuine feelings by your words and actions, he'll respond."

"I want to believe you," Linda said. "But I'm so used to everything being miserable, I've become pretty damn cynical."

"You can get out of that rut. All you have to do is hope. And try."

She closed her eyes and tilted her head back. The sunlight felt deliciously warm on her skin; as she luxuriated in the glow, she considered Alice's advice. Could she try to revive her marriage? She wanted to stay with Thomas, but she wondered whether the struggle to find happiness with him would be worth it. Thomas was a seemingly incurable workaholic. Sometimes he could be self-centered, distant, and amazingly thoughtless. In spite of his flaws, she believed he really loved her. Over the years, he had often shown his feelings for her, in almost imperceptible ways: his silent, steadfast support of her freelance writing career; his habit of coming to her defense whenever someone assailed her unfairly; the way he often held her close late at night, when he thought she was sleeping. There were lots of other things he did, too, small but telling tokens of his emotions. Could she convince him to stop handing her the occasional love tokens and give her everything he had?

She believed she could. It would take determination, love, and tons of patience. She had the determination and love, but she wasn't sure about the patience. After ten years of frustration, her reservoir of patience felt depleted. But maybe she could hang on a bit longer. Maybe.

She opened her eyes and looked at Alice.

"Okay, I'll do it," she said. "I'll take your advice and work to bring Thomas around."

Alice smiled. "Good. I knew you weren't a quitter, Lin."

"Still . . . what if it doesn't work?"

Alice hesitated. "I'm sure it'll work. But if you do everything you can to prove that you love him, and he keeps acting like a stranger, then you might have to put yourself through one of the most painful things in this crazy world of ours: a divorce."

They were trapped.

Disbelieving, Jason stared at the barricaded door.

He was afraid to move—almost, in fact, afraid to breathe. Holding his breath, he looked at Shorty and Brains. Terror shone in their eyes, and they stood as still as wax figures, as if the slightest movement would draw the attention of the unearthly intruder and provoke a violent reaction.

Silence gripped the room in a vise.

Don't hurt us, Jason prayed. *Whoever you are, please don't hurt us.*

The stereo system that occupied a long mahogany shelf along one wall turned on, rows of buttons lighting up. A hip-hop song played at medium volume. As Jason watched breathlessly, the volume knob twisted all the way around to the maximum level. Heavy bass thundered from the speakers, the walls and windows shook, and Jason's teeth rattled.

Propelled into action, Brains rushed to the stereo. He ripped the power cord out of the wall socket.

The music played on.

Brains looked dumbly at the cord in his hand.

Incredibly, even though the volume control had been cranked to the limit, the music continued to get louder. Booming, pounding, hammering, the speakers literally jumped on the shelf; the music grew distorted and fuzzy. Jason covered his ringing ears, but that didn't help much. The volume continued to escalate, and grey smoke began to churn from the speakers. Both speakers suddenly spat orange sparks and short-circuited with a nerve-snapping bang, falling silent at last.

The three of them uncovered their ears.

"Damn," Shorty said, "That was—"

The bed jerked.

Like a bronco with a wasp up its tail, the double bed began to buck and bump, rising up, and then slamming onto the floor with enough force to nearly knock Jason off balance. The bedsheets slid off the mattress in a tangle, pillows bouncing onto the carpet. The bed rose higher each time the entity snatched it into the air and threw it down, until it smacked both the ceiling and the floor, like a pinball trapped between a couple of bumpers.

To Jason, the noise was almost as amazing as the sight of the possessed bed. He thought he could feel blood oozing from his punished ears.

Finally, the bed dropped and remained still.

Jason, Shorty, and Brains exhaled. But they did not move, Jason sensing, as Brains and Shorty probably did, that this bizarre exhibition of power had not yet concluded.

For a moment, stillness.

Then, instead of concentrating on one object, the poltergeist went wild, attacking everything in the room. The ceiling lamp shattered, glass raining to the carpet. The closet popped open, and shirts, jackets, jeans, shoes, and other assorted pieces of clothing flew out like birds, darting through the air in every direction, bombarding Jason and the others, who shielded themselves with their arms. In the same fashion, the bureau burst open, T-shirts and socks and boxer shorts taking flight and joining the fray. Desk drawers shot out like torpedoes and whacked into the walls, spilling their contents as they flew. Both bed pillows split open, releasing a blizzard of feathers. The windows opened and shut, opened and shut, curtains billowing and flapping. On another shelf, a glass tank filled with goldfish ruptured, and water and fish poured out. Then the bed sprang into life again, bucking and hopping like a piece of furniture in a fun house.

Crouched in a corner, buried under mounds of clothing and debris, Jason could not take it anymore. He fought to his feet and shouted in his loudest voice: "You crazy motherfucker! Stop this shit right now! I mean it!"

He was aware of how foolish he sounded—he didn't have any power over this thing—but his words seemed to have a magical effect. The destructive spirit instantly departed: the bed quit jumping, the windows stopped opening and closing, the curtains ceased flapping, and every piece of clothing wafted to the floor in lifeless piles.

Jason blinked, stunned, as silence settled over the room once more.

Both of them smothered under clothes, Shorty and Brains crawled into the open.

Tremors shook Jason, spreading through his legs and arms and rattling through to the core of his body. He hugged himself tightly, feeling as if he might fall to pieces like a cheap toy.

With a gasp, Shorty buckled over and vomited loudly. Brains patted his cousin's back and murmured words of comfort. But Brains, too, appeared to be deeply shaken.

"Let's get out of here, fellas," Jason said, his voice brittle due to his dry throat. "We've gotta go outside, get some fresh air. I feel like I'm gonna pass out."

Although his legs quaked, Jason made it to the door. Brains and Shorty trudged behind him.

In their shell-shocked condition, it took all three of them to move the bureau that blocked the doorway. They filed outside solemnly, like mourners leaving a funeral.

Three hours later, after they had cleaned up the wreckage in the bedroom, Jason, Shorty, and Brains had a meeting in the den. A strategy meeting. They had to decide on a plan for dealing with the Stranger. Until they learned this entity's name and purpose, referring to him as "the Stranger" seemed appropriate, because both its identity and motivation eluded them.

They had baked two frozen Tombstone pizzas and brought them into the den on big pans. Jason was starving, and the fellas were, too. They greedily dug into the food as they talked.

"We should call a minister," Shorty said. He paced, cap turned backward, a slice of pepperoni-and-cheese in his small hands. "That's what we should do, man. Call up Minister Thompson from my church. Only a man of God can kick a demon's ass."

"Who said the Stranger is a demon?" Jason said, sitting on the couch. "I mean, he seems to be some kind of spirit, but not all spirits are demons. Are they, Brains?"

"That's correct," Brains said from his perch on the stairs. "Basically, a spirit is a supernatural being. It can be either good or evil, an angel or a demon or maybe a poltergeist. The possibilities are broad."

"We don't know exactly what he is," Jason said. "All we can be sure of is that he's really powerful."

"Very powerful," Brains said. "So powerful that I wonder

if a minister could help us, assuming that one would believe our story in the first place. I doubt it."

"If we don't turn to God, who do we turn to?" Shorty said. He stopped pacing in the center of the room and regarded them pleadingly.

"We handle it ourselves," Jason said. "Your minister probably won't believe us, and no other grown-ups will believe us either. Think about it. A spirit writing words on my mirror, then coming out of a Ouija board to rip apart a bedroom? I'd think it was a wacky story myself if I wasn't living it. We can't rely on anyone else. We have to fight back on our own, fellas."

"I agree." Brains pushed his glasses up on his nose. He gulped down a bite of pizza. "So what's our strategy going to be?"

"Lots of prayer," Shorty said. When he saw Jason and Brains frown, he said, "Okay, okay, we can do more than pray. Why don't we get a weapon?"

"What kind of weapon?" Jason said.

"A knife," Shorty said. "I have a blade we can use, a real long-ass one. It has a sheath that you can clip to your belt, too. It's not the greatest thing, but it's something. How's that sound, fellas?"

"How's a knife going to hurt a spirit?" Jason said. "A spirit is like a ghost, right? You can't stab a ghost."

"We *think* the Stranger might be a spirit," Brains said. "We don't know for sure. He could be a man who's able to move objects with his mind. I've heard about people who can supposedly do that. It's called telekinesis."

"Tele-ki-what?" Shorty said.

"Telekinesis," Brains said. "Have you seen those people on TV who can bend spoons and stuff? Obviously, whoever the Stranger is, he's a lot more powerful than the average spoon-bender, but my point is, he could be human. And if he's human, a knife could hurt him. It's better than nothing."

"Well, okay," Jason said. "We arm ourselves with the knife. I just hope we don't have to use it."

"Then we have the weapon stuff settled," Shorty said. "Now, how about action? What're we gonna do?"

"Before we get into that, I need to tell you guys something," Jason said. "About another weird problem I've been having."

"Another one?" Brains said. He looked at Jason incredulously. "That shocks even me."

"This one isn't like the word-on-the-mirror thing," Jason said. "It's different. I've been having a nightmare."

"What's it about?" Shorty said.

Jason told them everything about his recurring dream. He was relieved finally to be able to relate it to someone; the details poured out of him. In light of what had happened that day, the nightmare, while disturbing, was not nearly as terrifying. Reality had become more frightening than his darkest dreams.

"What do you think?" Jason said. "Is the stalker in my nightmare the Stranger in real life?"

"I'd bet on it, Jason," Brains said. "It has to be him. I'm glad you told us about that dream. I think I know what we should do."

"What?" Jason said.

"We stay at my house tonight. And we sleep in shifts. Remember how the Ouija said the Stranger is coming for you? It seems logical to me that when the Stranger comes for you, he'll come at night, like he does in your nightmare. By sleeping in shifts, one of us will be awake when the Stranger appears, and maybe we'll be able to stop him. Or maybe we won't. But until we've solved this, it'd be foolish for you to sleep alone, like a sitting duck. Agree?"

"Yeah," Jason said. "For now, I think we've got our plan. Arm ourselves with that blade, and sleep in shifts. Seems good to me. Is that alright with you, Shorty?"

"Yeah, man. It's cool."

"Great," Jason said. "When can you get your knife?"

"I'll get it now," Shorty said. "I have to drop by the crib and pack some stuff for tonight anyway."

"Same here." Jason finished his last slice of pizza and stood. His memory of what had happened in the bedroom weighed heavily on his mind, and the fact that they were up against someone who did not appear to be an ordinary man evoked shivers of sheer dread. But with a plan of action to protect themselves, maybe he and the fellas had a chance. Whoever he was, whatever he was, the Stranger would not win without a fight. Not with anything less than a full-scale war, Jason vowed silently.

CHAPTER SEVEN

like father, like son.

Standing at the window of his girlfriend's North Chicago apartment, holding a cigarette and gazing into the night, Thomas pondered his father's cruel words. Since he had left the nursing home earlier that day, Big George's words had followed him like haunting spirits, making it nearly impossible for him to concentrate on work or anything else. He told himself to put them out of his mind, to dismiss them as yet another example of Big George's dementia, but he could not expel them from his thoughts. Because he secretly worried that Big George might be right.

He took a draw from his cigarette. He had been chainsmoking for the past several hours. It was unusual for him. He had not tasted nicotine in years.

He heard the bedroom door open behind him. Footsteps whispered across the plush carpet. Then two slender, copper-colored arms slipped around his waist, embracing him from behind.

"I didn't know you smoked," Rose Mason said in a whisper, her lips near his ear.

"There's a lot you don't know about me." He took a final draw from the Kool and extinguished it in a glass ashtray.

Rose dropped her hand to his groin, rubbed gently. "Maybe so. But I know the most important things about you."

He took away her hand and turned to face her. She was nude. She had a beautiful body: lithe, shapely, full in all the right places, her caramel skin as smooth as a peach. Ordinarily, the sight of her set his hormones aflame. But he could not summon any desire.

"Rose, I might have to disappoint you tonight," he said. "I'm not in the mood."

"I'll get you in the mood. You don't have to do a thing. Lie down, and I'll take care of everything."

She would, too, if he allowed her. He could lie down and let her fuck his brains out, then get dressed and leave, and both of them would have got exactly what they sought from this one-dimensional relationship. She got fantastic sex with a virile man whose stamina matched hers. He got to slip out of the demanding role of Thomas Brooks, hardworking entrepreneur, devoted son, inept husband and father, and assume the position of a man whose sole responsibility was to get it up. Rose required only great sex and trite conversation, and that was all he delivered. Their relationship was almost sinfully superficial—and relaxing. Whenever he left her apartment, he always left with the belief that he had released air from a stress balloon that often seemed dangerously close to exploding.

Nevertheless, as therapeutic as sex with Rose might have been, it was *wrong*. He was married and deeply in love with his wife. He had no business being in this woman's bedroom.

That is, unless he was really the womanizing dog Big George claimed both of them were.

Like father, like son.

Those damned words again. Mocking him. Challenging him. Daring him to prove them wrong.

Like father, like son.

He resolved that he had to break this cycle. Right here. Right now.

Rose had unbuttoned his shirt. She started to slip it off his shoulders. He stopped her.

"Hold on," he said. "We have to talk."

"Can it wait?"

"No. We have to talk now."

"Come on, baby. You haven't been here all week."

"It's only Tuesday."

"It feels like Friday to me."

"Damn, girl. Is sex all you think about?"

"I have needs, Thomas. I'm not gonna hide the fact that I need a man a few times a week. A female can't be shy these days, or she won't get shit."

"I guess so." He walked past her and sat on the bed. "You're honest."

"Damn right, I am." She sat beside him. She stroked his chest, kissed his neck.

He gently pushed her away. "But it's time for me to be honest, too."

She drew back. "What do you mean?"

"You probably don't care, but I have to tell this to someone. I talked to my dad today. Like usual, he chewed my ass out over anything that came to mind. But he said something I've never heard him say before, and it bothered me. It still bothers me."

"What did he say?" she said, watching him but, judging from her expression, not earnestly interested in his confession. She wasn't interested in anything if it wasn't about her. Her conceit was one of several unpleasant personality traits he had been willing to overlook because the sex was so good.

"My dad said I was just like him," he said. " 'Like father, like son,' is how he put it. He accused me of cheating on my wife, the same way he'd cheated on my mother."

"So, he was telling the truth."

"I can't stand the fact that I'm like him. I hate my father. It's terrible to say that, but it's true. There's nothing I love about him. When he told me that today, I saw how much like him I've become, and I hate myself for letting it happen. I can't take it anymore; I've got to change. So . . ."

"I get it." Her face darkened. "You want us to stop seeing each other."

"Rose, I'm sorry. But we have to. I can't do this anymore."

She glared at him.

"I'm sorry," he said again, knowing how lame he sounded— like all of the other married men who used women for sex, then cast them aside when the affair became inconvenient. He sounded like a manipulative dog, the kind of man whom women despised and nice guys loathed because he gave *all* men a bad reputation.

Shit, he needed another cigarette.

Rose went to the closet and removed a blue silk robe. She covered herself, returned to the bed.

"This doesn't surprise me," she said. "I knew you'd leave sooner or later. Men always do."

He stood and buttoned his shirt. "I didn't mean to use you."

She laughed. "Please, you make it sound like you've broken my heart. I never loved you, baby. You were a good fuck, nothing more, nothing less."

"Thanks a lot."

"Don't get an attitude. We used each other, and that's that. You'll go home to your wife, and I'll go on to the next man." She snapped her fingers. "You're dismissed."

"Is that all? That's so . . . cold."

"Oh, you're dripping with self-righteousness, ain't you? Are you gonna tell your wife about me, Mr. Do-right?"

He shrugged. He had not yet considered whether he would tell Linda about any of this. The subject floated like a giant storm cloud in his mind.

Rose chuckled. "Nah, you won't tell her. After you get over this little guilt trip, you'll be out looking for pussy again. Don't call me next time, all right?"

"There won't be a next time."

She curled up on the bed and crossed her legs. She smiled sweetly.

"Thomas, do me a favor, okay? Get out of my mother-fucking apartment."

"You don't know me," he said, compelled to explain that his rejection of her was not a mere temporary awakening of conscience. There would be no next time, no more "like father like son." He was putting this crap behind him for good.

"Are you gonna make me call the cops on you?" Rose said. "I said to get out of my fuckin' apartment!"

He got out of there. Rose didn't give a damn about his morals, and he shouldn't expect her to care. They hadn't been friends; they'd been sex partners. Nothing more.

As he walked across the parking lot to his Buick, the idea that he'd used the woman purely for sex, and had let her use him in kind, disgusted him. He'd always used protection when he was with her, and had been tested recently (without Linda's knowledge, of course), but he felt filthy nonetheless. The thought hadn't bothered him before, but it bugged him now. Christ, what was wrong with him? He'd been behaving so irresponsibly, he was fortunate that he'd gotten off the hook with Rose so easily.

He climbed in his car. Under a clear night sky, he drove away from the apartment building and headed north, toward Spring Harbor.

By ending his association with Rose, he had taken a step

toward proving to himself that he was not like his father. But another obstacle loomed, and he could thank Rose for reminding him of it. Was he going to confess to Linda?

He had to sit down and think it over, ponder every angle of the issue, then determine the best course of action. *Action* was the key word. He would have to do something. If he did not take action and do the right thing, he feared he would eventually wind up like his father. Sick. Bitter. And alone.

Electric-blue lightning seared the sky, and thunder grumbled like an angry god.

Lying in his bed, clutching the bedsheet to his chin, Jason looked out of the nearby window at the building storm. Elm trees swayed in a fierce wind, and darkness pressed against the glass—a burned-out blackness that reminded him of ashes, death, and the end of all hope. He turned away from the window. Watching the turbulent night only sharpened his anxiety.

He stared at the dark ceiling, shivering, though the room was warm.

He told himself to be brave, to face his fear like a man, but his voice sounded weak and unconvincing.

Thunder clashed, shaking the walls. Lightning ripped apart the darkness, ghostly flickers playing over the furniture.

When he thought he might be spared from the terror that night, he heard the fateful sound: a door downstairs opening, then slamming shut.

His heartbeat accelerated.

He looked at the bedroom door. It was locked. But a locked door never seemed to make a difference. He checked out of habit and foolish hope.

Then he heard the footsteps. They clocked across the floorboards, each step loud and sharp, as if the walker wore a pair of combat boots. The stalker marched slowly, methodically, like a sadistic executioner approaching a doomed victim. With each strident footfall, Jason's heart pounded harder.

He yanked the bedsheet over his head.

But covering himself seemed like a pathetic attempt at protection, hardly better than lying out in the open. He had to think of something else.

He threw off the cover and swung his legs to the side of the mattress. He slid his feet to the soft carpet, stood.

He heard the footsteps reach the bottom of the stairs. The invader began to climb the steps.

Frantic, Jason hurried to the door. Noticing his oak desk, he gripped the side of it and, straining, pushed it in front of the door. It probably would not stop the stalker, but it was better than nothing.

Thunder boomed in earth-rocking fusillades. A gust punched the window, like a furious spirit demanding entry.

The footsteps arrived at the head of the stairs.

He looked around wildly for a place to hide. Inside the closet? Behind the curtains? Under the bed? None of those spots seemed safe, but he had to choose one—quickly. He heard the stalker shuffling across the hallway, drawing closer to his room.

He dropped to the floor and scrambled underneath the bed.

Although the stale air under there felt cooler, he was suddenly sweating much more than before. Cold perspiration poured off him. Combined with the cool air, the icy sweat drove a numbing chill into his body that compelled him to curl into a fetal position, shivering, hugging himself for warmth.

Lying on his side, he had a view of those few inches near the floor not concealed by the hanging bedspread. At the moment, he saw only the oak baseboard at the bottom of the wall facing him, but that would change soon. The stalker was coming.

The doorknob rattled.

He tensed.

The doorknob turned again. Back and forth, back and forth. He imagined the knob, gleaming brass rotating left and right, and with each squeaky turn, he cursed the stalker. Although the stalker twisted the knob stubbornly, he would not enter through the door in the conventional manner. He was merely teasing Jason.

The doorknob quit rattling.

Jason listened.

He heard a soft hiss, like air escaping a balloon.

Then he heard footsteps inside the bedroom. So much for the desk's usefulness as a barricade.

The stalker walked to the closet at the foot of the bed. Jason heard the closet door squeal open.

He swore silently.

The stalker likely knew where he was hidden. But he wanted to prolong the search, raise Jason's terror to a fever pitch. Jason wanted to fight back, wanted to grab the guy and pulverize him for playing these mean-spirited tricks, but he cowered under the bed, not daring to move. What sane person would attack a man who could walk through doors?

The closet squeaked shut.

Trembling so badly he was certain he would give himself away, he tried to hear where the stalker would head next, though from past experience, he knew exactly what would happen. He listened out of a vain hope that his fears would not be realized.

The stalker walked across the room, to the windows. He ruffled the curtains.

Jason ground his teeth.

For a moment, silence, as though the stalker were deliberating where to look next. Then, Jason heard the inevitable: footsteps approaching the bed.

He drew himself into a tight ball.

He desperately wished he could fold up into himself and

vanish. Or shrink as tiny as a gnat. Anything to get out of there. His heart banged wildly.

A pair of sleek black leather boots stopped beside the bed, inches away from Jason's face.

The boots shone in the darkness, emitting a strange, silvery glow.

Jason heard the sound of movement: the visitor beginning to bend down.

He clenched his hands into fists. He was caught between wanting to see the stalker's face and never wanting to know the man's identity.

Slowly, the stalker lifted the hanging bedspread. Higher, higher, higher . . .

The instant Jason would have seen the face, he shut his eyes and screamed, exploding out of the nightmare.

"Hey, you all right?" Shorty said.

Heart thudding, Jason groaned. He lay curled up like a pill bug and wedged under something. He unclenched his hand, touched the object above him. It felt like a table.

"You crawled under the card table," Shorty said. Crouched on the floor, he peered at Jason, his face a black oval in the dark den. "Damn, that nightmare of yours must be an ass-kicker. You okay?"

"I'm alive, but I feel awful." He squeezed from underneath the furniture. "Man, how embarrassing. I was hidden under there like a little kid afraid of the bogeyman."

"Don't worry, I ain't gonna tell anyone," Shorty said.

Outside, thunder bellowed. A continuous sizzle of rain pattered on the roof. Jason went to a window and lifted the drape. The stormy night had a burned-out look that reminded him of his nightmare. Shivering at the similarity, he dropped the curtain.

"What time is it?" Jason said.

"Almost four in the morning. Ain't nothing happened. We're the fools here, man. The Stranger's probably snoring like everyone else."

"Maybe so. But I think sleeping in shifts is a good idea. In case something does happen."

"Anyway, it's your turn to watch," Shorty said. "Four o'clock, remember?"

"Yeah."

Shorty handed him the flashlight and the sheathed knife. Jason clipped both items to his waistband.

"Watch your back, don't fall asleep, and if you see anything, holler," Shorty said. "I'm taking my butt to bed."

Shorty slipped inside his sleeping bag, which lay beside Brains, who slept soundly on a pallet. Brains's shift had been from ten o'clock until one; Shorty's had been from one to four; and Jason's ended at seven. Jason had slept six hours, but he felt as if he could use six more. His muscles ached from all of yesterday's activities.

According to their plan, the designated watcher had to make a circuit of the house every thirty minutes, checking all vacant rooms such as the living room, dining room, and kitchen, and enclosed spaces such as the laundry room, closets, and bathrooms. Shadowy niches were to be inspected with the flashlight, and close attention was to be given to all doors. Not knowing the true nature of their adversary, they had to guard themselves as though anticipating a physical threat. But if their nemesis proved to be something unearthly, their plan might be a waste of time: the stalker in his nightmare could walk through doors. . . .

Don't think about it, Jason cautioned himself. *It's only a dream.*

He began his circuit. He went to the laundry room, which was located just off the den. He shone the flashlight within. He saw a clothesline from which dangled a few shirts and blouses. A washer and dryer. A large sink. Containers of Tide and Clorox standing on a small table. A plastic laundry basket. But no Stranger. He closed the door.

He already had the feeling that he had a long shift ahead of him.

He swept the flashlight beam across the dark corners of the den. Nothing.

He climbed the stairs to the first floor, emerging in the kitchen. The refrigerator hummed. Raindrops drummed against the skylight. Flashlight in hand, he searched the area, pausing at the back door to see if there were any signs of forced entry. He found nothing suspicious.

He sighed. He had a *very* long shift ahead of him.

He checked the rest of the ground floor. The breakfast nook. The dining room. The living room. The bathroom. The coat closet. The front door. Nothing.

He went upstairs. He trod quietly, not wanting to awake Brains's parents or sister, none of whom had any idea what was going on, and all of whom thought the three boys just wanted to hang out overnight, play video games, and eat pizza. He checked Brains's bedroom. Couldn't check his sister's room, so scratch that one. Couldn't enter his parents' room, either, so forget that one, too. The bathroom. The guest room. The hallway closet.

Nothing. Nothing. Nothing.

Although he should've been glad the Stranger had not visited them, he gritted his teeth in frustration. He should be sleeping, not searching for someone who would probably not appear. He could imagine the Stranger laughing at their wasted efforts.

He clicked off the flashlight and took the stairs to the first floor. As he left the last step, the telephone rang.

He jumped at the sound.

He read his watch. Fifteen minutes past four. Who would call at this hour?

The phone rang again.

Worried that the ringing would wake everyone, he rushed into the living room. A telephone sat on the end table. A bright-red light on the phone pulsed in unison with each ring.

He snatched up the handset.

"Hello?" he said.

Dead silence.

"Hello?" he said again, ready to hang up if the caller did not speak immediately.

Silence.

Then a deep, smooth voice: "I know what you need."

"What?" he said, convinced he had heard wrong.

"I know what you need . . . Jason."

His fingers tightened around the handset.

"Who is this?" Jason said.

A ripple of low laughter.

"Hey, who are you?"

"I know *exactly* what you need, Jason."

Jason was struck by something in the voice. Something . . . familiar. But he couldn't place what had ignited a spark in his memory.

"What are you talking about?" Jason said. "How do you know what I need?"

"Because I know you."

"But I don't know *you*," Jason said. "Who are you?"

"Remember."

At the mention of that word, Jason's heart began to jackhammer.

"Yes, it's me," the voice said, the caller's true identity still eluding Jason's mental grasp. "The Stranger."

CHAPTER EIGHT

Jason's heart boomed so loudly, he was certain the noise would wake everyone in the house. The Stranger had called him. But where was he calling from?

Brains's family had Caller ID connected to their telephone. The small plastic display sat on the table, along with the lamp and the phone. Holding the handset to his ear with one hand, he clicked on the table lamp. He lifted the indicator device to the light.

The digital display read, *"UNAVAILABLE."*

Jason bit his lip.

As though aware of what Jason had tried to do, the Stranger chuckled.

"You cannot trace the call, Jason. Not to where *I* am calling you from."

"Where are you calling from?"

"Fantasyland," the Stranger said. He laughed.

Fantasyland?

Jason was not sure whether he was being honest or not.

He was inclined to doubt him. Calling from Fantasyland? The idea was ridiculous.

"I'm coming for you, Jason. Soon. We have some unfinished business to conclude."

"I don't know what you're talking about. Tell me what's going on. Who are you? Why are you messing with me? What do you want?"

"Patience, patience. For now, I will give you one answer, Jason: I know you. I know what you need, I know what you want, and I'm going to give it to you."

"But what—"

"I'm going to give it to you."

The phone clicked.

The line had gone dead.

Jason stood there gripping the handset. Sweat saturated his face. His mouth was dry.

Rain ticked on the roof.

In the distance, thunder rumbled.

He replaced the handset on the cradle.

Rational thought seemed impossible. He tried to organize his thoughts and failed. The Stranger's oddly familiar voice kept playing in his mind, his ominous words repeating themselves over and over.

I know what you need, I know what you want, and I'm going to give it to you.

Jason gazed out the living room window at the stormy summer night, wondering what secrets awaited him—and wondering if he really wanted to know.

I'm going to give it to you.

Immediately after he hung up the telephone, Jason awoke Shorty and Brains. He told them what had happened.

"Jesus," Shorty said, his eyes wide. "If I'd gotten that call, I would've shit on myself. Were you scared?"

"Of course, I was scared," Jason said. He paced across the den, too wound up to sit. "I'm still scared. I can't stop thinking of what he's going to do next."

In fact, he could not stop asking himself a lot of questions about the Stranger. Who was he? Why was he bothering him? Was he a spirit, or was he something else? Why was he hiding his identity? Where had he called from? What was that "unfinished business" he had mentioned? What had he meant when he said he was going to give Jason what he needed and wanted? What was the ultimate purpose of this mystery he had sucked Jason into?

On the sofa, Brains had been cleaning his glasses with his T-shirt. Clearing his throat, he slipped on his eyeglasses.

"Well, Jason," Brains said, "we might not know what the Stranger plans to do next, but I know what I'm going to do. I'm going to arm you with a better weapon. Have you ever used a handgun?"

Jason stopped pacing. "A gun? No way. You have one?"

Rocking in the recliner, Shorty chuckled. "Man, Brains is a damn sharpshooter; he ain't the clumsy nerd a lot of people think he is. You know his pops is in the army, right? He taught Brains how to shoot before he taught him how to read. And Brains was reading books at three."

"As usual, he exaggerates," Brains said, rolling his eyes. "But my dad did give me some lessons about firearms, and I have access to a good pistol. I'll teach you how to handle it. I think you need to start carrying a gun, Jason. There's no telling what the Stranger is going to try."

"What if I get in trouble?" Jason said. "It's against the law to carry a gun."

"Man, how're the cops gonna find out?" Shorty said. "You plan on robbing a bank?"

"No, but . . . a gun?" Jason said. "That's serious, fellas."

"I've thought about it quite a bit," Brains said. "It *is* a serious step, which is why I didn't suggest from the start that we carry firearms. I wanted to see how far this business with the Stranger would go first. I think it's gotten serious enough. The Stranger is obviously going to continue his weird mission, and it promises to get more intense."

"Good point," Jason said, the Stranger's ominous promise echoing in his thoughts. *I'm going to give it to you.*

"I honestly don't know whether a gun will even matter against someone like the Stranger, but what other choice do we have?" Brains said. "Wooden stakes and holy water? I prefer a gun, thank you."

"You've convinced me," Jason said. "But please make sure you teach me well. And it has to be a gun that's small enough for me to hide in my clothes. Because if I get caught . . ."

"Your mama will wear your ass out," Shorty said.

"You know the deal," Jason said.

Brains smiled grimly. "Don't worry, I'll teach you well. It'll be a small gun that you can conceal, too."

"What about you guys?" Jason said. "Are both of you going to have guns?"

"Damn right, we will," Shorty said, and Brains nodded. "The Stranger seems to just care about you, but since we're helping you, he might try some shit with one of us. We ain't taking any chances."

"Exactly," Brains said. "The biggest chance that I'll be taking will be swiping three handguns—and ammo—from my Dad's collection. I doubt that he'll notice. He only cleans his firearms a couple of times a year, and he doesn't go hunting anymore."

"I feel better knowing both of you are gonna be armed," Jason said.

"I have another idea, too," Brains said. "I think it'll be wise for us to change where we sleep each night. If we stay in one place, we might become careless from getting used to the same old routine. But if we move around, it'll help us stay alert. We've already slept at my house. I figured we could sleep at yours next, Jason."

"Oh, no," Jason said. "That's a bad idea."

"What's wrong with staying at your crib?" Shorty said. "You got giant cockroaches? Monster rats?"

"Well . . . never mind," Jason said. He had never told them about his relationship with his parents, and he was in no mood to talk about it. "It should be okay, but I can't promise that my mom will let you guys sleep over. She's . . . unpredictable."

"She's fine; that's what she is." Shorty whistled. "Man, one day I came over there, and she was lying in the backyard in this skimpy swimsuit. I almost had a heart attack. I know she's your mom and all, but she's got a body on her that won't quit."

"You don't know her," Jason said. Shorty had been infatuated with his mother since the first time he had seen her. If only he knew the truth.

Shorty shrugged. "Anyway, if she says no, we can go to my crib. No big deal."

"Thanks," Jason said. He turned to Brains. "So. When do we begin target practice?"

For the first time in months, Thomas dropped by his house during the afternoon. He felt guilty about leaving The House of Soul—in his thoughts, he could hear Big George threatening him—but he had to speak to Linda.

He parked his car in the garage. He took a long pull off his cigarette, ground it out in the ashtray. If he followed through on his plan for this conversation with Linda, that would be his last smoke.

He pressed the remote control clipped to the sun visor. The big garage door thumped shut behind him.

He stared at the door that led to the kitchen.

He had spent last night on the living room couch, searching for an answer to his dilemma, and when dawn arrived, he knew what he had to do: tell Linda about his affair. Living with the secret was impossible. He viewed himself as an imperfect but honest man; if he hid his adultery, he would not be able to look in the mirror without hating what he saw. Big George's piercing remark—*"Like father, like son"*—had snapped him out of his delusional belief that the affair was good for his mental health. Big George's words presented a challenge, too. Would he tell Linda the truth and prove himself a better man than his father? Or would he keep his secrets, as Big George would have, and continue to cower under his father's shadow?

He was a better man than his father. He had to be; he couldn't tolerate the thought that he was on the same level as Big George. He had to do the right thing. A real man lived by a code of honesty. It was time for him to prove his manhood—to himself.

He got out of the car and entered the house.

Linda stood near the kitchen counter, pouring coffee into a mug. Wearing a summery white blouse and peach shorts, she was as lovely as she had been when they first met in high school. He wished he had more time to spend with her. But there was always the restaurant sitting on his shoulders like a stone gorilla, demanding all of his attention, time, and energy. One of these days, he vowed, he would show Linda how much he loved and appreciated her. One of these days.

She turned. "Am I dreaming, or have you come home from work before midnight?"

"I have to talk to you. The restaurant isn't going anywhere."

"If you're saying that about your job, I must be dreaming." She motioned to her coffee. "Want some?"

"Sure." Why was she being so cordial? For a couple of

days after an argument, she was usually moody, and yesterday they'd had a real nasty fight. Her friendly demeanor seemed odd.

She handed him a brimming mug of java. She wrinkled her nose. "Have you been smoking?"

"A little."

She studied him. "Whatever you plan to tell me must be bothering you. You only smoke when you're stressed out."

"It is important, Linda."

"Then let's sit down. I have a few things I need to say, too."

They sat at the dinette table. He gazed into his coffee, pondering how to begin. Unable to summon words immediately, he glanced at her.

Her brown eyes were clear, her gaze forthright, as though she had tapped some well of inner peace since their confrontation yesterday. She had never reacted like this. He looked away from her, shifting in his chair. What was going on here?

"What's bugging you?" she said.

Now was the time to tell her the truth.

But as he regarded her, he suddenly knew he was not going to confess. Not right now. He had to mull over this strange transformation in her attitude, determine a different approach to exposing his infidelity. If he spoke prematurely, before he understood her unusual behavior, he might regret it.

Or maybe he was only making excuses for himself. No matter how carefully he worded his confession, it would not alter the terrible truth. He had cheated on her, plain and simple. Was there actually a tactful way to tell your wife that you've been sleeping around?

She watched him expectantly. He had to say something. He launched into the obvious.

"I want to apologize for yesterday," he said. "I made a big

mistake when I grabbed you. I lost control of myself, and I'm sorry. You had every right to slap me. I promise that I'll never lay a hand on you again. Can you please forgive me?"

"Not yet."

"Not yet?"

"First, I have a few promises of my own to make."

He pushed the cup aside. "What are you talking about?"

She didn't stop to explain. "Number one: I promise to show you, in every way I can, that I love you."

He frowned. The conversation had taken an unexpected turn.

"Number two: I promise to support your career."

"Now *I* must be dreaming," he said.

"Number three, and this is the big one: if you don't start treating me and our son the way you should've been treating us all along, I promise to divorce you."

He reared back. "Where the hell did that come from?"

"Ten years of misery, baby." She folded her arms. "Now that you have my promises, I forgive you."

"Wait a minute, that's bullshit, Linda. You can't force me into anything."

"I'm not forcing you. The choice is yours. More than anything, I want us to become the family we used to be. But if you don't get your act together, it won't happen, and there's no sense in us being married."

"You're putting the blame on me, like you always do." He pushed away from the table and walked to the door. "I don't want to hear it. I'm going back to work."

She got up. "Hold on, listen. I'm not blaming you for everything. I admit, some of our problems are my fault. But I'm committed to doing better, Thomas. For us to get back on track, you have to do your share, too."

He spun around. "Woman, what do you want me to do? I bust my ass trying to support us, I don't have time to live a normal life. If I get lazy, that place'll go to hell so fast it won't be funny, and we'll lose everything."

"We've already come close to losing everything. I'm not talking about money, I'm talking about our family."

"You're not hearing me. I can't *risk* changing my work habits."

"I see. Then you value your work above your family."

"Hell, no. You and Jason are the reasons why I work so hard."

She shook her head. "No, baby. I know the real reason why you work so hard. You're brainwashed."

"What?"

"Yes—brainwashed. Your dad's brainwashed you. You're a workaholic like he was, because he taught you that's how a real man runs a business. But a real man works hard, then comes home and spends quality time with his family. You work hard, but you've forgotten your duty to us. Think about it. When was the last time you saw Jason?"

Thomas leaned against the counter. He sighed. "Last week, if I remember correctly. Damn, that's pathetic, isn't it?"

"He's a good kid," she said, "but he needs you. I need you, too. I only wish you needed us."

"I do need you, both of you," he said. "I figured I'd have a chance in the future to spend time with you, do the family thing. There're so many people out there struggling to make ends meet, and I don't want us to ever be like that."

"We're a long way from poor, Thomas."

"True. But the very thought of poverty . . . it scares me. You know how I grew up, Linda. In a three-room shack crawling with roaches and rats. A nightmare. When Dad opened the restaurant, we finally climbed out of that hell, and I feel like I owe The House of Soul and my dad for saving us."

Her eyes were kind, understanding, filled with love. So much love that his heart kicked.

He went on. "You ever heard that saying, 'once poor, never rich'? It fits me. I'm worried that if I cut down my work hours, I'll be turning my back on my job, my father—and I'll lose everything. I want to make so much money that we'll never have to worry about being poor—ever."

"You can waste a lifetime chasing that dream," Linda said. "Thomas, you already bring home twice what you earned only four years ago. We've got plenty of money socked away in our investment portfolio, and enough saved for Jason to attend almost any college he wants. Face it, we're doing very well for ourselves."

"Doesn't matter. Anything can happen. The stock market can crash; banks can fold; the restaurant can go under—and everything we have would be wiped out, forcing us to live in a shelter or, even worse, survive on the streets, picking our dinner out of garbage cans and begging for spare change. Why are you looking at me like that?"

"You need to relax, honey. Forget the doomsday scenarios and live. Enjoy life. Enjoy your *family.*"

"I hear you. You're right. But . . . hell, maybe I am brain-washed. I probably sound like a nutcase to you."

Arms folded over her chest, she watched him, silent.

He bowed his head. "I'll work on cutting down my hours," he said. It was the right thing to say, but he wasn't confident about his ability to follow through; the familiar fear of losing everything gnawed at him. "But I can't change my habits overnight. I hope you have patience. I have a long way to go."

She stepped into his arms and hugged him fiercely. At first he did not respond, for as an adulterer, he did not think he deserved his wife's embrace. But the feeling of her against him, so warm and firm—so *alive*—overwhelmed him. He drew her closer and kissed her brow, loving her sweet scent and everything else about her and cursing himself under his breath.

"All of us have a long way to go, honey," she said, her head resting on his chest. "But if we go together, we'll be fine. I have faith. Our relationship's been at rock bottom for so long that we can only go uphill."

"You're right," he said, though he didn't feel as if he was due to travel uphill. As he ruminated on the shameful truth he had left unspoken, he felt as if he were plummeting into a cold, dark place of unrelenting torment . . . and inescapable guilt.

After Jason repaired his bike with spare parts that Brains had found in his garage, he rode home around five o'clock. He planned to ask Mom whether his friends could sleep over. He disliked having to ask her for any favors, but if he refused to ask, the fellas would want to know why, and he did not want to expose his turbulent relationship with Mom. It was easier to ask her and get it over with.

The .22 that Brains had given him rested in an ankle holster, which Brains had also loaned him. Earlier that day, Brains had taught him the fundamentals of using the handgun: how to load it, the correct shooter's stance, how to aim and fire the weapon, and other basic techniques. Jason did not feel confident enough to battle the Stranger one-on-one, but he felt safer than he had before. His jeans concealed the weapon.

He had also spoken to his girlfriend. After he apologized for not calling her yesterday, he reaffirmed his promise to take her to the Fourth of July carnival that Friday. She had been talking about the carnival for days, and though he had been enthusiastic about it originally, with all this stuff with the Stranger going on, his interest had waned. But if he wanted to keep her happy, he would have to take her. Life goes on.

Once he reached the house, he pushed his bike toward the garage, intending to park it inside since he would be home for the rest of the day. He opened the side door. As usual, his father's car was not there, but his mother's Nissan was inside. Sunbeams streaming through the garage window revealed something else in there, too.

He stopped. He told himself that he could not be seeing this. But he prayed that it was actually real.

A Randolph Street M9000. It leaned on its kickstand in front of the car, chrome frame glittering in the sunshine, as shiny and new as a model that had just rolled off the assembly line.

The white Mylar balloon that was tied to the handlebars read in big, blue letters:

HAPPY BIRTHDAY!

CHAPTER NINE

Trembling, Jason stared at the Randolph. He admired it from various angles, not touching it, irrationally afraid that it would dissolve like a phantasm under his fingers. Every sleek inch of the chrome bicycle had been obsessively polished; seeing its dazzling luster, it was easy to believe that it had never been touched by a human hand, as though the sheer power of his wishing had created it from empty air.

Finally, he clutched the handgrips.

It's mine. It's really mine.

Sometimes, dreams did come true.

He rushed toward the house to thank his mother. When he reached the door that linked the garage to the kitchen, he halted.

He had not told either of his parents about the Randolph. Assuming they would never buy it, he had kept his mouth shut.

He had not spoken of the bike to Granddad, either. Granddad might have bought it for him, but Jason would have felt uncomfortable asking for such an expensive gift.

In fact, he had not even mentioned the bike to Shorty and Brains.

The only person to whom he had confided his wish was Mr. MacGregor, the owner of the bike shop. Not only did Mr. MacGregor not know his birthday was coming soon, there was no way he would have given him one of his store's finest products. It was impossible.

So . . . who had given him the Randolph?

The answer struck him. It was incredible yet sensible, mysterious yet obvious. The phone call last night. The curiously familiar voice. The Stranger.

I know what you need, I know what you want, and I'm going to give it to you.

He looked at the bicycle, at the Mylar balloon proclaiming "Happy Birthday."

I'm going to give it to you.

The Stranger had given him the bike. He was certain. He suddenly felt sick.

He stumbled to his mother's car and sat on the bumper. Bent over, he breathed deeply. His heart slammed so hard, his chest hurt.

Again he glanced at the bike, the balloon.

I'm going to give it to you.

Who was the Stranger?

Why was he doing these things?

Jason would have done anything to end this, anything to quell the terror that had grabbed hold of him yesterday morning and tightened its grip on him with each passing hour.

He stood. In need of fresh air, he left the garage and walked along the side of the house.

He ordered himself to think. Being scared would not help him. What was he going to do?

He thought of a source that he and the fellas had not explored yet: the cops. Earlier, they had not possessed any evidence that could have aided the police in an investigation. But the Randolph was proof. Maybe the cops could lift fingerprints from it, or hair, saliva, blood—anything, because the smallest clue could lead to the perpetrator's doorstep. Yeah, the cops. The cops would prove that none of this was as weird or frightening as it appeared to be.

Or maybe, as he feared, they would prove nothing at all.

The white-and-green sedan bearing the insignia of the Spring Harbor Police Department parked in front of the house.

The policeman met Jason and his mother near the garage. Jason related how he had discovered the Randolph, but he left out the other things the Stranger had done. He wanted help, not ridicule. He hoped the clues gathered from the bike alone would be enough to catch the enemy.

"I've been on the force seventeen years, and I have to admit, that's one of the strangest stories I've ever heard," the officer said when Jason had finished.

"I feel the same way," Mom said, standing beside Jason. "If I had heard it from someone else, I would have dismissed it as a joke. But Jason wouldn't make up something like this. He's mature for his age."

Jason smiled briefly at her.

Mom had pulled her car out of the garage, providing a clear path to the bicycle, which Jason had left sitting in its original position. Hands clasped behind him, the cop walked slowly around the bike.

"Impressive, very impressive," he said. "Whoever polished this did an incredible job. As though they were determined to gain your approval." He regarded the Mylar balloon. "That's a nice touch. Happy birthday. When's your birthday, kid?"

"July nineteenth," Jason said. "I'll be fourteen."

"Really? I've a fourteen-year-old son. He'd flip if he got a birthday gift like this." The cop bent down and examined the chrome frame. "No city registration sticker, engraved name, or serial number on here. Odd."

"You think it might've been stolen?" Mom said.

He rose. "Maybe, maybe not. I'm going to check around. Excuse me for a couple of minutes, folks." He returned to his sedan. Jason saw him speaking on a cell phone.

Jason turned to Mom. "What do you think?"

"It's weird, honey," she said. "Very weird."

"That bike costs fifteen hundred dollars," he said. "I've been wanting it for months."

She cocked her head. "You have? Why didn't you tell me?"

"Yeah, right. You wouldn't have bought it for me."

"I might have."

"Whatever, Mom."

"How can you be sure of what I'll do unless you ask? From now on, if you want anything, you tell me. I won't promise you that I'll get you everything you ask for, but at least give me a chance, Jason."

"Sure."

"I'm not like I used to be. I keep telling you. One of these days, I hope you'll believe me."

"The cop's coming back," Jason said, glad that they could change the subject.

"I've talked to Mr. MacGregor, who runs the only store in the city that sells these bicycles," the officer said. "He hasn't reported having any of his bikes stolen. According to police headquarters, no one in town has reported a stolen Randolph, either."

"Maybe someone bought it," Mom said. "Jason says he visits Mr. MacGregor's store often. Mr. MacGregor might have told someone about Jason, and that person might have bought the bike for Jason, for whatever odd reasons."

The cop shook his head. "I pursued that line. No good. MacGregor hasn't sold one of those bicycles in months."

"Why does it matter whether it was bought or stolen?" Jason said. "Can't you just lift the fingerprints from it and identify the guy?"

"The law doesn't work like that, kid," the cop said. "Before I can call in a fingerprint technician, we need a strong reason to believe a crime has been committed. This is a bizarre occurrence, certainly, but I don't see any proof of wrongdoing."

"You're kidding," Mom said.

"I wouldn't kid about this, Mrs. Brooks," he said. "These days, most police departments in the country have huge backlogs of cases that need attending to: serious cases of homicide, rape, child molestation, you name it. The cops in Spring Harbor are under the same pressure. Our suspicion of criminal conduct has to be solid before we can justify the manpower needed to begin an investigation. I don't mean to make light of your fears, but I'd get laughed out of my department if I requested a fingerprint man for this. It looks as if someone's simply given you a gift, kid. There's no law against giving birthday presents."

Jason stared at him. "That's it? You can't do anything?"

"I'm sorry, kid," he said. "My hands are tied."

"But couldn't Jason be in danger?" Mom said. "We don't know who did this. We don't know what might happen next."

"I understand," the cop said. "It's frightening. Especially now, when there seems to be a psychopath living on every block. But like I said, no law's been broken."

"And you can't do anything until you *suspect* a law has been broken," Mom said, punctuating her statement with a loud sigh.

"Sorry, Mrs. Brooks," the officer said.

Mom looked at Jason. "I guess we'll have to handle this on our own."

"I guess so," Jason said, though he had no intention of involving his mother any further. She was the last person he wanted to have caught up in his business.

The cop's eyes softened. "If you want, I'll impound the bike. We'll wait a while and see if one is eventually reported missing, and if not, either you can pick it up or we'll sell it at an auction. It's up to you."

"Take it," Jason said. "Keep it. I don't ever want to see it again."

"All right, kid." The policeman went to the Randolph. He punctured the Mylar balloon with a pocketknife, flipped up the kickstand, and rolled the bike to his patrol car. After he secured it in the trunk, he turned to them.

"Once again, I'm sorry I couldn't be of much help."

"You did what you could," Mom said.

"Which wasn't anything, unfortunately." He opened his car door. "You folks take care. If anything else happens, call us immediately."

"We will," Mom said. "Thanks."

Nodding at them, the officer slipped inside his cruiser. He drove away, the bike jutting from the trunk, sparkling in the sunlight as the sedan rolled out of sight.

Jason had never been so relieved to see a Randolph Street M9000 disappear. Once the bike of his dreams, it had become part of his nightmares.

Freshly showered, clothed in a monogrammed black bathrobe with gold trim, Thomas hesitated at the closed door of the master bedroom. Inside, Linda was probably reading in bed. And anticipating a night of passionate lovemaking.

In spite of their talk that afternoon about reviving their relationship, Thomas didn't plan on fulfilling her sexual expectations. Sex, within the institution of marriage, was sacred, the ultimate means by which a couple celebrated their union. How could he make love to Linda while living a lie that mocked the very concept of marriage? If he were an honest man, he would abstain—and reveal the truth. That was what he had to do tonight, or else he would sink so deeply into this pit of deceit that he might never climb out.

Bracing himself, he opened the door.

Linda sat in bed, reading by the buttery glow of the bedside lamp. Except for the personalized monogram, her robe matched his exactly. The marital harmony that their clothing suggested intensified his guilt. As an adulterer, he had no business wearing this robe.

Linda placed the book on the nightstand. She came to him.

"I love the way you smell after you shower," she said, her arms encircling his waist. "So clean and strong. If you were a bar of soap, I'd rub you all over me—everywhere."

She raised her face. He lowered his head, touched his lips against hers. Her mouth was warm and soft, ripe for kissing. She nibbled gently at his lower lip. He ran his tongue across her teeth, and she pressed herself more tightly against him, the warmth and firmness of her body stirring his desire. He slid his hands down and cupped her hips . . .

. . . and heard Big George's raspy voice whispering like a snake in his ear: *Like father, like son. . . . You just like me, Tommy. . . . Just like me . . . Like father, like son.*

He pulled away from Linda.

"Linda, I'm sorry. I . . . can't. Not tonight."

"You can't what?"

"Make love to you."

"Why not?"

Because I'm a low-down dog and making love to you would only make me feel worse, he longed to say but didn't. He merely sat on the bed. "I'm . . . too tired. It's been a long day."

"Too tired? You came home from work earlier than you

have in years. How can you suddenly be too tired? Especially now?"

"I don't know, but I am." It was a lame reply, but he could not say anything else; a block of wood seemed to have lodged in his throat. He lay on his back.

She sat beside him. "Something's bothering you."

He did not respond.

She touched his hand. "When you're upset, I am, too. Come on, baby. Tell me what's on your mind."

He sat up and looked at her. He almost told her the truth. But as he thought about how much she meant to him and how deeply he loved her—and most of all, how much the truth would hurt her—he could not say the words his conscience urged him to speak. He could not risk telling her something that might tear her away from him. Because without her, he would be hollower than he already was.

"Thomas," she said, arms crossed.

"It's nothing, sweetheart. I'm just tired."

"Is it another woman?"

He almost choked. "What?"

"Have you been sleeping around?" She watched him closely.

He pulled one of her legs onto his lap and massaged her calf. "Come on, be realistic. Considering the hours I've been working, when would I have time for an affair? Assuming, of course, that I'd be stupid enough to have one in the first place." He lifted her foot, kissed it. Her pretty feet, with their meticulously pedicured, red-painted toenails, had always been sexy to him, and kissing one of them helped him avoid her perceptive eyes.

"If you were cheating on me, do you know what I'd do?"

He stroked her thigh. "Do we really need to talk about it? Relax, I don't have anything going on."

She was silent. Then: "Am I the problem?"

"Hell, no. You're as gorgeous and sweet as ever. *I'm* the

problem. I need to get my act together, put my priorities back in order. Give me some time, that's all I ask." He lay down again, sighing heavily.

She was quiet. She squeezed his hand. "I suppose you're right. Sorry I grilled you."

"That's okay. I'm the one who's sorry."

She smiled wanly. "I'll survive."

He smiled, too. But he had never hated himself more. Like a devilish line of falling dominoes, one lie led to another. Damn it, why did he have to lie to maintain her faith in him? How long could he keep up the act? What would be the final result of all this deception?

He did not know. But he suspected that he would get little sleep that night.

"Can we talk for a moment?" she said. "It's about Jason."

"Sure." He was eager to remove the focus from himself. "What's on your mind?"

"A couple of hours after you left the house this afternoon, we discovered a bike in the garage. It happened to be a new bike that Jason really wanted, but he had never told me about it. Apparently, a stranger gave it to him. The stranger tied a birthday balloon to the handlebars, too. Isn't that weird?"

"It sure is. What did you do?"

"We called the cops. They weren't any help—only said that leaving an anonymous gift isn't a crime. But they took the bike away. Jason didn't want it anymore. He seemed very upset by the whole incident."

"Strange. Does he have any idea who would've given him the bike?"

"No. That's what worries me. There're so many wackos loose on the streets. I hope this doesn't lead to something else."

"Your dad probably bought the bike for Jason. You know how he loves to spoil him."

"I thought about that. Dad said he didn't know that Jason wanted the bike. Jason never told him about it."

He shrugged. "Then I'm clueless."

She bit her lip. "Jason and his friends are up to something, Thomas. You know they're sleeping over tonight. He's never had friends stay overnight. I think they're planning something."

"Boys his age are always planning something. They're probably planning to sneak in a few girls."

She swatted his arm affectionately. "Be serious. I'm worried."

"Then what should we do? Put a spy camera in the garage? Hire a private detective to track Jason and his buddies? Lock Jason in his room for the rest of the summer?"

"How about you talk to him and see what he's doing?"

"I thought you already talked to him."

"I did, but . . . he never tells me anything. If I asked Jason to tell me if the sky was blue, he'd find a way to avoid answering me. Can you talk to him, honey? Please?"

"I'll talk to him." He yawned. "Tomorrow."

"That makes me feel better." She smiled. She kissed him softly. "Good night."

"Good night."

She clicked off the bedside lamp and settled on her side of the mattress.

Thomas folded his hands behind his head. Although he had brushed off Linda, he wouldn't be able to do it much longer. Happily married couples made love. Frequently. He would either have to make love to her, thereby committing another conscience-wrecking trespass, or give her the truth, at the possible cost of their marriage.

Neither choice held any appeal for him. And time would not wait for his decision.

At three o'clock in the morning, two hours after Jason had begun his watch, he heard the telephone ring in his mother's office.

Until the phone rang, the night had been uneventful. Mom had agreed to let Shorty and Brains sleep over, and Shorty had pulled the first shift; he reported only seeing Jason awake from yet another nightmare, curled up under a table in the living room. In the past, Jason had suffered the dream once a week. Since finding the message in the bathroom, he'd had the nightmare every night. Clearly, events were building to a head, and as he rushed into the room to answer the telephone, he wondered if this call would be the bomb that would explode the mystery at last.

The office was dark. The telephone sat on the curved wing of the desk, beside the computer. A green button on the keypad blinked in time with each ring; it emitted an eerie, alien glow in the blackness.

Neglecting to switch on the light, Jason grabbed the handset.

"Hello?" he said out of habit, for he knew who had called.

Silence.

Then he heard that strangely familiar, smooth voice.

"Did you like your gift, Jason?"

The terror that had gripped Jason during the Stranger's first call did not seize him this time.

"Cut the games, okay?" Jason said. "Who are you?"

The Stranger chuckled.

"I hope you enjoyed your present," the Stranger said. "I have more gifts for you, more of your secret wishes to fulfill."

"What secret wishes?"

"You know what they are."

"Okay, maybe I do," Jason said, having no idea what the Stranger meant, saying it only to induce him to reveal more information. "But how do you know what I want? How did you know I wanted that bike?"

"Because I know you, as I've told you before. I know everything about you."

"But *how?* I don't know anything about you."

"Yes, you do. Deep in the recesses of your soul, you understand everything about me."

More riddles. "Are you some kind of spirit?"

"Aren't we all spirits, Jason?"

"That's not what I meant. Are you a demon, a ghost, a poltergeist?"

"I am all of those manifestations. I am none of those manifestations."

"Look, let's get to the point. What's your name?"

"The Stranger." He chuckled.

Striving to keep his composure, Jason said, "Come on. Tell me. Please."

"That would spoil the fun," the Stranger said. "I know how you enjoy an engaging mystery. I don't want to ruin such a fine time for you."

"You won't be ruining anything for me. I'm not having any fun."

The Stranger laughed. "I believe your nose grew an inch, my friend."

"Friend? Are you saying that you're my friend?"

"Of course I am."

In spite of his assertion, Jason was not assured.

"A friend from when?"

"A long time ago. Years in the past."

Jason shook his head. "But I didn't have any friends years ago. Shorty and Brains are the first real friends I've ever had."

"You insult me, Jason."

"If you're such a great buddy of mine, why are you doing this stuff to me?"

"I have not harmed you."

"You're scaring me, driving me crazy."

"My intent will become clear soon, Jason. Very soon, I promise you."

"When?"

"Soon. Have patience, my friend."

"Stop calling me your friend. We're not friends."

"We are friends. You simply cannot remember."

"Why don't you help me to remember, *friend?*"

The Stranger paused.

Awaiting a response, Jason clutched the handset so tightly it seemed it would snap in half.

"Very well," the Stranger said. "I'll help you remember."

The line clicked, fell silent.

The Stranger had hung up.

Jason hung up, too.

The office was quiet.

Jason felt light-headed, as though he had snapped out of a dream. Their conversation had had a dreamlike quality, flowing randomly in all directions like a wild river, never making sense at any given point. He wiped cold sweat off his brow. The Stranger had hinted that he would give him some kind of clue, but he was glad that, for the present, the ordeal was over.

He turned to leave the room, to tell Shorty and Brains what had happened. The moment he moved, however, the laser printer beside the telephone switched on.

Whirring, humming, clicking, buttons flashing and beeping, the printer ran through its setup cycle.

Jason took a step back, studying the inexplicably animated machine. The Stranger's final words, *"I'll help you remember,"* blared in his thoughts. Was the clue about to appear?

A sheet of paper was sucked out of the paper bin. It disappeared in the guts of the machine.

Watching intently, Jason inched closer.

Slowly the paper rolled out from underneath the hood. It dropped into the awaiting tray.

As suddenly as it had turned on, the printer shut off. The room darkened once more.

Jason picked up the page. Unable to read it in the darkness, he flicked on the light switch.

The message consisted of a single word, centered on the page:

COMA

"Oh, man," Jason said. "I don't believe this."

Heart throbbing, he dashed out of the room to wake Shorty and Brains.

The Stranger had promised to help him remember. But rather than granting him a revelation, he had reminded Jason of something he wished he could forget.

"It started with an argument between me and Mom, this past March," Jason said to Shorty and Brains, who sat huddled around him on his bedroom floor. "Mom used to drink a lot, and on that day she was pretty smashed. Whenever she was drunk, she'd get on my case about little, dumb things, and that's how it began. She said I hadn't taken out the garbage."

Shorty and Brains leaned forward, listening. Although it was three-thirty in the morning, they appeared to be wide awake. As Jason recalled those events in March, his own sleepiness drained out of him. He was back in the past, vividly reliving that fateful day.

"But I had already taken out the trash," he said. "I mean, I always did my chores on time. But Mom wasn't listening to me. She dragged me into the kitchen. She pointed to the garbage can. It was full. That kinda shocked me, but I figured she had just cleaned through some rooms and found more garbage that she stuffed in the can, then accused me of

never taking out the trash in the first place. She'd do anything to start a fight. That's how she acted back then.

"Anyway, I told her I had taken out the trash before, but
she said I was lying and slapped me. She shouted at me, ordered me around, and I don't know, man—something
snapped in me. I hated her. Hated her for drinking all the
time and pushing me around, for always treating me like I
was nothing, just her little slave. She'd been doing it for
years, and I was fed up, you know?

"So I stood up to her and told her to take out the garbage
herself. It was crazy to say that, but I had to. I couldn't let
her beat up on me anymore.

"That really did it. Mom snapped, too. She attacked me
like a wild animal. I tried to hold her off, but we wound up
wrestling. We fell on the floor. I got off her, and she came
after me, screaming that she was going to kill me. I've never
been so scared. I ran out of the house, flew across the backyard, and started climbing the big tree back there. She shouted
for me to come back, but I ignored her. I guess I wanted to
get away for a while, let things cool down. So I climbed the
tree, and . . . and . . ."

Jason stopped talking.

"And what?" Shorty and Brains said at once.

He shrugged. "Well, I don't remember this, but Mom
says it started raining while I was in the tree, thunder and
lightning and all, and when I started to climb down, I slipped.
She says I probably fell twenty feet. I blacked out. An ambulance came and took me to the hospital. I was in a coma for
three days. But like I said, I don't remember any of it. All I
remember is waking up three days later, after coming out of
the coma. My memory of what happened between the time I
climbed the tree and woke from the coma is blank. Gone."

"But isn't a memory block common for a person who
awakes from a coma?" Brains said. He pushed his glasses up

his nose. "I've heard that a person will usually have no memory of what happened right before he blacks out."

"It happens," Jason said. "My doctor said I shouldn't worry about it, and that it was probably best that I not remember falling out of the tree. He said the reason I couldn't remember is because the trauma of the whole thing might be too much for me to handle. I guess it's a good memory block."

"Maybe it would be good for the average kid," Shorty said. "But it ain't for you, man. You've got this crazy-assed stranger to deal with."

"I think the Stranger has something to do with my memory block," Jason said. "He keeps saying that he knows me, and he really does seem to know stuff about me. But I can't remember him. I bet that when I went into that coma my memory of him got erased, just like my memory of my fall out of the tree. The coma wiped out all of it. It kind of makes sense."

"Perfect sense," Brains said, nodding. "All along, the Stranger's been telling you to remember him, as though, deep in your mind, you know who he really is. Now he's given you another clue: the word *coma* on that paper. As if the key to remembering him lies in exploring what the coma did to you. That means we have to find a way to go into your mind and dig into that memory block. The answer to the Stranger must be in there."

"But how can we get in your head, man?" Shorty said. "I ain't a doctor. Brains is smart as hell, but he ain't one, either."

"No, none of us are doctors," Jason said. "But I know someone who's smart enough to be one."

"Who?" Brains said.

Jason told them, unable to hide a smile of pride.

"My grandfather."

CHAPTER TEN

Although Jason had two living grandfathers, whenever he thought of "Granddad," he invariably thought of his mother's father, Samuel Weaver. Samuel was the most remarkable man Jason had ever known, the embodiment of kindness, wisdom, patience, and every other virtue Jason could imagine. On the other hand, his dad's father, Big George, was the polar opposite, and Jason visited him only when his parents forced him to go. But he never tired of visiting Sam.

Granddad lived in a spacious neo-Victorian house on the west side of town. The house rested on an acre of landscaped grounds, far back from the quiet, elm-shrouded road. A spear-point wrought-iron fence encircled the yard.

He usually met Granddad for breakfast once a week, normally on the weekend. Although Granddad was retired, he maintained a busy schedule on weekdays, performing duties at his church, leading a community service program, and golfing with his retired buddies. Jason was grateful that Granddad was available to meet when he called him that morning.

When Granddad opened the door, he smiled.

"Well, well, I haven't seen you for a while." He ushered Jason inside. "You must be a busy man this summer."

"Yes, sir, I have been." Granddad was the only man he addressed as "sir." "I'll try to visit more often from now on."

"I wasn't complaining, son." Granddad closed the door. "I'm glad you finally have some friends. It's bad for you to spend too much time by yourself. Or with a feeble old man like me."

Jason smiled. Feeble old man. Granddad was sixty-eight, but today, in a short-sleeved, striped oxford shirt, olive twill pants, and black Rockports, his solid six-feet-two frame was as impressive as a man's half his age. True, his short hair had grayed, and his dark-brown skin had a generous web of wrinkles, but his sable eyes shone with vitality as well as with the indomitable spirit that had transformed him from a penniless Southern laborer into a vastly successful—and now, happily retired—entrepreneur.

"You're right on time. I just finished cooking breakfast," Granddad said. "Cooked up a storm this morning, too. Lena would be proud."

"I bet she would." Jason savored the tantalizing aromas that wafted through the hallway.

Jason noted, as usual, how openly Granddad spoke of his deceased wife. He had been seven years old when his grandmother died—not mature enough to comprehend death, but old enough to understand that his grandparents had been exceedingly close. Far from being reluctant to discuss his beloved Lena, Granddad talked of her, with love, on almost every occasion that he and Jason were together. In a way that was inexplicable to Jason, it was almost as if, in Granddad's mind, his grandmother had never died.

In the dining room the table was set: a platter of country ham and sausage, a pot of grits, a bowl of scrambled eggs, and a plate-ful of fluffy buttermilk biscuits, beside which stood a jar of homemade peach preserves.

"Hey, you weren't lying, Granddad," Jason said. "You threw down this morning."

Granddad chuckled. He poured orange juice for himself and Jason. "Man, if my doctor saw me doing this, he'd have a fit. My blood pressure's already high, and there's enough fat in this food to choke a horse. But I have to indulge every once in a while. Once a Southern boy, always a Southern boy."

Jason sat down and fixed his plate. As he ate, he did not talk much. He was trying to determine the best approach to the subject of memory blocks and how they could be overcome. That he could not tell Granddad *why* he needed the information complicated the matter. He could not speak of the Stranger to his grandfather for two reasons. Number one: Granddad, a highly rational man, would never believe his story unless he supplied proof. Number two: he did not feel safe telling Granddad about the Stranger, because he did not want the Stranger to target Granddad. Although the Stranger might limit his attention to Jason, Jason could not be sure. It was safer for Granddad to stay ignorant and uninvolved.

After breakfast, they went into the library, where they settled into comfortable armchairs in front of the fireplace. Thousands of books filled the polished oak shelves. A genuine Charles H. Alston painting hung above the mantel. The plush lavender carpet looked soft enough to sleep on, and the crisp smell of paper scented the air. Even without a flickering fire, a good book, and a mug of hot chocolate, this was easily the coziest room in the house.

"So . . ." Granddad stretched out his legs and slipped a toothpick between his lips. "What did you need to ask me?"

"How did you know I needed to ask you something?" Jason said.

"You didn't eat much this morning, and you didn't talk

much, either. That's unusual for you. I figured you had something on your mind."

"I do. But I'm not sure how to bring it up."

Granddad leaned forward. "This must be serious."

"It's not a joke."

"Lay it on me."

Jason pulled a brass-plated poker out of the stand of fire irons and turned it in his hands. "Okay, if a person wants to remember something but he can't, like the name of a song, for example, what should he do?"

Granddad stroked his chin. "Before I answer that, tell me something. Does this have anything to do with your getting that bike yesterday?"

"Sort of." Jason turned the poker.

"Sort of?"

Jason shrugged and kept turning the poker.

"Because that's a mighty odd question you shot at me," Granddad said. "Your finding that bike was bizarre, too. They have to be related, though only the Lord knows how."

Jason kept turning the poker.

Granddad sighed. "All right, we can drop it. But if you're in any kind of trouble—*any* kind of trouble—I'm here for you. Okay?"

"Yes, sir."

Granddad leaned back in his chair. "Now, there're two ways to get information out of your memory. The first and safest way is to simply let what you've forgotten come back to you naturally. That happens to everyone all the time. You try to remember the name of a song, or a movie, and it won't come to you. Then, a few hours later, when you aren't consciously thinking about it anymore, it suddenly pops into your mind."

"Yeah, that's happened to me before."

Granddad nodded. "There's a second method, as I said. But I don't recommend it, for a number of reasons."

Jason's heartbeat accelerated. "What is it?"

"Hypnosis."

"Oh, I've heard of that. What's wrong with it?"

"In your case, a lot. Hypnotic regression, which is usually what's used to crack a memory block, should only be performed by a qualified hypnotherapist. Regression is tricky, and not any Joe Blow can do it. Your first problem would be finding someone competent to regress you."

Jason swallowed. "Is there anything else wrong with it?"

"There sure is. Look, there's a reason why you forget a thing in the first place. Maybe it's not important. It might be, for instance, the details of what you watched on TV two weeks ago. It's irrelevant to your well-being, so it's wiped out of your consciousness.

"But," Granddad said, "what if you forgot this incident because having it readily available in your memory would be *dangerous* to your mental health? Such as a trauma that you've repressed because it's painful to remember. If I hypnotized you and attempted to draw that through your block, we could have trouble. You could lose the peace of mind that you've gained since the event occurred. Certainly, that doesn't happen often—reliving a trauma is helpful in many circumstances—but like I said, it's a tricky matter. What you need to understand is this: Sometimes you forget the information to forget the pain. And most times, you're better off that way. Got it?"

Jason's fingers were curled tightly around the poker. He relaxed them. "Yeah, I've got it. Thanks."

"Are you going to tell me what this is all about?"

"I'm sorry, but I can't. Not yet."

"You're the boss," Granddad said. "But if you're trying to recall something, chew over it for a little while, then stop thinking about it. If it's something you really need to remember, it'll come back to you, in its own time. Don't mess with hypnosis, son. I told you about it only because I think you deserve to know, and because I think you're smart enough *not* to try it. Besides, the memories released during a trance are sometimes more fiction than fact. If you stay patient, it's more likely that whatever you recall will be genuine."

"What if I can't wait?"

Granddad's brow furrowed. "What are you involved in? You have me worried, and even more confused."

"It's complicated, Granddad. Too complicated. I mean, I don't know everything about it myself. But I promise that once I tie it all together, I'll tell you about it."

Granddad sighed, obviously frustrated by Jason's reluctance to share the entire story.

Desiring to change the subject, Jason said, "Are we still on for breakfast this Saturday?"

"Of course we are. We have breakfast every Fourth of July morning."

"I wanted to make sure."

Granddad chuckled. "Funny, I thought you only wanted to change the subject."

Jason smiled.

"You can't lead me off the track that easily, Jason. You've got this old man's imagination running like a wild horse. I'm going to lose sleep trying to figure out what you're doing."

"You'll never guess," Jason said. "Believe me."

Before Granddad could ask him what he meant, Jason excused himself to leave. He thanked his grandfather for breakfast and answering his questions. He hurried to depart, not only because he wanted to escape further probing by Granddad, but also because he knew exactly what he needed to do next: start research on hypnotic regression.

A pang of regret shot through Sam as he watched his grandson ride away. Sometimes he selfishly wished Jason lived with him instead of with his daughter and son-in-law. Life was as precious as ever, but since Lena's passing, interminable loneliness had been Sam's companion.

In the library, sitting in his favorite chair before the fireplace, Sam resumed his reading of an engaging contemporary novel entitled *The Hearts of Men,* penned by a talented young author named Travis Hunter. But after a minute of reading, he closed the book. His conversation with Jason vexed him. What was the boy hiding? Secrecy was not in Jason's nature, and he'd asked an odd question. Sam could not imagine what Jason might be entangled in. Today's youths lived in a troubled age, but Jason had shown an uncanny knack for steering clear of the thorns out there.

Sam decided that he would call Linda later. If something was actually amiss, she might know about it.

He picked up the Hunter novel once more . . . then rested it in his lap again. Now that his mind was attuned to problems, he could not resist mulling over one of his own.

Seven years ago, a week before Lena died, he began to have a recurring dream. In the dream, he stood in a grassy, seemingly boundless field; a silvery haze delineated the distant horizon. Lena was hundreds of yards ahead, recognizable by the yellow dress she had worn on their first date. Suddenly, struck by a premonition of danger, he ran toward her, shouting her name, warning her that something terrible was going to happen. But as if Lena stood on some invisible magic carpet, she began gliding away, moving faster than he could run, waving, waving, waving at him. Soon, exhausted as much by his despair as by his exertion, he staggered to a halt. But Lena kept drifting farther and farther away, disappearing into that silvery haze, and, he understood somehow, out of his life.

For six consecutive nights, he had that nightmare. On the morning of the seventh day, he woke to discover that Lena had died in her sleep. A heart attack.

A few days ago, he had begun to have another recurring dream.

In this one, he was in the same vast field, and Lena was far ahead, as before. He ran after her, and she sailed toward that mysterious mist. But this time he traveled faster than she did, and he did not lose his energy. When he finally reached her, they embraced . . . and vanished together in the fog.

Although he rarely drank liquor before dinner, he needed a drink. He went to the wet bar, which was tucked in the hallway between the family and living rooms. He reached for the merlot, his usual dinner wine; then he opted for Scotch whiskey instead.

Scotch in hand, he looked out the library's big window at the clear blue sky, as though the heavens could answer the two questions that plagued him:

How was he going to die?

And when?

After leaving Granddad's place, Jason went to see Brains. When it came to research, Brains was better than anyone Jason knew. A hopeless Internet junkie, Brains was so skilled at digging up information online that high school students paid him to do research for their papers. Jason had no doubt that Brains could get the real deal on hypnosis.

Jason told Brains what Granddad had said.

"Hypnotic regression," Brains said, nodding. He sat in front of the computer in his family's study. "I thought about that. As a matter of fact, after I left your house this morning, I came in here and started some research."

"Why did I expect you to say that?" Jason smiled. Brains always amazed him.

Brains shrugged. "Still, what you found out from your granddad gives me some things to follow up on. I didn't know all of that stuff he told you. It should help."

"Good." Jason pulled up a chair. "Then I guess I'll have to be hypnotized. How long will it take you to find enough information for us to do it?"

"I don't know, Jason. A few hours probably."

"Any way I can help?"

"Sure, you can sit here with me and read what I stumble upon, share your thoughts, take notes, stuff like that."

"How about Shorty?" Jason said. After leaving Jason's house that morning, Shorty had gone home to do chores. "Should we call him over?"

Brains waved his hand. "No. Mike doesn't have the patience for this kind of work. He hates to sit still. We'll give him a call after we're done."

"Okay."

"How about you? Do you have time? Like I said, this may take a while."

"Yeah, I can stay. Even if I didn't have time, I would put off everything to do this. This is the most important thing in my life right now."

Brains looked at him. His expression was somber.

"I know," he said.

Late in the morning, Linda was in the kitchen washing dishes when the telephone rang.

"Hello?" she said.

"Mommy?" It was a child who sounded like Jason, but different somehow. A few years younger than her son, perhaps.

"Jason?" She said out of habit. Then: "Who is this?"

"I'm lonely, Mommy. You left me here all alone."

Linda's eyes narrowed. This child couldn't be Jason. The kid sounded as if he were no older than seven or eight.

"Why do you keep drinking so much, Mommy?" the boy said. "You're mean to me when you're drunk. You're a fuckin' bitch when you're drunk!"

The phone almost fell out of Linda's hand. Her knees buckled, and she leaned against the counter to keep from spilling to the floor.

It took her a moment to regain her voice.

"Who is this?" she said. "Is this a joke? Did someone pay you to call me and say that?"

The child laughed—high-pitched, mischievous laughter that raised the hairs on Linda's neck.

Her hand that gripped the phone grew clammy with sweat.

"How did you get my number?" she said. "What do you want?"

"You and Daddy hate me. Daddy only cares about his stupid restaurant, and you only care about getting drunk. I hope both of you rot forever."

Such virulence sounded weird coming from a child, but it was no less disturbing. Linda could not help thinking: this kid, whoever the hell he is, is reading my mind. He knows about my drinking, knows about every mean thing I used to do to Jason, knows the entire history of our screwed-up family.

But how could anyone, other than Jason, know such private details about their lives? When she'd been drinking, she hid it from everyone, including Thomas. Only Jason had known, and he certainly wouldn't have told some foulmouthed kid who seemed to believe that she was his mother.

The lack of any rational explanation reinforced her intuitive feeling that there was something very wrong—and very strange— about this phone call.

"I only want you to play with me, Mommy. Put down the bottle and play with me, you bitch!"

The child burst into another round of giggles.

Chilled, her hand shaking, Linda slammed down the phone. She hugged herself. Her heart whammed. *Jesus.*

Although she could not shake her sense that something

inexplicable had happened, she was a woman of reason and sought a rational explanation. The only sensible answer was that someone had put the kid up to playing a cruel joke. Jason was the only one who possessed the family knowledge to engineer such a thing, and though he was bitter about how she'd treated him in the past, he was not a vengeful kid. She could not believe that he was responsible.

Then what was the answer?

The phone rang again. Linda hesitated, then picked it up.

"I'm in the backyard, Mommy," the child said. "Will you come outside and play with me?"

"Listen, kid, I don't know who asked you to do this, but it's wrong. It's bad. You don't call strangers and talk like this—"

"Come outside, please, please, please?"

Linda hung up. Cold sweat covered her forehead, and she wiped it away with the back of her hand.

The phone rang. She did not pick it up. After about the tenth ring, the telephone lapsed into silence.

She leaned against the counter and sighed.

Right then, a sip of Jack Daniel's would have hit the spot.

Immediately, she banished the thought. She hadn't had a drink in months, and she had been doing fine. She didn't need a drink to handle stress. That was the old, I-feel-sorry-for-myself Linda's way of coping. The new Linda dealt with problems by confronting them head-on, although she'd be damned if she knew how she could confront a strange kid who reminded her of Damien from *The Omen.*

I'm in the backyard, Mommy. Will you come outside and play with me?

The window above the kitchen sink overlooked the back-yard. The drapes were pulled across the glass.

He's not really outside, she thought. He was only taunting her, speaking nonsense.

Nevertheless, she parted the drapes and looked outdoors.

It was a bright summer morning, seemingly void of malevolence. There was no one on the wooden deck. No one running across the lawn. She looked at the towering oak tree, which Jason had loved to climb when he was younger, and stopped.

A small, childlike figure sat high up in the leafy boughs.

She blinked, thinking she was fooled by shadows and the shapes formed by the leaves. The figure was still there, perhaps forty feet above the ground, perched like a monkey on the branches. She was too far away to make out any details.

Illusion, she thought. *My eyes are playing tricks on me.*

Then the figure shifted, rose.

Come outside and play with me, Mommy.

She heard the request clearly, as if the kid had whispered into her ear. She spun around, convinced that someone was in the kitchen. But she was alone. She turned back to the window.

Something floated from the shadowy tree boughs where the figure resided. It was a bright-yellow ball the size of a basketball. Never touching the ground, it sailed across the yard toward the house—not with speed but slowly, like a balloon drifting on air currents. It floated across the deck railing and then dropped to the deck floor, bounced a couple of times, and then lay still.

Linda gripped the edge of the counter. Her knuckles were bone white.

Let's play, Mommy, the voice said. *Let's play catch. Come outside.*

Linda snatched the drapes across the window. She backpedaled across the kitchen.

There was no way—*no way*—she was setting foot outside the house. Hell, no. She was curious about who—or what—had called her and perched in the tree waiting for her, but she wasn't a fool. It would have to break inside the house to get her, because she was not taking the bait.

Gripping the back of a chair, she waited for several minutes, watching the window.

Nothing happened.

She said a quick prayer, then mustered all of her nerve and went to the glass. She pulled back the drapes.

The yellow ball was gone. The figure that had been nestled in the tree had vanished, too. It was a gorgeous summer morning, with no hint of anything amiss.

I'm going crazy, she thought. *What did I really see out there?*

Maybe the backyard episode was a hallucination. She was certain that she had not dreamed up the phone conversation with the child, but she could explain it away as only a prank call. Just some weird kid.

Come on, girl. Be honest with yourself. You didn't imagine anything, and it wasn't a prank call. Something else is going on . . .

She firmly resolved to put it out of her mind. She had a writer's overactive imagination, and if she did not let go of this, she would drive herself crazy.

But she could not help thinking that something strange had happened yesterday, too: Jason's anonymous admirer leaving the bicycle in the garage. It was human nature to search for patterns, and she had the wild notion that all three incidents—the disturbing call, the backyard visit, and the bike—had originated from the same mysterious source.

Jesus, she was creeping herself out.

Put it out of your mind, girl. Everyone has lived through an incident that can't be logically explained. How about the time you got the call from Mama—the morning after she died—and she told you to look after Daddy? You didn't lose your mind then, and you aren't losing it now. Accept that these things happen, and don't ask why unless you can handle the answer.

The phone rang. The sudden ring almost tore a scream out of her.

Warily, she answered. It was only Alice, thank God.

"Hey, I've got a question, Ms. Romance Writer," Alice said. "I'm trying to come up with a good plot twist for my two lead characters, after the scene where they come back from the cruise. . . ."

Although Linda had housework to do and needed to spend some time on her own book, she was eager to talk to Alice and get her mind off what had happened. Nothing could draw her back to the real world as well as a conversation with her girl. She switched to the cordless phone, walked outdoors, and sat on the front steps, chatting away. Unknowingly, Alice had rescued her again.

Rows upon rows of data blurred across the monitor in Brains's study. Jason had filled several pages with notes, and Brains had downloaded more than a dozen documents to his computer's hard drive. Jason and Brains had a mighty task before them: in less than a day, they had to become experts on hypnotic regression. They had made significant progress since that morning. Jason was confident that, by the evening, someone—most likely, Brains—would be able to successfully lead him through a regression.

"My head is starting to throb," Jason said. He leaned back in the chair, rubbed his eyes. The clock on the desk read a quarter to one. "Want to take a break?"

"No." Brains's attention did not leave the screen. "If you want to rest, that's fine."

"Do you want something to eat?"

"Some chips, maybe. They're in the pantry."

Jason brought back the potato chips and placed them on the desk. Brains did not reach for them. He was so immersed in his research that he probably did not realize that Jason had ever left the room. His concentration was mind-boggling.

Jason was glad Brains was on his side. As he watched Brains's fingers fly across the keyboard, optimism filled him. They were going to beat this thing, he believed. They were going to bust the mystery wide open. They were going to put an end to the Stranger's stupid game, and his life was going to return to normal. He would not be surprised if they resolved everything that night. They were rolling forward quickly.

Energized by the thought, he pushed aside the chips, grabbed the notebook, and resumed his research.

A couple of hours later, firmly settled in reality once more, housework complete, Linda settled in front of her computer to work on her novel.

It didn't go well. For an agonizing hour, she typed in short bursts, struggling to find her flow. Although her current project was a departure from the category romance novels that she had been writing successfully for years, the book had been proceeding smoothly. Tough days had been rare, and there was usually an underlying cause for her lack of concentration.

She knew why she couldn't focus on her book that day. Earlier, while eating a light lunch, she had been reading the current issue of *Essence*. One of the feature articles was entitled, "Infidelity: What to Do if He's Cheating on You." It threw her imagination in gear and made her face up to a suspicion that had plagued her since last night.

Thomas was hiding something.

With a sixth sense that all wives developed, she could detect her husband's moods, and she believed that something distressed Thomas—something he wanted to keep secret.

She had questioned him the night before, but he had not opened up, and though she had mentally analyzed their conversation dozens of times, she could not decipher the source of his unease. Her imagination had taken over. Instead of spinning out words for her novel, it weaved a disturbing explanation for Thomas's odd behavior: he was sleeping with another woman.

She wondered if she was being too reactive, letting the *Essence* piece affect her too deeply. But . . . the possibility of infidelity was real. Thomas was a successful, attractive man. He would have gotten his share of opportunities to mess around. She did not believe he would stoop that low, but she was getting suspicious. No telltale signs had passed under her nose—lipstick on the collar, a whiff of unfamiliar perfume, credit-card bills for mysterious purchases—but she knew how Thomas acted when he harbored a secret. Evasive, distracted, and tired. The same way he was acting lately.

Eyes narrowing, she pushed away from her desk.

If Thomas was seeing another woman, their marriage was finished. Period. She was willing to tolerate almost any mistake Thomas committed. But not an affair. Never.

At the thought of such a thing, her hands began to sweat.

Realizing that she was on her way to convicting Thomas before he'd had his day in court, she decided to get out of the house and do something to quell her anxiety. She went shopping.

Jason and Brains had finished their research. Eager to put their plan in gear to end the Stranger's game, Jason went home to grab some clothes for the night. He would also ask Mom whether he could spend the night at Shorty's, since Shorty's place was their next base. He was certain that Mom would agree to let him sleep over. Lately, she was so afraid of denying him whatever he asked for that she would've agreed to let him take a trip around the world on his own. He didn't know whether it was a good thing for her to give him so much freedom. But right then, he needed all the freedom he could get to regain control of his life.

Surprisingly, Dad was home. When Jason walked through the front door, he discovered Dad sitting on the sofa in the living room, puffing on a cigarette. Weird. He didn't know that Dad smoked. Well, there was a lot that he didn't know about Dad. He was hardly ever there.

"Hey, Jason." Dad quickly put out the cigarette. "What's up?"

"What're you doing here?"

"Believe it or not, I live here. I like to drop by from time to time, make sure the house is still standing." He chuckled.

"Oh. Where's Mom?"

"I don't know. She probably went to the store."

"Man. I needed to ask her something."

"What's up? Maybe you can ask me. The last time I checked, I had parental rights."

Jason shrugged. "I wanted to spend the night at Shorty's— I mean, Mike's—house tonight."

Dad pursed his lips. "What are you guys into, Jason? Your mom suspects something."

Great. He was sure that Mom had told Dad about finding the bike in the garage. The last thing he needed was for his parents to be dipping into his business. They would only make things more complicated. They wouldn't believe him, anyway.

"We aren't into anything. Mom gets carried away."

"What's the deal with you finding that bike in the garage?"

"I don't know who put it in there. Don't have a clue. Do you?"

Dad looked dumbfounded for a moment. Then he said, "No, I've no idea."

Jason began to walk toward the stairs. "So can I spend the night at Shorty's?"

"That's fine, son. Does your mother have the number to your friend's house?"

"It's on the board in the kitchen."

"Good. Have fun this evening."

In his bedroom, Jason packed his clothes in his duffel bag. When he had packed everything he needed and had walked downstairs again, he found Dad still sitting on the couch. Dad had lowered his head as if in prayer. He didn't seem to hear Jason leaving.

"Bye." Jason opened the front door.

Dad didn't say anything. He only sat there with his head bowed, as if he were in a trance.

"Whatever," Jason said under his breath. Both of his parents were crazy. He wished, not for the first time, that he lived with Granddad, not with these strangers masquerading as his family.

He shut the door harder than he'd wanted to, but he doubted that Dad had heard the sound.

At Gurnee Mills in Gurnee, one of the largest shopping malls in Illinois, Linda shopped for about two hours. Not a believer in spending money out of sheer boredom, she mostly window-shopped. Between stops at stores, she nibbled at a chocolate-chip cookie, and by the time she was ready to leave, she had bought a shirt for Jason and a set of place mats for the dining room table. She had also bought some peace of mind; during the drive home, she anticipated getting back to work on her book.

When she parked in the garage at three-fifteen, she was surprised to find Thomas's Buick there. Thomas was in the kitchen. Of all things, he was cooking.

"Someone give me a camera," she said. "I have to snap a picture of this."

He grinned. He wore a dark-gray T-shirt and jeans that fitted him so well Linda wanted to slide up behind him and pinch his butt.

"You forget, I run a restaurant," he said. "I can throw down when I want to."

She inhaled deeply. "You're cooking fish? It smells great. But isn't it early for dinner?"

"It's better to eat now." He opened the refrigerator and removed a block of cheddar cheese. "Then we won't have to stop till much later."

"Won't have to stop what?"

Standing at the counter, he grated the cheese. "I've planned a light meal. Tossed salad, blackened salmon, pasta, and a bottle of Chardonnay. Easy to digest, won't slow us down."

"Are we going to be running a marathon?"

"I talked to Jason, too. I really don't think anything's going on with him, baby. If there is, he sure didn't give any clues. But he does want to sleep at a friend's house tonight. I told him it was okay. He's already picked up his things. We can reach him at his buddy's place if we need to."

"Thomas, are you listening to me?"

He added the grated cheese to a huge bowl of salad. "Go ahead and wash up, Linda. Dinner'll be ready any second."

She started to speak, knew it would be useless, and decided to keep quiet. When she returned downstairs after freshening up, Thomas had finished setting the table. The food looked delicious.

She sat down. He poured wine for both of them. He filled her plate with salad, then filled his own.

"All right," she said, "stop avoiding the issue. Why're you doing this? What's the special occasion?"

He smiled. "There's no special occasion, baby. I love you. That's all the occasion I need."

She would have needed steel wool to wipe the smile off her face. Apparently, he had dealt with whatever secret he'd been guarding. Or maybe he'd never had a secret. It must have been the cynic in her, restlessly probing for nonexistent problems. Shame on her for doubting him. To think that she'd suspected another woman!

They fell easily into conversation, and the talk was better than the food. It had been months since they sat down and talked without conflict. They talked about good times, friends and family, places they had been and places they wished to go. She became so engrossed in their discussion that her plate seemed to clean itself.

"Hey, you look ready for dessert," Thomas said.

"You made dessert, too?"

"Of course, I did. I think you'll enjoy it more than dinner."

"What is it?"

He smiled. "Close your eyes."

She shut them. She heard plates and silverware being conveyed from the table to the sink. Then silence.

"Okay, you can open them."

Thomas was standing beside her chair. He had stripped down to a pair of low-rise red silk briefs.

She sucked in a deep breath.

"I didn't give the dessert a taste test," he said. "You're gonna have to tell me if it's sweet enough."

She tore her gaze away from his beautiful body and looked into his eyes. "You think you're slick. 'Easy to digest, won't slow us down.' " She giggled. "Baby, even if you weren't as sexy as you are, you're sweeter than any dessert could ever be."

He smiled, came to her. She rose out of her chair to meet him.

"But I'd still like a taste test," she said.

Go through the physical motions, and the mind will follow, Thomas thought as he stood in the kitchen wearing only silk briefs, watching Linda rise to embrace him. Good sexual performance relied on state of mind as much as it did on health, and since he was in excellent shape, his guilt presented the only obstacle to his satisfying Linda. He had gone through the motions of being an exciting lover: preparing a delicious meal, being a good conversationalist, and then stripping and presenting himself as dessert. He did those things not only to romance Linda, but, just as important, to put himself in the mood. To rise above his pangs of conscience and attain that crucial level at which instinct took over. A level he had been unable to reach the night before.

Linda slipped her arms around his waist. They kissed deeply.

"I want you so much, it's killing me," he said, praying his body would cooperate with his words. He kissed her neck, explored her marvelous shape with his hands. Although he felt a growing desire, he did not feel that irrepressible sexual drive he needed in order to give Linda what she deserved.

After all, that was all he wanted to do: give his wife what she deserved. Finally resolving that Linda's contentment was more important than his self-esteem, he no longer considered telling her of his adultery. Why make her suffer for his mistake? The cliché was true: what she did not know could not hurt her. The truth would hurt him, maybe for a long time. He would have to live with it. He would simply have to focus on being the loving husband that this fine woman in his arms deserved.

They kissed and touched for what seemed like forever; then, by unspoken mutual agreement, he carried her to the bedroom.

He placed her on the bed and undressed her. When she was nude, he stood back and regarded her. Prolonging the sweet tension. Building up his own excitement.

"You have a beautiful body," he said, and it was true. They had been married for years, of course, but it had been ages since they had been nude in front of each other. In the past, on those rare occasions when they'd had sex, they had performed in darkness, neither of them undressing completely. He was pleasantly surprised at how well she had maintained her figure. As he took in her gorgeous body and imagined how she would feel against him, he felt himself becoming harder than ever before. He rolled down his briefs.

"My goodness," she said, apparently experiencing a similar surprise. "You look like a chocolate Adonis. If you don't get on this bed with me right now, I'm going to scream."

He stroked himself a little, teasing her. "Do you really want it?"

She laughed. "Come here!"

He stretched out beside her on the bed. She pressed onto him, enveloped him in her body heat. He kissed her lips, her neck, her breasts. He slid his fingers across her legs, traced circles on her firm hips. He had forgotten the pleasures of her body, and rediscovering her silken skin, sleek legs, lovely hips, and warm, full breasts thrilled him. He could get used to making love to her again. Her body was a hammock, and now that he had immersed himself in it, he only wanted to stay there, close his eyes, and rock, and rock, and rock. . . .

By eight o'clock in the evening, they were ready to hypnotize Jason.

Shorty's house was their base for the night, and they elected to perform the regression in his bedroom. They placed a recliner in a corner and put a padded chair a couple of feet in front of it. They positioned two nightstands on opposite sides of the chairs and planted a brass lamp on each.

To record the event, Shorty had borrowed his parents' compact camcorder. Shorty would film the proceedings. Brains would be the hypnotist.

Shorty gave the room a once-over. "Looks like everything's set. Are you ready, fellas?"

Brains cracked his knuckles and sat in the padded chair. "I'm ready."

Jason eased into the recliner. His heart beat way too fast; Granddad's warnings echoed in his thoughts. But he said, "I'm ready, too."

Shorty switched on the lamps. He shut off the ceiling light.

He turned on the camcorder and focused the lens on Brains and Jason.

"Showtime," Shorty said.

CHAPTER ELEVEN

Brains had never been so nervous. Although they had prepared as much as they could that day, he felt incompetent, the way he might have felt in a chess match against a grand master. He was supposed to be Jason's rock, the one upon which Jason could depend to guide him through this session safely. But he needed someone to guide *him*. Studying hypnosis on the Internet was not enough.

But he could not express his anxiety. Both Shorty and Jason thought he was brilliant, the one with all the poise and knowledge. Sometimes he disliked wearing the "whiz kid" label, but he mostly enjoyed the respect his supposed intelligence accorded him. Perhaps his desire to maintain the fellas' admiration was the kind of motivation he needed to keep himself together and do a good job tonight.

More important, he wanted to unravel the mystery of the Stranger. The Stranger was, to Brains, like a perplexing mathematical theorem that begged for a solution. Brains would not rest until he had discovered the answer.

"Okay, Jason," Brains said, "lean back in the chair and relax.

Rest your hands in your lap, palms up. Close your eyes. Take a deep breath. Let it out slowly."

Jason obeyed his directions. Brains waited a few seconds, allowing Jason to get comfortable.

"Now, Jason, I want you to imagine a blue balloon. Imagine it floating just in front of your feet. Can you see it?"

"Yes." Jason kept his eyes closed.

"Good. Now the balloon is starting to float up and over your body. As it passes over you, your tension and anxiety drain away. The balloon floats over your calves, and your calves relax. It drifts over your knees, and your knees relax. It floats over your thighs, and your thighs relax. It passes over your stomach, and your stomach relaxes. It floats over your chest, and your chest relaxes. It drifts over your neck, and your neck relaxes. It passes over your face, and your face relaxes. It floats over your scalp, and your scalp relaxes. And now it's hovering above your head. It starts to sail upward, higher and higher into the sky, and as it drifts away, so does all of your tension and anxiety. Soon the balloon is out of sight, and you are completely relaxed."

Jason was slumped in the recliner, breathing softly.

"You are in a very deep, very relaxing sleep," Brains said. "And you will answer some questions for me. While I ask you these questions, you will remain in that very deep, very relaxing sleep until I order you to wake up. Do you understand?"

"Yes."

"Good. Jason, do you remember the watch I showed you earlier?"

"Yes."

"I have that watch in my hands now." Actually, he did not. "Can you see the watch in my hands?"

"Yes." Jason's eyes remained shut.

"Great. But see, this is a unique watch. It's a magic watch. It controls the flow of time. Now, I'm starting to turn the watch hands backward. The hands go around and around the dial, farther and farther back. Can you see the watch hands spinning backward?"

"Yes."

"Now something magical is happening. As the watch hands turn backward, time itself begins to flow backward, too. It isn't ten minutes past eight anymore; it's now eight o'clock. And now it's seven o'clock in the evening . . . six o'clock . . . five o'clock . . . four o'clock . . ."

Gradually, Brains guided Jason back in time. He regressed him to that important weekend day in March, about three o'clock in the afternoon, twenty minutes before his calamitous fight with his mother. None of them was eager to have Jason relive his terrible fall out of the tree. If Brains could retrieve the information they sought without having Jason experience that trauma again, they would be satisfied.

"Where are you, Jason?" Brains said.

"I'm in my bedroom," Jason said. "Sitting at my desk."

"What are you doing?"

"Reading a magazine."

Brains nodded. "What have you done today?"

"I did my chores, then had breakfast at my grandfather's. We talked a couple of hours, and when I left his house, I went to the beach since the weather was nice. I hung out there for a while, skipped rocks across the water, daydreamed; then I came back home. I've been in my room reading magazines since I've been here."

"Did you do anything else? Meet any friends, maybe?"

"I don't have any friends."

He said that too quickly, Brains thought. As though he wanted to avoid the subject. Almost as though he were hiding something.

"You don't have a single friend?" Brains said.

"No. I told you that."

"You honestly don't have one friend?"

"I said no, didn't I? Do you have wax in your ears?"

"Why are you getting testy about this? I only asked you a simple question."

"You asked a nosy question."

"I get the feeling that you're hiding something, Jason. Are you?"

Jason did not reply. Eyes closed, brow creased, he shifted in the recliner.

"You have to answer my questions honestly," Brains said. "Do you have any friends?"

"Why do you want to know?"

"I want to know so I can help you, Jason. The more honest you are with me, the more I can help you."

"I don't need your help. I already have someone to help me."

"Who is that?" Brains said. "Who helps you?"

"I shouldn't tell you. You'll blab it to everyone."

"I'll keep it secret. I promise."

"Promise?"

"Yes, I promise. Now, tell me: who helps you?"

Jason spoke in a whisper: "My friend."

Brains glanced at Shorty and smiled. Jason had to be referring to the Stranger. It was the only sensible assumption.

Filming everything with the camcorder, Shorty gave Brains the thumbs-up sign.

Brains returned his attention to Jason. "What's your friend's name?"

"I can't tell you."

"You have to tell me, Jason. You have to be honest and open with me."

"No." Jason's lips formed a firm line.

"Okay. Then tell me where your friend lives."

"You can never go there."

"Why can't I?" Brains said.

"Because it's impossible. For you, anyway."

"Is it impossible for you to go there, too?"

"No."

"Then how can it be impossible for me?" Brains said. Jason shook his head. "You'd never understand. Ever."

"Does your friend live in this world?" Brains said, aware of how foolish he sounded, but not wanting to leave any question unasked.

"I can't tell you that," Jason said.

"Is your friend human?"

"I can't tell you that."

"Why not?"

"Because if I do, he won't be a secret anymore. He has to stay secret, always."

"All right," Brains said. "How long have you known this friend?"

"A long time. Since I was four years old."

"Are you close to him?"

"Extremely."

"You said earlier that he helps you. How does he help you?"

"He's always there for me," Jason said. "He knows me better than anyone. I can depend on him for anything."

"Do your parents know about this friend?"

Jason chuckled. "No."

"Does anyone else know about him?"

"No one does. Not even Granddad."

"Why do you hide him from everyone?"

"Because no one will understand him."

Brains leaned forward. "I'll understand him, Jason. You can trust me. Tell me more about him."

"I can't tell you anything else. I've already told you too much."

"You don't have to worry. I'm not going to give your secret to anyone."

"I know you won't, because I'm not giving it to you."

Brains sighed. He took a sip from the water bottle he had placed under his chair. Beside him, Shorty shrugged, mouthed the words *good try, man.*

Jason lay in the chair, relaxed.

Why was he compellcd to conceal the important details about the Stranger? What did Jason fear would happen if gave the complete truth?

Brains had no idea. This entire thing was getting weirder every minute. Because Jason had clammed up, Brains saw no alternative but to move him forward in time, to his fall from the tree. Maybe more clues waited there.

"Jason, it's now three-twenty on that same day. What are you doing?"

Tension drew Jason's face taut. When he spoke, his voice was pained. "I'm arguing with Mom. She's drunk, and she won't leave me alone. Why does she keep beating on me?"

Rather than get embroiled in that mess, Brains quickly moved Jason five minutes forward.

"What are you doing, Jason?"

Jason panted. Tears squeezed from his eyes, trailed down his face. "Running away, out the patio door, across the backyard, to the big tree. Mom's shouting at me to come back, but I'm gonna ignore her, 'cause she'll kill me if she catches me. I just want to get away for a while, let her calm down some. I jump up, grab a tree limb, then start climbing. Mom's calling me, but I shut her out; I shut out everything. All I want to do is climb to the top of the tree and forget what happened."

As he climbed in his memory, Jason's face twisted with the effort of his concentration. His breaths came in gasps. His hands clenched and unclenched, ascending the imaginary tree.

At last, Jason sighed. His muscles relaxed.

"There," he said. "I'm finally at the top, resting between a couple of limbs."

"What are you going to do up there?" Brains said.

"Not much. I rest my head against the trunk, look up at the sky, and see thunderclouds. I can smell rain coming, but I'm going to stay up here anyway. I just want to clear my mind and forget everything. I close my eyes, let out a deep breath, and just listen to different sounds around me. Birds, a car honking, dogs barking, the wind blowing. Then, I hear a voice."

Brains literally jumped forward. "Whose voice?"

"My friend's."

"Your friend is talking to you?" Brains said.

Jason nodded.

Brains leaned on the edge of his seat. Shorty, too, had moved forward with the camcorder.

"What does your friend say?" Brains said.

Strangely, Jason smiled.

"He says . . ." Jason said, and then his tone abruptly changed, becoming deep, sonorous, and nothing like his natural voice.

"I'm here."

Jason's eyes snapped open.

His eyes were white; his pupils had rolled back in his head, as if he were a voodoo priest possessed by an ancient spirit.

Brains stared at the whites of Jason's eyes.

"What the hell . . . ?" Shorty said, and then his words were drowned out by a tremendous boom of thunder, a shattering blast that sounded like a bomb heralding the end of the world.

Brains shot to his feet. He did not know what was going on, but he had to regain control of the situation.

Jason lay slumped in the recliner, the whites of his eyes gazing blindly. A thread of drool inched down the corner of his mouth.

Was he possessed by the Stranger? Could the Stranger do that? Jump inside Jason's body and take control?

"Are you there, Jason?" Brains said. "Do you hear me?"

Jason only lay there, drooling and breathing softly.

Thunder bludgeoned the night, rattled the windows.

"Brains," Shorty said.

"What?" Brains spun.

"Check out your watch, man."

The digits of Brains's watch were frozen at 8:31.

"Has it stopped?" Shorty said.

"Yes."

Shorty motioned to the camcorder in his hand. "The timer on this thing's stopped, and my watch has, too." He looked around the room. Beyond the corner they occupied, darkness reigned. "Man, something weird is going on. Can you feel it?"

"Something does feel different," Brains said, searching the darkness. He bent down and pulled the .22 out of his ankle holster. He was not convinced that the gun would harm the Stranger, but it was the only weapon he had. "Something's very different. But I don't know what it is."

Wind slammed into the windows.

Like Thor's hammer, thunder smashed the sky.

"How the hell can this be happening?" Shorty said. "Jason's been hypnotized, not us."

"I don't know, but I have to wake him up," Brains said. He turned to Jason. "Jason, you will wake up now! Do you hear me? You will wake up!"

Jason did not respond. He seemed comatose.

Brains grabbed Jason by the shoulders. He shook him. "I order you to wake up, Jason! Wake up now!"

Eyes white and strange, spittle creeping down his chin, Jason remained locked in the trance.

Outside, a gale shrieked. Thunder bellowed with such power that Brains expected the house to collapse.

Shorty clicked on the ceiling light. He parted the drapes at a window. "Oh, shit. Look out here."

Brains joined Shorty at the window. The overcast sky was the blackest he had ever seen, as black as it might be if the sun burned out and brought endless night to the solar system. Neon-blue lightning flashed and tore across the charred clouds, which churned like the bubbling contents of a sorcerer's cauldron.

In spite of the gloom, all of the surrounding homes were unlighted, as though everyone had vacated the town in fear of some catastrophic storm. The neighborhood *felt* empty, too. It was easy to believe that they were the only living people in the entire city.

But that was insane.

Rain struck the glass. Shorty and Brains flinched backward.

Like a giant stomping on the roof, thunder crashed.

Fierce winds howled, whined, and skirled.

A gritty taste had swelled in Brains's mouth—one he was not accustomed to. The taste of fear.

Yet fear was justified. Never in his life had Brains heard such bone-rattling thunder, or seen a sky burned as black as an iron skillet. Somehow, the Stranger must be influencing the weather. And if he could command the elements of nature, he was nothing less than a god. Only a fool would not fear him.

Brains could sense the Stranger's presence there, too. Somewhere nearby. A tangible aura of power suffused the air.

"Stand next to me," Brains said to Shorty. Together they formed a barrier in front of Jason. Brains held the gun before him, arms straight and locked, as his dad had taught him. Although he had trained with firearms for many years, in the face of this enemy he felt pathetically vulnerable.

Silently they waited.

Hard rain punished the house.

Thunder shook the walls as if they were constructed of cardboard.

Sweat crept down Brains's back. Beside him, holding up the camcorder in a valiant attempt to film this madness, Shorty had clenched his teeth.

Another peal of thunder made the floor tremble.

Then the lights went out.

Later, when darkness had fallen over the world like a great swatch of purple-black silk, Thomas reached across himself and traced his finger along the side of Linda's face. His heart clutched. Although they had made love with great passion and tenderness, that act of profound sharing failed to express adequately the depth of his feelings for her.

Linda's eyes opened. She touched his hand, kissed it.

"I love you," she said.

"At least *you* do."

She frowned. "What's that supposed to mean?"

"I've accepted something."

She bent her arm, rested her head on her hand.

"Go on," she said.

"I've accepted the fact that your happiness—and Jason's—is more important than mine."

"Placing your family's welfare above your own is fine, honey. But are you happy with yourself, too?"

"What makes me happy is making you and Jason happy. If I can do that until the day I die, that's enough for me."

She laid her head on the pillow. "That sounds nice. But in a way, it also sounds like you hate yourself."

He ran his fingers through her curly hair.

"Well?" she said.

"I'll be honest with you. In some bad ways, I'm exactly like my dad. I've tried to deny it, but there's no point in doing it anymore. It's in my blood. Like father, like son."

"Like hell," she said. "You're nothing like your dad. You have his workaholic habits, but you're getting over them."

"That's not all we have in common."

"Yes, it is. Listen, Thomas. You're a sweet, generous, thoughtful man—and your dad isn't. Stop comparing yourself to him. Hearing you talk like that bothers me, because it's not true."

Her words, intended to be loving and encouraging, were like hammer blows on his soul. Thanks to Big George's mastery of deceit, Mama had thought the same thing about Big George, though Thomas had known it was an outrageous lie. Big George would sometimes take Thomas with him when he visited his girlfriends, always sealing the visits with the threat that he would kill Thomas if he told Mama. As a boy, Thomas had vowed that he would never deceive his own wife as his father had hoodwinked his mother, but look what had happened. Just as his father had done, now he lived a lie, too—while his wife praised him as a sweet, generous, thoughtful man.

Like father, like son.

It was true. Lord help him, it was true.

His pain at the realization must have been evident, because Linda looked at him with concern.

"Are you okay?" she said.

"You're too good for me, Linda," he said, shaking his head. "I love you with all my heart, but you're too damn good for me."

She put her finger to his lips.

"Please, don't talk like that. I'm not too good for you, you're not too good for me. We're perfectly matched, understand?"

He did not reply.

She leaned closer.

"Understand?" she said.

"Yeah, baby. I understand."

"Good."

She kissed him softly, tenderly.

"Now, if you really want to understand how perfectly matched we are, you'll make love to me again," she said.

They made love again.

Lying in the darkness, holding her body close, he shut his eyes and slid into sleep. He dreamed that he was seventy years old and living in a nursing home. Sick. Bitter. Alone.

Darkness filled the room.

"Don't move, Mike, don't you dare move," Brains said. "Forget about the lights, he's controlling them, anyway. We can't be separated, not for one second."

"I ain't going anywhere," Shorty said.

The lights clicked on.

Then they blinked off again. And on again. And off. On. Off. On. Off. On. Off. On. Off. Faster and faster, on and off, in mindless repetition.

Due to his sight being temporarily impaired, colorful shapes swam like schools of fish in Brains's field of vision. He gripped the pistol tighter. He hoped the Stranger did not attack or do whatever the hell he planned to do. He wanted to be able to see what happened.

He had the impression, too, that the Stranger was only showboating. The thunder, lightning, wind, rain, this light show—it was like bragging, the behavior of a spoiled brat showing off his toys. Still, Brains's fear was genuine. Showboat or not, the Stranger possessed awesome power deserving of respect.

The lights turned on again. This time, they remained on.

Before Brains could register relief, the bedroom door shuddered.

"It's him," Shorty said.

Brains swiftly trained the .22 on the door across the room, finger around the trigger.

The Stranger began to hammer the door. His blows shook the entire door: *thud-thud-thud-thud-thud* . . .

"Let's push the bed against it!" Shorty said.

Brains holstered the pistol and joined Shorty beside the bed. They planted their feet on the carpet, bent down, and pushed.

The bed would not budge.

Impossible.

It was a twin-size bed, encumbered only with sheets and a pillow, but it would not move one centimeter. Brains and Shorty redoubled their efforts, sweated and cursed as they strained, but they may as well have been trying to uproot a tree.

Brains went to his chair, thinking he could lever it under the doorknob. But the chair would not move either.

They tried the windows, the sole route of escape. They were unlocked. But they would not open.

It was as if they were trapped in some nightmare world, a land in which the Stranger was a god, and Brains and Shorty were helpless captives.

Fierce hits bombarded the door: *thud-thud-thud-thud-thud-thud-thud* . . .

Brains and Shorty edged in front of Jason. Jason was sprawled in the recliner, head lolling, legs splayed before him. His chest rose and fell slowly.

"Jason, wake up!" Shorty said. He opened Brains's bottle of ice water and dumped the water on Jason's face.

Jason did not awaken.

The crack of splitting wood called their attention away from Jason. A fissure mapping the length of the door had appeared.

Thud-thud-thud-thud-thud-thud . . .

More cracks crazed across the door.

Brains aimed the gun. He had an absurd desire for the door to give way, so he could see what the Stranger looked like. If he could only *see* him, he might not be half as frightened as he was now.

The bolts popped off the doorjamb and clattered to the floor.

Brains held the .22, held his breath.

One last, savage whack: *thud!*

Like a chopped tree, the door fell forward, Brains's finger sweating on the trigger, about to fire . . .

And the instant the door should have struck the floor, Brains found himself sitting in the chair, in front of Jason.

"What the fuck?" Shorty said. He was back in position beside Brains. The camcorder rested on his shoulder.

Brains's mouth had dropped open. He shut it, swallowed.

He pulled up his pant leg. The .22 he had clutched only seconds ago gleamed in his ankle holster.

He examined the door. It had only a few nicks and scratches, the same markings it had borne for years. He opened it. He heard Shorty's parents watching TV downstairs.

Shorty lifted the window. "It doesn't look like there was a storm outside. I don't see a drop of rain on the glass, and the sky's clear."

Brains attempted to move the bed. It shifted easily.

He read his watch. It read 8:32, which meant only one minute had passed since he had last looked at it. He was sure he had checked the time about five minutes ago. All of those weird things could not have occurred *within one minute*.

His heart pounded painfully.

Jason groaned. His eyes had rolled back into their normal position. Brains noted that Jason's face and shirt were dry, too, though Mike had dumped a bottle of water on him to try to rouse him from the trance. The water could not have evaporated so quickly. *Impossible.*

Blinking slowly, clearly disoriented, Jason looked at them. "Hey, fellas, what's going on?"

"You don't know?" Shorty said.

"The last thing I remember is sitting down, then Brains telling me to close my eyes. Why? Did something important happen?"

"Yeah," Shorty said.

"What?" Jason said.

Shorty looked at Jason, then at Brains.

"We don't really know," Shorty said.

In Shorty's basement, after Brains and Shorty related to Jason what had happened, Jason rose from the sofa and paced. His mind was spinning.

"Then this is what we know, fellas. I've had this friend since I was four years old. I can go to wherever this guy lives, but no one else can go there. I used to be really close to him, felt I could depend on him for anything. And lastly, I don't want to tell anyone about him, because I'm scared no one will understand." He stopped pacing, shook his head. "Well, even with knowing all of that stuff, I can't tell you who the Stranger is, or why he's doing these things. It's a mystery to me."

"I figured as much," Brains said, sitting on the sofa. "We weren't able to tear down your memory block. We were interrupted."

"Ambushed" is a better word," Shorty said, seated beside Brains on the couch. "When the Stranger came, he tore shit up."

"Did you catch it on tape?" Jason said. "Maybe if we watch what he did, we can find some more clues."

"I got everything," Shorty said. "I'll show you."

Shorty walked to the VCR, which sat atop the TV. He switched on the machine and inserted the videotape on which he had filmed the hypnotic regression. He pressed PLAY and returned to his seat.

Jason sat on the overstuffed chair beside the television and watched.

On the large screen, Brains was sitting in front of Jason and speaking to him.

"Okay, Jason. Lean back in the chair and relax."

Shorty picked up the remote control and fast-forwarded the cassette. Colorful images twitched and blurred. He pressed *Play* again.

On the screen, Brains talked.

"Jason, it's now three-twenty on that same day. What are you doing?"

Tension draws Jason's face taut. When he speaks, his voice is pained.

"I'm arguing with Mom. She's drunk, and she won't leave me alone. Why does she keep beating on me?"

Viewing that segment of the recording twisted Jason's stomach. Thankfully, Shorty fast-forwarded the tape again. He pushed PLAY.

On TV, ensconced in the recliner, Jason spoke.

"There," he says. "I'm finally at the top, resting between a couple of limbs."

"What are you going to do up there?" Brains asks.

"Not much. I rest my head against the trunk, look up at the sky, and see thunderclouds. I can smell rain

*coming, but I'm going to stay up here anyway. I just
want to clear my mind and forget everything. I close
my eyes, let out a deep breath, and just listen to different sounds around me. Birds, a car honking, dogs
barking, the wind blowing. Then, I hear a voice."*

Brains jumps forward. "Whose voice?"

"My friend's."

"Your friend is talking to you?" Brains asks.

Jason nods.

Brains leans on the edge of his seat.

"What does your friend say?" Brains asks.

Jason smiles.

*"He says . . ." Jason says, and then his tone abruptly
changes, becoming deep, sonorous, and nothing like
his natural voice.*

"I'm here."

Suddenly, electric snow consumed the screen.

"Hey!" Shorty rushed toward the TV.

The instant he reached the television, the screen cleared.

The camcorder focused on Jason slumped in the recliner.
But Shorty, out of view, spoke.

"What the fuck?" Shorty says.

*Brains's mouth has dropped open. He shuts it,
swallows.*

The camera abruptly panned to the floor. Then it was shut
off. Snow filled the screen again.

Shorty switched off the VCR and television. He stood in
the center of the room, fists on his waist.

"Shit, I don't get it," he said. "I got everything. But nothing that the Stranger did is on there. It's been erased, man."

"If it was ever on tape to begin with," Brains said. "But I

guarantee you, Jason, it actually happened. Whatever it was."

Jason looked from Shorty to Brains. "You say your watches froze?"

They nodded.

"And you saw this really fierce storm that ended in a flash, without a trace that it had ever hit?"

They nodded.

"And the Stranger made the lights go crazy, pounded on the door, and trapped you guys in the room by making it impossible for you to move anything?"

"Hell, yeah, man," Shorty said.

"That's exactly what happened," Brains said.

Jason tapped his lip.

"I have an idea," he said. "It's a wild one, but listen. If all the amazing stuff you guys saw had happened in the real world, Shorty would have recorded it. But it didn't show up on the tape. So maybe it took place . . . somewhere else."

"Somewhere else?" Standing in front of him, Shorty frowned. "Like where?"

"I don't know," Jason said. "I guess somewhere different from here. Different from here, but the same in a lot of ways. Kind of like a . . . parallel dimension."

Shorty and Brains looked at him speculatively.

"It's a crazy idea," Jason said. "But the only other answer is that you guys hallucinated everything. Just imagined it all. I know you don't buy that explanation. I sure don't."

"I don't either," Shorty said. "Man, I was wide awake."

"Besides," Brains said, "how could both Mike and I hallucinate the same incident, down to the smallest detail? The idea that we could have shared a delusion is really unlikely. On top of that, why did our watches freeze at eight-thirty-one? My theory is that it's a *signal* that we've entered another zone or dimension, in the same way that your ears popping is a signal that you're entering a different altitude. The moment everything went back to normal, my watch ticked onto eight-thirty-two, and I know at least five minutes had passed."

"Five minutes of hell," Shorty said.

"Yeah, the time thing sounds like a signal to me," Jason said. "The storm might be a sign, too. We should look out for that stuff, in case we're pulled into that place again."

"I hope we aren't," Brains said. "The Stranger seems to be a god there. I couldn't move a flimsy chair."

"I couldn't open a damn window," Shorty said.

Jason clasped his hands. "Do we agree on this alternate-world idea? Do both of you believe that's what it is, another dimension?"

"I do," Shorty said.

"I don't know what else it could be," Brains said. "I don't think there's scientific proof to support the existence of alternate dimensions—nothing that I know about, anyway—so I'll accept it as an unsolved mystery."

"Good," Jason said. "Then maybe we've nailed down one mystery. I figure we should give the place a name, make it easy to refer to. How about . . . Thunderland?"

"Thunderland." Shorty nodded. "Works for me. I ain't never felt thunder that strong, man. I thought the ceiling was gonna crash down on us."

"I agree, the name fits, Jason," Brains said.

"Okay," Jason said. "I hate to say this, but I have a feeling that we'll be in Thunderland again soon. I think the Stranger was only giving us a taste of it. Since we have some idea of what it is, maybe we'll be ready next time."

Brains and Shorty nodded grimly.

A week ago, Jason would have dismissed a conversation like this as insane. But as the Stranger drew them deeper into his enigmatic scheme, it became increasingly easy to believe the unbelievable. What would he do next to push the boundaries of their minds? If he continued to pile improbability upon improbability, would they ever reach a breaking point? To Jason, it seemed that a world in which anything was possible was a world of madness. Already, the world was a lot madder than it had been last week.

A headache throbbed above his right eyebrow. Probably his brain straining to process and organize these harrowing, incredible events—mind overload. Based on everything they had experienced, he would've expected one of them to have passed out from the sheer terror, to have deteriorated into a human vegetable. But they were hanging tough. They were too frightened to slip, lower their guard, get soft. Fear could be the most powerful motivator in the world.

In fact, he doubted he would sleep that night. He was too drunk on adrenaline to relax.

Shorty sat on the couch. "I'm not sleeping, fellas. I can't. This is getting so wild I can barely keep up. I'm too damn hyper to sleep, I'll pull all the shifts tonight."

"I'm wound up, too," Jason said. "But you shouldn't watch all night, Shorty. If you do, you'll be dragging tomorrow."

"He won't be alone," Brains said. He removed his glasses, massaged the bridge of his nose. "I'm not sleeping either. I need to calm down, sort out these issues. I'll help Mike watch."

"Well, all right," Jason said. "Then we'll all stay up together and watch." As he regarded his wrung-out friends, his headache intensified. He could feel the gears of his brain grinding and turning fitfully. Like a stressed engine struggling to avert breakdown.

Thomas was not sleeping well. A few minutes past two o'clock in the morning, he climbed out of bed. He grabbed his house robe from the hook on the bedroom door, wrapped it around himself, and shuffled downstairs.

These damn dreams, he thought as he went to the kitchen. In each dream he'd had that night, he drove around Spring Harbor while Jason sat beside him in the car. He stopped at the homes of various women. After he visited each girlfriend, he grabbed Jason's throat and threatened to kill him if he told Linda. Jason would only stare at him silently, fear and hate burning in his eyes. It was likely the same glare that, as a child, he'd given Big George after he made his rounds to his women.

Thomas wondered if he would ever sleep soundly again.

In the kitchen he fixed a bowl of corn flakes, then headed to the living room. He switched on the TV, turning the volume low so as not to disturb Linda. He settled in the recliner and flipped through channels, slowly eating the cereal. There was nothing on TV worth watching, but anything was preferable to viewing the nightmares that filled his mind's eye.

As he raised the spoon to his lips, the telephone rang.

Startled, he looked at the phone on the end table beside him.

Who could be calling at that hour? Was there an emergency?

Maybe Big George is dead, he thought, with a spark of hope. He reprimanded himself for thinking such a thing.

The phone rang again. He picked up the handset.

"Hello?" he said.

"Hey, baby." It was a woman's voice that he did not recognize. "How are you doing?"

"Who is this?" he said, frowning.

"That's no way to greet a lady, sweetie."

"When I get a call at two in the morning, I forget my manners. Now will you tell me who you are?"

She chuckled—a low, throaty sound. "I'm whoever you want me to be, honey."

This is crazy, he thought. *An obscene call from a woman.* He had no idea who she was, and he would have remembered her. She had a smooth, undeniably sensuous voice; she would have made a bundle as a phone-sex operator.

"Are you lonely tonight?" she said. "Want me to give you some company?"

"I'm married."

"Married men get lonely sometimes. Every man can use a friend on the side . . . every now and then."

Guilt churned through him. This woman, whoever she was, could not possibly know about his affair, yet he had the strange feeling that she knew about him and Rose.

"I would be a perfect friend, sweetie. You'd like me. I have what you love in a woman: smooth brown skin, a lean, toned body, nice breasts, a tight ass."

"I don't think so." He could not believe this conversation. He should hang up. But her voice . . . he'd be damned if she didn't have the sexiest voice he'd ever heard. As if by magnetic force, her alluring voice kept the handset pressed against his ear.

"Oh, I think so. I think I want to ride you, baby. I want to take you inside me and squeeze you until you beg for me to let go, and then I want to put my nipples in your mouth and let you suck on them. Would you like that?"

He did not answer. Could not answer. His heart knocked.

"Then I'll kneel before you and take you in my moist, warm mouth. Does your wife do that for you, baby? I bet she doesn't. I'll run my lips and tongue all over it, work it in and out, make chills of pleasure ripple through your body . . ."

"Look, whoever the hell you are, don't call me again," he said, and hung up. His hand shook.

The phone rang.

He snatched it up. "Hello?"

"I'm in the backyard, sweetie," the woman said. "Why don't you come out to meet me?"

"Go to hell!" He slammed down the phone.

Heat flushed his face. That crazy-assed woman had punched

his buttons. Her honey-smooth voice and her vivid descriptions of the acts she would perform had fanned his desire to a fever pitch. He was angry at himself for listening to her, for succumbing to lust so easily. He was acting like a damn animal, not a responsible, committed husband.

Like father, like son.

He wanted to go to sleep. He didn't want to dream, think, or do anything else. He wanted to sleep like a stone and wake up some time tomorrow. He only wanted some peace.

Thankfully, the phone did not ring again.

All hopes for relaxation gone, he clicked off the TV and went to the kitchen to place the bowl and spoon in the sink. Above the sink, there was a window. It provided a view of the backyard.

I'm in the backyard, sweetie. Why don't you come out to meet me?

Although he was certain the woman had only been teasing him, he peered out of the glass. Thick mist filled the yard; it roiled and churned in phosphorescent waves.

Through the mist, he thought he glimpsed a figure standing near the big oak tree.

It couldn't be her. He had to be imagining this.

As he watched, the figure approached the house. The fog seemed to part in its wake. Because the fog concealed the ground, however, it appeared that the figure was walking on air.

Now, that was really crazy.

The visitor drew closer, revealed by the light glowing on the back porch. It was definitely a woman, and she had described herself accurately: brown-skinned, a lean, taut physique, full breasts. She was completely nude. Ravishing.

He wanted to look away, couldn't. He wanted to run, but his feet seemed to be nailed to the floor.

If this was a dream, it was the most lifelike dream he'd ever experienced.

As she came closer, he saw that her face was as beautiful as her body: large, almond-shaped eyes, a generous mouth, and lustrous dark hair.

Standing only five feet away from the window, she beckoned for him to come outside.

He looked to the back door beside him. It was only two steps away. Two steps, and he could have this incredibly erotic woman in his arms. He could imagine them together on the grass, fucking like dogs.

His mouth was dry.

He looked at the woman. She placed her hands on her breasts. Smiling, she kneaded them slowly, lovingly.

He could feel his hands on her breasts. Could see himself licking the dark nipples, sucking greedily.

"Come on, Thomas," the woman said. He heard her voice clearly, almost as if she were whispering in his ear. "You did it with Rose. Aren't I more beautiful than she is?"

"Yes, but . . . hey, how do you know about Rose?" he said. "How do you know my name?"

"I know plenty of things, sweetheart. I know what you need right now. Me."

A chill passed through him. Weird. This was some weird shit.

The back door was two steps away. But he was not going out there. His body hungered for this fabulous-looking woman, but he would not allow himself to indulge his lust. Not only was it wrong; some subconscious feeling told him that it was dangerous. What kind of woman called at two o'clock in the morning and then showed up in someone's backyard? How could she know his name and know about Rose, too? He had not told *anyone* about Rose.

Too many questions. No logical answers. That meant it was time to end this encounter. He wasn't some fool in a horror movie who willingly walked into strange shit.

He glanced at the woman again—and then pulled the

drapes across the window. He made sure the back door was locked, too.

He stood against the counter for a few minutes, waiting for something to happen—for her to glide like a ghost through the door, maybe. Nothing happened. Gradually, his heartbeat slowed.

By morning, perhaps he would not remember this incident. He did not want to remember it. He did not want to dwell on things he could not rationalize away.

He would not tell Linda about it, either. Why worry her? She would only suspect that he had dreamed it up, anyway, and the last thing he needed was for her to think that he dreamed of other women.

He switched off the kitchen light and returned upstairs. Linda was asleep. Quietly he lay beside her.

"I love you, baby," he said. He kissed her softly on the forehead. "God, I love you so much."

As if she had heard him, she scooted into his arms. He held her close. Lustful visions still flashed like photos in his mind: the woman in the backyard—inviting him, tempting him.

It didn't really happen, he assured himself. *It was only a bad dream. And I won't think about it anymore.*

Eventually, the disturbing images faded, and he drifted off to sleep.

CHAPTER TWELVE

Friday morning, Thomas and Linda enjoyed breakfast in bed. Fruit, toast, eggs, and orange juice. Like honeymooners, they took turns playfully feeding each other, stretching a meal that would normally take ten minutes into a half hour. They made love after breakfast—a slow, tender session that, in Linda's mind, somehow surpassed the hot passion of the previous night. Around nine o'clock, they mutually agreed it was time for both of them to get to work. They shared a long, liquid kiss at the door, then Thomas left for the restaurant, Linda standing at the window watching him leave, a serene smile on her face.

When she turned to go to her office, she was still smiling. Since yesterday, she and Thomas had talked, held each other, and loved more than they had in years. The past twelve hours seemed like a romantic fantasy, too sweet to be true.

But it's really happening, she thought. *We persevered through the bad times, and this is our reward for staying together. It's only going to get better.*

She settled in front of her computer to work on her novel.

She wrote with unusual speed and focus. When she looked up at the clock, she was surprised to see that she had worked past noon. She would have continued to work, but she had learned that it was always better to take a break before inspiration dried up. Besides, she was hungry.

Before heading to the kitchen, she checked the mailbox. The mail appeared to consist of bills, credit-card offers, and a book from one of the many book clubs of which she was a member. After a closer examination, she noticed that the large padded envelope that she had assumed contained a book did not bear a return address. The only address written on it was hers. It was printed in square, black letters.

Curious, she tore open the envelope.

A videocassette slid out.

Nothing was written on the tape's label. Odd.

She popped the videotape into the VCR. She pressed PLAY and stood in front of the TV with her arms crossed.

She could not believe what she saw on the screen.

Thomas and another woman. In bed.

At one o'clock, Jason opened the front gate of the Sawyer residence. He strolled across the walkway, climbed the steps to the porch, and stood there with his finger poised over the doorbell.

He did not want to take his girlfriend to the carnival. Having slept only three hours the previous night, he was tired, hardly up to the half-mile walk to the county fairgrounds, where the carnival was located. He was tense, in no mood to eat, talk, laugh, shout, play, and otherwise act as though he were a typical teenager having a good time. Worst of all, he could not blot the Stranger out of his thoughts. Thoughts of the Stranger spread like a virus through his mind, crippling his ability to think of anything else.

He would have liked to cancel his date, but he had

promised Michelle that they would go. Used to living with parents who, for years, had casually broken promises they made to him, he was determined to stand by his word. He didn't want to be anything like his crazy family.

They would stay at the carnival for only a couple of hours. In a public place filled with hundreds of people, what could go wrong, anyway?

Nothing, of course.

He pressed the doorbell.

The door opened. Michelle stuck her head out.

Jason summoned his best smile.

"Hey, sweet thing," he said. "How's it going?"

She frowned. "I know you're not talking to me."

"You're the only one here."

"I'm not a 'sweet thing,' for your information. I'm an intelligent, responsible young woman."

"You forgot *pretty.*"

"Huh?"

"Intelligent, responsible, and *pretty* young woman."

She smiled shyly.

"Okay. Since you said that, I forgive your 'sweet thing' comment."

"Did it really bother you?"

"No, not coming from you. But if some other guy had said it, I'd have wanted to smack him. You can get away with saying almost anything to me."

"Really?" He rubbed his chin thoughtfully.

"Don't get any ideas. I said *almost* anything."

"Calm down. I was only going to tell you how beautiful you look today. So I'll say it: Michelle, you look beautiful today."

"You're too nice," she said, but it was obvious that she was eating up his flattery. It made him feel good to see her smile. The past couple of days had been full of storm clouds; it was nice to see a little sunshine.

"Ready to go?" he said.

"Yep." She closed the door behind her and came outside.

He wasn't merely acting flirtatious when he complimented her. With her dreamy brown eyes and bright smile, Michelle was the finest girl in the school. She wore a yellow blouse, white shorts, and sandals. He couldn't help noticing how well her clothes hung on her blossoming figure.

Sometimes he was surprised at how comfortable he had grown with Michelle in the two months that they'd been dating. He did not consider himself to be a ladies' man, but somehow, being around her brought out his confidence. She had a calming effect on him.

On their first date, he had been anything but calm. Anxious in the presence of such a pretty, popular girl, he had stumbled over his words, made comments he later realized were stupid, and had been terrified at the thought of even holding her hand. When the date was over, he was convinced that she would never go out with him again, and that she would, in fact, tell everyone what a loser he was. To his astonishment, she agreed to another date. He soon began to relax around her. She was very pretty, but she was equally sweet. He wondered how she had ever made him nervous.

"What are you looking at?" she said as they walked down the porch steps, side by side.

"You. I've missed you the past few days."

"I've missed you, too. What have you been doing?"

"Breaking into houses, joyriding in stolen cars, and stealing candy from babies."

"You're so silly. Seriously, what have you been doing?"

"Not much. Hanging out with the fellas, nothing special."

He hated to lie to her. But he could not risk telling her the truth and involving her in his problems. He valued their relationship too much to endanger her.

"I wish I could hang out," she said. "Mama's trying to kill me this summer. She's got me doing everything, from scrubbing floors to helping her paint the bathroom. Since I'm going out of town tomorrow to visit my cousins in Atlanta for a couple of weeks, it's like she wants to work me to death before I go."

"We'll have fun at the carnival. It'll be a good break for both of us."

"What do you need a break from? Playing video games all day?" She giggled.

"Hey, video games can wear you out."

"Uh-huh. Sure."

"Really."

"Whatever you say. Don't let me tell Mama. She'll call you over to do some *real* work."

"As long as I'm with you, I wouldn't mind." It was corny, but so what? He wanted to be carefree for a change.

"Aw, you're such a sweetie," Michelle said. She took his hand in hers, squeezing it gently as they walked.

Warmth spread through Jason. How could he have thought about canceling their date? With all that he had faced recently, he needed a couple hours of fun and laughter. Michelle was the perfect solution for his abraded nerves. As long as they were together, he would be happy and nothing would go wrong. Nothing.

Fifteen seemingly endless minutes later, the images on the television flickered into electric snow. Linda gazed blankly at the screen. She rose from the sofa and shut off the TV.

Slowly, she returned to the couch.

She had to sit. She felt off-balance, shaky.

She leaned back on the cushions. She stared at the ceiling.

Numbness lay like a marble slab on her body. She closed her eyes. She squeezed her hands into fists. Her heart began to hammer, beating so hard her entire body throbbed in unison with each pound. Sweat formed on her face in cold beads, her mouth dried up like a sun-scorched pond, and a single thought boiled in the depths of her storming mind, erupting into her consciousness with such power that she shouted it aloud.

"How the hell could he do this to me?"

Hadn't she been busting her ass lately to rebuild their relationship? Hadn't they talked about the importance of each of them doing their share if the marriage was to work? Hadn't he given her his word that he had remained faithful to her?

Yes, all of those things had happened. But one fact nullified everything: Thomas only cared about himself.

Unable to sit, she sprang off the couch.

She didn't give a damn about the woman who had filmed their little rendezvous. It could've been any woman. She didn't blame her. She blamed Thomas. The bastard. The selfish, cheating, manipulative bastard. He'd been acting really funny the past few days. Finally, she knew why.

That asshole!

She paced through the house, cursing. Tears began to spurt from her eyes, and her weeping only made her more furious, more unsettled. She felt as if she would literally explode.

Wandering in a daze, she happened by the telephone in the kitchen. Without hesitation she snatched the handset off the cradle. Dialed The House of Soul. Hung up after the first ring, before anyone had answered.

To hell with calling him.

She was going down there.

If she remembered correctly, Thomas had set up a VCR at the restaurant, in the employee room, where the staff took breaks and watched training tapes. She didn't care what he might be doing when she arrived—didn't care if the president was in there chowing on greens, rib tips, and corn bread. She was going to march in and demand that he watch this tape. If he refused, she would play it anyway for his employees, and if they wanted, she'd buy popcorn and soda for their enjoyment as they viewed the show.

She was close to losing all control of herself. She didn't care. If she tried to restrain her emotions, if she began to actually think about this madness, she would go crazy—before Thomas had been burned by the flames of her wrath.

She ejected the videocassette out of the machine and jammed it into her purse. Rushing out the front door, she got in her car, gunned the engine, and sped to The House of Soul.

The carnival was in full swing when Jason and Michelle arrived. Drenched in golden sunlight, the fairgrounds rocked, jumped, and twirled to the tune of a thousand people caught in an ecstasy of fun. The Ferris wheel, the Tilt-a-Whirl, the Dive Bomber, the Whip, the Caterpillar, the Whirl-Wind. Cotton-candy kiosks, pokerino parlors, ring tosses, taffy-apple stands, and bottle pitches. The mouthwatering aromas of hot dogs, hamburgers, pizza, taffy, cotton candy, and pretzels. Bright colors everywhere; loud music pumping, pumping, pumping from scores of speakers; kids laughing, shouting, and screaming with glee. So much excitement and energy, it was impossible to absorb it all at once; you could only step in and let the atmosphere sweep you away.

"I love coming here," Michelle said. Looking around, she grinned. "I wish I could live at a carnival."

"I hear the freak show needs new help," Jason said. "You might want to sign up."

She pinched him in the ribs.

"Hey, I thought you said I was beautiful."

Grimacing, rubbing his side, Jason said, "I thought *you* said I was being too nice."

"I was kidding, Jason. I love compliments. Who doesn't?"

"Thanks for telling me."

"I love taffy apples, too."

"That's nice."

"It'd be nicer if you bought one for me."

"Will you give me a kiss if I do?"

"Maybe. A quick peck on the cheek."

"I was hoping for a French kiss."

"Keep hoping, baby. It ain't happening here."

He sighed. "I can dream, I guess."

At a taffy-apple stand, he bought apples for both of them. They took big, sloppy bites of the treats as they walked down the crowded midway, surveying the amusements, trying to decide which ride to try first.

"There, let's get on that." She pointed.

She was pointing at the Ferris wheel. It was the biggest one he had ever seen, like a wheel from a chariot a mythical god might use to traverse the heavens. As if burning slowly from within, the metal spokes and rims gleamed, though the burning phenomenon was created by nothing more remarkable than reflections of the sunlight. Each gently swinging gondola looked occupied, and a long line curved to the booth at which the tickets were taken.

"The line's long," he said.

"All of the lines are long. We have to start somewhere. That seems like a good place."

"Why's that?"

"It's romantic," she said. "Think about it. You're high in the air; there's a cool wind; the sun's warm on your skin; you can see the country for miles around . . ."

"And you can feel your stomach about to turn inside out and make you throw up on your girlfriend," he said.

She wrinkled her nose. "Okay, that's nasty."

"Sorry, but it might happen."

"Are you scared?"

"What? I'm not scared." He knew what *real* fear was, and getting on a Ferris wheel didn't come close to what he'd been through lately. But he'd play along with her.

"Prove it," she said.

"All right, I will." He took her hand and led her toward the ride. They got in line.

"What a typical guy." She smiled. "You can't admit that you're scared of anything."

"I wanted to try the Ferris wheel anyway."

"Sure, Jason." She kissed him on the cheek. "Don't worry, I won't tell anyone. It's our secret."

"Thanks. I was worried about that."

They waited in line. Everything was going perfectly, more perfectly than he could have anticipated. There was nothing to worry about. Everything would be fine.

Thomas was seated at the desk in his office, working on an inventory report, when Linda knocked on the door.

Seeing her face at the square window in the door broke his concentration as effectively as a rock shattering glass. He'd plunged so deeply into work that he had forgotten the problems that plagued his personal life. The sight of Linda's face brought everything back up, like bile.

Why was she visiting him here? What did she want? Whatever it was, couldn't it wait until he got home?

She knocked again.

"Thomas, it's me," she said. "Will you open the door, please?"

Reluctantly he closed the file on his desk. He would see why she had come, then get her out of here. With only a few hours remaining until he went home for the day, he wanted to savor all the time he had left in his comfortable, secluded world of work.

He opened the door.

"What a surprise," he said. "You're visiting me at work. Next thing, you'll be wanting a job here."

"I need to show you something. I couldn't wait until this evening."

"What is it?"

"You'll see. Come on." Beckoning him, she turned and walked down the short hallway, into the employees' break room.

The area was furnished with a long pine table, several padded chairs, and a shelf stocked with magazines such as *Ebony, Jet, Essence,* and *Black Enterprise.* A built-in media center housed a stereo, VCR, twenty-seven-inch television, and several videotapes, most of which featured restaurant-training seminars.

The room was empty.

"If you interrupted your writing to show me this," he said, "it must be something important."

"Oh, it is. I promise." She removed a videotape from her purse, switched on the VCR and TV, and inserted the cassette. He frowned. What was she up to?

"You might want to sit down." She smiled. "This is gonna knock you out."

"Okay." Still frowning, he pulled out a chair and sat.

She pressed PLAY and took the seat beside him.

Snow filled the screen. Then the tube cleared, and the content of the recording appeared.

His eyes widened.

On the screen, he and a black woman—it had to be Rose—were in a bed. The woman sat astride him, her slim, naked back facing the camera, but his face was clearly revealed. Eyes squeezed shut in rapture, his lips moved soundlessly, hands sliding over her legs. Letting her ride him like a cowboy, enjoying every second of it . . .

Shit. Oh, shit!

He shut off the TV.

Slowly Linda stood. She was not smiling anymore.

"Baby, I can explain," he said.

"Isn't that what husbands always say when they fuck up? 'Baby, I can explain'? You can do better than that."

He groped for words. "It's over with me and that girl. It was never anything to begin with—just sex."

"Just sex?"

"There were no real feelings between us—nothing like that. Linda, I swear, she was only an escape from the pressure—the constant pressure, a way out of the stress I get from this goddamned job and my crazy daddy—and it was wrong, all wrong, and you have every right to be pissed, all the right in the world to be absolutely furious. But I'll never, ever cheat on you again, I promise."

She stared at him.

He lowered his eyes, gazed at the floor.

"That's all you can do?" she said. "Stare at the floor like a total sucker? You can't even look me in the eyes. Some kind of man you are."

"Linda, I promise—"

"Shut up."

He shut up.

She unzipped her purse. His heart clutched, because he was certain that she was digging for a gun, knew she would draw it out and blow his guts against the wall without hesitation . . . but she only pressed EJECT on the VCR, took out the videotape, and slipped it inside her open bag.

He sighed.

"You thought I was gonna shoot you?" she said, as uncannily aware of his thoughts as ever. "I feel like killing your ass, but it's not worth it—I'd end up spending the rest of my life in jail. I'd much rather spend the rest of my life without you."

"What?"

"It's over, Thomas. I thank your girlfriend for sending me this tape and waking me up at last. You'll never change. You don't care about me, and you don't care about Jason. All you care about is yourself, this restaurant, and your daddy. I don't have time for you anymore." She moved to leave.

"Linda, wait." He touched her arm.

She spun. "Don't you ever touch me again, you bastard. Do you hear me?"

"Baby, please. Don't do this."

"I haven't done anything to you. You did this to yourself. You're the one who slept with that bitch and told the lies. All *I'm* doing is what any woman with brains would. Divorcing you."

"Divorcing me? Hey, no, you can't do that, not after all we've been through."

"I can't, huh? Watch me."

With that, she turned and stormed out.

The line moved faster than Jason expected. They reached the ticket booth after they had been waiting for only five minutes.

They gave the tickets to the attendant, slipped through the turnstile, and walked across the wooden floor toward the last empty gondola. After they slid onto the wide seat, another attendant snapped the safety bar in place, rattled it to ensure it was locked, and hurried to the control station at the edge of the platform.

"Man, I've got butterflies," Jason said. "I've never ridden one of these before."

"Are you scared?" she said.

"Me? Please. It's just a ride."

"You look scared to me."

"Well, I'm not." He tried to smile. He was not genuinely

afraid, but he was nervous. "I'm not really scared. I'm excited, I guess."

"Sure, Jason."

"Honest. I have butterflies of excitement, not fear."

"I believe you." She turned away, a faint smile on her face. Then she glanced at him. "Do you want to hold hands?"

"I thought you'd never ask." He found her hand and squeezed it. She laughed and patted his hand reassuringly.

Music blasted from the surrounding speakers. The Ferris wheel jerked once, twice, and began to turn. He watched the floor recede slowly underneath them, their gondola creaking slightly on the thick steel pins that connected it to the wheel rims.

"I love this," she said. "Wait until we get to the top. You won't believe the view."

"I can hardly wait." His stomach trembled as their basket continued to rise.

Michelle scooted closer to him. For him, heaven got no better than that. He draped his arm across her shoulders, loving the feel of her warm body against his. Leaning into him, she sighed contentedly.

The giant wheel kept revolving, their gondola rising higher above the carnival.

"I heard that it's good luck for a couple to kiss at the top of a Ferris wheel," she said.

"Where'd you hear that?"

"From some friends. It's a girl thing."

"That figures. Girls have rituals for everything."

"Do you want to do it?"

He looked down. They seemed to be about fifty feet above the ground and steadily ascending. "If I'm conscious by then, yeah."

"You know, Jason, we've never really kissed before. We've always just given each other pecks on the cheek."

"You don't have to remind me."

"Maybe we should make this one the real thing."

"A real French kiss?"

"Yeah, I guess so."

"Hey, that sounds good to me. Sounds *great* to me."

"Have you ever kissed a girl on the lips?"

"Nope."

"Good. That makes two of us."

"You mean you've never kissed a girl on the lips, either?"

"No, dummy. I've never kissed a boy on the lips."

"So this'll be the first time for both of us," he said. "Good. That way, you won't know if I'm no good. Nothing to compare it to, you know?"

"If I feel your tongue halfway down my throat, then I know you're no good. There are some signs, boy."

"Oh, well, it was only a thought."

They continued to rise.

Cool wind blew, gently swinging their gondola.

Above them, the passengers in the highest basket released a chorus of ecstatic screams.

His stomach quivered, not only with the rush of being high above the earth, but in anticipation of the approaching special moment with this special girl.

Finally, they hit the top.

"Here we are." She leaned back and put her hand on his chest. "Let's close our eyes and do it at the count of three."

"All right." He shut his eyes.

They counted together: "One . . . two . . . three!"

Unsure what to expect, he leaned forward.

He met only empty air.

Certain that they had done as clumsy adolescent lovers do in a movie and simply misaimed their lips, he opened his eyes. He assumed he would see the same oops-let's-try-again look on Michelle's face.

But she was not there.

In fact, the entire carnival was deserted.

The Ferris wheel had stopped, leaving the basket in which he sat at the utmost peak.

That was not the only thing that had stopped. The digits on his wristwatch had frozen at 1:39, too.

CHAPTER THIRTEEN

As if a wizard had cast a powerful spell, a thunderstorm had instantly replaced the sunshine and clear skies. Mallets of thunder pounded the earth, lightning bullwhipped the coal black sky, and a gale shrieked across the carnival, rocking Jason's gondola like a tugboat in a tempest.

Disbelief had frozen Jason as still as his watch digits. Gripping the cold safety bar, he gaped at the miraculously transformed world. Although Shorty and Brains had told him all about this strange place, seeing it himself for the first time had driven his heart into his throat and squeezed sweat from his pores. He found it hard to believe this was actually happening.

Flashes of lightning enlivened the darkness.

Thunder steamrolled across the day.

Thunderland. The name fit so perfectly.

He needed to get out of his seat and away from the Ferris wheel. The metal wheel was the tallest structure in the area. Staying seated was to risk getting fried by a bolt of lightning.

He leaned sideways, peered over the lip of the gondola.

God, he was high up in the air. His stomach curdled.

He considered waiting there until the storm calmed, but that was a dangerous idea. This wasn't the normal world, in which all storms eventually ceased. Here, the thunder and lightning might rage forever.

He would have to get down. It was the only sensible choice.

It's like climbing a tree, he thought. He had spent his childhood clambering up and down the big oak in the backyard. He'd become as agile as a monkey . . . though he had fallen out of the tree in March, in a thunderstorm like this one.

Don't think about that.

He thumbed the latch on the safety bar. He pushed the bar away from him.

His heart had already been beating fast. Now it continued to beat fast—but it knocked harder, too.

He didn't dare look down again.

Slowly he pushed off the seat. He grabbed the nearby rim. Twining his legs around the nearest spoke, he slid down slowly . . . slowly . . . until his feet touched a crossbeam that braced the spokes.

He paused, panting.

Thunder rolled.

Lightning flared, an ultrabright burst that drove needles of pain into his eyes. He blinked, temporarily blinded.

When his eyesight cleared and he resumed his descent, a tide of wind rushed toward him. It shook the Ferris wheel down to its foundations, rattled it savagely, and he feared the wheel might tear loose from its ground supports and roll like a runaway tire across the carnival. He pressed his face against the cold spoke and held fast with his legs and arms, his muscles throbbing with the effort.

The gale abated.

But the other storm elements continued the onslaught. Before he could gather his bearings, another burst of thunder blasted the sky, and lightning licked a charred cloud that seemed to be only a few feet overhead.

In spite of the turbulent weather conditions, he had to get moving. If he waited for a period of calm, he would likely be either electrocuted or flung away by a gust.

He slid off the spoke, to the crossbeam underneath, then moved across that beam to the next spoke. He continued that method of beam-to-spoke, spoke-to-beam, gradually moving downward. His confidence grew. As long as the day remained dry, he could reach the ground with no problems.

When he was perhaps thirty feet above the carnival, en route from a crossbeam to a spoke, thunder crashed again, harder than ever before. As if the explosion signaled the rupture of some immense, celestial container, a flood of icy rain dropped straight down from the black sky.

The Ferris wheel quickly became slick.

Rain splashed into Jason's eyes, blurring his vision. His clothes grew as heavy as a suit of lead.

He wanted to choke the Stranger and demand to know why he forced him to endure this. If the bastard wanted him to die, why didn't he strike him down and save both of them all this trouble?

The rain fell harder.

Regardless of the slick metal, he had to continue his descent. The weather would only grow worse.

Carefully he navigated to the next spoke. It was only a couple of feet away, but it seemed ten feet away, for the lightning and veils of rain cast the world into weird, flickering, uncertain perspectives. Twice, his feet skidded an inch or two on the wet beam, and the near-accidents touched off vivid fantasies of him flying off and cracking his skull like a melon on the earth below.

Finally reaching the spoke, he clung to it tightly.

Not much farther to go. Twenty-five feet, maybe less.

Rain showering him, he edged down to the next crossbeam. He reached for the nearby spoke.

Wind wailed, shoved him hard, and threw gritty rain into his eyes. Blinded and knocked off balance, he teetered; then both of his feet slipped off the beam. He lunged for a girder, a cable, a strut, anything that would help him regain his balance, but his hands found no holds. Screaming, he plunged backward, away from the Ferris wheel.

In the seemingly suspended period of time that marked Jason's fall, he imagined his body as a big, thick pillow that would strike the ground with only a feather-light thump. He saw himself landing on his back and feeling jubilation as he realized that he'd sustained no injuries whatsoever. His fantasy was hopeless, he knew, like the optimistic yet doomed thoughts of everyone on the brink of a lethal accident, but he imagined it anyway—imagined it so intensely that, in his mind, his miraculous landing had become fact. He experienced it so vividly that his desired outcome seemed *inevitable*.

Imagining feverishly, he squeezed his eyes shut, bracing himself for the agony of the impact.

Nothing happened.

Heart hammering, he opened his eyes.

He lay on the ground. Puddles bubbled around him.

High above, shadows cloaked the Ferris wheel, pulsating eerily with each discharge of lightning.

He lay there, cold raindrops splattering his face.

He lifted his arm, flexed it. It was okay, not broken.

He wriggled his fingers. They were fine, too.

He did a mental inventory of the remainder of his body, trying to detect any injuries. Nothing hurt. He was in good shape.

And he had fallen from a height of more than twenty feet.

And had not felt the impact.

As if what he had imagined during his fall had become reality.

Trembling, he sat up.

He did not know how this discovery would affect his attempts to solve the mystery of the Stranger; in fact, he was not convinced that it was more than a freak occurrence. But . . . if he could create whatever he imagined in this quasi-world, that meant he had some control. No, not control—power. Power. The power to fight back and maybe win this bizarre game the Stranger had made him play.

Excitement coursed through him.

He got to his feet. He searched the concourse, wondering how he should test his newfound ability. Then he saw a large canvas tent, standing a hundred yards ahead.

The huge, colorful banner read: *FREAK TOWN.*

It was not the idea of a freak show that had hooked his attention. What grabbed him was the open, fluttering flap that formed the tent's entrance, and the pale-yellow radiance that emanated from within.

Inexplicably, he was drawn to the tent. He did not expect to see any carnival freaks inside. He anticipated something much more extraordinary—although he could not explain why he expected to see anything at all.

Once he reached the entrance, he halted.

The rainfall had ceased. The sky was still black with swollen thunderclouds, but the lightning and thunder had stopped as well. The cool wind that blew sporadically was soft, refreshing.

From his position a couple of feet beyond the doorway, he saw that the pale-yellow incandescence was emitted by rows of lightbulbs. The naked bulbs dangled above the roped-off walkway and the dozen or so stalls behind the ropes.

He stepped inside the chamber.

The motionless air was thick with humidity. It smelled of wet canvas and sawdust.

"Is anybody here?" he said.

No answer.

It seemed empty, but he could not discard his feeling that something awaited him in there.

He strolled down the walkway, peering into each stall he passed. All of the stalls were empty. Except the last one.

On the blanketed platform of the last compartment, Michelle reclined languorously.

"What are *you* doing in here?" he said.

"Waiting." She sat up, ran her fingers through her hair.

"Waiting for who?"

"For you." She smiled.

He approached her. "Hold on, this isn't making any sense. First of all, do you know where we are?"

"Sure."

"Where are we?"

"The carnival, silly."

"That's not what I meant. I meant this place, this world— where is it?"

She giggled. "This world? You're the one who isn't making any sense, Jason."

"Okay, forget about that. Tell me how you got here."

"I walked with you. Do you remember?"

"Yeah, I do. But before I came here, we were riding the Ferris wheel."

"Yes. About to kiss." Giggling, she scooted closer to him.

He dragged his hand down his sweaty face. "I'm confused. As a matter of fact, I think I've gone crazy. None of this is making any sense at all."

"Sure, it is."

"No, it isn't. I mean, when I first saw you here, you said that you've been waiting for me."

"I have been waiting." She moved closer until she sat directly in front of him. Her knees pressed against his legs.

"But how did you know I was going to come in here in the first place?"

"Because I know you."

"What do you mean?"

She picked up his hand, rubbed his fingers. "I know you as well as you know yourself."

"Come on. I like you, but we've only known each other for a couple of months."

Smiling, she shook her head. "No, longer than that. Much longer."

"What does that mean?"

Instead of answering, she wrapped her arms around his neck, drew him forward, and kissed him softly on the lips. Her lips were warm and sweet, and he felt a strong urge to forget about everything and go on kissing her forever. He slid his hands down to her waist, then to her hips, while her soft hands kneaded the back of his neck.

Their lips parted.

"That was a first kiss to remember," she said.

"It was," he said, breathing hard. "It really was. But you haven't answered my question."

She kissed both corners of his mouth. "I'll answer it later. When I've finished."

"When you've finished what?"

"Doing things for you." She kissed his chin.

"What are you going to do for me?"

"Give you things. Fulfill your most secret wishes. Like I promised you the other night."

A chill seized him.

"What did you say?" he said, the unthinkable flashing in his mind.

Not answering, smiling as if amused at his sudden horror, she lowered her hand to his crotch, unzipped his jeans, and slipped her fingers inside his boxer shorts. She squeezed him gently. That soft pressure and the feeling of her smooth, warm hand filled his chest with a delicious tension. He moaned.

Slowly, she stroked him up and down.

"Oh, God," he said. In spite of his terrifying knowledge of this girl's true identity, he was unable to push her away and run. She had discovered his sexual fantasy, had taken his hand and enticed him to *live* it, and he was helpless to resist. Overwhelmed by the power of his own secret desire.

With every fluid motion of her expert hand, a flash of pleasure shot through him. His knees weakening, he leaned against her. She curled her free arm around his waist and leaned back until she lay on the blanketed platform and he lay beside her.

She placed her hand on his chest, pushed him onto his back.

"I can't do this," he said. "I shouldn't do this."

She helped him remove his shirt.

"I have to get out of here," he said. "This is nuts."

She sat up and began to take off her tank top.

"This is insane."

She whipped off her shirt, then slid off her shorts, too.

He gaped at her nude body. Her body was fabulous, better than he had dreamed it would be. As he stared at her, the front of his boxer shorts rose into a pyramid. He blushed.

"Looks like a friend wants to be let out." She rolled his jeans down his legs, freeing him.

"I can't do this," he said, aroused anyway. "I just *can't.*"

She straddled him, placed his hands on her hips, and lowered her face to his. She kissed him.

"You can," she said, and started to prove her point.

When Jason awoke, he was sprawled on the platform, alone. His pants and shirt lay crumpled beside him. The sweet scent of Michelle's perfume hung like a lingering spirit in the humid air.

No, not Michelle's perfume. *Its* perfume. The Stranger's.

Grimacing, he sat up. The idea of having done it with the Stranger, regardless of the beautiful body he had assumed and the pleasure he had given him, was sickening. He had a compulsion to wash himself, to scrub until his skin was raw, as though by giving himself a thorough cleansing he could wipe the experience out of his memory. Something within him felt dirty.

He put on his shirt, zipped his jeans. Jumping off the platform, he left the stall and stepped onto the roped-off walkway.

When he had approached the tent, he had sensed a presence within. Now he sensed nothing.

He wanted to track down the Stranger, learn who he was and why he was doing these things, but he did not know where he had gone. Soon after he climaxed, things had got blurry and he passed out. When he awoke, the Stranger had vanished.

The prospect of searching the carnival for the Stranger was daunting. In this nightmare place, the Stranger was king. There was no telling what obstacles he might throw at Jason in an attempt to keep him away.

Because he had no alternative, Jason walked down the passageway, toward the fluttering flaps of the entrance. Each naked lightbulb that he walked under mysteriously extinguished itself when he passed it, the darkness behind him tightening into a black womb.

He arrived at the tent doorway. A dilapidated ticket booth stood beside the entrance. It was empty.

No one was in sight.

Outside, the carnival was silent.

He stood inside the doorway, soaking up the peculiar atmosphere of the place. Where, exactly, was this amusement park located? In another dimension? In a dream world?

Figuring that a walk would kick his mind into gear, he stepped outside . . .

and found himself sitting in the gondola on the Ferris wheel, beside Michelle. She frowned at him.

"I thought we agreed to kiss on the count of three," she said. "You sat there with your lips puckered. I ended up kissing your shirt."

He blinked. "Huh?"

"If you didn't want to do it, you should have told me," she said. "I would've understood. I admit, kissing on a Ferris wheel is kind of silly."

He stared at her, heart ramming against his rib cage. He looked around.

The basket in which they sat had passed the top of the wheel. It descended slowly, creaking gently.

The carnival was crowded, music and other noises bursting from everywhere.

The day was clear, sunny, warm.

His watch functioned. It read 1:39, and the seconds steadily ticked away.

His clothes were dry, too, even though, only a short while ago, he had been walking through rain.

He slumped in the seat.

He wondered how much more of this he could endure.

She leaned toward him. "You look terrible. Are you feeling okay?"

"Michelle, I think I need to go home."

Her eyes were compassionate. "You feel bad? Is the Ferris wheel making you sick?"

"I think so. Or it might have been something I ate. I don't know. But I want to go home and lie down for a while." He didn't enjoy lying to her, but he could not give her the truth. He did not want to involve her. And because she would probably decide he had lost his mind if he gave her the real story, he might risk losing her friendship, too.

Disappointment flickered in her eyes. "We can go. But remember, I'm going out of town tomorrow to visit my cousins in Atlanta. I won't see you again for a couple of weeks."

"I know. I'm really sorry. I'll miss you."

"Don't be sorry, sweetie. It's not your fault." She squeezed his hand. "Now please, stop talking so much. To feel better, you'll need all the energy you can get."

He kept quiet. He would need all the energy he could get, but not to heal. The way things were turning out, he would need it for another purpose: to survive.

CHAPTER FOURTEEN

Feeling ashamed and adrift after Linda left the restaurant, Thomas dragged himself back to his office. He couldn't have been more stunned if a physician had announced that he had contracted cancer and had only one month to live. His life was over.

Something, however, nagged at him and begged to be checked out. He grabbed the telephone off the desk and punched in a number.

On the third ring, Rose answered.

"Rose, this is Thomas."

"What do you want? No, I ain't meeting you nowhere."

"I'm not calling to ask you to meet me. I only want to ask you something. Did you ever, uh, send a video to my wife? A video of us together?"

"What?" Her confusion sounded genuine. If she was acting, she was good—she was real good. "I wouldn't record shit like that. I ain't even got a camcorder."

"Please be honest with me, Rose."

"Thomas, I'm at work. I don't have time for your stupid-assed questions. Is that all you wanted?"

"Yeah, that's all. Sorry to bother you." He hung up.

Rose had to be lying. If she had not sent the tape to Linda, then who was responsible? He had *never* been with another woman outside of his marriage.

Although the logical answer was that Rose had secretly recorded one of their sex episodes, the explanation failed to erase his unease.

Because the woman in the video was not Rose. Rose had a large, vivid tattoo of a blood-red rose imprinted on her back. The woman in the recording did not wear a tattoo. Linda had taken away the tape, but he did not need to review it to recall what he'd seen.

But if the woman was not Rose, then who was it?

He thought about the strange, almost unearthly woman who had been in the backyard late last night, tempting him.

It could have been the same person. Their bodies were the same—lean and shapely—and they shared the same skin tone.

His heart thudded. He was entertaining an impossible scenario, and he must leave it alone. He had only been with Rose. Rose was in the video, and he was sure that, in his shock at seeing himself exposed on tape, he had simply missed seeing her tattoo. Rose had simply lied to him on the phone.

Yes, it was Rose, trying to get revenge for his dumping her, by wrecking his marriage. Oh, she was sneaky. But he didn't blame her. He was at fault for pursuing an affair with her in the first place.

He pushed away from the desk. He needed to get out of the office, get some fresh air. Or else he would start listening to that insistent little voice in his mind again, spinning its impossible scenarios.

* * *

Thomas left The House of Soul and began driving. He drove without any particular destination in mind. An irrepressible urge to travel— somewhere, anywhere—held sway over him. Maybe he needed to get away for a while and organize his thoughts. Or maybe he searched for something he thought he might find during his drive. He could not explain his intentions. He simply guided the steering wheel, balanced his foot on the gas pedal, and drove along the smooth city streets.

Cruising through Spring Harbor, with the afternoon sun casting warm, golden rays on the town, he realized he was nearing a familiar place. Green Meadows Nursing Home. How ironic. He smiled bitterly.

He parked near the entrance.

He did not know why he had come there. This seemed to be the worst possible time to see his father.

His gaze traveled up the brick building and found Big George's fourth-floor room. The drapes covered the window, as always. Inside, Big George spewed bitterness and hate, as always. Nothing ever changed. Did he expect this visit to be any different from the others?

Unable to understand his actions, feeling almost as though he were a puppet manipulated by unseen fingers, he entered the nursing home. He took the elevator to the fourth floor.

He walked into his father's room.

"You again," Big George said, propped up in his bed by pillows. "Shit, Tommy. I thought you already visited once this week."

"You have a good memory, Dad. I visited a few days ago." Thomas closed the door. He sat on the overstuffed chair beside the bed.

"Why are you back so soon?" Big George said. "I thought I warned you about leaving my place in the hands of those stupid niggers you hired. Didn't I?"

Thomas sighed. "Yeah, you warned me. I guess I don't listen. We share that trait, don't we, Dad?"

"What the hell are you talking about?"

"Remember what you said? 'Like father, like son.' You were right—we do have a lot in common. Like the way we cheated on our wives, for example."

Big George's eyes widened. "So you do have a girl on the side! I knew it! You're a dog if there ever was one, boy!"

"I sure am," Thomas said, nodding. "A dog. Just like you."

"Bow-wow-wow!" Big George said. Tears streaked down his dark, prunelike face as a fit of laughter convulsed him. Thomas found himself laughing, too, though he did not know why he laughed. Was he laughing at the sight of his father, a seventy-year-old man, barking like a dog? At the tragic bond that he shared with Big George? Or at the sorry depths into which he had sunk, a pit so deep that laughing was the only alternative to crying?

"Like father, like son," Big George said. Chuckling, he extended his withered arm and clapped Thomas on the shoulder. "Glad you finally admitted it, son. Ain't nothing wrong with getting all the pussy you can. It's in a man's nature. Just don't get caught!"

"Linda caught me, Dad."

"She caught you? How?"

"My girlfriend sent Linda a videotape of us in bed. I had no idea that she had filmed anything. She was sneaky."

"Was Linda pissed?"

"She was furious. She said she's divorcing me."

At this news, Big George laughed.

"What's so funny?" Thomas said.

"You," Big George said, shaking his head. "I swear, you might be my son, but you can't do anything right. You're too stupid to know how to pull the wool over a woman's eyes. You mean well, but you're a disgrace to my name, boy. I wish I'd had another son, he would've been better than you."

Thomas's next words tumbled out before he could catch them. "I wish I'd had another father."

"What did you say?" Big George's eyes narrowed to black darts.

By speaking those words, he had crossed a line in their relationship, and he sensed that he could not turn back. He repeated himself. "I wish I'd had another father."

Big George glared at him.

Then he punched Thomas in the mouth.

Startled by the blow and his father's unexpected power, Thomas fell out of the overstuffed chair and dropped on the floor. He put his hand to his lips. He felt a thread of blood.

Above him, Big George slowly climbed out of bed. His clawlike hand closed around the weathered wooden cane leaning beside the nightstand.

"I'm gonna kick your ass for that, boy," Big George said. He planted his big, shriveled feet on the tile floor. His hands tightened around the cane. "I'm gonna whip your black ass like I used to in the old days."

Holding his bleeding lip, Thomas inched backward along the floor. Part of his mind shouted at him to stand up like a man, but another part of him felt ten years old again, compelled to lie down and take his beating like a good little boy who had made another dumb mistake deserving of a whipping. As he warily watched his father clamber to his feet and grip the cane in both hands, he repressed the desire to call for Mama.

"Gonna tear your ass up!" Big George said. He swung the cane.

It whistled through the air and thwacked against Thomas's leg. Darts of pain shot up his thigh, and he bit back a cry. Grimacing, he scooted away.

"Got a lesson to teach you, Tommy," Big George said. "A good, long, painful lesson."

Big George shuffled forward, his blue pajamas billowing like loose sails around his emaciated frame.

His leg pulsating, Thomas turned over and crawled away from his father.

Grunting, Big George slammed the cane onto his back.

Agony fanned through Thomas's body. He clenched his teeth.

"Don't you ever speak to me like that again!" Big George said. "I don't care how old you are, I'm still your daddy. I brought you into this world, I can take you out."

He smashed the cane into Thomas's shoulder.

Blood flooded Thomas's mouth. He had bitten his tongue.

Panting, his pajama top sodden with sweat, Big George raised the cane.

"You gonna thank me later for beating you, Tommy. You been acting lost lately, like you forgot what I taught you. You need this whipping to clarify things for you. I'm the man, boy, and I'll always be the man. This cane upside your head is gonna knock that fact into you."

He swung the cane toward Thomas's head.

In a burst of energy, Thomas blocked the stick. He seized the end of it and snatched it out of Big George's fingers.

"Nigger!" Big George said.

Using the cane to support himself, Thomas rose.

"What you gonna do?" Big George balled his hands into fists. Spittle sprayed as he spoke. "Hit me with it if you got the guts. Hit me, goddamn it!"

"No way, Dad." Thomas dropped the cane to the floor. He kicked it under the bed.

"You pussy, you think you a man now?" Big George said, spit spraying Thomas's face. He whacked Thomas with the back of his gnarled hand.

Thomas rocked sideways, but he maintained his balance.

"Speak up, boy. You think you a man?" Big George clouted Thomas in the jaw again.

Thomas took the blow, then turned back to his father.

"Answer me, nigger! You think you a man?" Big George's hand whipped toward Thomas.

Thomas stopped it in midair.

Cursing, Big George tried to strike him with his other hand. Thomas snared that one, too.

Hands locked together, they stared at each other.

"I am a man." Thomas gazed at his father, who stood a few inches shorter than he did. "My own man."

Big George spat in his face.

"Look," Thomas said, not wiping away the spittle as it slid down his cheek. "You're seventy years old and hobbled by a stroke. I'm thirty-eight, and I can bench-press four hundred pounds. If I wanted to, I could kick your ass all over this nursing home without breaking a sweat. Before I give in to the urge to do that, you better sit down."

Thomas released Big George's hands.

His father glared at him. His thin chest heaved.

Then, scratching his bald head, he turned and shuffled to the bed. He sat on the edge of the mattress.

Standing over his conquered father, Thomas felt jubilant. He had dared to confront Big George, a man who had never backed down from anyone, and he had won. But it was not over yet. To truly break free from his father's controlling shadow, he needed to do two more things.

"Now we're going to have a talk," Thomas said. He sat in the overstuffed chair, across from Big George. "This time, you're going to listen to me. You won't interrupt me until I'm finished."

Big George said nothing. He picked lint off his pajamas.

"I know you're listening. You'll definitely hear what I'm going to say. I'm selling The House of Soul."

Big George jerked up. "No."

"Yeah, I see that got your attention," Thomas said. "I bet you don't believe me. But it's true, I've decided to sell The House of Soul. I don't need that place in my life anymore."

"You can't do it. I won't let you."

"You can't stop me. You made me the owner, remember? You can't do anything but stand aside and watch me sell it."

"Why do you want to sell it?" Big George said. "What's wrong with you? That's your business, boy. Do you know how many black men dream of having a business? Do you know how fortunate you are?"

"Maybe I am fortunate to have the restaurant. But I don't have peace of mind. I'm good at the job, but I never wanted to own a restaurant. It was your dream, not mine. You forced me to live your dream. I refuse to do it anymore."

Big George glowered at him. "You're going to live your own dream, huh?"

"That's right."

"You're going to try to be an architect, ain't you?"

"Very good, Dad. I'm surprised you remember."

"How the hell could I forget? That was all you ever talked about when you were a kid."

"I've always wanted to be an architect," Thomas said. "Remember those drawings I'd put in notebooks when I was younger? Those notebooks you'd make me throw away?"

"I remember," Big George said. "When I made you throw that shit away, I was trying to do you a favor and save you the trouble of learning the hard way that you ain't got what it takes. As I see now, I was wasting my damn time."

"I don't expect you to support my decision," Thomas said. "But I plan to attend college, get my degree, and go forward from there. It'll take a few years—and a lot of hard work—but I'm gonna do it."

"You're betraying me," Big George said, and actually managed to appear stricken. "You know that, you ungrateful bastard? After all I've done for you, you do this to me. Betrayal!"

"Let's not talk about betrayal. As far as I'm concerned, you betrayed me the day I was born."

Big George's wounded look deepened.

Thomas, on the other hand, felt as if an enormous burden had eased off him. His father's injured pose did not worry him, for it was just that: a pose. A skilled manipulator, Big George could fake any emotion he thought would help him get what he wanted. He wanted Thomas to keep the restaurant so he could continue to live his fantasy through him. If making Thomas feel guilt-ridden would help him accomplish that goal, he would put on an act worthy of an Oscar nomination.

"You might as well give up the act," Thomas said. "You won't make me feel guilty about this."

Instantly, Big George's pitiful expression changed to reflect what he really felt, which was anger. "What the hell brought all of this about? Are you doing drugs? Yeah, that's it. You're messing with that crack shit, ain't you?"

"No. I've just been doing a lot of thinking the past few days. At last I know who I am, where I'm going, and what's most important to me. It took a long time, but I've finally become a real man."

Big George rolled his eyes.

"There's one last thing," Thomas said.

Big George grunted. "What?"

"For my entire life, I've hated you."

"I know that, boy. I don't give a damn. So why are you telling me?"

"Well, I don't think I hate you anymore."

Big George chuckled. "Oh, you love me? Is that part of your new life, too? Get a new job, then start putting on a bullshit love act for your old man?"

"No, that's not it. I don't hate you anymore because I've released the hate, let it go. It was hurting me more than it was you—controlling my life."

Big George nodded listlessly.

"Although I don't hate you," Thomas said, "I don't love you, either. I don't like saying that, but I'm being honest. You never did anything to deserve my love, Dad, even though I tried everything to get love from you. So for the rest of our relationship, I'm just going to be *tolerating* you."

Big George had closed his eyes.

"I know you're listening," Thomas said. "I know you really don't give a damn about how I feel. But I had to tell you. If by some miracle you develop into a normal human being with normal feelings, you'll know what you have to overcome to win me over."

Big George yawned.

Thomas stifled the urge to laugh at his father's childish antics. Jesus, this man was pathetic. How had he lived in fear of this poor excuse for a man?

The weight that his dad had burdened him with for all of those years had departed. For the first time ever, he felt free. When he stood, he had to check the sudden desire to leap into the air and click his heels together like a happy cartoon character.

"By the way, remember I told you that Linda said she's divorcing me?"

His eyes opened. "Yeah. I hope she goes through with it."

"Anyway, I'm going to try to convince her to give me another chance."

"Gonna feed her some good lies, like I would do?"

"No, I'm going to admit that I made a big mistake,"

Thomas said. "I'm going to apologize. I'm going to beg her to forgive me. I'm going to promise that I'll never do it again. I watched you do that routine with Mama whenever you made a mistake. I remember all the steps."

"Like father, like son," Big George said.

"Not anymore, Dad. Because unlike you, when I talk to my wife, I'm going to be *sincere,*" he said, and turned away from his father and walked out.

CHAPTER FIFTEEN

At Brains's house, in the den, Jason recounted the carnival incident for Brains and Shorty.

"That's amazing," Brains said. Sitting on the recliner, he regarded Jason with awe. "Falling off that Ferris wheel without a single bruise to show for it. Incredible. Only because you *imagined* yourself falling safely."

"Yeah, that's how it seemed to work," Jason said from his place on the couch. "But I didn't get a chance to see if I could do other stuff there, just by using my imagination. The next time any of us are in Thunderland, we'll have to try it. I mean, if it really works, it could help us. It's power."

Perched on the arm of the sofa, Shorty said, "Yeah, maybe so, but it ain't shit compared to the Stranger's power. Man, he comes out of a Ouija board and raises hell, he goes around invisible leaving gifts for you, he calls you on the phone from who knows where, he pulls us into some dream world where he runs the show, and *now* he's turned into your girl-friend. Shit, that's power, man. How the hell can we beat that?"

"We can do two things," Brains said. He pushed up his

glasses on his nose. "The Stranger's said that he wants to fulfill Jason's secret wishes, and he's done two things for Jason so far. My guess is that he'll try to give Jason a third wish, too. The Stranger seems to consider himself a genie or something like that, and you know that genies always grant three wishes."

"I wish this guy *was* a genie, man," Shorty said. "I'd rub the magic lamp and put his ass back in there."

Brains chuckled. "Anyway, assuming that Jason has another wish to be granted, if we can predict Jason's next wish, maybe we can set a trap for the Stranger." He looked at Jason. "Get it?"

"I get it," Jason said. "But I have no idea what my next wish is. The only thing I'd really thought about was getting that bike. Sure, I fantasized about doing it with Michelle, but I wasn't dreaming about it all the time or anything. I don't really know what he's going to do next."

"Don't you wish for a million bucks?" Shorty said. "Or to take a trip to the moon, something like that?"

Jason shook his head. "Sorry. No."

Shorty shrugged and looked at Brains. "Forget that, then. Okay, Brains, you said we could do two things. What's the other one?"

"You'll say it's crazy," Brains said.

"It can't be any crazier than everything else we've been through," Jason said. "Go ahead and tell us."

"Okay. You should fall out of a tree again, Jason."

Shock propelled Jason off the couch. "What?"

Brains spoke calmly. "When you fell out of the tree in March, you went into a coma that erased your memory of the Stranger. Basically, falling out of the tree somehow knocked the Stranger *out* of your conscious mind. If you fall again, maybe you'll knock the Stranger back *into* your conscious thoughts. You'll reverse the memory block by reliving the accident. Understand?"

"No, I don't understand at all." Jason returned to the sofa. "That's the nuttiest thing I've ever heard, Brains. You want me to go into another coma?"

Brains shrugged. "You might not go into a coma this time."

"Right, I might go into a casket," Jason said. "No, I'm not doing it. What do you think, Shorty?"

"You want me to be honest?" Shorty said.

"Yeah."

"You should do it," Shorty said.

"Are you serious?" He stared at Shorty, then at Brains. They appeared sane and reasonable. Why, then, were they suggesting that he take such a foolish risk?

"Want to know why?" Shorty said. His voice hardened. "Because the Stranger's a mean motherfucker, that's why. Remember how he tore up Brains's room when you guys used the Ouija? Remember how he scared the mess out of me and Brains when you were hypnotized? Remember how he's been playing with us, teasing us, since all of this shit started? I know, he acts like he's this great old buddy of yours, granting you these wishes and all of that shit—but he's got a mean streak, man. He's cold-blooded as hell, and he's going to really start showing it soon. I can feel it. You should take that fall before he hurts someone."

Jason sat in silence, soaking up Shorty's words.

Brains and Shorty watched him, equally silent.

"All right, I guess I see what you mean," Jason said. "I'm worried that the Stranger might hurt someone, too. But what if I jump out of a tree, hit my head, black out, wake up, and still don't remember anything about him? Or what if I knock my head hard and black out—and go into a coma and never wake up again? I'm not sure I can take the risk."

"It has to be your decision," Brains said. "We can't make it for you."

"Think about it, man," Shorty said. "You don't have to decide this minute."

"No, I need to make a choice," Jason said. "If the Stranger keeps busy like he has been, I might not have time to think about this later. I'll choose now."

He slipped his hand into the front pocket of his jeans. He withdrew a quarter. He held the shiny coin in the air.

"What's that for?" Brains said.

"The way I see it, there's a fifty-fifty chance that doing the fall will get rid of my memory block. So, there should be a fifty-fifty chance that I'll agree to do it. The best way to split the odds equally is to flip a coin. That's what I'm going to do." He stood.

Shorty and Brains rose. They gathered around him.

Holding the quarter in his hand, Jason said, "Heads, I fall. Tails, I don't."

"Man, I hope you know what you're doing," Shorty said.

Jason flipped the coin in the air, caught it in one hand as it dropped, and slapped it onto the back of his other hand.

Slowly he took away the hand that covered the quarter. *Heads.*

"Look, girl, I'm telling you," Alice said on the telephone to Linda, "you need to cool off before you dash off to a lawyer and start divorce proceedings. Don't be rash. Give yourself time to chill."

"Chill?" Linda said. She held the handset to her ear, pacing the kitchen. "How can I chill when all I can think about how is many nights Thomas spent with that whore? When I wonder about what diseases he caught from her and passed on to me?"

"Girl, you need to think about whether you really want to go through with this divorce thing," Alice said. "Yes, Thomas made a big mistake, and you're hurt and mad as hell. But before you do anything, you need to sit down and talk to him. Give him a chance to explain his side. He said he left that woman."

"He's lying," Linda said. "Don't you see? All he ever does is lie to me."

"I know what happened," Alice said. "I bet he dropped that woman and she got pissed, so she figured she'd get revenge by wrecking your marriage. She probably filmed that tape months ago, and was waiting for a chance to send it to you. You're reacting exactly the way she wants you to, girl."

Linda stopped pacing and leaned against the counter. "I don't care about what she's thinking. I'm only concerned about Thomas. Why did he lie to me? That's all I want to know. Why didn't he tell me the truth?"

"Would you have wanted to hear the truth, Lin?"

"Hell, yeah."

"Please. Now you're the one guilty of lying."

"Well, maybe I am." Linda shrugged. "I'm just . . . I don't know how I feel. I'm mad, hurt, and still crazy about Thomas all at once. He's been so sweet lately, everything's been so perfect." She ran her fingers through her hair and sighed. "Why did this have to happen?"

"I can't tell you," Alice said. "All I can tell you is this: give yourself time to cool off, then sit down and talk to Thomas. Don't run off and do something you'll regret later."

"I'm sick of thinking about this, Alice. Right now I feel like having a drink. If you'll excuse me, I'm going to hang up now and pour some Jack's."

"Don't overdo it," Alice said. "And if you have a drink or two, keep your ass out of your car. It would break my heart if I read about you in tomorrow's paper."

"I'm not going anywhere."

"Good. I love you, Lin."

"Love you, too, Alice. As usual, thanks for being my shoulder to cry on. Good-bye."

Linda hung up. Lord, she craved a drink, thirsted for the tranquility that only getting drunk could bring. She had promised Jason that she would never drink again, but this was a unique situation. It was okay this time. She would only do it once.

Yeah, right. That's what everyone says when they start drinking again. Who do you think you're fooling?

She blocked out those disturbing thoughts. On the dinette table, she placed a bottle of Jack Daniel's, a bottle of Sprite, and a large pitcher filled with ice cubes. She mixed the liquor and soda in the container, going heavy on the whiskey. She poured the concoction into a tall glass.

As she was taking her first smooth sip, Thomas entered the kitchen through the connecting door to the garage.

"Linda, what are you doing?" He came to the table, frowning.

"What the hell does it look like I'm doing?"

"Planning to drink. Too much. Way too much."

"Congratulations, you smart asshole. Want a cookie?"

She gulped her drink in an exaggerated manner, tipping the glass high, slurping, and then belching. Watching her silently, Thomas didn't appear half as astounded as she expected him to be. Well, he could kiss her ass. Whether he was there or not, she was going to get wasted.

He pulled out a chair and sat. "I didn't come here to argue. I came here to apologize."

"Oh, really? I thought you came to fuck me and record it on video, so you could play it back tonight for your girl-friend."

He cringed. "I told you, I broke up with her."

"You've told me a lot of shit that wasn't true."

"You're right, I have. I'm not denying it. I've been a lying, manipulating bastard, and I don't blame you for doubting me. But it's different now. *I'm* different now."

"That's what they all say." She reached for her glass. When she grasped it, his big hand closed over hers.

"Please, listen to me," he said. "Stop drinking and listen to me."

"I told you not to ever touch me."

"Linda, come on—"

"Get your hand off mine."

He sighed. He withdrew his hand.

She took another pull of her drink.

"Drinking won't solve anything," he said. "Our problems won't just go away."

"No, but I wish you would."

"I'm not leaving, Linda. We've been married too long for us not to work this out."

"I don't want to work it out. All I want is a divorce."

"You don't mean that. You want us to stay together every bit as much as I do."

"I get it. You're a mind reader now. You've gone from being a complete dog to a sorry-assed mind reader in one day."

"I know you're hurt, sweetheart," he said. "After what I've done, you have every right to feel hurt. But all I ask is that you meet me halfway. I can't do it by myself."

Why did he have to sound so damned reasonable? So willing to compromise and sacrifice? Why wasn't he like this before? It pissed her off that he had to be backed into a corner like this before he woke up.

"No," she said. "It's too late for that. You had your chance, and you blew it."

"Meet me halfway," he said again. "We've been through a lot together, baby. We can grow past this."

His level-headedness annoyed her. He was too smooth, too practiced. He didn't really understand what he had done to her, to them. He didn't understand the depth of her wounds.

"No," she said. She stood, picked up her glass and the pitcher.

He rose. "Where are you going?"

"To get drunk. In peace." She walked down the hallway, went inside her office, shut the door, and locked it.

He knocked.

"Open the door, honey. Please."

She sat at her desk, in front of the computer.

He rapped again.

"Please, Linda. Let me in."

She gazed at the blank computer screen, arms crossed over her chest.

"I'll do anything to convince you that I deserve another chance," he said. "Anything to convince you that I'm sorry, that I really love you, and that I plan to show you that I do, every day."

"Go away, Thomas. Pack your bags and leave."

"What if I sing for you, like I used to? There's not much else I can do from behind this door."

"Don't waste your breath."

But he began to sing anyway, and more surprising than his impromptu performance was that he sang her favorite song, which she thought he had forgotten: "If Only for One Night," by Luther Vandross. Thomas had a good voice, too: deep, rich, and steady. She had forgotten how good his voice was.

He finished the tune. "Do you want me to do another? Or are you going to let me in so we can talk this out?"

Lips pressed together, she stared at her liquor. Alice's advice rang in her mind. *Give him a chance to explain his side. . . . Sit down and talk to Thomas. . . . Don't run off and do something you'll regret later.*

She inhaled a deep breath. She was trembling. Hot tears streamed down her cheeks.

"Please, Linda. I'm begging. Please let me talk to you."

She wiped her eyes, sniffled. Finally, she got up and unlocked the door.

The elm in Brains's backyard appeared to stand about forty feet tall. Lush green leaves, filigreed with deep-orange evening sunshine, flourished in abundance. Scores of sturdy limbs and branches jutted from the ancient-looking trunk, which provided a large array of handholds, stumps, and crevices. Several leafy boughs hung above the ground, most of them well within Jason's reach.

"I can't believe I'm going to do this." Jason gazed at the elm. "Falling out of a tree on purpose. Have I gone crazy?"

Standing beside him, Brains said, "Do you want to change your mind, Jason? If we brainstorm for a little while, maybe we can think of another plan."

"But your idea of how doing this might work makes sense, Brains. A warped kind of sense. Anyway, I flipped the coin, and it was heads, so I have to do it."

"All right," Brains said. "It's your move."

"How high you gonna climb?" Shorty said.

"About twenty feet," Jason said. "That's around the height I fell from the first time. I want to copy the first fall as much as I can."

"Twenty damn feet." Shorty shook his head. "Shit, I wish I hadn't backed you up on this, Brains. I should have kept my big mouth shut."

"I didn't hear you give us any brilliant ideas," Brains said.

"Yeah, well, your idea ain't brilliant, it's stupid," Shorty said. "You're gonna get Jason paralyzed or something."

Anger flaring in his eyes, Brains went to grab Shorty. Jason stepped between them.

"Knock it off, fellas. Sure, Brains thought of this, but *I* decided to do it. Both of you need to step back and let me climb this tree in peace."

Grudgingly Brains and Shorty retreated to the patio. They watched him, Shorty shifting from foot to foot, Brains clutching his cell phone, likely ready to call an ambulance the instant Jason hit the ground.

Jason walked under one of the drooping boughs, jumped, and snared the branch in both hands. He pulled himself up and onto the tree. Already he was about six feet above the earth. He would not need to climb much higher.

His legs straddling the branch, he scooted toward the wide trunk. Once there, he rose into a standing position. With one hand wrapped around a branch above him, the other gripping a limb beside him, and both feet planted on stumps protruding from the trunk, he climbed the elm as though it were a ladder. Rough bark scraped against his hands. Wind-whipped leaves blew into his face. Ants scrambled onto his body, and two squirrels high above ceased their scampering and regarded him curiously. Grunting, sweating, and panting, Jason blocked out all distractions and concentrated on climbing, pleased to discover that he still had the tree-scaling skills he had developed years ago.

Finally, when he sensed that he had ascended high enough, he stopped. He looked down.

He was about twenty feet in the air, give or take a foot or two. The height from which he needed to fall.

Thomas walked inside. He looked around the room appreciatively. "I'm going to set up my own office like yours. The moment I stepped in, I felt like whipping out a pencil and working on some designs."

Linda returned to her seat. "Working on some designs?"

He sat across from her on the small sofa. He nodded. "That's right. That's what architects do: design buildings."

"For your information, you're not an architect."

"As of today, I am. Planning to be one, anyway."

She gaped at him.

He looked back at her, lips curved into a subtle smile. "You're not," she said.

"Yes, I am."

"You can't."

"Yes, I can."

"What about the restaurant?"

"I'm selling the restaurant."

"I don't believe you. What about Big George?"

"I've already talked to him. He doesn't want me to do it, of course. He thinks I'll only make a fool out of myself, but I don't care what he thinks. This is my life. Not his."

Linda had never heard him talk like that before, but for years she had dreamed of hearing him speak such bold, confident words. She couldn't believe it. Was he planting another lie? Was this his roundabout way of slithering back into her heart?

"What about us?" she said.

"The capital gain we'll get from selling The House of Soul will support us comfortably for years while I go to college and get my new career started. Plus, there's your writing income. Unless I become the most unsuccessful architect on earth, and unless you never sell another book, I don't see us having any money problems whatsoever."

"I wasn't talking about money, Thomas."

"I know," he said. "But before I answer your question, I'd like for you to come sit next to me."

She searched his eyes.

He withstood her scrutiny without a trace of unease.

She moved onto the couch, beside him.

"Now, what about us?" he said. "Well, we could have dinner together each night, for starters. Me, you, and Jason, of course— he's an important part of this. We could always make time for one another—sometimes just to talk, sometimes just to sit quietly together, sometimes just to gripe about whatever's bugging us. We could go on picnics. That's one thing I wish I could've done with my own family when I was a kid, 'cause they seem like so much fun. We could go fishing. I've always wanted to take a fishing trip, and I want to teach Jason how to fish, too. We could go to museums, ball games, art galleries, restaurants, fairs . . . damn, Linda, there're hundreds of places we could go, thousands of things we could do together. But the very best thing we could do can be done anywhere: we could love one another and show it, without shame or fear or hesitation, because loving is what being a family is all about. Even if I fail in my goal to become an architect, if I have you and Jason by my side, I'll be a success in the one career that matters more than all the others combined."

Almost out of breath, he stopped talking.

She regarded him quietly.

"Will you stay with me?" he said.

"It's not that easy, Thomas. I can't get over something like this so quickly."

"I understand," he said. "You have scars that might take months—maybe years—to heal. I violated the most basic foundation of our marriage. Trust."

She only looked at him.

He held her gaze. He touched her cheek tenderly.

This time, she did not resist his touch.

"But I love you," he said. "I don't want to sound melodramatic, but baby, I love you so much I literally can't go on without you. Nothing I achieve would matter if you weren't there to share it with me. Without you, life just wouldn't be worth as much any damn more. I'll ask you again: will you stay with me?"

She touched his hand, which still rested on her cheek.

Could she trust him? Could she put her heart on the line again for this man whom, in spite of the pain he had caused her, she loved as much as life itself? Would the inevitable struggle to rebuild their marriage be worth it?

She took his hand away from her face.

"I need some time, Thomas. This is . . . a lot for me to handle. You have to understand. Please don't pressure me."

"I'll give you time, space. Anything you need. I only want to be with you."

Tears tugged at her eyes. She loved this man so much, and her love for him made the pain that much sharper, like a razor twisting in her gut.

"Leave me alone," she said. The tears had begun to flow. "Please. Leave."

The guilt in his eyes seemed to match her anguish. Seeing his guilt did not give her any pleasure. His pain was her pain, too.

He gently took her hand, kissed it. "I love you."

Her eyes blurry with tears, she watched him walk out of the room. Part of her wanted him to leave the house for a few days, and perhaps permanently; another part of her longed for him to stay at her side forever.

She took her drink off the desk and returned to the sofa. She stretched her legs across the cushions. She began to raise the drink to her lips. . . . Then, she stopped and stared into the glass.

The liquor glimmered, dark and pungent. Like a magic potion. Or a poison.

She flung the glass across the room.

It struck the wall and shattered upon impact, a dozen shards clattering to the floor . . . liquor streaming like rivulets of tears down the wallpaper.

Twenty feet in the air. Time to fall.

But as Jason gazed down there—the ground looked *so* far away—something in him shrank. Could he go through with this? Did he have the courage?

What would Shorty and Brains think of him if he chickened out? What would he think of himself? Would the Stranger later do something terrible that would make him regret giving up?

He told himself to stop thinking so damn much. He did not need to debate. He needed to act.

Grasping branches in both hands to support himself, he stepped toward the tip of the limb on which he stood. He intended to walk to the end, shut his eyes, and let himself drop. As he moved closer to the tip, the limb dipped a few inches under his weight, swayed left and right, but it did not snap.

He almost wished it would snap beneath him. At least that would be a real accident, more in spirit with the concept of reliving an unintentional fall. What he was attempting now felt too planned, almost like a parody of the true incident. But he could not turn back.

He reached the edge of the limb.

Below him, the hard ground seemed much more than twenty feet away. It seemed to be *two hundred* feet away.

It's only my imagination. It isn't that far. I'll survive. I lived through it once; I'll make it again.

Across the yard, on the patio, Brains and Shorty watched.

I can't chicken out. They're depending on me.

His heart trip-hammered. Sweat had glued his shirt to his torso.

He looked at the ground.

God, this is so crazy. But I have to do it.

He shut his eyes.

All right, now let go. Let go of the branches and fall.

He loosened his grip.

He felt himself slipping forward . . . forward . . . forward . . .

But at the last instant, he seized the branches with such haste that his knuckles popped.

He exhaled. He opened his eyes.

He could not do it. A leap of faith like this was beyond him.

He pulled himself backward, away from the brink. He descended the tree.

Shorty and Brains met him at the bottom. Both of them wore puzzled expressions.

"What's up, man?" Shorty said. "You were on the edge, ready to go for it. What went wrong?"

"I went wrong," Jason said. He was unable to meet their eyes. "I don't have the guts, fellas. Sorry."

He was afraid that they would rebuke him and criticize his cowardice, but they did not. They put their arms around his shoulders. They walked him back inside the house, neither Brains nor Shorty speaking, somehow understanding that no words could have alleviated Jason's guilt. Or could have freed him of his fear that, because of his own weakness, something terrible was going to happen.

CHAPTER SIXTEEN

Saturday, the Fourth of July, began with postcard-perfect weather. The sun shone warm and bright, and the cloudless sky was a lustrous blue, as if it had been polished the night before in preparation for the holiday. Cool breezes rolled off Lake Michigan, the wind scented by the aroma of barbecue simmering on hundreds of grills throughout the city.

As he had done on every Fourth of July morning in memory, Jason ate breakfast at his grandfather's house. It was just the two of them, but he did not want to be there. Although he loved Granddad's company, he felt as though he lived two lives. One life revolved around his attempts to demystify the Stranger; the other life consisted of maintaining relationships with people who knew nothing of his struggles. Separately, each life brought unique burdens. In tandem, they were almost unbearable. At every moment of the day, he felt himself being pulled in several directions. He would not be able to tolerate the strain much longer without snapping.

He picked over his food. He had no appetite and no willingness to fake one. He watched Granddad eat and tried to sustain his end of the conversation.

Although he believed Granddad was curious about what he had been doing the past several days, Granddad neither questioned him nor mentioned their last discussion, during which they had talked about hypnosis. His chatter was ordinary, touching on topics such as what they might eat at the cookout, which relatives and friends they might see, and what activities they might occupy themselves with after the feast was over.

Maybe he had accepted Jason's desire to keep his troubles secret. Or maybe he sensed that Jason's affairs might be too disturbing to know. Whatever the reason, Jason was glad that he did not bring up the subject.

After breakfast, as they took the dishes to the kitchen, Granddad put his hand on Jason's shoulder. He smiled—an embarrassed smile that Jason had seen before. Before Granddad had spoken a word, Jason predicted what he would say.

"Guess what I have for you," Granddad said.

"Let me think." Jason set his plate on the counter. "An errand."

"You must be telepathic, son," Granddad said. "I know I do this to you every year, but I always seem to forget something."

"What do you need?" Jason said.

"Lighter fluid for the charcoal. I thought I had bought some, but I must have forgotten." He fished a crisp ten-dollar bill out of his wallet and handed the money to Jason. "Keep the change. With what you'll get back, you should be able to buy yourself a couple of books, maybe some ice cream."

"Come on, Granddad. Ten bucks doesn't go *that* far anymore."

"Are you implying that I'm out of touch?" Granddad looked at him sternly. "That I'm some feeble-minded relic of a man?"

"That's exactly what I'm implying, sir."

"Ah, get out of here, man!" Smiling, he handed Jason another ten-dollar bill and shooed him away. "Don't come back here until you know how to speak to your elders with respect."

Jason went outside and mounted his bike. He had accepted that for most of that day he would have to behave as though he were a normal kid enjoying the Fourth of July. In his family, missing the big Fourth cookout was akin to a Catholic priest missing Sunday Mass. No one ever skipped it. He didn't consider blowing it off.

Besides, what would he do if he skipped the picnic? Stay home and leap out of the tree? He had proved yesterday that he lacked the guts. A loser like him deserved to suffer by sitting all day at the family barbecue.

The grocery store was packed. Herds of customers milled through the aisles, their shopping carts groaning under the weight of last-minute holiday purchases. He picked up a container of lighter fluid and then stopped at the magazine and book area.

He smiled ruefully as he surveyed the paperback thrillers. While many of them seemed fascinating, he doubted they could match the story of his life. Real life had become ten times stranger than fiction.

Although he did not have the peace of mind to read, he bought a mystery novel. The idea that he would eventually have the opportunity to enjoy it encouraged him and fueled the optimistic notion that he would get through all of this alive.

When he stepped outside the supermarket, the grocery bag in one hand and a can of Pepsi in the other, his optimism diminished.

Before entering the store, he had parked his bike in the bicycle stall at the corner of the building. Now the stall was empty. Someone had stolen his bike!

Brandon Massey

He could not believe it. He turned around, thinking he must have actually entered the building from the opposite direction. What he saw when he swung around made him drop the Pepsi.

Blake Grant. The bully.

Blake sat on Jason's bicycle, less than ten feet away, blocking Jason's path to the supermarket entrance. He rolled back and forth, back and forth, only a few inches each time, like an angry bull gathering strength for a mad charge. Except for one new feature, he looked exactly as he had when Jason had eluded him in the forest earlier that week. Sleeveless black T-shirt, faded jeans, scuffed combat boots. Tanned, bulging muscles. Hawkish face. The tightly wound ponytail. And the black eye patch.

"You thought I forgot about you?" Blake said. He motioned to his new feature, a splint on his nose that he must have got as a result of the kick Jason had delivered while on his way over the car lot fence. "Do you think I could forget after this?"

Jason opened his mouth to say something and discovered he could not speak. Something cold and wet soaked his feet. He looked down and saw the cola he had dropped. Its foaming contents oozed into his shoes.

He looked up. Blake had edged forward a few more feet. His single eye blazed like a hot sapphire.

"I've been looking for your ass all week, and I've finally found you. You're not getting away, dude. Don't try to run."

Someone clutched Jason's shoulder from behind. Startled, Jason dropped the grocery bag.

"Keep your mouth shut," a voice said, close to his ear. It sounded like Bryan Green, Blake's pal. "You're gonna come with us, got it?"

"Yeah," Jason said. Travis Young, the fat kid, walked up behind Blake. He grinned at Jason, but it was the mean, hard grin of someone who got off on inflicting pain—like a kid who enjoyed squashing bugs.

The three boys crowded him, sweaty, breathing hard, primed for violence. Jason didn't have space to run or even to swing a fist.

"We're gonna take a trip to the woods behind the store," Blake said. A switchblade appeared in his hand as if by magic. "If you give me any shit, Brooks, I'll skewer you like a shish kebab."

"Yeah, sure, anything you say. Just don't kill me."

Blake laughed. "Don't worry, dude, if you stay cool, I won't kill you. I'll only do what I've been wanting to do all along: kick your ass so bad that, when I'm done, you'll wish you were dead."

He poked Jason in the stomach with the knife. Jason held back a cry of pain. Travis grabbed one of his arms; Bryan grabbed the other.

"Get moving," Blake said.

As they rounded the side of the supermarket, moving out of view of the people in the parking lot, Jason heard a noise like keys jingling on a chain. The next thing he knew, Travis and Bryan wrenched his arms behind his back, and they slapped a pair of cold handcuffs onto his wrists.

Like a match enkindling tinder, the click of the engaging handcuffs ignited Jason's imagination. What were they going to do to him?

Imagining their possible schemes escalated his anxiety. His tongue felt stuck to the roof of his mouth, as if he had tried to eat a spoonful of glue. Sweat streamed down his chest and back.

He attempted to force apart his bound wrists. No good.

He still wore the .22 in the ankle holster, concealed under

his jeans. He would've used the pistol to scare the kids away if his hands weren't chained. So much for the usefulness of a gun.

About two hundred yards behind the store, thick forest thrived. The huge elms, oaks, and maples cast such deep shade that it seemed as though night had fallen underneath their leafy boughs. The area looked deserted, too.

Dark, desolate woods. Bound hands. A knife at his back. What did all of that add up to?

Maybe a beating. Or maybe murder.

The thought of murder did not seem to be a product of his overactive imagination. Sure, Blake had promised that he was only going to beat him up, but how reliable was a promise from a person like him? A kid who, from all available evidence, was as psychopathic as a convicted killer? His chances of winning the state lottery were greater than the chances of Blake's word meaning anything.

And these days, kids slaughtered one another all the time. Bullies no longer stole your lunch money and sent you home with a black eye. Instead, they stole your money, your jewelry, your designer clothing, beat you half to death with a pistol, then used that same gun to blow your brains out just for the hell of it. Blake could do anything to him. *Anything.*

His heartbeat raced.

They left the asphalt behind the supermarket and entered the forest. Dank shadows embraced them like old friends, and the humid air smelled of rotted wood and dead things. Tall weeds crunched underneath their feet, clouds of buzzing insects fleeing out of their path.

For an instant, Blake eased the blade off Jason; Jason heard him slam the bike to the ground. Then Blake was on him again, pressing the knife in his back.

"Are you getting scared?" Blake said. "Are you about to piss your pants?"

Jason did not reply. He did not want to hear the fear in his voice, afraid that hearing it would somehow intensify his terror.

Blake poked him with the blade.

"Answer me, boy. Are you scared?"

"Yeah, man, I'm scared, okay? Who wouldn't be scared?"

"Did you hear that, dudes?" Blake chuckled. "The dickhead's gonna shit his pants."

Travis and Bryan, both of them gripping Jason's arms, laughed.

"I'm gonna get you for kicking me in the nuts, asshole," Travis said. He giggled. "I'm gonna smash your balls until you puke."

Bryan tightened his hot grip on Jason's arm. "I'm gonna beat you just because I feel like it. I haven't kicked anyone's ass since . . . oh, yesterday, I guess." He laughed.

I'm dead, Jason thought. *I'll need plastic surgery after these guys finish with me . . . and if Blake goes overboard, maybe a casket.*

Deep in the forest, they reached a small clearing. The area had a look that made Jason suspect this was a hideaway for Blake and his buddies. Tamped-down grass. Obscene messages etched into the bark of surrounding trees. A mound of ashes and charred wood in the center, the ghost of a recent campfire. Cigarette butts, beer bottles, and empty potato chip bags littering the ground.

"Home at last," Blake said. Jason felt the knife leave his back, then a sharp whack against the side of his head. He cried out and stumbled forward, but the two boys did not let him go. They laughed while his head throbbed in pain.

"Goddamn," Blake said, behind Jason. "I smack him, and he whimpers like a girl. You're a pussy."

"Fuck you," Jason said.

Blake grunted. Jason heard the click of Blake sheathing his blade. Putting it away in favor of another weapon?

"Turn that asshole around, dudes," Blake said. "The fun's about to start."

Roughly they spun Jason around to face Blake. Blake slipped gleaming brass knuckles onto his fingers. Grinning, he clenched and unclenched his hand.

"We're gonna start out with some face rearrangement," Blake said. "After that, Travis'll crush your nuts; Bryan'll do whatever the hell he wants, then I'm taking another turn. We believe in everyone getting an equal opportunity to kick ass, don't we, boys?"

"Hell, yeah!" Travis and Bryan said.

I'm dead, Jason thought.

Thunder rumbled.

Jason's heart began to pound harder. He recognized the thunder. It was unmistakable.

They were in Thunderland.

The Stranger must be there, too. What was he planning to do now?

The woods, already dark, darkened as thunderclouds covered the sky.

"Shit," Bryan said, looking skyward. "Dude, it's gonna rain."

Thunder clapped, a deep-throated boom that made the trees tremble.

"I don't give a fuck about some storm," Blake said. "I'm kicking your ass, Brooks, even if the sky falls down on me."

Lightning flickered, briefly illuminating the woods.

Thunder crashed, rumbles that spread like shock waves across the ground.

Blake scowled at the stormy sky. He glared at Jason. He clenched his fist.

A strange power entered Jason's body.

*   *   *

A blast of shocking coldness struck the top of Jason's head, rushing under his scalp and streaking through his brain, leaving his nerves icy and numb. Freezing energy flowed like ice water down his face, coursing through his neck, spreading through his shoulders, shooting into his arms, hands, and fingers. Intense power flooded his chest and stomach, streaming down his thighs and calves and finally into his feet, where it hit his toes and made them feel as frigid as if they were buried in snow.

Invaded by that chilling, alien energy, Jason's body abruptly felt as though it had been given a massive dose of Novocain. He could not feel the boys holding his arms anymore, though they still held him tightly. He could not feel his feet on the ground. He could not feel anything.

He tried to turn his head. He could not.

He tried to speak. He could not open his mouth.

He was not only numb; he was unable to control his body, too.

Somehow, the Stranger must have done this to him. But how? Why?

One eye gleaming hatefully, Blake came forward, brass-knuckled fist cocked.

An invisible force drove Jason's hands apart, snapping the handcuffs in half. As if guided by puppet strings, Jason's hands whipped around in front of him, breaking the holds of both Travis and Bryan.

Bryan and Travis stood frozen, shocked expressions on their faces.

Oh, no, Jason thought. As he stared at his freed hands, he had a dreadful realization. Something so terrible, he could not bear to think about it.

Blake had halted with his fist raised. "What the hell?"

"This is what the hell," the Stranger said, using Jason's mouth, Jason's voice. As Jason watched in horror, he seized

Bryan's head with both of his own hands. He twisted savagely. The sound of cracking bones filled the air. Bryan dropped like a rag doll to the ground, his head sagging between his shoulder blades.

Gaping at Bryan's corpse, Blake backpedaled.

No, Jason thought. *No.*

"More secret wishes to fulfill," the Stranger had said. He had given Jason the bike of his dreams and a fantastic sexual experience with a replica of his girlfriend. Now it was time to grant him another wish: getting rid of the bullies who had terrorized him.

Jason had wanted to be rid of Blake and the others, but never in his darkest dreams had he wanted it to happen like this.

A fierce thunderclap resounded; then rain began to fall. The downpour snapped against the trees and glittered like silver chains in the flickers of lightning.

Travis turned to run. In one quick motion, the Stranger made Jason stoop, grab a beer bottle, and bring the bottle down on Travis's head. The bottle shattered against his skull, and Travis shrieked and fell to the earth. He lay there, groaning.

Jason stepped forward. With incredible force, he stamped his foot onto the kid's back. The boy's spinal cord popped like a rubber band, and his moans immediately ceased. *Dead.*

Jason wanted to vomit but could not. He could not control his own stomach.

Blood spattered his hands. Blood he had spilled with his own hands. *Oh, God.*

He caught movement in the corner of his eye. Involuntarily, his head swiveled.

Blake was taking off.

The boy ran fast but sloppily. He bumped into trees and bushes, blinded by the rain and his own terror. Even a seemingly fearless bully like Blake sensed when something supernatural was happening, and he had the good sense to flee.

For once, Jason felt pity for him. In spite of his unwillingness to continue this slaughter, Jason's body began to pursue Blake.

He ran with inhuman speed and agility, taking impossibly long and powerful strides, effortlessly dodging trees and shrubbery, not hampered at all by the pounding rain. In seconds, he was on Blake's heels.

"You can't get away," the Stranger said through Jason. "The more you run, the more pain I will give you when I murder you."

"All right, you motherfucker!" Blake stopped running and whirled around. "You want a fight? I'll give you one!"

Blake flicked out the switchblade. He lowered himself into a fighting stance.

"Come on, you crazy fucker," Blake said. He lunged at Jason.

As easily as if Blake had moved in slow motion, Jason caught the hand that gripped the knife. He squeezed. Bones popped. Blake yelped, the knife dropping from his broken fingers. Still clutching Blake's ruined hand, Jason drew back his fist and hammered it into Blake's nose.

Blake howled.

Jason wanted to cry, too, at that act of cruelty, but he was not in control; he was only an observer in his own body. He released Blake's hand.

Blake put both hands to his smashed nose. He stumbled backward, shrieking in agony.

The Stranger made Jason bend down and retrieve the switchblade. Raindrops glimmered on the sharp, deadly knife.

Please, God, don't let the Stranger force me to do this, Jason pleaded. *Give me the power to stop this.*

Blake had backed into a tree. He covered his nose, weeping. Blood drenched his hands.

Jason stalked toward him. He grabbed the boy's wet hair and raised his head, making him look at him.

"Are you scared?" the Stranger said through Jason. "Are you gonna piss your pants?"

Face smeared with blood, Blake stared at him, terrified.

Jason raised the switchblade to Blake's face. Blake's eye widened.

"Were you actually going to use this on me?" the Stranger said.

"No, dude, no," Blake said. He spat blood. "I only wanted to make you listen, you know . . . throw a scare into you. I've never stabbed anyone. Honest, dude."

"Neither have I," the Stranger said. "Honest, dude. But I've always wanted to."

He rammed the knife into Blake's chest.

Blake gasped, spluttered, wheezed. Blood seeped from his lips. He fell forward against Jason.

The Stranger made Jason twist the blade around in Blake's chest, then yank it out. He shoved Blake away. The kid's corpse fell lifelessly to the ground.

Jason regarded his bloody hands. The Stranger, who claimed to be his friend, had made him into a killer. He would never be able to escape the guilt. This would haunt him forever.

Thunder crashed across the sky. Rain plopped onto Blake's corpse.

Still controlled by the Stranger, Jason turned away from Blake's body. He dropped the blood-stained knife . . .

And he was standing in the small clearing. The open handcuffs lay at his feet. His hands were clean, dry.

Shafts of sunlight pierced the forest canopy, bits of blue sky visible through the leaves. A flock of large, curious black crows perched on the tree branches.

Blake, Travis, and Bryan lay on the ground, scattered around him like forgotten, broken toys. None of them moved. Their eyes gazed sightlessly at the sky.

"Oh, God," Jason said. Hesitant, he stepped forward, in full control of his movements once more. He bent beside Blake. He noted that Blake's body did not have any of the wounds he'd suffered in Thunderland. There was no blood anywhere, no knife tear in his shirt. Was he still alive, in a comatose state?

Jason placed his fingers against Blake's pale neck, seeking a pulse.

Nothing. The boy's flesh was cool.

Jason snatched away his hand. Turning, he saw the other two kids sprawled on the ground, their faces languid, eyes as glassy as marbles.

They were gone. All three of them.

He crawled away and vomited explosively.

Blake and his friends are dead, and I killed them.

Tears spilled out of him. Although he hadn't liked Blake or his buddies, they hadn't deserved to die. And the fact that the Stranger had forced his body into committing the vile act sickened him to the core. He wanted to run—run far away and as fast as he could, escaping the Stranger and what the Stranger had forced him to become: a killer.

Using a tree to support himself, he got to his feet.

In the branches above, crows squawked. Jason looked up. He saw dozens of crows, big ones almost the size of falcons, lined up like soldiers. Each of them seemed to be looking down at him, their sharp black eyes condemning him.

But they were only birds. They couldn't be accusing him. Still, he started thinking: what would happen to the bodies of Blake and his friends?

He didn't want to ponder the question, but he couldn't avoid it. He couldn't bury them himself, which meant someone would eventually find their bodies. The discovery would be a major story in a small, sleepy town like Spring Harbor. There would be an investigation. People would be questioned. Witnesses might come forward.

He might be convicted as a murderer.

There was no way out of it. This was no longer a game or a puzzle. This was murder, and he was going to be held responsible.

Run.

The whispered command came to him so softly that he questioned whether it was an actual voice or a thought in his own mind.

Above, the crows jittered and squawked excitedly. The tree boughs were heavy with them; there were so many of them now that their bodies blocked out the sunlight.

Run, Jason. Now.

He heard the voice clearly. It wasn't his imagination. The voice was familiar: it was the Stranger. Although Jason's watch did not stop and he did not hear thunder rumble, the Stranger's presence permeated the air; a numbing coldness enveloped him as if the door to an immense freezer had been opened. Jason shivered, goosebumps breaking out on his skin.

A crow swooped out of the trees and landed on Blake. Wings fluttering, the crow jabbed its beak into Blake's eye.

Jason's stomach roiled. Dread weighed down his limbs like sand.

Crows fed on dead things, but how had such an enormous flock of them arrived so quickly? The instant he had snapped out of Thunderland, he'd noticed the birds aligned in the tree boughs, as though they had foreknowledge of the massacre. Crows did not behave like that—unless they were somehow being controlled.

The idea of someone like the Stranger being capable of manipulating an army of crows did not seem far-fetched at all.

Another bird slashed through the air and attached itself to Bryan's neck. It greedily attacked the throat.

Last warning, Jason . . . The Stranger's voice was as clear as if he'd been standing beside him.

Jason looked up . . . and saw the platoon of crows dive off the branches and funnel to the earth in a dark, roaring wave, driven by a single mind, a sick hunger. He covered his head with his arms and raced out of the clearing, directly through the teeming mass of birds. Wings flapped against his face, and beaks grazed across his skin, but the crows did not attack him. Inexplicably manipulated by the Stranger, the carrion eaters cared only about the three corpses; they swarmed across the bodies, feeding, and would do so perhaps until little trace of the corpses remained.

Jason ran with a scream trapped in his throat and did not stop running until he reached the edge of the forest.

He found his bike at the rim of the woods. He pushed it out of the forest, hopped on it, and returned to the supermarket.

The grocery bag that he had dropped lay on the pavement where he had left it. He tucked it under his arm.

He couldn't go back to Granddad's house yet, not after something like this. He rode directly to Brains's place.

"We've got to call a meeting," Jason said to Brains the moment he answered the front door. "Where's Shorty?"

"He's at home," Brains said. He stepped onto the porch. "What's going on? Why do we need to have a meeting?"

"Before I tell you why, you better sit down," Jason said, sitting on the porch swing. Looking puzzled, Brains sat beside him.

Jason told him what the Stranger had done to Blake and the other boys.

"Oh, my God," Brains said, his eyes huge behind his

glasses. "This guy is . . . crazy. I can't believe he killed those kids."

"It's my fault," Jason said. "If I'd jumped out of that tree yesterday, maybe—"

Brains grabbed Jason by the arm. He shook him hard. "That's bullshit, Jason. Do you hear me? So what if you didn't take the fall out of that tree? *You* didn't wish anyone dead, and you didn't kill anyone. The *Stranger* used you to murder those guys, and he'll have to answer for it. You won't. Do you hear me?"

"I hear you," Jason said. "But I feel sick. God, why did he have to kill them? I only wanted them to leave me alone. I didn't want them dead!"

Brains released Jason's arm. "I know you didn't. It's the Stranger's fault—he uses some kind of warped logic that I'll never understand. You just stay tough, Jason. You've shown a lot more courage than most people would have. I respect you more now than I ever have before, and you were already high on my list of respectable people."

Jason smiled halfheartedly. "Thanks."

They sat in silence.

Around them, the neighborhood geared up to celebrate the Fourth: barbecuing, cutting grass, blasting party music. People happily ignorant of the terror roaming within the town.

Finally, Jason rose. "Come on, let's call Shorty. I don't know what we're going to do next, but we'd better think of something. Soon."

CHAPTER SEVENTEEN

Shorty's mind was whirling when he finished talking to Jason on the telephone. The Stranger had killed Blake and his buddies. Man, that was sad. As he feared, the Stranger was starting to show them what he was really about. He was an evil, insane . . . damn, Shorty didn't know what to call him. He was just a *thing* that should not have been allowed into the world.

Before Shorty had answered the phone in his bedroom, he had been munching on a barbecued rib that he'd sneaked off the backyard grill. He had been ravenous before, but now the sight of the half-stripped bone sickened him. He hadn't liked Blake or either of his boys, but they were only kids. They had not deserved to die. Thinking of them gone forever spoiled his appetite.

He slapped on his Chicago White Sox cap and went outside. Since Brains lived across town, it usually took about ten minutes to reach his house. As Shorty pedaled his bike across the city streets, he thought about his girlfriend. He wanted to see her. They had been going steady for a month, and they had kissed—really kissed—only the week before, for the first time ever. The memory of her luscious lips had stayed with him, and he yearned to drop everything, visit her, and drown himself in her kisses. He was tired of this Stranger shit.

But he had to stick with Brains and Jason. He could never desert them. They were like brothers to him.

Five minutes into his trip, as he moved to cross Northern Road, he braked to a stop.

He could not believe what he saw.

Northern Road, a four-lane thoroughfare that formed the hub of Spring Harbor's downtown, was completely deserted. No cars were parked in front of the stores; all of the restaurants, shops, and gas stations appeared to be closed; and not a single vehicle rolled along the blacktop. It resembled the business district of a modern-day ghost town.

Although he suspected what he would see, he checked his watch. He was right. The digits were frozen.

Damn.

His hands tightened around the handlebars.

He rarely had nightmares, but he had experienced several lately. The worst of them was exactly like this. Trapped in Thunderland. Isolated with the Stranger. Powerless.

Charcoal clouds swarmed in the sky and amassed into a thick, bulging mantle. Like the footsteps of an approaching giant, thunder resounded.

Was he really alone there? Or were Brains and Jason awaiting him at Brains's house, as they were in the real world?

One way to find out. Go there. Where else could he go, anyway?

Steeling himself for the journey ahead, he started riding across Northern Road.

When he neared the center of the street, explosive thunder cannonaded the clouds, and a freezing downpour gushed from the resulting breaches. The rain felt like frozen needles on his skin. He swore under his breath at the Stranger.

On the left side of the next road, the First Bank of Spring Harbor loomed, a rectangular brick building with a huge parking lot. The parking lot was empty except for a shiny black car that idled in front of the bank.

Shorty stopped, staring.

Similar to a BMW sedan yet bearing none of the markings of the famous auto, the sleek, jet-black vehicle faced the street, the urine-yellow headlamps burning holes in the sheeting rain. Tinting as dark as onyx filmed the windows, and the chrome grille gleamed. The windshield wipers swept slowly across the glass, in a hypnotic motion that beckoned him to come closer and take a look inside the car.

He shook his head as if clearing away dust.

It was obvious who sat inside the vehicle. He did not need to sneak up and peer through the window like some fool in a horror movie. Hell, if someone had offered him a million bucks to peek inside, Shorty would have told him to shove the money where the sun didn't shine. Such a powerful aura of evil surrounded the sedan that Shorty would not have been surprised to see the Devil himself sitting behind the steering wheel.

The car's engine revved. Like a panther that had awoken with a big appetite.

In what was probably a lame attempt to pacify the driver, Shorty took his feet off the pedals. He coasted slowly down the sloping road, dragging his shoes on the slick pavement, watching the car as he might watch a Doberman pinscher. When he passed through the headlight beams, he shielded his eyes, yet he felt a heat similar to that he experienced whenever he stood before a pile of burning leaves.

Out of the hot glare at last, he slammed his feet onto the pedals and raced pell-mell down the street.

The car roared and thundered after him.

* * *

Thomas had not slept at all the previous night. He'd lain on the living room sofa, feeling worse than he'd ever felt in his pathetic life. He was scared to death that he would lose Linda. He had finally taken steps to assume control of his future, but it might be too late for him to keep one of the two people in his life who mattered the most.

Linda did not speak to him during the rest of the evening, did not even look at him. The next morning, she was the same. It was as though he were invisible to her.

He was invisible to his son, too. Earlier that morning, Jason had come downstairs and left the house without glancing at Thomas or saying a word. Thomas had no idea where the boy was going.

He felt like a spirit walking among the living. The painful truth was that he deserved every bit of it. Nevertheless, he yearned to communicate with his family.

In the past, he had kept The House of Soul open for business on the Fourth of July. This year, he allowed the restaurant to stay closed for the day. His staff were appreciative. He was in no mood to work.

Late that morning, Linda was in the kitchen, preparing food for the family's holiday cookout. He wanted to talk to her. He could not stew in silence any longer.

He went to the kitchen doorway and watched her. She went about her business, fixing deviled eggs at the counter. She hummed a tune softly. She did not look at him.

"Linda," he said.

She ignored him.

"Linda, please. I need to talk to you."

"About what?" She continued to work on the eggs.

"We can't go on like this."

She said nothing. Her attention was focused on preparing food.

"Jason needs us," Thomas said. The words popped out of him, unplanned.

Abruptly Linda stopped. She appeared to be surprised. "What made you realize all of a sudden that our son needs us?" she said.

Thomas shrugged. "He seems . . . distant. He walks around the house like we're not even here. Seems to come and go as he pleases."

"There's a lot that you don't understand about Jason," she said. "I don't understand him myself half the time. He's smart and stays out of trouble, and he loves his granddad— he went to Dad's house this morning for breakfast. But after you get past the basics, he's an enigma. I still think that he's up to something with his buddies, but it's impossible to get him to share any information."

"It's my fault that he behaves like that," Thomas said. "If I'd been there for him when he was younger, like a father is supposed to, all of us would get along better."

"It's not all your fault. I share the blame, too. I neglected Jason while you were neglecting me." She looked away from him, but he caught a glimpse of shame in her eyes.

Thomas entered the kitchen and sat at the dinette table. He buried his face in his hands.

His family was a mess. He despised his father, his wife had lost faith in him, and his son ignored both of them. How had he ever let this happen? He wished he could travel into the past and correct every misguided decision of his that had led to these circumstances.

Linda came to the table. "We can't dwell on the past, Thomas. As hard as it is to overcome our mistakes, we have to let them go and think about the present."

He looked in her eyes, and he almost asked if she had forgiven him. But he kept his mouth shut. He couldn't push her. In time, she would forgive him. They had to concentrate on the member of their family with whom both of them needed to rebuild ties: Jason.

"We'll work with Jason," he said. "He needs to be our top priority."

"It won't be easy. You can't imagine how far away he is from us. Sometimes it scares me. It's like he has no use for us."

"We'll bring him around, no matter what it takes. I have to believe that, deep down, he wants to have a relationship with us. He doesn't want to be hurt anymore. We have to prove to him that we want to save our family. That's the only way he'll let us in."

"I hope you're right. I really, really do." She smiled briefly. At the sight of even a small smile from her, his heart picked up speed.

Things were going to get better. Perhaps not today, but one day.

Lightning blazed the sky, almost bright enough to blind Shorty as he furiously pumped the bike pedals.

He urged himself on: *Ride, man. Ride your ass off. Get to Brains's place, so the three of you can face the Stranger. Don't worry that Brains and Jason might not be there, because they should be; they will be; they have to be.*

As if he were a fugitive fleeing across a prison yard, the car's headlights captured him.

Shorty skidded around a corner, almost smacking into a telephone pole. He regained his balance and stole a glance behind him.

The sedan careened around the corner, tipping sideways like a car in an action movie, the two tires that remained on the pavement spinning and smoking. After the vehicle completed the turn, the airborne wheels banged back onto the street. The searing headlights found him again.

He bounded onto the sidewalk.

The pursuing car vaulted the curb and tore across the ground, dodging trees and fences as deftly as a motorcycle. The sidewalk on which they raced trembled, the vibrations rattling through the handlebars and into his hands.

Shorty cycled into a front yard, then into the backyard of the same property. The Stranger did not follow, but Shorty kept moving. He cut across several backyards, entered an alley, followed that gravel path for a few blocks, went through more backyards, crossed a street, rode across another alley, another backyard, and then stopped under a vacant carport beside a large Victorian house, which was as dark as every home he had seen there.

Heart thudding, he listened closely.

Other than the sound of rain drizzling onto the roof of the carport, he heard nothing.

Although terror coursed like kerosene through his veins, he could think clearly enough to recognize his location. He was about two blocks from Brains's. Roll onto the street ahead, turn left, pass two stop signs, go a little farther, and he would be at the door. That wasn't far, was it? He could make it. He was fast. Too fast for the Stranger.

Okay, if you're so fast, get your ass out there.

He crept down the driveway until he had a clear view of the road. He peered right, left. No sign of the Stranger.

Maybe he had lost him. Or maybe the Stranger was playing with him, letting him enjoy a fake sense of security before he stomped him. The asshole loved to play games. He was worse than a bratty kid.

But Shorty sensed that waiting for something to happen would be a bad idea, so he got moving. After checking both ways again, and again seeing no one, he shot toward Brains's.

He had Brains's house—where lights shone—in sight when he heard the Stranger's car, roaring louder than ever.

He looked behind him. The black car screeched around the corner, in the same stunt-car fashion that it had earlier.

He pumped his legs hard, splashing through cold puddles. The Stranger's hated headlamps found him. Shorty rode harder. He could not die, not here, not like this. He was too young to die; he had years and years of living left, and he had never treated anyone badly, so life could not be this cruel to him. God would have mercy on him and deliver him from this monster.

He bounced across a flooded gutter and jumped over the curb. Brains's well-lighted home stood three houses away.

The headlights intensified, burning his back. He heard the car growl hungrily. He could not look behind him. He could only ride and hope.

He rode into Brains's yard. He could feel the car at his back, the heat from its grille spewing like flames from the nostrils of a dragon. The porch beckoned, twenty feet away but seemingly much farther. He lowered his head, gritted his teeth, and forced every ounce of strength he had remaining into his throbbing legs.

When he was about ten feet away from the steps, he felt the car smash into the bike's rear tire. Thrown off balance, he flew over the handlebars, sailed through the air, and smacked onto the hard ground and rolled like a crash-test dummy across the lawn.

He blinked slowly. His body was a snarl of pain. Blood, grass, and mud obscured his vision. He wiped his eyes with one scraped, bleeding hand . . . and wished he had left the grime over his eyes.

The black sedan rumbled toward him.

He tried to scramble away but could not move. His body felt broken, useless.

He gnashed his teeth. Suddenly, he was not frightened anymore. He was pissed off at God. Why did he have to die like this?

As the car rolled over him, crushing the life out of his

body, darkness enveloped him, and his enraged question fell on the deaf ears of a great void.

Jason and Brains sat on the veranda swing, waiting for Shorty to arrive. As they waited, they did not speak much. The death of an acquaintance, whether loved or disliked, influenced you to sit still and quietly contemplate life—and how abruptly it could end. Jason had seen many mysterious happenings, but death was the greatest mystery of all, and he could not understand why God had let Blake and his friends fall into that unfathomable void.

Immersed in those thoughts, he contemplated the wooden strips of the porch floor.

Brains tapped his arm.

Jason jerked up. "What?"

"Did you hear that?" Brains said.

"Hear what?"

Closing his eyes, Brains paused, listening. He said, "A weird noise. Like a jet flying somewhere far away, but different, somehow."

Jason listened.

"I hear it," he said. "What is that?"

Brains shrugged, but his eyes remained attentive. The noise grew louder. It sounded like an approaching airplane. An unusually loud airplane.

"It's probably a military jet," Jason said. "This is the Fourth of July, Brains. You know they have air shows and stuff today. I bet that's all it is."

"Yes," Brains said. "You're probably—"

A powerful gale arose, stopping Brains in midsentence. Cold and sharp, the wind tore across the veranda, whipping the bench from side to side and rocking the hanging plants. The odd, jetlike roar doubled in volume.

Jason and Brains jumped up. Expecting the worst, Jason looked at his watch. The digits ticked steadily.

They leaped onto the sidewalk. They scanned the crystalline blue sky. No airplanes flew overhead.

"What's going on?" Brains turned in circles, gazing skyward. "What is that noise?"

A premonition grabbed Jason's stomach. "Shorty."

Before Brains could ask what he meant, the roar escalated into an eardrum-piercing scream, the gust swirled like a mad dervish around them, and then Jason heard a deafening *whoosh!*

Covering their heads, they dropped to the grass.

Less than ten feet away from the porch, a few feet above the ground, an invisible force ripped open an aperture in the air, as if the real world were merely fabric that could be torn apart. The otherworldly hole was a ragged circle the diameter of a garbage can. It pulsed and glimmered, the surrounding air charged with alien energy that raised the hairs at the nape of Jason's neck.

Although fear prevented Jason from getting to his feet, he gazed into that supernatural portal, and it was like viewing a storm through a window. He realized that he was looking into Thunderland.

Beside him, Brains, too, stared raptly at the spectacle before them.

Just as Jason wondered if the Stranger might emerge from the hole and slay them, a Chicago White Sox cap whirled out like a Frisbee.

Shorty . . .

Bile rose in the back of Jason's throat. He tasted it, as bitter as grief, and choked it down.

The spinning baseball cap plopped onto the steps.

Instantly, the shimmering door to Thunderland closed. The wind and the strange noise ceased. Silence reclaimed the day.

Slowly, he walked to the hat. He picked it up. It felt damp. He examined the tag. The letters written on there in black ink read *M.J.*

Brains looked at the cap, then at Jason. He said only one thing.

"Mike."

CHAPTER EIGHTEEN

More than fifty relatives and friends showed up for the holiday cookout at Sam's house. Sam gave them the run of his spacious home, but mostly everyone gathered in the huge backyard, where they socialized and enjoyed the smorgasbord of food: barbecued ribs and chicken; hot dogs, Polish sausage, and hamburgers; baked ham; spaghetti; macaroni and cheese; collard greens; green beans; black-eyed peas; potato salad; sweet-potato pie; chocolate cake; homemade ice cream; and much more—enough dishes to ensure there would be plenty of leftovers for the following week.

Thomas was a true soul-food lover, but he had not eaten anything. He was overwhelmed by the sight of all the people there, most of whom he had seen only a few times in the past several years. Like a fool, he had always allowed the restaurant to take precedence over family social affairs. Finally aware of how precious these occasions were, he worked the crowd as though he were a politician running for election, not interested in eating, deriving pleasure solely from renewing ties with old friends and family.

His enthusiasm didn't rub off on Linda. She was solemn, almost as though they were having a family meal after someone's funeral. She avoided Thomas in favor of the company of her relatives and friends.

He sighed. *Patience.* He would have to be patient and loving to the end.

He found Jason in a remote corner of the yard. Alone, Jason sat in a lawn chair, a plate of untouched food at his feet. He did not turn when Thomas approached.

Linda approached Jason, too. Her attention was riveted on their son, not on Thomas.

Thomas tapped Jason's shoulder. "The food's disappearing fast. And *I* haven't eaten yet, either. You better clean your plate and get over there again before I do, or I guarantee there won't be a scrap left."

Jason remained silent. He did not look at him.

Thomas blushed. After he had neglected his son for years, what kind of response did he expect? *Hey, Dad, thanks for letting me know. Wanna race to the table? Last one there's a dirty rib tip!* It was natural for the boy to be standoffish.

Linda touched Thomas's arm and squeezed gently, as if to say *"good try."* He smiled at her, but worry knotted through him. He wondered if they really would be able to draw Jason back into the circle of their family. Jason would turn fourteen this month. Many kids, eager for greater independence, started rebelling at that age. If Jason was already this far from them, Thomas was afraid to imagine how far he might drift in the future, if they did not pull him back. But pulling him back was a delicate, complex matter. If they poured on the love and affection, they might repel him. If they exercised a lighter touch, he might slip away. They had to strike the perfect balance. Linda seemed capable of doing her part, but Thomas doubted that he could fulfill his role. For him, fatherhood was almost foreign territory.

Nevertheless, he had to try.

"Since you're not hungry, do you want to play volleyball?" Thomas said. "I see your cousins starting a game right now. I haven't played in a while, but I'd be more than willing to play with you."

Again, Jason did not respond.

Confused, Thomas glanced at Linda. She frowned. Stepping forward, she rested her hand on Jason's shoulder.

"Are you okay, honey?" she said.

Jason did not speak, did not look at them.

Maybe Jason was not being stubborn. Maybe his silence had nothing to do with them at all.

Thomas walked in front of him, kneeled so they were face to face . . . and flinched when he saw the look in his son's eyes. He had seen that look before. Ten years ago, he had seen the same look in Big George's eyes when the physician announced that, because of his stroke, he had to retire from The House of Soul. It was the look of someone who had suffered a crushing loss.

What in God's name could have happened to Jason?

Searching for evidence that would answer the question, Thomas noticed that Jason clutched a Chicago White Sox hat in his lap. Did it belong to him? Thomas knew little about Jason's taste in clothes, and he had no inkling of Jason's favorite sports teams.

What a poor excuse for a father he was. Even he and Big George had shared a love for the Chicago Bears.

Knuckles as white as bleached bones, Jason gripped the cap in the manner of a tense child gripping a teddy bear.

"What's wrong, Jason?" Thomas said.

Jason's response was almost inaudible: "Nothing."

Linda bent beside the chair, rested her hand on Jason's shoulder. "Whatever it is, you can tell us. Talking about it might help."

"It won't help," Jason said. "Because you won't believe me."

What a strange thing to say. Linda glanced at Thomas. Her apparent bewilderment mirrored his own.

Thomas pointed to the baseball cap. "Is that yours?"

Jason glared at him. "Do you remember buying it for me?"

"Well . . . no."

"Then it's not mine."

"Your mother could've bought it."

"She could have, but she didn't. I don't wear hats, and she knows it. Obviously, you don't."

Thomas cleared his throat. *Stay cool,* he reminded himself. *Be patient with the boy.*

"Obviously, neither of you can see that I don't feel like talking." Jason glared at both of them. "Leave me alone. Please."

"Son, we only want to help," Thomas said.

"You can't help me." Jason shook his head firmly. "No one can help me."

"You're acting weird," Linda said. "What's going on?"

Jason dragged his hand down his face. Thomas had never seen a kid appear so wrung out. He looked like a battle-weary soldier.

"Okay," Jason said. "You'll probably think I'm crazy, but I'm gonna tell you. It's gotten too serious. I don't have anything to lose by telling you about it. You might need to know, too, because things might start happening to you, if they haven't already."

"What kinds of things?" Thomas said. Inexplicably, he thought about the incident the other night: the strange, sensuous woman calling him in the middle of the night and showing up, like a ghost, in the backyard.

Jason leaned forward. His expression was so intense, it was hard to believe he was only thirteen. He spoke in a whisper.

"A man . . . a spirit . . . a thing, whatever you want to call it, has been terrorizing me and my friends for the past few days," Jason said. "We call it the Stranger, because we don't know its name, or what it is. The Stranger gave me the bike that I had always wanted. Remember, Mom?"

"Yes, I do." Linda's eyes were wide. "I thought it was only a coincidence."

"No coincidence," Jason said. "The Stranger's done other things, too. He's powerful, and he knows a lot about me. He says that he wants to fulfill my 'secret wishes,' but I don't know why. I can't figure out anything about him, and I'm running out of time. Today, he's . . . killed four people so far. Including Shorty."

"Come again?" Thomas said.

"Call Shorty's parents if you don't believe me," Jason said. "Someone found his body downtown, next to his bike. They'll probably say he had a heart attack or something, because when you die there, your body in the real world seems to just shut down. No one will ever know who really . . . did that to him. Except me and Brains."

"You can't be serious," Thomas said. "Four people dead in a small town like this? It would be all over the news, son."

Immediately, Thomas regretted making the statement. Jason's jaws clenched, and he pushed himself out of the chair.

"I knew it would be a waste of time to tell you," Jason said. "Grown-ups never believe anything kids say. You think we make up stuff like this."

Linda flashed an angry look at Thomas; then she turned to Jason. "Honey, please, tell us what happened. We'll believe you. Tell us everything."

"Sorry, Mom," Jason said. "Time's running out. Something's gonna happen again soon. I can feel it. I need to go."

"Where are you going?" Thomas said. "What are you going to do?"

"You wouldn't believe me anyway," Jason said. "All I'm

telling you is, be careful, and pay attention to clocks and thunder. If the clock hands freeze and you hear thunder rumble, you're in trouble. You better grab a gun and be ready to blow somebody away."

Puzzled, Thomas began to ask what he meant, but Jason spun around and rushed out of the backyard, dumping his plate in a garbage can. Thomas got up to chase after him. By the time he reached the driveway, Jason was on his bike, racing down the street.

Thomas gave up running after him. What the hell was the boy talking about? His story was ridiculous. Had he always possessed such an overactive imagination?

He and Linda had a lot of work to do with Jason. Not only did they need to reel him back into their family; they had to reel him back to reality.

Shaking his head sadly, Thomas returned to the backyard.

As Jason rode his bike home, consumed with grief and guilt and tormented by questions of what he would do since the Stranger had murdered Shorty, he resolved that he was going to attempt the fall from the tree. Again.

Desperation had pushed him to make the decision. He had to learn the truth about the Stranger before the fiend harmed someone else. Falling out of the tree again was his only hope of restoring his memory and unraveling the mystery.

At home, he parked his bike in the garage. He went into the backyard and walked under the big oak.

This was where it had begun. This was where it had to end.

He jumped up, grabbed a branch, and climbed.

When he estimated that he had climbed about twenty feet, he stopped. He surveyed the ground below.

Although he had been in this same position previously, on the elm at Brains's house, the prospect of striking the hard earth was no less frightening. His heart clutched, and his throat tightened, making it difficult to breathe.

As he did yesterday, he asked himself if he could go through with this. Did he have the courage? Was it a stupid idea? Should he try something else?

Rather than ponder those questions and risk losing his resolve, he forced himself to act. He closed his eyes, said a short prayer, and pushed away from the tree. For a moment, he teetered among the limbs, leaves brushing his face, and his feet scraping against bark . . . then he abruptly pitched forward into empty space.

Falling, he squeezed his eyes shut tighter, as if he could escape into the darkness underneath his eyelids before he experienced the pain of the impact. Although the blackness beneath his eyelids was deep, when he struck the ground, the darkness into which he sank was far deeper.

Jason awoke in his bed. The curtains concealed the windows, enclosing the room in purple-black shadows. Except for distant ripples of thunder, silence governed the day.

Groggy, he blinked. He had no idea how he had got there, or where he had been minutes before. He recalled attending the cookout at Granddad's house, but the memory was so vague, he might have been there days ago.

He turned to look at his wristwatch and winced. The side of his head ached. He touched the afflicted area. He felt a prominent bump.

As he gingerly rubbed the injury, everything came back to him.

Everything.

Not only the memory of his intentional fall out of the tree earlier that day, but everything he had been searching for.

The Stranger's identity. The details of their relationship. Every piece of information that had been erased from his mind when he plunged into the coma in March. It had all come back.

Heedless of the pain in his skull, he sat up.

His hands shook.

He had solved the mystery. At last.

His jubilation was tempered by the fact that the Stranger had murdered four people before Jason had found the courage to take his revelatory leap from the tree. Four kids killed before he had discovered the simple, obvious truth. His excitement faded.

A clash of thunder rocked the house. Jason took note of his watch. The digits were frozen at 3:21.

He rushed to a window and parted the drapes. Galleons of thunderclouds cruised the sky, and cords of electric-blue lightning sputtered like live wires across the clouds. Trees bucked, punished by the fierce wind.

Once again, he had been cast into Thunderland. He was certain that he had been brought into his room and placed in the bed by the same entity who had thrown him into this world. He was not a stranger anymore.

An acrid odor filled the air. Jason spun around.

Tendrils of black smoke curled under the bedroom door and crept into the room.

Fire, he thought with alarm. *The house is burning!*

But this wasn't the kind of smoke that indicated flames nearby. Dark, thick, roiling, the smoke billowed under the door and gathered in the center of the room, churning slowly—less like smoke than like a cloud, a miniature thunderhead that had fallen out of the sky.

Amid the swirling mass of vapor, a figure began to materialize.

Jason had backed up against the window. He drew short, quick breaths.

Amazingly, the visitor appeared to form from the smoke itself; when his body solidified, the cloud vanished.

Jason gaped at him.

Mr. Magic smiled.

"No, you are not dreaming," Mr. Magic said. "I'm back. And this time, I'm real."

CHAPTER NINETEEN

On the night of July 19, nearly fourteen years ago, Linda Brooks gave birth to Jason Samuel Brooks. Weighing in at seven pounds, Jason emerged with a caul covering his head—a thin membrane of skin regarded in legend as a sign of paranormal ability. His family, though aware of the myth, did not believe in it. After the caul was surgically removed, his parents took him home, and he was a normal child in every respect. For a while.

For Jason's first four years, he enjoyed an ideal upbringing: a family with sufficient financial resources; a nice house in a peaceful neighborhood; good food always served on time. Most important, closely knit parents who loved him dearly and expressed their love at virtually every opportunity. But in the winter of his fourth year, those blissful circumstances changed.

It began when his grandfather, George Brooks, was struck down by a major stroke that forced him to retire from his restaurant. Assuming the demanding management position that Big George had held, Thomas threw himself into The

House of Soul. He worked long, grueling hours, weekdays and weekends, obsessed with continuing the legacy his father had begun. Linda, struggling to cope with her husband's constant absence, imprisoned herself in her work as a writer, and, consumed by self-pity, acquired a taste for hard liquor.

Jason's harmonious family life was shattered.

He had always been a shy child. But then, with each of his parents locked within their separate worlds and spending little time with him, his natural shyness increased dramatically.

Even before Jason's family disintegrated, he had been an imaginative boy, easily enraptured by fanciful tales of kingdoms, dragons, princes, and magicians. Especially magicians. On his fourth birthday, a few months before his grandfather's stroke, his parents took him to see a famous stage magician performing in Chicago. The show enthralled him, and the magician's appearance imprinted itself on his mind. Jason was of the age when many children create imaginary playmates. It was therefore natural for that magician, who had thrilled him so, to form the basis of his imaginary friend.

He named his playmate Mr. Magic. The simple name seemed fitting. Playing with Mr. Magic quickly became a daily activity.

In fact, because Jason was habitually ignored by his mother and father, playing with Mr. Magic became his primary activity.

Nearly all children who had an imaginary friend shed those companions for real friends when they began attending school. But not Jason. Lacking the self-confidence to form friendships with other children, he contented himself with Mr. Magic. Mr. Magic never yelled at him, hit him, broke promises, or made him suffer any of the terrible treatment he had received from his parents—treatment he believed he would get from all other people he dared to open up with. Kind, reliable, honest, funny, and loving, Mr. Magic was perfect—everything he could ever have wanted in a companion. Jason saw no reason to end their relationship and brave the hazards of reaching out to others.

Mr. Magic was real, in Jason's mind. His powerful imagination had imbued Mr. Magic's image with a clarity equivalent to anything in the real world. Jason could see him, hear him, touch him, and smell him as though he were an actual person. Nonetheless, he kept Mr. Magic secret from everyone. They would think he was weird. They would not understand.

No one understood.

No one except Mr. Magic.

Jason believed they would be best friends for life and that they would never outgrow each other. Then, on a day in March, as Jason descended from the oak tree during a storm, he fell and hit his head on the ground. After three days in a coma, he awoke—with no memory of Mr. Magic and the special relationship they had shared. He quickly developed the social skills and interests of a healthy thirteen-year-old boy. To him, Mr. Magic was dead and forgotten.

But Mr. Magic had his own plans.

Eyes wide, Jason moved away from the figure standing in front of him. He backed up against the bed and dropped onto the mattress.

He sat up, tried to speak. But he could neither think of anything to say nor draw the breath necessary to form words.

Watching him, Mr. Magic chuckled.

Jason's imaginary friend, Mr. Magic, had resembled the stage magician whom he had once seen perform years ago. Tall and lean, with chiseled features and chestnut brown skin, his playmate had sported a whimsical costume: a black top hat, black tuxedo with white ruffled shirt, bow tie, flowing black cape, polished black shoes, a thin, dark cane. An almost comical outfit, really, and one that Jason had found amusing and comforting.

The Mr. Magic that stood before Jason in the flesh looked similar to Jason's imaginary friend and was dressed in the same flamboyant garments. But there were differences. This Mr. Magic was taller; a year ago, a forward on the Chicago Bulls, an athlete who stood six feet eight, had visited Jason's school, and Mr. Magic was clearly as tall as the ballplayer. Mr. Magic's hands were grotesquely long, his fingers like giant crab legs. There was something weird about his eyes, too. His eyes were brown, but something seemed to . . . *wriggle* in the whites of the entity's eyes, as if tiny worms slithered around his pupils. When Jason stared more intently, the wormy things vanished. He wasn't sure what he had seen. In fact, he wasn't sure of anything he was seeing right then.

"How?" Jason said, at last able to talk. "How can you be here? You aren't *real*."

"You underestimate yourself, Jason," Mr. Magic said in his inimitable, sonorous voice. "Your imagination is extraordinary. It breathed life into me as God breathed life into Adam. True life. I am far more than the imaginary friend you've always considered me to be. I am as real as anyone you've ever met, and I always have been."

He certainly seemed to be real. When he moved, his shoes made slight indentations in the carpet. Shadows swarmed over his clean-shaven face, and the flickers of lightning that came in through the window flitted across his voluminous cape. Jason also thought he could smell him. No longer smelling of smoke, Mr. Magic's scent reminded him vaguely of Old Spice.

"But you were only in my mind," Jason said. "It should be impossible for you to be here, living and breathing like a real person. Impossible."

"Almost nothing is impossible," Mr. Magic said. "The

universe is filled with nearly infinite possibilities. Remember, too, not only is your imagination unusually vivid; you were also born with a caul. A legendary sign of paranormal talent."

"Yeah, I remember, my mother told me all about it," Jason said. "But it's just an old legend. It doesn't mean anything."

"It means that you possess great power," Mr. Magic said. "Whether you choose to believe so or not."

"Enough power to create you and then give you the ability to jump out of my head and into the real world?"

"Well, it did not work quite like that," Mr. Magic said. He pursed his lips. "Let me see . . . when you fell out of the tree in March, and, unfortunately, forgot about me, I missed you so much that I decided to *cross over,* I suppose you could say. Cross over from the land of dreams, where you created me and where we shared our adventures, to the land of flesh and blood.

"I discovered, however, that crossing over in the manner I wished to was impossible," Mr. Magic said. "It seems the universe does have rules that govern these issues. The nearest I could get to the dimension in which you live is the alternate world you and your friends have entered on several occasions. You named it quite aptly, Jason: Thunderland."

"Thunderland," Jason said. "I guess we were right about it being another . . . dimension."

Mr. Magic nodded, smiling. "You always have been an intelligent boy. I can appear in the 'real' world, but my powers are limited there. It's taxing to assume a physical form, though I have done it on occasion. I prefer, however, to limit myself to phone calls, simple messages, things of that nature.

"But in Thunderland, I am a god. Nothing is beyond my

capabilities. The world is completely uninhabited, except by those whom I choose to bring there. It's my private playground, in a sense. Doesn't that sound exciting?"

"Sure, whatever you say," Jason said. He was amazed at how easily he had adapted to this most improbable of circumstances. His imaginary playmate coming to life? You could not get any crazier than that. But he accepted Mr. Magic's existence. He did not understand how it was possible—he probably never would—but he accepted it. Like the average person who did not understand a thing about nuclear physics yet accepted the reality of the nuclear bomb. To Jason, it was really that simple.

He sensed, too, that it was not important to worry too much about how Mr. Magic had become real. Obviously, Mr. Magic had a plan. He needed to learn the plan and do whatever was necessary to ruin it, so that he could go back to living a normal life. That was the important concern.

"I could ask you a million things, but I really want to know the answer to one question," Jason said. "Why are you doing all of this stuff to me and my friends?"

"You wish to know my motives?" Mr. Magic said. Tapping his cane on the carpet, he sat on the windowsill. "Very well, I'll explain. I gave you the bike, gave you sex with the girl, and killed Blake and his despicable friends because I want you to see that this new life of yours is a mistake. You can be happier with me than you ever can be with any of your friends and family. By doing you these favors—granting you three secret wishes, if you will—I had hoped to show you the truth. The truth being that you need only me. No one else."

"You think you've been making me happy?" Jason said. "Are you crazy? You've only scared me and confused me for the past week."

"Be honest, Jason," Mr. Magic said. "You were delighted when I left the bike in your garage, you moaned with pleasure when I thrilled you with the girl, and you would have eagerly bathed in Blake's blood if I had provided a tubful. You know it's true."

"That's bullshit," Jason said. "Yeah, I liked the bike, but only until I found out that you had given it to me. And the sex was exciting, but afterward, it made me sick. And I never wanted Blake and those guys dead. I only wanted them to leave me alone."

"I granted your wish," Mr. Magic said.

"I didn't wish for you to kill them," Jason said. He swallowed. "And I definitely didn't wish for you to kill Shorty."

Mr. Magic chuckled. "Ah, your buddy Michael. Michael I murdered for a different purpose. I murdered him to liberate you."

"Liberate me?"

"Precisely. To liberate you from the feelings you nurture for other people. To free you from the chains of love. Relationships are stifling, Jason. Your loved ones demand time, energy, money, commitment, kindness, love, understanding—an endless list of fussy, selfish requests comparable to the ransom demands of a mad bomber. For what? What results from your perpetual attempts to please these taskmasters? Nothing. Death. Ashes. Yes, loved ones die, my friend. They suffer heart attacks, get crushed in car accidents, and are slain by the numerous psychotics who prowl your streets in this sad age. Somehow, some way, they all die, and everything you have given them perishes with them. It all rots in the grave. Perfectly useless, wasted effort on your part.

"But I do not die, Jason. I will exist forever. You gave me everlasting life. I will never leave you."

Jason shook his head. "I didn't understand a word you said."

"It is quite simple. I plan to liberate you, to set you free from your prison of ordinary, human concerns. The most effective way for me to achieve that goal is to terminate the relationships you are presently ensnared in. Hence, my disposal of Michael. Your liberation is essential, Jason. You must be a free soul before you can come back to me."

"What do you mean, come back to you?"

Mr. Magic, still sitting on the windowsill, leaned forward on his cane.

"I mean, join with me. Not roam with me in the fantasy world, as we did in the past, but merge with me as if we were separate flames uniting into one enormous fire. A roaring fire that will ravage your world as no war in history has ever done. Nothing is quite as exciting as murder, Jason. No childhood game can compare to the thrill of gripping a living, beating heart . . . and bursting it in your bare hands."

Slowly Jason blinked. Mr. Magic was nuttier than they had expected. Jason understood, right then, that reasoning with Mr. Magic was impossible. He was as mad as any dictator who'd dreamed of world domination.

When Jason spoke, he tried to prevent his voice from quavering. "Why do you want to destroy the world?"

"In Thunderland, I have tasted godlike power," Mr. Magic said, "and I have enjoyed it immensely. But as I said, that place is devoid of life. Your world, however, overflows with the living. The prospect of exercising divine power there is indescribably thrilling. Furthermore, considering your world's present sorry state, it is ripe for a bit of, shall we say, cleansing. Why wait for God to do what we can do ourselves?"

"But you said that your powers were limited in my world."

"That is correct," Mr. Magic said. "Alone there, my capacities are restricted. But with you, I would be invincible."

"So you need me to conquer the world?" Jason said.

"You are a vital component," Mr. Magic said, nodding.

Not only was he insane; he was a selfish, manipulative son of a bitch. He didn't suspect it, either. He thought he was charming. He was a case study in pure insanity.

"Forget it," Jason said. "I'm not coming back to you. I don't need you, and I don't want you. If you're so great, destroy the world by yourself."

Mr. Magic threw back his head and laughed.

Outdoors, thunder cracked.

Rain marched across the roof, streamed like tears down the windows.

"Don't need me, don't want me?" Mr. Magic said. "You are an intelligent boy, but you don't understand what we mean to each other. We are part of each other, inseparable; the link we share is unbreakable. You will realize that fact after I've liberated you. That exciting time is drawing near, Jason. Several others will die tonight."

Jason shot off the bed, hands clenched into fists. "What others are you talking about?"

"The ones you love most, of course," Mr. Magic said. "Surely, you know who they are."

"Tell me."

"It's not your concern," Mr. Magic said. "From this moment onward, your only concern is me. You will enjoy being with me again, Jason. You may experience grief and anger over the deaths of your loved ones, but that will pass, I assure you. Once we unite, we'll have so much fun together that soon you won't even remember them."

Jason shook. "You're crazy."

Mr. Magic only smiled, as though Jason were a dim-witted child who did not comprehend anything he had said.

Mr. Magic pushed off the windowsill. God, he was so tall. The peak of his top hat was only inches beneath the ceiling.

"How about some magic, Jason?" Mr. Magic grinned. He raised his cane.

Then he cast the cane on the carpet.

"Oh, shit," Jason said, backing up and staring at the stick.

But it was no longer a stick. When it struck the carpet, the wood transformed into a long, shiny creature that seemed to be a hybrid of a snake, a centipede, and a figment of pure fantasy. It had the length and gleaming black scales of a serpent, and dozens of tiny, jittering legs along both sides of its sinuous body. A pair of bulbous black eyes adorned its head, and when it opened its mouth, small fangs glistened.

The beast crouched on the floor between Jason and Mr. Magic. It hissed. Its large, glistening eyes focused on Jason.

Hot terror had pinned Jason against the door.

"Keep that thing away from me," he said. Fear thickened his throat, like mucus. "Don't let it touch me."

Mr. Magic chuckled. "My goodness, you are trembling. Why are you afraid? We are friends, Jason."

"Just keep it away." Looking from the snake-centipede-thing to Mr. Magic, Jason stealthily reached behind him and grasped the doorknob. Escape was his only option. He didn't know where he could escape to in this strange world, but he obviously could not trust Mr. Magic. Previously his friend, he had become a demon.

"Do not fear me, my friend," Mr. Magic said. "I will not harm you. Unless, of course, you give me reason to do so. But that will not happen, will it? You will be a good boy, yes?"

"Yes," Jason said, and twisted the knob and tore open the door.

Whip-quick, the creature leaped off the floor and bit him.

CHAPTER TWENTY

The cookout ended around eight-thirty. The leftovers were divided among friends and relatives, lawn chairs and picnic tables were packed away, garbage was bagged and tossed into the Dumpster, and the stereo was turned off and returned inside the house.

Linda was glad to be going home. She enjoyed cookouts, but putting them together was so much work. She was exhausted. After she and Thomas helped clean up, they said their final good-byes to everyone, and Thomas drove them home.

Night had fallen over the city. Kids playing with firecrackers crowded on sidewalks and congregated in the streets, creating enough bangs, shrieks, and pops to match the sounds of a nation at war. Like devotees making a pilgrimage, families laden with coolers and blankets trudged toward the park to watch the citywide fireworks display, which would commence at nine o'clock.

Driving, Thomas glanced away from the road and looked

at her. "Okay, we haven't really talked about this yet. Give me your honest opinion on Jason's story."

She was glad that Thomas had brought up the subject of Jason. Jason was one of the few subjects she could discuss with him without feeling angry and bitter.

"I don't know, Thomas," she said. "It sounds unbelievable, and Jason has always had an extremely vivid imagination. On the other hand, he and his friends have been up to something the past few days, like I've suspected. They've been spending the night at one another's houses every night. Don't forget, someone really did give Jason the bike, too. We don't know who's responsible."

"But a spirit?" Thomas said. "A spirit that's running around killing folks? Come on."

"We haven't called his friend's family yet. If they tell us that the kid really is dead—and I pray that he isn't—that would be a strong sign that Jason's telling the truth. I don't have their number with me, but it's at home."

"Then we can call them when we get in. I prefer to believe that Jason's making up this whole story. Maybe he's doing it for attention."

"Jason's not like that, Thomas. Besides . . . something weird happened to me recently."

"What happened?"

"I got a call," she said, "from a child. The kid sounded younger than Jason, but he talked as though I were his mother, and he taunted me about some things that only Jason could know about. Then he invited me into the backyard to 'play with him.' I didn't go out there, but I looked out the window. I saw someone in the tree . . . then a ball floated out of the tree, toward the house." She shivered. "I moved away from the window. A couple of minutes later, when I looked outside again, he was gone, and so was the ball."

"That's some strange shit, Linda."

"You're telling me. That's why I'm inclined to believe at least part of what Jason is saying."

Thomas rubbed his chin. "All right, I have to admit that something weird happened to me, too. *I* got a call the other night."

"You're kidding," she said. "Was it a kid?"

"No, it was a woman. She had a memorable voice—very sexy, I have to say. And she knew things about me and you. Even crazier, she knew about my umm . . . affair."

"She did?" Linda stared at him. "I didn't know about it, and I live with you." Her anger came back in a hot rush. She drew a breath. *Don't get sidetracked,* she reminded herself. They were talking about Jason and these bizarre incidents, not their marriage.

"That's not all," he said. "After I hung up on her, she showed up in the backyard. She was butt-naked, baby. She tried to get me to come outside, too. Of course, I didn't. I went back to bed."

"I can't believe all of that happened and you didn't tell me about it," she said.

"You didn't tell me what happened to you, either."

"Touché," she said. "I didn't want to admit to myself that it had actually happened. I tried to convince myself that I was daydreaming."

"Same here. I was half convinced that I had dreamed the whole damn thing, so I didn't bring it up. But since our experiences were similar, in a way, there must be a connection."

"Yes, there must be," she said. "But I'll be damned if I know what it is. We'd better talk to Jason as soon as we get in. We need for him to tell us everything."

"Agreed. I can't see how any of this stuff would connect and make sense, but he might know something that could tie it all together."

Thomas turned onto their block. Sitting on a slight hill, surrounded on both sides by towering elms, oaks, and maples, their modern two-story home looked deserted. The black windows stared blankly into the night, and the porch lamp was off. Was Jason here? Or was he on his mysterious mission?

Linda reached above her and pressed the remote control clipped to the sun visor, opening the garage door. As Thomas pulled into the garage, she saw Jason's bike leaning against the wall. He was here. Good. She was anxious to sit him down and clear up this strange business.

When they entered the kitchen and called for Jason, he did not answer.

Thomas headed upstairs to Jason's room. Downstairs, Linda searched for a note, thinking he might have departed without taking his bike. She found nothing.

"He's not in his room." Thomas came down the steps. "Did you find a note from him?"

"No."

"I wonder if he came home when he left your dad's house. He said he felt that he was running out of time, remember?" Thomas ran his hand through his hair. "Shit, I wish I had listened to him."

"I'll call his friend's parents," she said.

She read Mike Johnson's phone number off the list of numbers tacked on the Peg-Board beside the wall phone. She had punched in three digits before she realized the line was dead.

"Thomas, pick up the phone in the living room. This one isn't working."

Nodding, Thomas left the kitchen. From the other room, he said, "This one's dead, too."

Thunder rumbled. A whooping gale thumped the walls, snuffled at the edges of the windows.

Chilled and not certain why, Linda hurried toward the living room and Thomas. He met her in the hallway.

"It's probably pointless, but I'll check the phone upstairs," he said.

"I'll go with you," she said, not wanting to be alone, and unable, too, to understand her onset of anxiety.

In the master bedroom, another telephone sat on the nightstand. As Thomas had guessed, that one was also dead.

Another club of thunder hit the night. It was the most powerful crash Linda had ever heard; the force of the reverberation actually knocked her off balance. Gripping the dresser for support, she peered outside a window. The sky sagged under the weight of heavy, oil-black thunderclouds. Lightning throbbed against the backdrop of the heavens, resembling the luminous veins and arteries of some huge, otherworldly beast.

She turned to Thomas. "The storm could have knocked out the phone lines."

"I can't recall that ever happening," he said. "The electrical lines, sure, I've seen that. But the phones? That's a new one. The storm started only a couple of minutes ago."

"Well, what else could it be?"

Thomas did not answer. He glanced at his watch.

"The second hand's stopped," he said. "Check your watch, Linda."

She looked at her Timex. It read 9:14, and the hands were frozen.

"Mine has stopped, too," she said.

"Good Lord," Thomas said. "I don't believe this."

"You're thinking of what Jason said earlier, aren't you?" she said. "Something about it being dangerous when the clocks stop and thunder rumbles."

"Exactly. I don't know what any of it means, but I remember his advice." He opened the closet and removed a wooden case from the top shelf. He opened the box.

Inside, a .38 gleamed darkly.

"A precaution," he said when she looked at him questioningly. He carefully took the revolver and several bullets out of the case. "Jason warned us to arm ourselves. I don't know who—or what—we're up against, but we'd be crazy to ignore his advice."

"I guess that now you believe everything he said."

"This is some strange shit, baby. I don't know what's happening. I'm clueless. I don't *want* to believe Jason's story, but it looks like he was on the money."

"I hope he was wrong. Judging from what he said, someone might try to attack us."

"We'll be ready." He loaded the ammunition in the revolver. Ordinarily, the sight of guns made her nervous, but she was grateful that he was prepared. She wished she had a gun of her own, though she had no idea how to use one.

"What's our plan?" she said.

"Get to my car phone. Call his friends. If they can't give us any answers, we call the cops."

"Sounds good to me," she said.

Like God clapping His mighty hands, thunder blared. A gust screamed—a haunting, humanlike cry.

Then a fury of rain hammered the house. Clattering, splashing, and hissing, it was most intense cloudburst Linda had ever witnessed.

Clutching the .38, Thomas went to the doorway. While Linda waited near the bed, he ducked outside and checked both ways.

"All clear." He returned to her. "Come on, let's get the hell out of here. The longer I stay here, the more worried I get. I know something's happened to that boy. I don't want to waste a second messing around."

"I'm right behind you," she said.

They moved outside the bedroom and crept toward the stairs, Linda searching in every direction for a threat she could not name, in a house that seemed nothing like the place she called home.

* * *

Brains neither heard nor felt the portentous thunder when it first struck. Sitting on his bed, he paged slowly through a family photo album. He stopped and stared for long stretches of time whenever he found a photograph in which Shorty appeared. His grief, as potent as it had been that morning when he had seen Shorty's baseball cap spin out of the supernatural hole, had rendered him oblivious of the outside world.

In every picture, Shorty seemed happy. Although he had been photographed in a variety of places—in front of a roller coaster at Six Flags Great America, near a heap of gifts at Brains's tenth birthday party, eating barbecue at a cookout a few summers ago—his cheery, easygoing nature had been captured flawlessly in each photo. Except for Brains's own memories, nothing reminded him so poignantly of his missing cousin.

No. Not missing cousin. *Dead* cousin. Because Brains had not witnessed Shorty's death, part of him harbored the hope that he was still alive, maybe trapped in some corner of Thunderland. But it was only dumb, childish optimism. Mike's body had been discovered downtown, near Northern Road. He was dead.

Dead.

Brains wondered when he would be able to accept Mike's death. He kept believing this was a nightmare from which he would awake to find that everything was okay.

He turned the last page of the photo album. Sighing, he closed the book and placed it beside him on the rumpled bedspread.

He lay on his back, gazed at the ceiling.

He felt dead himself. Hollow, numb, weak. He did not want to do anything. He only wanted to lie there and breathe.

Nevertheless, the pistons of his brain fired up again. For the first time that day, his thoughts advanced past pondering Shorty's death. He asked himself what he was he going to do.

He had to do something. Although he had never experienced the loss of a loved one, he intuitively understood that mourning, as proper and natural as it was, had its limits. Eventually, one had to salvage the pieces and move on with life. Brains could no more wallow forever in grief than he could stay submerged underwater for eternity. While it might ordinarily be acceptable to mourn Mike for a long time, with the Stranger on the prowl, Brains couldn't afford to—or else he might share Mike's fate.

What was he going to do?

Call Jason? Would that do any good? Most likely, it would not. Jason was probably as lost and grief-stricken as he was.

What was he going to do?

Suddenly, he heard thunder.

He bolted upright in bed. He checked his watch.

The digits had stopped at 9:14.

He jumped to his feet.

The question of what he was going to do had gained new urgency. He was in Thunderland. He had been so immersed in grief that he had not realized that his surroundings had changed. He could not afford to zone out like that again.

Reminding himself that the Stranger had quit the game-playing and had begun to kill, Brains decided that, first of all, he should arm himself. Jason had said that whatever a person imagined in Thunderland instantly became fact, but Brains could not put his faith in something like that. He needed something solid. A gun.

Cautiously he left his bedroom. He slunk into the dimly lit hallway.

In the real world, his family had been downstairs talking. Now he heard only the storm: thunder rolling, rain hammering the roof, wind buffeting the house. Being alone here frightened him, but he was thankful that his family had been spared the horror of this place.

He went into his parents' bedroom, switching on the light

as he entered. He pulled out the nightstand drawer. A shiny .45 rested within, the final and ultimate element of his father's extensive security preparations.

He took out the revolver. It was loaded. He found extra ammunition at the bottom of the drawer, inside a case. He filled his pockets with ammo.

He was not sure whether the weapon would hurt the Stranger. But he felt safer.

Feeling as exhausted as he used to be after a long day of work in the Mississippi cotton fields, Sam Weaver stepped outside shortly after nine o'clock, holding an icy bottle of Heineken in one hand and a bag of roasted peanuts in the other. Every Fourth of July, after the guests had left his home, he liked to sit on the patio and watch the town's fireworks. After his tiring cookout-managing duties, he needed to unwind. He also derived a childlike delight from the colorful, creatively arranged explosions.

With the patio light shut off so he could enjoy the pyrotechnics to the fullest, darkness gathered around his property. He navigated his way across the deck to the glass-topped table, placed his snacks on top, and sat in a wicker chair.

He noticed the empty seat beside him. Lena, his deceased wife, used to enjoy the Independence Day fireworks with him. He was so accustomed to her company that sometimes, after an especially awesome explosion, he would turn to that seat, expecting to see excitement on her lovely face—only to find that she was not there. He had been a widower for seven lonely years, but he retained an assortment of habits from his married life.

Sighing, he looked away from the chair. He took a slow swallow of the cold beer. *Delicious.*

He searched the dark sky. The light show had not begun yet. He glanced at his watch. It read 9:14.

Although the event was scheduled to begin at nine o'clock, he was unconcerned. The folks might have been mired in technical difficulties. On one such occasion, the fireworks had started thirty minutes late, and that year's display had been the most spectacular ever, as if the park district had decided that it needed to outdo itself in order to compensate for its tardiness. If another late start would result in a show half as exciting as that other one, he did not mind waiting a little while.

He leaned back and relaxed, alternately sipping beer and eating peanuts.

When nothing had happened in the skies, he checked his watch again: 9:14.

He frowned. That couldn't be right. He had read his watch earlier—at least five minutes earlier—and it had flashed back those same digits. Hadn't it?

He held up his beer. Could the alcohol have muddied his perceptions? No, the bottle was half full, and anyway, he wasn't such a sap that one beer could have set his head spinning. Too much booze was not the source of the problem.

He did not relish the idea, but perhaps the problem was in his own mind. He was sixty-eight and evidently in good health, but he was plenty old enough to creep into the beginning stages of Alzheimer's. He lived alone, which meant he could already be having all kinds of lapses and not be aware of them. This incident could be only one in a series of mental missteps, notable primarily because it was the first time he saw proof of his affliction.

Sweet thought, Sam.

Then again, he might be getting carried away. The watch could simply be malfunctioning.

He tinkered with the buttons. The digits did not change. Apparently, the problem really was in his watch, not in his head.

Thunder resounded through the night.

Alarmed, Sam looked up. Gas-jet blue lightning flashed, the stark light briefly illuminating the backyard. Another rumble of thunder rolled across the sky.

Wasn't this the perfect unwinding session? Something happened that made him temporarily fear that he was a step away from the nearest nursing home, and then a thunderstorm ruined all hope for the fireworks. Lord have mercy, he should just take his old, tired butt to bed.

A cold gale swept across the deck.

Like boulders colliding, thunder banged.

The air suddenly felt heavy with pent-up rain.

He quickly got up. He grabbed the peanuts and the Heineken and fled inside the house by way of the sliding screen door.

The instant he shut the door, rain fell. It did not begin slowly; it began in a torrent, striking the glass with a fury that brought to mind Biblical lands flooded by forty-day-long downpours. No doubt, if he had been a second later getting inside, he would've been drenched.

Darkness filled the kitchen. He dropped the bag of peanuts on the counter beside him, walked to the light switch near the refrigerator, and flicked it on.

His dead wife was sitting at the dinette table.

CHAPTER TWENTY-ONE

Sam's hand, in the process of lifting the beer to his lips, halted at his chin.

Although the bottle was ice-cold, he abruptly felt much colder.

It was Lena, his wife, who had been in the grave for seven years. Lena, dressed in a bright-yellow blouse, her long black hair curly and lustrous. Lena, her face youthful and beautiful, her brown eyes shining with the love they had always held whenever she had looked upon him. Lena, sitting there watching him quietly, seemingly as real as the tile on which he stood.

Sam thought he felt a heart attack coming on. He touched his chest. His heart still beat, but it pounded wildly.

A moment ago, as he had sat on the deck pondering the frozen watch digits, he wondered whether his mind was breaking down, and he had decided that his fears were baseless. But this disconcertingly realistic vision of Lena proved that something truly was wrong with him. It had to be mental disease, Alzheimer's—something like that. He refused to consider any other explanation. Because any other explanation would drive him crazy in earnest.

The hallucination of his wife spoke: "Sam, do you recognize me? It's Lena."

Pangs twisted through his heart. The damn thing's sweetly musical voice sounded exactly like Lena's.

He suspected that talking to a creation of his own mind might endanger his fragile mental condition, but perhaps by speaking to it he could dissolve it, in the same manner that a police negotiator could use words alone to persuade a violent criminal to surrender.

"I know who you are," he said, and he was pleased to hear that his voice was strong, controlled. "And I know *what* you are. You're an illusion. My real wife is gone to God."

"I'm not an illusion, sweetheart," she said. "I'm really here. The good Lord knew how much we missed each other. He brought me back so we could be together again."

"God doesn't work like that."

"God works in mysterious ways, sugar."

"Not in those kinds of ways," he said. "You're only a creation of my own mind, a ghost I dreamed up. I want you to go away. Now."

Instead of vanishing, the Lena-illusion pushed away from the table and walked around it.

He saw that the illusion, which mirrored how Lena had appeared in her mid-thirties, wore high-cut white shorts that showed off the wonderful figure she had possessed at that age.

It began to walk toward him.

Sam had been holding the beer bottle loosely. He tightened his grip around the neck.

"You've missed me, haven't you, sugar?" the Lena-illusion said, slowly drawing closer. "You've missed me a lot. Especially at night, haven't you?"

"I told you to go away." He raised the bottle.

It continued to come closer.

"Yes, I know you've missed me at night. You're tired of sleeping alone in that big, cold bed. Aren't you, baby? Don't you miss us keeping each other warm at night? Don't you want us to hold each other again? Don't you?"

He kept telling himself to fight this sick fantasy, but his resolve was crumbling. Since Lena's death, he had not had a sexual relationship with another woman, for he believed it would be an act of infidelity. But thoughts of sex occasionally visited him. He was older, but he certainly was not dead. Sometimes he wondered how it would feel to hold a woman again. How it would feel to kiss. To make love.

"Don't you?" the Lena-illusion said. Smiling seductively, it continued to close the gap between them.

He struggled to suppress his sexual urges and think rationally. He must not allow this thing to seduce him. Sex with a hallucination? Lord, that would propel him into complete madness. The only way to preserve what sanity he had left was to resist the pull of his libido and somehow get this alluring specter out of there.

"No," he said in what he prayed was a firm voice. "No, I don't want to touch you again. Stay away from me."

The Lena-phantom ignored him. It came closer, stretching its delicate hands toward him.

"Come to me, Sammy." Its slender fingers groped for him, only inches away.

Terrified of the touch of this nameless thing, he dropped the bottle and ran.

With the surefooted swiftness of a man half his age, he flew up the winding staircase, streaked down the hallway, and slammed into the bathroom. Shut and locked the door. Gripped the sink with sweaty hands, gazed into the basin, panting.

He had never been so disturbed.

How could his mind have conjured such a thing? Was he

that ill? Sweet Jesus, if he had plunged this far over the edge, who knew what might happen next?

Chills swam like icy eels through his veins. His greatest fear had always been losing his mental stability, his presence of mind. Because he'd learned at an early age that a man was only as strong as his mind, he had spent his life educating himself, developing his powers of perception, and strengthening his will. To be tormented by hallucinations was a nightmare of tragic proportions.

To dispel the inner coldness, he turned the faucet handle, releasing warm water into the sink. He bathed his face.

After washing, he dried himself with a towel. He examined his face in the mirror. He looked tired but normal, not at all like a man who would be haunted by sick illusions. Better still, his racing heartbeat had slowed.

Nevertheless, tomorrow morning, he would visit his doctor. He loathed going to physicians, but letting an illness of this degree go unchecked was tantamount to driving blindfolded on an expressway during morning rush hour. He was in grave peril—from himself.

Booming thunder made the bathroom walls tremble. Rain rapped the window.

Out of curiosity, he checked his watch. It still read 9:14. Obviously, its battery had run down. Tomorrow, he would go to the jewelry shop and have the watch repaired.

He needed another drink, something more potent than beer. It was never his habit to deal with stress by consuming alcohol, but right then, nothing would have been as pleasing as a stiff shot of whiskey—a double shot, perhaps, to knock him out until morning and spare him the terror engineered by his own mind.

He opened the door.

An acrid smell filled the hallway. He looked to the spiral staircase. A large mass of noxious-looking black smoke churned up the stairs.

What was this? Fire? No, it could not be. Although the smoke roiled in thick waves, it retained its basic shape and did not dissipate like ordinary smoke. A blaze was not the cause of this; this was something else. Another hallucination?

As Sam watched, mystified, the enormous column of dark vapor writhed into the hallway. He thought he glimpsed hands in there . . . a face . . . legs. No, he was not seeing this. This was, absolutely, another demented illusion.

Because a giant-sized man materialized from the smoke itself.

"Hello, Samuel," the man said.

Sam froze.

The intruder was a lean, very tall man dressed in a black tuxedo, black bow tie, black top hat, and shiny black shoes. A cape flowed from his shoulders in a silky black wave. Strikingly handsome, with chestnut-brown skin, he tapped the carpet with a black cane, smiling at Sam like a guest who had arrived late for the holiday cookout.

"Who the hell are you?" Sam said.

"I am Mr. Magic." He smiled pleasantly. "I've come to kill you."

As Sam gaped at him, Mr. Magic drew back his cane and swung at Sam's head.

Sam raised his arms protectively and lurched backward. The cane slashed like a saber through empty space, leaving ribbons of air in its wake.

Although he had missed Sam, Mr. Magic laughed. He began to march into the bathroom.

Sam did not know who this man was, what he was, or why he wanted to kill him, but he knew what he had to do next: get his .357 out of the gun case under the bed and blow this bastard away. In this age of random, senseless violence, he had prepared for an attack in his home—though nothing could have readied him for a threat quite like this Mr. Magic character. Illusion or not, Sam had something for him.

Since this was the master bathroom, it had two doors: one opened to the hall; the other led to the master bedroom. As Mr. Magic charged inside, blocking the hallway exit, Sam spun around, yanked open the second door, hustled through, and slammed the door shut behind him and locked it before Mr. Magic could follow.

On the other side, Mr. Magic chuckled.

"I'll give you something to laugh about." Sam ran across the dark bedroom. He clicked on the bedside lamp and reached underneath the bed; his hand found the cool wood of the gun case. He pulled out the case and gratefully removed the polished, loaded .357.

He rose, the weapon trembling a little in his hands. He rushed to the other bedroom door that opened to the hallway, and slammed and locked that one, too.

He moved beside the bed, watching both doorways warily.

Rain drummed on the roof.

Grinding wheels of thunder drove across the night.

Just when he thought Mr. Magic had decided to enter by another route, black smoke, drifting under the door that led to the bathroom, slithered into the room.

"I'm ready for you this time," Sam said as waves of smoke poured inside. "Come on."

In spite of his tough words, the gun shook badly in his clammy hands. He realized—or, perhaps, accepted—that these were not hallucinations. The truth, which was far worse, was that he was up against something unearthly, some kind of supernatural fiend. He was a skeptic on such matters, but like everyone, he had witnessed incidents in his life that defied rational explanation. Although he had never seen anything on the scale of an entity like this, the universe was full of mysteries both wonderful and monstrous, and he would never attain complete knowledge of God's creation. This Mr. Magic character, though, seemed less like something from God and more like the spawn of the devil.

Quickly, the tower of smoke metamorphosed into the well-attired demon.

Lord, help me, Sam thought. *Please give your servant the strength.*

Mr. Magic stalked toward Sam.

"You take one step closer, and I'll blow your head off," Sam said. He aimed the revolver at him, hands still shaky. "I may be old, but I'll be damned if I roll over and die for you."

"Such tenacity," Mr. Magic said. "I like that. I had not anticipated much resistance from a doddering old man like you. You have piqued my interest, Samuel. I will enjoy murdering you."

"Go to hell," Sam said. He pulled the trigger.

The gun boomed, the recoil snapping painfully through Sam's wrists. A round blasted Mr. Magic's chest, but he did not bleed, scream, or even grimace.

Refusing to accept that the gun was useless, Sam squeezed the trigger twice more. Both rounds plowed into Mr. Magic's torso, but neither of them had any harmful effect. Mr. Magic strode forward, raised his cane in the air, and cast it upon the bed.

"What the . . ." Sam's words guttered into silence as he saw that the thing that had been the cane was now alive, squirming on the bed. Long and black, gleaming like some kind of snake, but with dozens of tiny legs along its body, and bubble-like eyes and needle-sharp fangs. It hissed malevolently.

Operating on pure instinct, Sam trained the revolver on the creature and fired. But the serpent beast was *fast*. As the bullet plowed into the bedsheets, cotton exploding in the air, the snake-thing scurried forward and launched itself at Sam.

Crying out, Sam swung the gun to bat away the serpent, but it attached itself to him. Its tiny legs, slick with slime, wrapped around his entire arm, and it must have had suction-type feet, because they pressed against his skin and started sucking, leeching the blood out of him.

"Jesus, Jesus, get off me!" Whirling his arm around, Sam felt blood draining out of him, the thing's repulsively warm body pressed tight against his skin. The creature sank its fangs into the back of his hand. A bolt of pain shot through him, and the gun dropped out of his fingers. He howled in agony.

Across the room, Mr. Magic laughed.

Filled with revulsion, yet determined, Sam seized the snake-centipede by the back of its slimy neck. It hissed and writhed, but he would not let it go. As if swinging a baseball bat, he whipped the creature's head against the bed post. The thing's skull snapped, and it fell away from his arm and onto the floor, leaving a residue of ooze and blood on his skin.

"Bravo," Mr. Magic said. He clapped his long, thin hands.

Lord, Sam thought. He was panting. *Please, let me survive this. Deliver me.*

Deliverance might be as close as the nearest door.

His heart feeling as though it would seize up and never throb again, Sam fled to the hallway door. He popped the lock and twisted the knob—but the door would not open. It seemed to be glued to the door frame.

Impossible! Sam thought. Open up, *damn it!*

A hand fell on his shoulder.

"Sammy," an eerily familiar voice said.

Sam turned.

The Lena-thing leered in his face.

He screamed. He shoved aside the damnable thing and ran, but it caught him by the back of his shirt. It jerked him toward it and wrapped its arms around his waist, hugging him from behind. Struggling to escape, he flailed his arms and stumbled forward a few steps, and then he hit the side of the bed and fell onto it.

The Lena-thing laughed. It crawled on top of him.

He grabbed fistfuls of the bedspread, straining to crawl away.

The Lena-thing roughly turned him over, forcing him to lie on his back. Sitting on his thighs, it lifted his shirt. It slid its hand underneath and touched his belly.

Its fingers were cold.

Repulsed, Sam squirmed, but he could not move from underneath the monster. It had him pinned in place.

"Gonna touch you the way I used to," the creature said, sounding exactly like his dead wife. It smiled. "Gonna make you feel so good."

The Lena-thing, balanced on his knees, moved its frigid hand in slow circles across his stomach.

"Get off me," Sam said, weakly. The creature's icy touch drove numbing chills to the core of his body.

"You've been looking forward to this for so long, ain't you, baby?" It grabbed one of his nipples in its freezing fingers, squeezed, and twisted. Sam cried out. The monster laughed.

Oh, Jesus, what a nightmare this was. Sam wanted to awake into the comforting, familiar world of family cookouts, breakfast with his grandson, reading good books by the fireplace, golf with his buddies, and church services. Without warning, for an inexplicable purpose, someone had pitched him into hell.

A spasm corkscrewed through his heart.

No, Sam thought. Another razor of agony cut across his chest.

It was the event that he had dreaded for years, ever since Lena had succumbed to the same fate: a heart attack.

Above him, crooning wordlessly, the Lena-thing unzipped his jeans.

"I'm gonna make it real good for you, Sammy," the Lena-thing said. It began to roll down his pants.

Sam ordered himself to fight against this monster's viola-
tion of his body, but his muscles did not obey; another flash
of agony seared through his heart, and then he felt himself
drifting away, *sliding* out of his body as though his skin were
only a light jacket. The walls of the bedroom dissolved. The
demon vanished. Sam found himself in a vast, grassy field
warmed by a golden sun.

In the distance, he spotted a familiar figure in a yellow
dress, steadily drifting closer.

The dream about Lena, he remembered. The real Lena,
his love for all time.

He traveled toward her, carried by wings of air.

Jason, he thought, hoping his final, desperate message
would reach his grandson by some kind of telepathy. He
loved many of his family and friends, but he and Jason
shared a special relationship, and he yearned to send the boy
one last piece of his heart before he left him. *I want you to
know that I'm proud of you. Remember that forever. . . .*

Thomas and Linda reached the garage. Along the way,
they found nothing to suggest that anyone had invaded their
house; neither did they find any clues indicating where Jason
had gone. Cold sweat had begun to soak Thomas's shirt. The
longer this disturbing ordeal lasted, the higher his anxiety
climbed.

He was grateful to have Linda beside him. The touch of
her warm hand on his arm gave him strength. He held up the
.38; she held up *him*.

She flicked on the garage light switch. Large fluorescent
tubes blazed into life.

The incessant clamor of rain, wind, and thunder echoed in
the large chamber.

Their cars, his Buick and her Nissan, sat seemingly undisturbed in their spaces. Shining a flashlight through the win-

dows, they checked inside each vehicle. Both of them were empty.

They got inside the Buick. Thomas removed the cellular telephone from the glove compartment.

"What's the plan if the phone doesn't work?" Linda said.

"It'll work. It isn't connected to the house lines."

"True. But what if it still doesn't work?"

He shrugged. "I don't know, I haven't thought about that. Why are you worried about things that won't happen?"

"I'm a writer, remember? Always wondering 'what if?' is second nature to me."

"Okay, well, try not to worry. Everything's gonna be fine. Let's take this one step at a time."

He pressed the phone's ON button. The green power light on the handset brightened.

"See?" he said. "We're in business. What's his buddy's number?"

She had written the phone numbers of Jason's friends on a slip of paper. She read one of them to Thomas. He punched in the digits and pushed SEND.

Before the line could ring once, the power indicator blinked out.

"No." He checked the battery, found it properly connected to the phone. Once more, he pushed ON. But the green button remained dark, and the handset issued only flat silence.

"This is nuts," he said. "How can it malfunction? It worked a second ago."

"Plug it up to the car's battery and see what happens." She handed him the device to connect the phone to the cigarette lighter.

He plugged in the cord. The cell phone still did not work. Fearing that the car battery might be dead, too, he twisted the key in the ignition. The Buick started.

"I don't get it." He shook his head. "It doesn't make any damned sense."

"I don't know what's wrong with these phones," she said. "But I say we stop wasting time trying to use them. Let's go to Darren's house. His place is closer than Mike's. We might find Jason there."

"Good idea." He shifted into reverse.

When they backed out of the garage, rain avalanched onto the car with a jarring crash, blurring the windows. Thomas clicked on the windshield wipers. But the wipers could not keep up with the frenetic rainfall.

Linda turned around in her seat, gaping. "This is incredible. Any minute now, we should see Noah's Ark."

"Tell me about it." He backed down the driveway and into the street. "I've never seen it rain like this."

She switched on the radio, presumably to muffle the roaring downpour. No noise came from the speakers. She raised the volume, changed from station to station. Nothing but silence.

Driving carefully, he said, "Something must be wrong with the communication systems around here. No phones, no radio, and probably no TV, either. A communications breakdown."

"How could that happen?" she said. "All of them operate independently of one another. They aren't gathered in a single building that could be blown up or something."

"I don't know what's going on. Maybe it's the storm, maybe it's an alien invasion, or maybe God got sick of our noise and decided to shut us up for a while. Linda, I have no idea, and I don't really care. I only want to get our boy."

"That makes two of us. Drive faster."

"I can't go any faster. These streets are like rivers. This isn't a powerboat."

Immense wings of water sprouted from the sides of the

Buick as it parted the churning lake that had flooded the road. Hard rain pummeled the car like a hail of bullets.

In no time, visibility had been reduced to zero. He drifted to the curb and parked.

"We can't drive in this," he said. "We have to wait until it calms down."

"Let me drive," she said.

"It's too dangerous. Your vision might be better than mine, but driving in this weather isn't safe. If we wait five or ten minutes, it'll probably have slackened off some."

"What if it doesn't?"

"Linda, please."

She grabbed his arm. "No, think about it, will you? *What if it doesn't?* We've got to have a plan. Jason's life might depend on how fast we act."

"Come on, we aren't in one of your books. You're getting carried away."

"Am I? Whose idea was it to bring the gun?"

Looking at her, seeing the determination on her beautiful face and the sharp intelligence in her eyes, made him remember why he loved her so much. She would not sit back and allow things to happen to her. She had to plan, initiate action. He never would have wished to change anything about her, but at that moment, when he felt confused and so worried he thought he might shit his pants, he wished she would just shut up.

"I brought an umbrella," she said, pointing at the black umbrella on the floor in front of her. "I spotted another one in the backseat."

"You want us to walk?"

"It's safer than driving blind. Considering the road conditions, we might travel faster by foot."

"How far away is Darren's house?"

"About half a mile. Maybe a little farther."

He looked out the windshield. In the deluge, he could

hardly see the front of the car, and the rain showed no signs of weakening. In fact, since they had left the house, it had stepped up its intensity.

"You win," he said. "We wait a few more minutes. If the weather doesn't improve, we'll start walking."

"Okay. I only hope that Jason, wherever he is, can afford to wait that long."

Brains was going on the run.

If, as he suspected, the Stranger could place psychic tags on intended victims just as a game warden could put electronic tracking devices on deer, by staying in the house he was making it far too easy for the Stranger to get a fix on his location and wipe him out. Leaving and keeping on the move might improve his chances for survival. Admittedly, it was a weak, unreliable plan, but he did not know what else he could do. He had decided that taking action of any kind was better than waiting to die.

Thunder bombed the night. Wind-driven rain lashed the house.

Because he would be moving fast and perhaps recklessly, Brains removed his eyeglasses and replaced them with his contact lenses, which he wore whenever he played sports. He went to the walk-in closet in his parents' bedroom and took out his father's raincoat. He pulled it on.

His dad owned a pair of galoshes that looked as if they would fit, too, but he opted to keep on his basketball shoes. He had to stay quick on his feet.

A big yellow flashlight stood atop the oak dresser. After verifying that it worked, Brains slid it into the raincoat pocket.

He opened the bedroom door, checked left and right. *Clear.* He eased outside and crept down the hall.

At the head of the stairs, he stopped. A sour smell made him cough. What was that?

Blackness swallowed the bottom of the staircase. He flicked the stairwell lamp switch.

A thick tower of ink-black smoke floated at the foot of the stairs. Slowly a figure took shape in the vapor—no, took shape *from* the vapor itself, as though the entity were some freak of nature.

The Stranger, he thought. *It has to be the Stranger.*

Brains raised the gun.

The man that formed from the smoke was lean, and tall enough to play power forward for the Bulls. He was dressed in a black tuxedo, top hat, bow tie, and shiny black shoes. In one frightfully large hand, he carried a black cane. A silky black cape billowed around him.

Was this really the Stranger? Was this the elusive entity that had terrorized them, the shape-changing beast that had murdered Mike and those kids? Was this really Jason's long-time friend and confidant?

If the answer to all of those questions was yes—and it had to be—then this wild adventure had taken a sharp turn into truly bizarre territory.

The man began to climb the stairs.

His hands trembling, Brains cocked the .45.

"Whoever you are, stop right there, or I'll shoot."

"I am Mr. Magic," the man said. His voice was deep, melodious. He ascended another step. "It's my pleasure to finally meet the great Brains." He chuckled.

Mr. Magic. *Jesus.* No wonder he was dressed like a stage magician. Brains would never have expected the Stranger to wind up being something like this. Not in a hundred years.

"Whoever you are, whatever you are," Brains said. "Stop, or I'll shoot!"

Mr. Magic only smiled. He spread his long arms. "Then fire away, Darren."

His voice was mellow, utterly calm. Water seemed to seep

into Brains's knees. Mr. Magic had transformed from a mass of smoke, for God's sake. Would a gun really harm him?

Mr. Magic took another step.

Brains sucked in a deep breath and squeezed off three smooth shots. The first two rounds hit the guy squarely in the chest. The third struck his shoulder.

But Mr. Magic did not bleed—did not so much as wince. Brains might as well have pelted him with feathers. *Damn*.

"My turn," Mr. Magic said, and flung his cane onto the steps. The cane mutated into something that looked like a black snake, but it had dozens of miniature legs, bulbous eyes, and wicked-looking fangs.

Whatever it was, it had never been described in Brains's science textbooks. Brains's eyes grew so large, he thought his contact lenses might pop out.

Like an angry cobra, the creature raised up and hissed, its hateful glare fixed on Brains. It raced up the stairs.

CHAPTER TWENTY-TWO

Propelled by dozens of small, shiny legs, the snake-creature scurried up the steps toward Brains.

Brains didn't try to hit the thing with a bullet. It was too damn fast. He turned and dashed to the nearest room, his bedroom.

Ice water gushed through his veins. The .45, his sole weapon, was basically useless. Jason had said that whatever you fantasized in Thunderland immediately became real, but Brains's mind pumped so quickly he could barely think, much less summon the concentration to imagine anything that might stop Mr. Magic. His only choice was to escape.

He heard the reptile-creature chasing after him, hissing, its legs pattering across the hardwood floor.

In the stairwell, Mr. Magic laughed.

Move, move, move.

Brains rushed inside his bedroom and slammed the door, locked it. Frantic, he looked around. He saw his bureau beside the door. He positioned himself beside it and shoved it hard, blocking the doorway.

The dresser obviously would not stop Mr. Magic, but it might buy Brains some time to run.

As Brains moved away from the makeshift barricade, the many-legged serpent darted from beneath the bureau. It was small enough to slither underneath the door.

Trying to run, Brains spun so wildly that he tripped over his own feet. He smashed against the floor. The gun popped out of his grasp.

Oh, you stupid klutz!

The snake-creature was quick to take advantage. It scrambled across the carpet and burrowed under the cuff of his jeans.

Brains screamed.

Hissing, the reptile-beast ran along his leg like a slick of warm oil, making his pant leg bulge. Pain suddenly stabbed his thigh.

Screaming, Brains hammered his fist against the knot in his jeans that had to be the creature's head. It hissed furiously, its body squirming, but it did not die. He felt its tiny legs squeezing against his thigh, as though trying to suck the blood out of him. It bit him again.

Growing dizzy with agony and revulsion, Brains rolled, snared the gun. He pounded the butt of the revolver against the reptile's skull, one-two-three-times, and finally heard a satisfying *crunch*.

Tears filling his eyes, he grabbed the foot of the bed and struggled to his feet. Dead, the serpent slid down his leg, its limp tail protruding from the cuff of his jeans. He snagged the end of its slimy body and yanked it out of his pants. Grimacing, he threw it across the room. The reptile-beast struck the wall . . . and when it hit the floor, it was a black cane once more.

Everything Brains had ever learned in school was useless. Book smarts didn't matter in Thunderland; the rules of biology didn't exist here. It was a world of strange, deadly magic.

Pure animal instinct alone would keep him alive. And instinct told him to haul ass.

"Are you and my little friend having fun in there?" Mr. Magic said from the hallway. He chuckled.

Brains hustled across the room to a window. Lightning flared, the ghostly incandescence casting his reflection on the glass and showing him a face that he scarcely recognized as his own. He looked nothing like the calm, self-assured young man he was accustomed to seeing in the mirror each day. He looked like a little kid who had seen the bogeyman.

Behind him, the doorknob rattled.

Hands shaking, he unlocked the window, pushed it up all the way. Icy raindrops slanted in through the screen, soaking his arms. He raised the screen as high as it would go. The opening gave him sufficient room to escape. Directly under the sill, latticework dropped to the sodden ground, glistening vines snaking over and under the wooden geometric web.

He slung one leg over the sill.

An explosion as loud as a thunderclap boomed through the room, and then the bureau lifted off the floor and hurtled toward him like an out-of-control truck, smithereens of the shattered door showering the carpet. He threw his other leg outside and clambered onto the latticework in time to avoid getting smashed. The dresser banged into the window frame, knocked away chips of wood, and fell onto its side, where it lay motionless.

Mr. Magic strolled through the ruined doorway, cape fluttering. He ambled casually, clearly in no hurry to attack Brains. His smug arrogance made Brains want to smash his face. This was only entertainment for him. Brains vowed that he would discover a way to gain an edge on Mr. Magic and survive.

But for now, he could only run. He began to climb down.

Rain battered his back and wind whipped his raincoat, but he managed to descend to the muddy, flooded backyard without a hitch. He sloshed forward a few steps, looked up to the window.

Backlit by the bedroom light, Mr. Magic gazed down at him. Because of the slanting rain, Brains could not discern the expression on his face, but he bet it was that stupid, arrogant grin.

He gave Mr. Magic the finger and ran.

Much to Linda's surprise, after a short while the rainfall slackened. It no longer bombarded the Buick with the frenzied vehemence that had made her wonder if Mother Nature had taken a hit of PCP. It had subsided to a persistent drizzle.

Rivers of water rushed into gutters, and debris drifted around the swampy streets like flotsam from a blasted warship. It would likely take hours for the roads to become suitable for driving, and she refused to wait for those ideal conditions. Flooded roads or not, they had to find Jason.

"Even though the rain's let up, we should walk to Darren's place," she said. "The streets are gonna be in bad shape for a long time."

"We can make it in the car," Thomas said. "We'll have to drive slowly."

"But it would take us forever to get to his house."

"I don't care. I don't want to walk. I've gotten a bad feeling about that idea."

"Why?"

"Because something isn't right about this place. You must have noticed it. For one, there's the thing with all the clocks stopping. Second, the phones and the radios being dead. Then, look at this storm. I don't know about you, but I've never seen it rain like this."

She nodded. He had voiced some of her same thoughts.

"There's another thing I noticed," she said. "Since we've left the house, we haven't seen a single person. This is Fourth of July night, Thomas. Even in the worst weather, someone should be out, driving, walking, or something. But look." She wiped away the condensation on the passenger window, which gave them a view of the outside world. Total darkness enveloped every house in sight. "The city looks abandoned."

"So what do you think is going on?" he said.

"In a nutshell? Some strange shit."

"Then we're on the same page. I don't know what's happening. For all we know, we could be in the Twilight Zone. I *do* know that I don't want to walk out in the open. I feel as if that would make us easy targets."

"Good point," she said. "Although I don't feel safe anywhere, inside this car included. If, like Jason thinks, we're in danger from some entity or spirit, it can probably reach us wherever we are."

"Listen to us." He laughed, shaking his head. "Both of us sound like we've gone off the deep end."

It was funny, in a way. They were adults living in a modern, well-ordered world, and they were discussing spirits and alternate dimensions as though they were members of some mystic sect. It would have been funnier to her if they had not been living this odd new reality.

The marital problems that she and Thomas had endured lately seemed remote, like the tribulations of characters on an old TV show. The sheer weirdness of what was going on, and their desperate need to find Jason, made everything else irrelevant. This situation was far more important than anything she'd ever faced in her life.

"All I really care about is finding Jason," Thomas said. "The car can take us to him faster."

"Agreed. Let's get moving."

He shifted the Buick into gear. They pulled away from the curb and rolled slowly into the submerged street.

Linda watched the houses that they passed. All of them were dark, eerily desolate. Thomas's fear of walking in the open seemed not only reasonable but wise. It was easy to believe that, if they set foot outside the car, something would snatch them and suck their lives away.

She shivered.

They reached Darren's house. Like all of the homes on the block, it was a well-kept, two-story contemporary model, complete with a big yard and a three-car garage. Like all of the others, it was dark, too. Her hope that they would find Jason there dimmed. She reminded herself to stay positive.

After they got out of the car, they stood beside each other on the wet lawn, glancing around warily. Thomas had drawn the .38, but she would not have felt safe even with the National Guard at her back.

A burst of lightning shattered the night into a million luminescent pieces. Thunder groaned, the ground trembling as though huge, subterranean creatures burrowed underneath the crust of the earth.

They sloshed across the sidewalk and climbed the porch steps. She pressed the doorbell.

Soft chimes rang within. But no one answered.

Thomas tested the knob of the heavy oak door. It turned. He gave the door a soft push. Sheer darkness greeted them. "Anyone home?" He poked his head inside the doorway.

No response.

"Are you here, Jason?" she said.

No answer.

Pushing the door open, they stepped inside. They methodically searched the house. It was tastefully furnished with upholstered furniture in earth tones, polished hardwood floors, lots of green plants, and several fine pieces of African-American art. Finding nothing of significance on the ground level, they ascended the staircase to the second floor. When they saw a nearby bedroom, they halted.

The door had literally been blown off the hinges. Slivers of wood, obviously from the ruined door, littered the carpet.

Deeper within the room, a bureau rested on its side beneath an open window. Rain drizzled inside.

"What happened in here?" Thomas said. He crunched across the rubbish, walked around the knocked-over dresser.

"It looks like there was a fight," she said. "Or a tornado touched down in here."

He surveyed the destruction. "I hope Jason wasn't around."

"I don't think he was," she said. "Call it motherly instinct, but I think someone else was involved. Probably Darren."

"Yeah, Darren . . . and the bad guy," Thomas said, examining a shard of wood.

The bad guy. The Stranger, as Jason had called him. As she viewed the chaos that had been wreaked in this room, the idea of such a dangerous personality did not seem far-fetched.

Chills overcame her. She hugged herself, trying to warm up.

Thomas dropped the sliver of wood. "I want to get out of here. There's nothing in here that helps us, and this place is starting to give me the creeps."

"Ditto," she said.

They left the house, closing the front door behind them.

"Where do you want to go next?" she said.

"His other buddy's crib. What's his name? Mike."

"What if no one's there?" she said.

"Then we go to the police station."

"What if no one's there, either?"

He put his arm around her as they walked back to the car.

"Then we start praying."

Brains ran as he had never run in his life. He ran through backyards, across alleys, over front yards and sidewalks. He splashed across flooded streets and tore across gardens, driveways, and patios. He climbed over fences and jumped over piles of trash. He had no destination in mind. His only goal was to run as far as his pumping heart would carry him.

As he ran, the rainfall ebbed, from a blinding shower to a drizzle. The wind, thunder, and lightning also abated, though they periodically declared themselves.

The night only grew darker.

Eventually, he eased into a jog. Then a brisk walk. Then he stopped.

He did not stop because he believed he had escaped Mr. Magic. In this fantastical realm, where Mr. Magic exercised godlike powers, escape was not a real possibility. He quit running because he needed to create a strategy. Unless he found a way to defeat Mr. Magic, his running would be wasted energy, and this would continue to be a lopsided game of cat-and-mouse.

He took stock of his surroundings. He was near Lewiston Avenue, a major road on the western edge of town. Every house and building looked deserted. Wounded from the beating the storm had administered, trees drooped, their broken branches littering the ground. A river of black water containing all kinds of debris streamed down the roadway, seeping into the gutters.

All in all, it was a scene that might have been painted by a landscape artist suffering from severe depression. He looked farther ahead. What he saw lifted his spirits.

Several hundred yards away, a covered pedestrian bridge spanned the width of Lewiston Avenue, in the same location that it occupied in the real world. It looked the same, too: suspended about twenty feet above the pavement; constructed of sturdy black steel, with girders and stiffening trusses; two sets of stairs, which allowed access to the walkway from either side of the street; a metal roof covering the center span. It was so identical in every detail to the real bridge that he would not have been surprised to see the same obscene graffiti imprinted on the girders.

In Thunderland, a sanctuary was too much to wish for, but the bridge was the next best thing. Once upon it, he would no longer have to run, which meant he could conserve his strength. He could survey the land from an elevated position, which would enable him to see anyone approaching before they reached him. Since flights of stairs were attached to both sides, he could not be cornered; when the need to flee arose, he could take the closest stairway to the ground.

His mind made up, he walked toward the bridge, grass squishing beneath his feet.

He came to the stairs. Raindrops glimmered like bits of silver on the steps and railing. At the top, tunnel-like darkness yawned.

He looked around. He was still alone.

He grabbed the cold railing. He climbed the stairs, his aching legs protesting at the effort.

On the walkway, a soft wind stirred about scraps of litter.

Drenched by perspiration and rain, the raincoat clung like a second skin to his body. He feared it would restrict his movements, so he removed the gun from the pocket and peeled off the coat. He dropped it to the floor.

At his house he had fired three rounds at Mr. Magic. He replaced the expended bullets with new ones.

Exhaling, he leaned against the railing. He was so tired; fatigue weighed heavily on his bones. If he survived, he would sleep twelve hours every day for a week recuperating.

Cool wind whistled down the passageway.

In the distance, thunder groaned.

The sound of footsteps drew his attention. Someone was climbing the stairs on his right, footfalls clanging softly on the metal steps.

He spun, raised the .45.

Darkness gathered at the end of the bridge. He was too far away to peer over the edge of the platform and identify who might be approaching.

Waiting, fresh sweat streaming down his face, he balanced his finger around the trigger.

A hat rose into view: a baseball cap that sported the Chicago White Sox logo.

It can't be, Brains thought. *No way.*

Mike Johnson, his cousin, hopped onto the bridge.

CHAPTER TWENTY-THREE

Brains did not lower the gun.

"Hey, man," Mike said. "What the hell are you doing up here? Put down the damn gun."

"You aren't Mike," Brains said. "My cousin is dead. I saw his body myself, in the real world."

"Dead? What?" He walked forward. "Man, I've been here for hours looking for you and Jason and dodging that crazy-assed Stranger. He's been chasing me all over the place. Where have you guys been?"

It sounded and looked like Mike. *Just like him.* He wore a Chicago White Sox cap, matching jersey, and shorts. Nike basketball shoes. Even a thin gold necklace with a small gold crucifix in the center. The resemblance to his cousin was perfect.

But it was not Mike. It couldn't be. Mike was dead, beyond all doubt. Brains had been present earlier that afternoon when his aunt and uncle had identified Mike's lifeless body.

"I know you're dead," Brains said numbly.

"What do you mean, I'm dead?" Distress lined his face. "How can I be dead in the real world but alive in this place? Tell me, Brains."

"I don't know," Brains said, realizing how little he really understood about Thunderland. Was it possible that Mike was alive in Thunderland but dead in the normal world? Could Mike be trapped in this alternate dimension?

What if I'm trapped here, too? Brains suddenly thought, and a crippling fear gripped his testicles.

"You don't know? Come on, man. You're smart."

"Not that smart." After the past few days, Brains didn't feel as though he knew a damn thing about anything. "None of this makes any sense to me. You look like Mike . . . but you can't be."

"Shit, man, you've lost it. Will you put down the gun? Stop aiming at me!"

Brains lowered the weapon. He wanted more than anything in the world for his cousin to be alive. Maybe this was Mike. He had admitted his inadequate knowledge of Thunderland. So why couldn't this be Mike? He was not going to blow away his own cousin based on an unproven assumption that this was really Mr. Magic.

"Thank God," Mike said, and blew out a whistle of air. He came forward. "Shit, you had me scared to death."

"Sorry," Brains said. "If you'd seen what I've seen here, you'd understand why I'm so jumpy."

"I understand quite perfectly, you gullible little fool," Mike said in a rich, sonorous voice that didn't fit him at all.

Terrible comprehension swept over Brains. He swung the gun upward, but he was too slow. The Mike-replica lunged forward and backhanded him across the face with superhuman force. Brains flew backward, the revolver tumbling out of his hand and spinning into the night. He crashed against the bridge floor, tiny white spots swarming in his vision. Intentionally he bit his tongue, and the sharp pain helped bring his vision back into focus. He did not dare lose consciousness.

"I expected a more intelligent response from you," Mr. Magic said, continuing to wear Mike's body. "The great Brains. You're a softhearted fool like the rest of your kind."

Brains spat out a tooth, blood streaming from his lips. His mouth ached. He had never been hit so hard in his life.

He might not have a chance in hell of defeating Mr. Magic, but he was not going to give up like a punk.

"You don't scare me," Brains said, though shakily. Sitting up, he gathered his courage: "You can kiss my ass. I'm not running from you anymore."

The Mike-replica laughed. "Such heroic words. I wish you could have heard your dear cousin's screams when I drove my automobile over his fragile body. Like you, he was quite a fighter. But in the end, he was weak, too."

Fury fell over Brains like a red hood. Screaming, he leaped up and charged the Mike-thing.

The blow came so quickly he didn't see it. One instant he was bearing down on the Mike-replica; the next, hurtling through the air. He slammed against the metallic floor, dizzy. Warm blood filled his mouth. Probably, he had lost another tooth.

Your arms is too short to box with God. In his delirium of pain, the phrase came to his mind, the title of a gospel play his parents had seen or something, and while he never would've regarded Mr. Magic as God, he was so overmatched in this fight that the expression was tragically apt. He strained to get up again and slipped, too weak, too beaten.

Grinning madly, the Mike-creature snagged Brains's ankles. Aware of what Mr. Magic planned to do, Brains kicked, fighting to free his legs. But he could not break the thing's powerful grip.

Mr. Magic took a step backward. He started to spin. Brains, sprawled on his back, started to spin, too. Around and around and around. The world blurred into grays, blacks, and violets.

In the midst of the spinning, Brains recalled when he was younger, when his big sister used to play with him by spinning him like this. It used to be so much fun, and he would laugh himself to tears when she finally released him and he flew across the yard like a pebble propelled by a slingshot. He wondered if he would ever see his sister again.

He did not see Mr. Magic let him go, for his world had revolved into a smudge of colors, but he felt the sudden release of his ankles. He felt himself flying in an immense, open space, and he realized that he had been cast not to another side of the bridge, but over the railing, to the hard street below.

Swiftly he plunged downward.

As he fell, he thought of Jason's advice about being in this place, which he had never bothered to apply: *what you imagine there becomes true.* Not wasting another moment, Brains imagined himself striking the flooded road and absorbing the impact without sustaining the slightest injury. He imagined himself hitting the water like a bath toy, splashing and bobbing to the surface. He saw *himself* as a giant bath toy, capable of falling twenty feet without suffering any harm. He saw himself living to tell about this event.

But the instant he collided with the earth, all he saw was darkness.

By the time Thomas parked in front of Mike Johnson's house, the water had, amazingly, almost completely run off the streets. Although he would have to exercise caution whenever braking or turning—the roads glimmered darkly, showing they were still wet—traveling at regular speeds was relatively safe. He appreciated the miracle that had caused this. In spite of the protection the Buick provided, driving slowly around this newly unfamiliar town had coated his forehead with cold sweat. He could easily imagine someone chasing after the crawling car, reaching it, and smashing a window and climbing inside.

He shut off the car. The engine ticked and pinged as it cooled.

"It looks deserted." Linda gazed out of the window at the Johnson residence. "Like every house we've seen."

He agreed. Curtains of darkness veiled the windows of the white two-story Colonial, and he did not see anyone moving either inside the house or around the yard.

"We have to check it out," he said. "We can't leave a single stone unturned."

She sighed. "I know. But I'm so worried about Jason and where he might be, I'm starting to feel sick."

"I feel the same way. But as far as I'm concerned, after all we've been through, we're destined to get through this and pull our family together again. We have to keep our hopes up."

"And our guards up."

"Right. Those, too."

She smiled a little, touched his face gently. She opened her door and got out. He followed.

A slow, cool drizzle, the kind that could go on for hours without a break, pattered to the earth. Gray-black clouds capped the sky.

As they walked on the path toward the house, the shriek of spinning tires pierced the night.

They spun in the direction of the noise.

A car whipped around a corner, a couple of blocks away. At that distance, Thomas could not ascertain many details—it appeared to be a large, dark sedan—but at once he recognized the feeling it gave him: fear.

He did not require a glimpse of the driver to understand why seeing the car had elicited that reaction from him.

Instinct told him everything. *This* was the bogeyman Jason had warned them about.

The skin at the nape of his neck tightened.

Headlights glaring, the vehicle—definitely a black sedan—roared forward.

Running was out of the question, and he did not like the idea of hiding in a nearby house or garage. Until they formed a plan, they needed to stay on the move. Sitting in one place was suicide.

He put a hand on Linda's shoulder. "Get back in the car."

She was an independent woman who did not take to being ordered around, but thank God, she did not protest or waste time asking questions. She hurried to the Buick. He followed closely behind her.

The black car was several hundred yards away. Closing fast.

She threw open the passenger's door and hustled behind the steering wheel. He got in, slammed the door.

She twisted the key in the ignition.

The Buick did not start.

"Shit!" Linda smacked the steering wheel, turned the key again. Nothing. The engine clicked uselessly.

Fresh sweat broke out on his face. Damn it, it figured that something like this would happen. They had stumbled into a nightmare, and in nightmares, things upon which you could ordinarily bet your life never worked when you most needed them.

Bright, urine-yellow light washed over them. He looked through the rear window, shielding his eyes with one hand to cut down on the glare. The sedan was a couple hundred yards behind, maybe closer, and it bore down on them faster than ever.

She gunned the engine again.

This time, it started.

The black car growled. Closer.

She mashed the accelerator, simultaneously wrestling the steering wheel to the right. The tires screamed against the slick pavement, and then the car shot forward like a kicked horse. Thomas snapped back in his seat. The Buick jumped over the curb and bounced onto the sidewalk.

Thomas twisted around in time to see the sedan speed across the spot they had occupied on the road, like a bull that had charged a matador and missed. They had been damned lucky. If they had moved a second later, they would have been crushed.

He strapped on his seat belt. The protection it offered might prove insufficient in a major collision, but it beat counting on luck to save the day again. Seeing what he had done, Linda engaged her safety harness, too.

The driver of the enemy car braked. The sedan skidded a few hundred feet, slid around in a complete circle, and stopped.

Linda cut the wheel to the left and hit the gas. They bumped over the curb and onto the road. She kept turning until they faced away from the black car, and nothing but the empty, dark avenue lay ahead of them. She tramped on the accelerator. The Buick scrambled for purchase on the wet blacktop, then exploded forward with such abruptness, it was a wonder neither of their necks snapped.

The town raced past in a murky blur.

He patted her shoulder. "Great driving. I couldn't have done better myself."

"Thanks." She glanced at the rearview mirror. "But it's not over. He's coming."

He checked for himself. Sure enough, the guy rolled after them, far behind yet gaining.

"You have any idea where we should go?" she said.

"Not the police station. I honestly doubt anyone's there."

"Me, too." She passed a stop sign without slowing. "We're on our own."

"How confident do you feel behind the wheel?"

She shot him a look. "I'm not a meek little housewife, Thomas. You don't have to take over."

"That's not what I meant. What I meant is, do you feel you can shake this guy?"

She sucked in a breath. "I can try."

"Good. Because that's what I want you to do—shake him. I don't see anything else we can do. If we can get him off our ass for a little while, we can hide out somewhere and cook up Plan B. What do you say?"

She flew past another stop sign. "It's a good idea. But we better start working on Plan B right away. I don't know what kind of car that guy has, but from the looks of it, it belongs at the Indy Five Hundred." She glanced worriedly in the rear-view mirror. "Look at him."

He did not have to look. The fact that the interior of the Buick was suddenly awash in urine-yellow light told him enough.

He unbuckled his seat belt. He took out the .38.

She saw what he was about to do. "What're you doing? Sit down."

"Don't worry." He pressed the button that rolled back the sunroof. "All I'm going to do is distract him with a few bullets, try to slow him down. Keep driving, and don't make any quick stops or turns without telling me first."

She opened her mouth, then shut it. From her expression, he knew she was not happy with his decision, but she would not fight him on it any longer.

He waited for her to hook around a corner. Then, gripping the .38 in both hands, he squeezed through the open sunroof. He planted his elbows on top of the car.

Cold rain and wind buffeted his face. The headlights of their pursuer's car nearly blinded him. He squinted, wishing he had a pair of sunglasses.

When his vision adjusted, he still could not make out any details of the driver. All he glimpsed was the shape of a head.

He focused the gun on the driver's side of the windshield. Praying that the Buick's motion and the wind would not throw him off target, he fired three rounds in rapid succession.

Golden sparks flared on the windshield, but the glass did not break—did not even fragment.

The Stranger, though he must have been aware of Thomas's attack, did not appear ruffled, either. His hateful sedan stayed on course, about twenty yards behind them.

Thomas swore. Not only did the bastard have bullet-proof glass; he was as fearless as a kamikaze pilot.

He aimed for one of the front tires.

Before he could fire, Linda touched his leg. "Hold on, Thomas!"

She swerved around a corner, tires squealing. He braced himself against one side of the roof. His stomach did sickeningly slow somersaults, and he feared the .38 would fly out of his hands, but when she completed the turn and straightened out the car, his nausea faded, and he had not lost the gun.

The black car careened around the corner. It locked onto them once more.

Focusing on a tire, he squeezed the trigger.

Sparks showered the front bumper. He had missed.

That came as no surprise. He had not visited a firing range in years. Hell, it was amazing that his first three shots had connected with the windshield. Under the circumstances, it would have been difficult for him to hit the side of a barn with a bazooka.

He aimed again, trying to ignore the punishing wind and bright headlights.

That time, the round ricocheted off the blacktop.

Undiscouraged, he loosed another shot.

The targeted tire ruptured with a *bang!*

He shouted triumphantly, almost losing the gun in his glee. The sedan drifted to the side, the blown-out wheel flapping. The gap between them quickly widened.

He slid back inside the car and refastened his seat belt.

"I hit one of the bastard's tires," he said to Linda. "He's falling behind like he's standing still."

She looked at the rearview mirror and smiled. "Thank God. I wouldn't have been able to stay ahead of him much longer. He was too fast."

"Keep the pedal to the metal. I want to get so far ahead of him it'll take him hours to find us."

"What makes you believe he could find us at all?"

"He found us before, he can do it again. We can't take anything for granted with him. Whoever he is, whatever he is."

The rear window exploded. Linda screamed, her hands flying off the steering wheel, and Thomas cried out and ducked down in his seat, though he had heard no gunfire. Fragments of tempered glass sprayed over them. Wind howled through the shattered window, sounding like the anguished wail of a hell-bound soul.

Cautiously, Thomas sat up, glass sliding off his back. Linda, bits of glass sparkling like Christmas glitter in her hair, had recaptured the steering wheel in time to prevent an accident. Blood glistened at the corner of her mouth.

"You're bleeding," he said.

She nodded. "I bit my tongue. But Thomas, how did he do that? I didn't hear gunfire."

"I guess he doesn't need a gun." He searched behind them.

The sedan was about a hundred yards away. The Stranger had used the moments during which they had been shocked by the exploding window to gain on them.

"I'll try to lose him again," she said. She hung a vicious left, onto Northern Road.

Halfway through the turn, two more explosions boomed.

Without looking, Thomas knew what had happened. The rear tires had been destroyed.

The Buick began to fishtail. Linda grappled with the steering wheel, straining to keep the car under control.

Stores, restaurants, and churches floated past, shrouded in foggy blackness that made them appear to be figments of a dream. The black car charged out of the rain, gaining fast.

"Go faster," he said.

"I'm trying." She had pinned the gas pedal against the floor, but the Buick puttered along at only forty-five miles per hour. Thomas heard flapping rubber and grinding wheel rims ringing out, sounding like ominous music.

The black car pulled alongside them.

Thomas tried to see the driver. But the tinted window was opaque.

He picked up the .38 off the floor. He aimed at the black glass.

The sedan lurched sideways, slamming into them. The gun popped out of his hands, and he knocked into Linda hard, causing her to lose hold of the steering wheel. The uncontrolled Buick cut across the street, bumped over the curb, and rolled into the parking lot of a gas station, heading toward the self-service pumps.

Frantically Linda hit the brake pedal, but too late. They smashed head-on into an island of gasoline pumps, splitting open deep ruptures in them, the front end of the car crumpling like an accordion. Thomas jerked forward, but the safety harness threw him back into the seat, preventing him from flying through the windshield. Linda, too, was saved by the seat belt.

With the recklessness of a drunk driver, the black car crashed into the pumps at a nearby island. Gasoline squirted out of the burst fuel dispensers and splashed onto the caved-in hood.

Gas also saturated the smoking Buick. The acrid odor brought tears to Thomas's eyes.

Linda forced open her door. "Come on! It's gonna explode!"

He went to open his door, but it would not budge. The collision with the stranger's sedan had mashed it out of shape, virtually fusing it to the car.

Linda had already escaped. She ducked back inside and grabbed his hands.

"Hurry," she said, pulling him out. Once he had got out of the wrecked vehicle, she wrapped her arm around his waist, he slung his arm over her shoulders, and they ran across the parking lot, away from the accident.

Boom!

A tidal wave of scorching heat shoved him forward. It pushed him faster than he could have ever managed to run—actually lifted him a few inches off his feet—and then drove both him and Linda to the hard, wet ground. The heat engulfing him was so intense, he barely felt the pain that flashed through his rattled body.

Lying there, he wondered if he was going to die. He wondered if he cared anymore.

Linda groaned. She crawled forward, away from the inferno.

He started to crawl, too.

They reached the damp grass in front of a hardware store. There, the air was merely warm, not hot, and it was possible to draw breaths without choking on any lung-searing fumes.

Breathing deeply, he savored the air as a dehydrated man might have savored fresh water.

He rolled onto his back. Through bleary eyes, he looked at the destruction they had fled.

It was worse than he expected. Rippling flames covered the gas station, the Buick, and the black car. Spires of smoke rose high into the stormy sky, and trails of burning gasoline spurted from the ruined pumps and sloped toward the street. As he watched, the flaming portico fell and crashed to the fire-blanketed concrete.

He was about to check on Linda when something in the conflagration caught his attention. A blob of black smoke, darker and thicker than the smoke that churned from the blaze, drifted out of the destruction. It rolled toward them.

Thomas sat up, wiping his eyes, desperately needing to clear his vision.

Beside him, her face smudged with dirt, Linda sat up, too.

The whirling pillar of sooty vapor dissipated . . . and a giant of a man miraculously appeared in its place. He wore a black tuxedo and a matching top hat. Like a stage magician on his way to an engagement in Las Vegas.

"I know I'm dreaming," Thomas said. "God in heaven, I've got to be dreaming."

Linda's mouth hung open, trapped in a silent scream.

The man walked right up to them, a black cape fluttering around him. He gracefully doffed his hat, and when he smiled, his teeth gleamed.

"At last, we meet," he said in a smooth, rich voice. "I assure you, my doomed friends, the pleasure is all mine."

CHAPTER TWENTY-FOUR

Jason. I want you to know that I'm proud of you. Remember that forever. . . .

Jason snapped awake to Granddad's voice echoing through his mind. He looked around, disoriented by a clattering, rhythmic noise and harsh yellow light. Shielding his eyes, he blinked slowly. When his vision adjusted, he saw that he was lying on the red vinyl seat of a fast-moving commuter train.

Granddad was not around. Jason must have heard his voice in a dream, though intuition led him to believe that something terrible had happened to his grandfather.

He sat up.

He was in a double-deck passenger car, the same kind he and Granddad often boarded when they traveled to Chicago. As far as he could see, he was the sole person on board. Darkness pressed at the big windows.

He checked his watch. The digits had stopped at 9:14.

He gasped. Nine-fourteen? When he had awakened in his bedroom after falling out of the tree, it had been about twenty minutes past three o'clock, and the watch digits had been frozen then, too.

Above his wrist he noticed two faint puncture wounds. He remembered—Mr. Magic's loathsome cane-creature had bitten him. Its venom must have knocked him out.

Apparently, after he blacked out, Mr. Magic had allowed him to sleep for several hours in the real world, and then he had returned him to Thunderland, at 9:14 that night.

But why?

When he tried to stand, his legs buckled, and he grabbed the back of the seat to keep from falling.

Once he regained his balance, he walked to one end of the car. He looked out the window. Tall trees lined the tracks, and railroad cross ties vanished beneath the swiftly advancing coach.

He noted that there was no door at his end. There was only the window. There were no doors on the sides of the car, either; the only door was located at the other end, and it appeared to lead into another passenger car.

He walked down there and slipped into the next compartment. It was as deserted and well lighted as the first car, and it also lacked any side exits. The only exit led to a third compartment.

The third car was identical to the first two, except there was no doorway at the end, and no window. He put his ear against the cool wall where the door should have been. He heard the locomotive—or something that sounded like an engine—humming, whirring, and clicking.

He returned to the first coach. He gazed out of the portal that overlooked the railroad. He guessed that the train was traveling around sixty miles per hour, maybe faster.

Why had Mr. Magic put him on it?

* * *

No matter what else she faced in the rest of her life, Linda knew she would never face anything that could compare with this night. Her perceptions of reality had been turned upside down and inside out. She had progressed beyond the denial stage, but it might be years before she could put this in perspective—if she lived that long.

She and Thomas were in the passenger coach of a speeding commuter train, in one of three double-deck cars coupled with the locomotive. Weary to the bone, still shocked to a degree, she had resigned herself to sitting on the vinyl seat near the front window. Thomas, however, paced the aisle, grumbling to himself, sometimes smacking the seats he passed. Like her, his face was streaked with dirt, his pants were soiled and torn, and his shirt was ripped in several places. Unlike her, he had not calmed down.

While they lay on the ground after crawling away from the burning gas station, Jason's bogeyman, who identified himself as Mr. Magic, had thrown his massive cape over them. When he snatched it away only a second later, they found themselves magically transported to the train.

The appearance of the entity and the instantaneous teleportation, by themselves, were enough to push Linda to the brink of her sanity. But there was more: addressing them in the train with the patient manner of a teacher, Mr. Magic claimed responsibility for the mysterious, disturbing calls and visits that she and Thomas had recently received; he had given Jason the bike; and he had fulfilled "more of Jason's secret wishes" as he put it. He was engaged on a zealous mission to win her son's loyalty, and she and Thomas were merely pawns in his game, toys for his amusement.

His fantastic story would've made Linda cackle until her throat bled if she hadn't understood that everything he said, every inconceivable detail, was true. She had seen plenty of proof. She didn't *want* to see or hear anything else, didn't want to spin theories on how any of this was possible. Her brain was ready to shut down.

Thomas continued to pace, grumbling.

"Thomas, please sit down."

"Hell, no." He glared at her. "We won't get out of this by sitting on our asses. We have to move, act, fight. You're not a passive woman. You should know better than to tell me to sit at a time like this."

"We've tried everything," she said. "There aren't any exits, the windows won't break, and we don't have the gun anymore. What else can we do?"

He crossed his big arms over his chest. "You're the writer. You tell me."

"We do what that thing told us to do: we wait and leave it up to Jason."

"To hell with that shit. He wants us to sit here and wait for the train to smash us to bits. Shit, there might not be another train coming down the tracks. He could have said that to scare us."

"You know he was telling the truth. Thomas, it's out of our hands. What happens to us depends on Jason and what he chooses."

For a moment, Thomas looked as though he would continue the argument, and then his shoulders sagged. He plopped down next to her and dragged his hand down his grimy face. "That's what scares me. I'm not sure the boy's gonna make the best decision."

"He will. Have some faith in him."

Thomas seemed doubtful.

"He has to," she said. "He's distant, but he doesn't hate us."

Thomas turned away from her.

She wanted to grab him and shake him, scream at him that their son was not a murderer and that, on some level, he loved them and would make the choice that would save their lives; but she did not grab Thomas, did not touch him. Because she did not know whether she believed everything she wanted to say.

Jason spun at the sound of an opening door.

"Ah, you are awake." Mr. Magic strolled into the coach. "How was your sleep? Refreshing, I hope?"

Jason had no patience for Mr. Magic's silly mannerisms. "Why did you put me on this thing?"

Mr. Magic wrapped one thin hand around a shiny support beam and rested his other hand on his cane. The cane did not transform into the creepy snake-centipede beast. It was a normal stick.

"I placed you upon this train because I believe in free will," Mr. Magic said.

"You call throwing me on here and trapping me inside giving me free will?"

"You misunderstand me," Mr. Magic said. "Admittedly, thus far, I have not granted you much choice in these matters. But that is about to change."

"How's that?" Jason said. "You're gonna let me choose if I want to die by stabbing or a bullet in the head?"

Mr. Magic chuckled. "You have quite a macabre imagination, my friend. No, the choice I am presenting to you is much easier. It is also infinitely more appealing, if I do say so myself."

"Go ahead," Jason said. He did not expect Mr. Magic to give him a choice he would want to consider, but if he could delay the inevitable battle by listening to him, he would. "I'm all ears."

"Good." Mr. Magic leaned leisurely against the handrail. "You have been unaware of this, but another train is traveling on these same tracks. On it are your mother and your father. As you are, they are trapped inside. Obviously, there are no engineers or other such people here to control the rails. Therefore, this train and your parents' will soon collide, ensuring the deaths of all aboard. Excluding myself, of course."

Jason stared at him, skeptical. But when Mr. Magic returned his stare forthrightly, Jason knew he had told the truth. Further, the comic-book-style disaster he described was typical of him. From the beginning, Mr. Magic had exhibited a flair for melodrama: the over-the-top action, the sensational event. His decision to use colliding trains as the climax of this mad adventure matched his style.

Jason went to the window. He saw only giant trees ranked along the tracks. If the other locomotive really thundered toward them, it was not close yet.

"Do not despair; all is not lost," Mr. Magic said. "You are being given a choice, remember? Here is my offer: you can choose to remain on this coach and perish in a dreadful accident. Or you can join me and, by doing so, save your own life and the lives of your parents."

"No way," Jason said. "Even if I joined you, you wouldn't save them."

Mr. Magic raised his hand. "I give you my word, Jason. Do you realize how many opportunities I've had to murder your parents? Originally, my plan was to destroy them, but I've had a change of heart. I believe their fate is best left in your hands. I promise: you join me, and they will be spared."

"What if you're lying?" Jason said. "You might have killed everyone already and be saying this only to trick me into giving in."

"Quite simply, you must trust me, Jason. Are you willing to bet your own life and your parents' lives on the nonexistent possibility that I am being deceitful?"

Jason did not answer. Mr. Magic had him beat on that score. He was not sure that Mr. Magic was being honest, but he was not going to wager anyone's life on the chance that he was lying.

"I did not think so," Mr. Magic said. "Now, what is your decision? Eternal life with me? Or death with your family?"

Jason chewed his lip, thinking of a ploy to stall Mr. Magic. But all he could think of saying was, "I need time to think about it."

"Nonsense." Mr. Magic waved his hand dismissively. "The answer is obvious. You're an intelligent boy; you should know the sensible choice." He walked toward Jason. "Consider this, Jason: What have your parents ever done for you? For almost all of your life, they've ignored you, neglected you, broken promises they've made to you, beat you, cursed you, in nearly every imaginable fashion have clearly shown that they don't care about you and, least of all, love you. Haven't they? Yes, they have. By their heartless acts, they forced you to withdraw into your bedroom, into books, into music, into yourself, into *me*. Yes, me. I exist because of your parents' abandonment of you. You created me, and I made your private hell bearable. I gave you laughter, joy, excitement, *acceptance*. Even when you grew older, when you reached the age at which most children cast away imaginary playmates, you stayed with me, didn't you? You stayed with me because I was your true friend. Because I would make you happy when no one else cared to try. Because I was always there for you. Because I *loved* you. I have said this before, Jason, and I shall say it once more: we are part of each other, inseparable; the link we share is unbreakable. If you turn your back on me, you will, in effect, be turning your back on your own soul."

When Mr. Magic finished speaking, he was standing only a couple of feet away from Jason. Jason took a step backward.

Mr. Magic smiled. He extended his hand.

"Will you join me, my friend?"

Jason gazed into Mr. Magic's eyes. He looked down at his open palm.

Although Mr. Magic had spoken truthfully about their past relationship, he had no problem making his choice.

He spat in Mr. Magic's hand. "Go fuck yourself."

For a seemingly timeless moment, Mr. Magic stared at him.

Then he slowly squeezed his extended hand into a fist.

"Very well, Jason." His lips tightened. "You've made your decision, and you will accept the consequences."

He snapped his long fingers.

The lights went out.

And Mr. Magic began to change.

Thomas was pacing again.

This time, he did not pace out of a restless urge to hatch a plan that would break them out of their bind. He had accepted that escape was impossible. Instead, he paced out of worry for their son.

"Jesus, I hope he does the right thing," he said, more to himself than to Linda, who still sat, head buried in her hands. "If I could only talk to him, let him know how I feel about him, how sorry I am for how I've treated him, I would be okay. This waiting is killing me."

"Your worrying is killing me," Linda said. She rose up. "Please, calm down. Everything is going to be fine."

"Is it?" he said.

"Yes, it is. I know Jason. Like I told you before, he's a good kid. He's just distant, and considering the terrible upbringing we've given him, that's to be expected."

"I don't know, Linda. At the cookout, he treated us like we were strangers."

"That's only because he had a lot on his mind," she said. "You've seen this Mr. Magic character. Can you blame Jason for being preoccupied?"

"No, of course not. But I wonder if it's as simple as you make it out to be."

She sighed. "Look, Thomas. Jason will not—"

The lights went out.

Linda did not finish her sentence. Judging from her abrupt silence, she had probably fallen mute with shock. Thomas walked toward her, moving cautiously in the darkness. He sat next to her. They held each other close. He hoped he was wrong, but the dying lights gave him the terrifying feeling that Jason had made a bad decision—the worst decision, the deadliest decision.

Mr. Magic was changing.

An eerie silver luminescence throbbed in the passenger car—not sufficiently brilliant to sting Jason's eyes, but bright enough to illuminate clearly the metamorphosing Mr. Magic. Jason had backed up to the window. He knew he should look away, climb the stairs to the upper deck, and run like hell, but he could not. Terror forced him to stand motionless and watch raptly.

The transformation started with Mr. Magic's eyes. As though his pupils were candlewicks, sapphire blue flames flickered into life in both sockets, blazing like the fiery eyes of a jack-o'-lantern. Then, as if affected by the same mysterious fire that had consumed his eyes, his face began to melt. It grew oily, elastic, as though his skin were mere rubber; and even as it sagged to the extent that Jason feared it would tear loose from the neck and plop into the aisle, it started to bulge, pulsate, and shift, all the while those malevolent blue eyes remaining intact and fixed on Jason. They pinned him under their unearthly gaze and dared him to turn and run.

The weird silver light continued to throb. Jason's heart seemed to boom in unison with it.

The mutation quickly reshaped Mr. Magic's familiar features. His nose and jaws stretched and swelled as though inflated with air, transforming into a long, crocodilian snout, replete with row upon row of sharp, shiny teeth. Big, wickedly pointed horns sprouted like obscene plants out of the top of his skull, tearing apart the top hat. His ears extended themselves several inches, the tips narrowing so that they appeared as sharply pointed as the horns. A forked, speckled tongue slithered from between his green-black lips and licked at the air.

Jason realized that he had climbed halfway up the steps leading to the upper deck. He did not remember moving.

The rest of Mr. Magic's body had joined in the transformation. He shook violently, arms twitching, legs jerking, his tuxedo shuddering as though whipped about by a gale. Then, much as his face had done, his clothes grew waxlike; they dissolved like oil into his trembling flesh, and his body started to writhe, pulse, and grow. His arms grew until they were twice their normal length. His hands stretched and curved into claws. His legs swelled as thick as tree trunks, and his feet increased in size, simultaneously becoming webbed. His expanding torso seemed to *explode* with muscles, and his shoulders broadened much wider than any football linebacker's.

A long, ropy tail, the needle tip curled like a scorpion's sting, quested around his ankles.

His skin was no longer brown and smooth. Horny, black-green scales covered his entire monstrous body. With each rhythmic pulse of the strange silver light, the scales shimmered.

Although Jason was morbidly fascinated by Mr. Magic's change into this new form, he was not surprised that he had re-created himself into such a creature. The day he had left that message in Jason's bathroom, initiating the campaign of terror that had engulfed Jason and his friends, he ceased being the gentle imaginary playmate of old. He had become a monster, and since he had nothing left to hide, no further need to curry Jason's favor, it was only appropriate that he finally reveal his true self.

Throughout the last half of Mr. Magic's metamorphosis, Jason had ascended the remaining stairs and emerged on the top deck. He lowered into a hunch. Stealthily, he crawled down the aisle, heading toward the other end of the coach. He intended to get out of this compartment and slip into the next car, not because there was anything in there that might help him, but because, if he could delay a confrontation by putting as much distance as possible between them, he might be able to think of a way out of this.

The beast's massive head turned. The glowing eyes found him.

"Jason," it said in a deep, guttural voice that reflected not kindness but intense, inhuman hate.

Jason did not answer or look back. He broke into a run.

The creature roared, the noise rattling the thick windows. It came after him.

Clackety-clack, clackety-clack, clackety-clack . . .

That mind-numbingly repetitive sound was like a drumbeat of doom to Linda. She had not given up on Jason. He was her son, her baby, and she would continue to give him the benefit of the doubt until she was dead . . . but the extinguishing of the lights seemed to hint at ominous tidings.

Thomas had left her side. He stood at the window, face pressed against the glass. He had not spoken for several minutes. His silence distressed her more so than the relentless noises of the train.

"Do you see it?" she said, not sure she wanted to know the answer, only needing to break the silence.

He did not respond.

"I said, do you see it?"

Again he did not answer.

Fearing what she might see, she got up and went to the window. Thomas edged aside, giving her room. She gazed out into the night.

Far away, visible as little more than a speck in the darkness, a light twinkled. She had no idea how long it would be before that other train reached them, but as she watched, the light grew—ever so slowly—brighter. Closer.

CHAPTER TWENTY-FIVE

The beast was coming.

Jason sprinted down the aisle of the upper deck. He reached the stairs, jumped, and landed so hard on the bottom that stakes of pain shot through his knees. Not daring to look back, he threw open the door leading to the next coach and staggered through.

The creature shrieked.

Jason glanced behind him in time to see the beast's needle-like tail whip forward and strike the door's window. The glass shattered, and he shielded his eyes in order to avoid being blinded by the flying shards. He ran into the second car.

Halfway through the compartment, he stopped running. He realized that if he was going to have any chance of defeating this monster, he would have to fight back. Simply putting distance between them would not resolve anything. It would only postpone his certain death. He had to take a stand.

The beast slowly pushed through the door.

He bent, pulled up the leg of his jeans.

Thank God, the .22 gleamed in the ankle holster.

He withdrew the handgun. He gripped it as Brains had taught him, positioning himself in the shooter's stance. Although he understood the importance of taking a stand, his hands trembled so badly, he feared every shot he fired would miss the mark.

Hissing, the creature emerged in the car. Its sapphire blue eyes burned like molten jewels, saliva glistening on its rows of crocodilian teeth. The thick tail snaked back and forth between its legs.

He squeezed the trigger one-two-three times, the gun's report loud in the coach, rounds hitting the monster's scale-covered chest with heavy thuds. Three tiny wounds appeared, but they neither gushed blood nor seemed to injure the beast. It strode forward without missing a step.

He backed up. Panic tugged at him, and he fought to maintain control of himself.

When his back met the door, he fired three more rounds.

Only two of them made contact. One struck the beast's shoulder; the other grazed its neck. Neither harmed it at all.

Knowing it was useless, he pulled the trigger again. The gun clicked. No more bullets.

The creature roared triumphantly. It charged forward, teeth bared.

Jason spun and rushed through the door behind him, into the last car. He climbed the stairs to the upper deck.

The creature stalked through the door. Its claws flexed eagerly.

Jason moved backward along the aisle, one hand sliding on the railing. The beast's head snapped in his direction. It charged forward and grabbed the metal railing in its claws. With a mighty jerk, it tore the barrier out of the wall. Steel shrieked. Screws popped loose. Jason tumbled forward with the railing, and the beast buckled and fell, too. It dropped backward and crashed into the lower-deck seats. The monster broke Jason's fall; he landed on its scale-armored chest, the rail the only thing separating them.

Terror and revulsion flooded through him.

The beast's forked, speckled tongue fluttered near his face. It hissed.

Its eyes glowed. The fall had taken the creature by surprise, but judging from its bright eyes, it had not been wounded.

He remembered the gun in his hand. He brought it up high, and jammed the muzzle into one of those burning eyes.

The beast screeched. It thrashed beneath him.

He twisted the pistol around in the socket. Acrid black smoke seethed from the wound, making him want to gag, but he gritted his teeth and continued to attack. He ground the gun deep, determined to reach the thing's brain and squash it into mush.

The creature howled, squirming furiously.

He forced the .22 down into the skull. *Die, you asshole. Die, die, die, die—*

Something whacked against his head.

Crying out, he rolled off the creature's chest and onto the floor. He groaned. He rubbed his throbbing head.

Through teary eyes, he saw the monster's tail, dancing about like a charmed cobra. So that was what had hit him.

He got up, using a seat to balance himself. Nausea quivered through him. He choked it down with a great effort.

The creature was pushing the railing off.

He saw that the eye he had pummeled had already repaired itself. It shone wickedly, mockingly.

He wanted to cry. He had tried everything, and nothing had worked. The bastard was invincible. What else could he do?

The monster shoved off the railing. It began to sit up. He looked to the door.

There was one last thing he could do, though it would not do any good.

Run.

Thomas and Linda stood side by side at the window.

Thomas found it hard to accept that everything he had worked for in his life had come down to this. He was no saint, but surely he deserved better. And if he did not, didn't Linda merit a better end?

He could not answer those questions himself. But the way things were going, he would get the opportunity to hear God answer them soon.

The light of the oncoming train was faint, but it would be brighter than he would ever want in a minute or so.

He glanced at Linda. She watched the approaching train, her lips moving continuously, as though she were talking to herself. He listened closely. He realized she was praying.

He looked at the steadily brightening light.

He began to pray, too.

Panting, glancing over his shoulder every few steps, Jason burst into the last passenger car.

He looked around wildly, wondering where he should hide, wondering if there was any point in hiding. He heard the beast bellowing, drowning out the *clackety-clack* of the train. It sounded as though it had entered the second coach. Within a minute, it would overtake him, and this battle would be over.

He wished he had saved the last round in the .22. If he had kept it, he would not be debating with himself. He would have resolved his present concerns with a simple bullet in the head.

The creature thundered. Closer.

He retreated to the front of the compartment.

Remembering the train his parents were on, he put his face against the glass. He could make out a yellow light, distant but gradually growing brighter.

He had hoped the trains would collide before the monster killed him. But it seemed that both disasters might occur at the same instant.

He heard a pitiful, whimpering sound. He realized the noise came from him.

There was nothing to do, nowhere left to run. He had tried everything. Everything had failed.

A thin fluid ran into the corner of his eye. Thinking it was sweat, he wiped away the substance. But when he caught sight of his hand, he saw blood on his fingers. He had probably got the injury when that bastard had popped him. . . .

His eyes widened.

With the edge of his shirt, he quickly cleaned away the blood. He raised his hand to his face.

Black-green scales covered his hand.

Horrified, he turned over his hand. His palm was normal. Only the back of his hand, the area between his wrist and his knuckles, bore the scales. A small patch of repulsive malignancy.

Screwing up his courage, he touched a scale. It felt hard, like bone. He wriggled his fingers. Oddly, he could not feel the scales on his skin, could not feel any additional heaviness. His hand felt normal, as if it had been like this for his entire life.

But it had not been like this for his entire life. The transformation must have taken place recently. When Mr. Magic had metamorphosed . . .

Jason's heart knocked as understanding settled over him.

I have said this before, Jason, and I shall say it once more: We are part of each other, inseparable; the link we share is unbreakable. If you turn your back on me, you will, in effect, be turning your back on your own soul.

He examined his hand.

We are part of each other, inseparable; the link we share is unbreakable.

He looked at his hand again.

If anything proved the truth of Mr. Magic's words, those scales did. The beast into which Mr. Magic had mutated wore the same shiny, two-toned armor. Which meant that, to a minuscule degree, Mr. Magic's transformation into that creature had occurred within Jason, too. It was due to the mysterious link they shared.

If Mr. Magic could indirectly cause changes to Jason's body, it was logical to assume that Jason could cause changes to Mr. Magic's body, too.

He wondered why he had not thought of it before. It was simple; it made sense. *He* had created Mr. Magic. He had formed Mr. Magic from the stuff of his own imagination. He, Jason, had breathed life into him and set him loose in the world of daydreams. He was, in truth, a god compared to him. He could do whatever he wanted to Mr. Magic. He could wipe him out of existence. Just as he had brought him to life.

All he needed to do was use the proper weapon. Not a gun or a knife—his own imagination. The means he had used to create Mr. Magic could be the tool he could use to destroy him.

No sooner had he reached the conclusion than the beast shoved aside the door. It growled. When it saw Jason, its sapphire blue eyes blazed with triumph.

"No escape," it said in a voice that was half snarl, half gurgle.

Jason did not run, did not turn away.

The creature rumbled forward, roaring.

Jason raised his hands so that the palms faced outward. He drew a deep breath.

Then, he *imagined*.

Shards of electric-blue energy crackled from his palms and struck the beast.

The creature howled and staggered to a standstill. Its glowing eyes, though filled with agony, seemed surprised.

Jason knew then, for certain, that he had uncovered the key to obliterating this entity. The creature had not counted on Jason's ever discovering how to hurt it. Clearly, it was astonished.

But it refused to accept defeat. It charged Jason, as though it could rip him apart before he managed to destroy it.

Jason steadied himself and concentrated. Bolts of blue energy erupted from his palms and enveloped the beast in a fiery web. The monster stumbled backward, roaring in pain, black smoke steaming from its cracked scales. Shrieking, it spun around and whipped its wickedly pointed tail toward him.

Jason shot a sphere of blue fire at the flying tail, blowing it in half in midair. A jet of yellow fluid spurted from the ruptured appendage, and the curled sting dropped to the floor, reflexively jabbing the air like a dying wasp.

The monster grumbled, wounded but not dead. Its severed tail lay useless at its feet, liquid seeping from the ragged end. A horrible stench invaded the air.

"It's over," Jason said. "You never did have the real power. You're the one who forgot what our relationship was really all about. *I* created you. Now I'm going to destroy you. Forever."

The monster screeched defiantly. It gathered itself for one final attack.

Jason raised his hands.

The creature charged forward.

A giant orb of brilliant white light exploded from Jason's palms. As the energy consumed the beast, earth-splitting thunder boomed, and an invisible force hurled Jason backward . . . away from the disintegrating creature, out of the train, out of Thunderland, and into a realm of perfect darkness.

Linda recited prayers that she did not know she had learned. Although she believed in God, she had never been a churchgoing woman, and she was surprised by how coming face-to-face with death could generate a powerful yearning for God's grace.

She clearly saw the light of the advancing train. It was less than a mile away. A locomotive of death.

By unspoken agreement, she and Thomas moved closer to each other. She found his hand, and he squeezed hers tightly.

There was no need to say anything, no need to reaffirm their love for each other. She could feel his love for her in the heat of his body, and she was certain he could feel her love for him, too. She had forgiven him for the wrongs he'd done. Holding on to bitterness and anger while teetering on the brink of death was impossible and pointless. She had never felt closer to her husband.

She only wished she could have held Jason one more time, to tell him she loved him and that she was sorry for everything—every terrible, foolish mistake she had made. She would've traded her life for one more chance to see him.

But the train was only a half-mile away.

Their coach began to rock.

Clackety-clack, clackety-clack, clackety-clack . . .

A few hundred yards away.

"Close your eyes, sweetheart," Thomas said.

She did as he said. In her final glimpse of the train, it seemed close enough to spit on.

Clackety-clack, clackety-clack, clackety-clack . . .

Lord, please forgive my transgressions. I know I have not lived a perfect life, that I have not lived in complete harmony with your laws. But I beg you to have mercy on me—

There was an explosion of brilliant white light, so searingly bright that Linda saw it even though her eyes were closed. She heard herself scream.

Suddenly, darkness and silence.

She was afraid to look around. She thought she might be in hell or, worse, in a black void in which she would float for eternity. She felt someone shaking her. She heard Thomas's voice.

"Sweet Jesus, baby. Look, look!"

She opened her eyes.

She was sitting in the Buick. Thomas was behind the steering wheel, and they were parked in the driveway of their house. In front of them, the automatic garage door had just finished opening. The night was clear and dry.

She looked down at herself. She did not have a single bruise or scrape, and her clothes were clean, as if she had merely been asleep for the past hour, not battling for survival. Thomas, too, appeared physically unaffected by what had happened.

Incredible. But what was most amazing of all was that they were alive.

She checked her watch. It read 9:14, but the second hand was not frozen; it swept around the dial at regular speed.

Giggling like a kid, Thomas switched on the radio. Luther Vandross sang "The Power of Love."

Both of them looked at each other. They laughed.

"How?" she said. "How did this happen?"

"I don't know," he said. "But I'm guessing that Jason had something to do with it."

"You think he's okay?"

"Let's go see." He drove the Buick into the garage. As he shut off the car, the door that connected the garage to the backyard opened. Looking weary, yet triumphant, Jason walked through the doorway.

Brains awoke in his bedroom.

Slowly he sat up in bed. The family photo album lay beside him, closed. He stared at it as he might have stared at an ancient artifact. He wondered who had placed it there, and why.

When he picked up the album and opened it, his memory of everything that had happened returned. He remembered shooting at Mr. Magic in the house and escaping by climbing through a window. Running for miles. Fighting Mr. Magic on the bridge. Mr. Magic hurling him over the railing. Falling, falling, falling . . . and imagining himself surviving the impact.

Imagining himself surviving the impact.

Excited, he leaped to his feet. He read his watch.

The digits had switched to 9:15.

He dashed out of the bedroom and ran outside.

Across town, colorful fireworks exploded in the clear night sky.

Giddy laughter overcame him. He sat on the veranda bench, rocked with giggles. He probably sounded like someone who had lost his mind, but he didn't care. He had been saved. By a miracle. Even if he laughed until tomorrow morning, that wouldn't express his sudden, profound happiness to be alive.

Sore and weary to the marrow, Jason shuffled toward his dad's car. Mom and Dad, looking nearly as exhausted as he was, got out of the Buick.

Jason stopped.

Pressed close together, Mom and Dad stopped, too.

Jason looked at them. They looked back at him.

Silence hung between them.

Dad said, "We made it, thanks to you, son. You saved all of us. How in God's name did you do it?"

"It doesn't matter," Jason said. "It's over. I don't want to dwell on the past. I want to let it go."

"Do you mean it?" Mom said. "Do you really want to release the past?"

He knew what she meant. Did he want to release the bitterness he held toward her and Dad? Did he want to grow beyond the painful memories? Did he want to take a chance and work toward building a better future with his family?

Mom and Dad watched him, their faces unsure.

But after the past several days, after a ghost from the past named Mr. Magic had torn down his old world of self-limiting beliefs and forced him to build a new world based on a fresh awareness of the limitless possibilities life offered—if only he dared to imagine them—Jason was certain of his answer.

"Yes, Mom, I do want to release the past," he said, and felt that, by saying those words, he had taken the first step toward a new, brighter future. "I really do."

He rushed into their arms and hugged them. They held one other for a long time.

In the hours after they escaped Thunderland, Jason discovered who had survived . . . and who had died.

Brains had lived. He related to Jason an incredible account of his battle with Mr. Magic, and his miraculous survival. Jason was simply relieved that his friend was still with him.

Michelle, Jason's girlfriend, was unharmed. She was visiting relatives in Atlanta and had no knowledge of what had happened, and once Jason confirmed that she was okay, he didn't tell her any details. Perhaps Mr. Magic had spared her because she was away.

Granddad was dead. They found his body on the patio of his house, slumped in a chair, a warm Heineken and a bag of peanuts sitting on the nearby table.

The paramedics stated that Granddad had likely died of a heart attack. Jason and his parents understood the true cause of Granddad's death. The incidents of that night would haunt them forever.

Granddad. Dead. When Mom found out, shock literally knocked her off her feet; Dad caught her and held her in his arms. Jason walked around numbly, feeling as though a vital organ had been ripped out of him. Oddly, he did not cry, though he expected that he should; he wondered if there was something wrong with him because he did not weep. Later, when Mom held him close and assured him that everyone grieved in his own way, and that he should allow himself to react in whatever fashion felt natural, the wisdom of her words settled over him. He found himself thinking of all the joyous times he had spent with Granddad, and he thought, over and over, of Granddad's words that had come to him earlier, as if in a dream:

Jason. I want you to know that I'm proud of you. Remember that forever. . . .

Had Granddad sent him a final encouraging message before he left this world? Jason chose to believe that he had, and it warmed his heart.

He was going to miss Granddad so much. He would miss Shorty, too. He regretted that Blake and his friends had died. All of those people had touched his life, for better or worse. Although he partly wanted to blame himself for everything that had happened, to shoulder such a responsibility would prevent him from ever having any peace.

He would be wise to release the guilt and move on.

CHAPTER TWENTY-SIX

Two years later, Linda gave birth to a child. Another boy. They named him Nathan. He was a healthy, beautiful baby. Although Linda's latest novel hit the bestseller lists and launched her career into the stratosphere, she was happy to take a break from her work and rediscover the joys of motherhood.

Much to his father's chagrin, Thomas sold The House of Soul for a substantial sum and pursued his dream to become an architect. A couple of years into his college studies, an internship led to a lucrative job offer from a leading firm. His talent, though not tapped until he was nearly forty, was remarkable. He accepted the job and began to attend classes at night, but spending time with his family remained his first priority.

At seventeen, Jason graduated from Spring Harbor High School near the top of his class. Scholarship offers from prestigious universities flooded his mailbox. He decided to attend Morehouse College in Atlanta. He was far away from home, but he could have felt his family's love from an infinite distance.

In his senior year at Morehouse, Jason returned home for Christmas break. Although he loved living on his own in a new city, he always enjoyed coming back to Spring Harbor. It was great to see his parents and Brains (who insisted on being called by his actual name, Darren), and he especially enjoyed hanging out with his little brother, Nathan. Nathan had recently turned five, and he was a lively, smart kid with endless energy.

On Christmas Eve, Jason and Nathan were in Nathan's room playing a video game at which Nathan was somehow managing to destroy Jason. Jason did not understand how Nathan always beat him. Kids these days seemed to be born with a special gene that gave them prowess in all things electronic.

"You're sorry, Jay," Nathan said to him. "I always beat you. I always beat my friend, too. He's old like you."

"I guess I'm an old man," Jason said. "Who's your friend? My chances of beating him are probably better than my chances of beating you."

"I can't tell you his name," Nathan said. He grew unusually calm. "It's a secret."

"Come on, you can tell me. I'm your big brother. You can tell me anything, Nate."

Nathan shook his head. "Nope."

"Fine, keep it to yourself." Jason waved his hand dismissively. He was sure Nate was only making up stories. Kids his age would say anything to get a reaction from an older person.

"Oops, be right back," Nathan said. "I got to pee-pee." He jumped to his feet and scrambled toward the door. Jason playfully swatted him on his shoulder. Nathan made a face at him, and then he darted out of the room.

Jason smiled. He loved that kid. He reminded him so much of himself, but he had his own unique personality, too.

He picked up the joystick. He selected the option to begin a new game.

The screen turned black.

He frowned. He checked the placement of the disc in the game console. It fit snugly.

He looked at the TV, planning to check the connection. Something had appeared on the dark screen. Several words printed in red, in large block letters:

I LOVE PLAYING WITH YOUR BROTHER,
BUT I MISS YOU.
WANT TO PLAY AGAIN, JASON?

Enjoy this sample chapter from Brandon Massey's upcoming novel, *Dark Corner*, available in January 2004 wherever paperback books are sold.

In the Beginning

Although William Hunter had lived his entire life as a slave on a plantation in the Mississippi Delta, he had never experienced anything like the horror he was about to face.

His muscles ached. His hands were sore, and dark with gunpowder. Blood—not his own—soiled his ragged shirt and pants.

Killing was hard work.

But they weren't done yet. The worst was still ahead of them.

He was part of a group of four men. One was a black man, a slave from the same cotton fields on which William had once toiled; one was a young white man, their slave master's son; the last man was a warrior from a Chickasaw Indian tribe.

They were an unlikely team, drawn together to battle a

common enemy. Only an hour ago, there had been seven of them. Two had been killed; the other, unable to endure the terror, had run away.

"We don't have much time till dusk," William said, looking to the edge of the forest, where the orange-red sun steadily sank into the horizon. "We must finish what we've begun."

The men grunted. Their faces, sweaty and spattered with blood, were grim with resolve.

William knew that every one of them was as frightened as he was, but they were determined to conceal their anxiety. True courage was doing what you had to do—without giving in to fear.

Almost as one, they shifted to confront the cave. The ragged mouth was large enough to admit three men. Sharp stones jutted from the ridge of the maw, like teeth.

Like fangs, William thought. A shiver rattled down his spine.

The fading sunlight did not penetrate the thick blackness that lay beyond the entrance. Stepping inside the cavern would be like plunging into a deep Mississippi night.

He hoped that their weapons would be sufficient. He was armed with a rifle. The Indian warrior had arrows, the heads wrapped in kerosene-soaked cloth. The other black man gripped a shotgun, and the white man had a revolver—and a supply of dynamite powerful enough to shatter the cavern walls, if need be.

All of them carried whiskey bottles full of kerosene. A cotton rag dangled from each lip, a poor man's fuse.

They'd done the best they could with the wreckage they discovered at the ravaged plantation, the place that, only yesterday, had been his home.

William had fashioned a torch from a broken broom and a towel. He struck a match and lit the makeshift wick. The fire sputtered, then strengthened into a healthy flame.

He advanced to the front of the group. Holding the torch

aloft, he looked at each man.

They were brave men. He did not understand how he'd become their leader. He did not understand much of anything that had happened since his old life had ended last night. He walked on instinct—and faith.

"One day, our children will thank us for this," he said. "Let us pray that they never have to follow in our footsteps."

The men nodded and murmured their agreement.

William Hunter turned to face the cave's mouth. This close, the stench of death wafted from inside like a dense fog.

He whispered a prayer, for himself and his men.

Then, he led them into the darkness.

Homecoming

At sunrise on Friday, August 23, David Hunter drove away from his town house in Atlanta with a U-Haul trailer hitched to his Nissan Pathfinder. The trailer contained clothes, two computers, books, small pieces of furniture, and other assorted items that held sentimental or practical value. He had left behind everything else at the town house, which, in his absence, would be occupied by his younger sister and her roommate.

In the SUV, David had a road map, a thermos full of strong black coffee, a vinyl CD case full of hip-hop, R&B, gospel, and jazz discs, and his four-year-old German shepherd, King. King lay on the passenger seat, looking out the window as they rolled across the highway. David tended to drive with one hand resting on the canine's flank.

They made excellent time. Traveling Interstate 20 West, they swept through Georgia and entered Alabama within a couple of hours. It was a fine day for a road trip. The morning sunlight was golden, and the cloudless sky was a tranquil ocean blue. Traffic was light and flowed smoothly.

After three hours on the road, sixteen miles outside Tuscaloosa, Alabama, David pulled into a rest area. He kept King on a leash as they walked along the grassy sward of the designated pet walk, but the dog was well behaved and didn't wrestle against the leash or try to force David into a run. King handled his business near a tree with the solemn dignity that befitted his name.

David was returning to the truck, planning to let the dog inside so he could go back and use the rest room himself, when he saw the man.

He leaned against a white Cadillac DeVille. Slender and brown-skinned, perhaps in his mid-fifties, he wore a green shirt and tan slacks. He talked on a cell phone, checked his watch.

From a distance of about thirty feet, the man looked like David's father.

David stiffened and stopped. King, brought to a halt, looked at David questioningly.

Although the day was warm and humid, a chill fell over David.

As if sensing David's attention, the man turned. He met David's eyes briefly, then looked away, continuing to chat on the phone.

The man was not Richard Hunter, his father. Of course it wasn't him. His father had died five months ago.

David sighed, went to the SUV, and let King climb inside.

I need to stop this, David thought, as he walked to the rest area washrooms. *I'll never see my father again. I have to accept it.*

He used the rest room, then returned to the parking lot. The man who resembled his father was gone. Whoever he had been.

David got behind the wheel of the SUV.

His cell phone chirped.

"Hey, it's your mama. Where are you?"

It was just like his mother to call the moment after he experienced an episode of weirdness.

"Hey, Mom. I'm right outside Tuscaloosa, Alabama. I passed the big Mercedes-Benz plant a little while ago."

"You're driving too fast. You shouldn't be that far already."

Although David was twenty-nine years old and had traveled extensively throughout the country, by air and by car, Mom never hesitated to dole out travel tips and cautions.

"I've been cruising at seventy-five. Traffic has been light." He paused, then added: "I'm at a rest area. I just saw a man who looked like Dad."

"Oh," Mom said. A note of melancholy crept into her voice. "Remember how the same thing happened to both of us, when your granddad passed? For a while, it seemed that once a month we'd see a man who looked exactly like him."

"I remember. But I feel different about this. Because there's always a chance . . ."

"David, honey, it's not good for you to think about that. I know it's painful for you, but you need to try to let it go. Your father is gone."

David swallowed. A monarch butterfly landed on the windshield, its colorful wings gilded with sunlight. It seemed to peer inside the truck at David.

His mother was right. He had told himself the same thing, many times. His father, Richard Hunter, was dead, and gone forever. Any stranger who looked like him was just that—a stranger.

But the circumstances of his father's death stirred a naïve hope that he might be alive.

Richard Hunter had not been an ordinary man. He was a writer, not merely good but brilliant; a Pulitzer Prize winner who evoked favorable comparison to the revered literary lions in the canon of African-American literature: Ellison, Hurston, Wright, Morrison. Richard Hunter had lived an adventurous, colorful life that matched his literary accomplishments. After a brief, disastrous marriage to David's mother that produced only one child, Hunter moved to Paris to write his first novel, an immediate best-seller, and thereafter embarked on a series of journeys that took him from Morocco to China, from South Africa to Nepal, from Australia to Indonesia, from Brazil to Denmark . . . his father's travels could've filled a dozen issues of *National Geographic*. Writing and publishing one best-selling novel after another, publishing essays in the *New Yorker*, crafting stage plays that opened on Broadway, and penning the script of an Oscar award–winning film, Richard Hunter had the proverbial Midas touch in the literary world. But his ability to sustain meaningful, long-term relationships seemed to be directly inverse to his writing talent.

David hardly knew his father. Throughout his dad's endless globetrotting, it was a rare event to receive so much as a postcard from him, to say nothing of a birthday or Christmas gift. He called or wrote David every few years, and visited less often. Although Hunter married three more times, and entertained countless girlfriends and mistresses, he never had another child. Often, David had thought that being Hunter's only child would have meant something to his father, but their relationship never developed beyond a superficial, awkward friendliness. David had learned more about Richard Hunter by reading about him in magazines than he had through direct contact with his dad.

But in March of that year, his father had been on a boat in the Gulf of Mexico, deep-sea fishing, when a storm swept him off the deck and into the ocean. An extensive search by the coast guard failed to recover his body. At the coroner's inquest, he was declared legally dead.

Richard Hunter's will revealed that he had bequeathed his money, property, and belongings to David—the total value of which equaled over four million dollars.

David was suddenly rich, granted a fortune by a man who was a relative stranger to him.

Nagging questions circled David's thoughts. Why did his father ignore him for his entire life, and then will him everything he had owned? Had his father loved him, but been unable to express his feelings? What kind of man had Richard Hunter been, outside his literary exploits?

And the question that haunted David most of all: Was his father really dead? His body had never been recovered, which gave David a fragile hope that, somehow, his father had survived the accident. But if Richard Hunter had survived, then where was he? Why hadn't he resurfaced to reclaim his life?

It was hard to speculate about stuff like that. One bewildering question led to a slew of others even more puzzling.

"I hope you learn a lot about your dad while you're in Mississippi," Mom said. "Like I've told you before, I don't think you need to make this trip, but I know you won't be happy otherwise."

Although his father had been a world traveler, between his journeys, he always returned to his hometown: Mason's Corner, Mississippi. There, he lived in a modest house that had been in the Hunter family for generations. The home had been vacant since his father's death.

"Well, like I've said, I'll be there for a year," David said. "Maybe not that long. It depends on how things go, what I find out."

"What do you expect to find out, David?" Mom said. Mom had asked him the same question before, but there was a desperation in her voice that he hadn't heard previously. "It's a tiny town with three traffic lights. What do you think you're going to learn there?"

David turned the key in the ignition. The engine hummed to life.

"I don't know, Mom," David said. "Maybe . . . the truth."

* * *

At a quarter past three o'clock in the afternoon, driving north on Interstate 55, David passed a road sign that announced the upcoming exit for Mason's Corner.

Anticipation tingled in his gut.

It had been about fifteen years since he had visited Mississippi. He had purposefully taken a longer route to Mason's Corner, traveling Interstate 20 West into Jackson, at the center of the state, where he then connected with Interstate 55 North, which would take him up to the northwest region, at the edge of the delta. He wanted to absorb the sounds and sights, and immerse himself in this place where his father's family had lived for so long.

Mostly, the land was covered with verdant hills that appeared to stretch to the edge of the world. At other times, maple trees and pine trees crowded the highway, their trunks festooned with kudzu. In many of the open stretches, he saw vast fields of soybean and cotton.

It was easy to imagine that this had once been a land in which cotton plantations had sustained the economy. The earth was so fertile it seemed anything might thrive in the rich soil. North of Jackson, David had stopped to refuel, and the warm, humid air was like the inside of a greenhouse.

The exit ramp for Mason's Corner came into view. He turned onto the winding lane, and entered a tunnel of trees that blanketed the road in dense shadows. Then, the trees thinned out and gave way to a suspension bridge. A sunlight-spangled river rushed in the chasm below. Two black children stood along the sandy bank, working fishing poles.

The bridge, about forty feet long, rattled and clinked as he drove across it. King poked his nose out the half-open window. He whined.

David stroked the dog's neck. "We're almost there, boy. I know you're fed up with riding in here."

Ahead, a blue sign read in white letters: Welcome to Mason's Corner, the Jewel of Mississippi. Pop. 3,200.

The town limits were marked only by small, erratically spaced homes. Rusty cars sitting on concrete blocks filled front yards, and clotheslines heavy with garments snapped in the summer breeze. People—everyone David saw was black—sat on porches and lawn chairs. They watched him drive by, and he thought he could hear what they were thinking: "Who's that guy moving here?" This wasn't like Atlanta. In a small town like Mason's Corner, a new resident would be noteworthy.

The road, Main Street, cut through the center of downtown—though calling the tiny business district "downtown" was being generous. While he waited at a traffic light, he looked around. Faded storefronts lined the road: a diner, a clothing shop, a florist, a furniture store. Old black men sat in chairs in front of a barbershop, talking and watching anyone of interest—all of them looked his way, their gazes lingering over the trailer. A scattering of cars and trucks were parked diagonally along the curb; a lot of people owned pickup trucks.

The light switched to green. He rolled forward.

He spotted other buildings: a People's Bank branch office, an elementary school, a library, the police station, a Baptist church, a BP gas station, a barbecue joint, a pool hall with a Old Style beer sign in the window. Farther ahead, there was a large park that had basketball and tennis courts, a baseball diamond, a playground, benches, and a pond that sparkled like quicksilver.

Everywhere, when he passed people, they looked his way and appeared to take note of the trailer. He could only smile. "Welcome to Mississippi," he said to himself. King chuffed.

David consulted his directions. The family home was located on Hunter Drive, which was coming up. He made a right turn, and found himself in a peaceful neighborhood of mature, leafy elms and modest houses.

The place was half a block down, on the left. A black mailbox at the curb had the name "Hunter" written in fancy script.

He pulled into the asphalt driveway.

Sitting in the idling truck, David stared at his new home.

A sensation of unreality washed over him. He had really done it. He had left behind his life in Atlanta and moved here, to the land of his fathers.

"My new home," he whispered.

It was a two-story house, painted eggshell white, with clapboard siding and forest-green shutters. According to Earvin Williams, his father's estate attorney, the home was almost eighty years old and had been constructed by a team of men that included David's great-grandfather. The place looked as though it had been kept in good repair. It had a screened-in porch, a two-car garage, and a tool shed, too.

The lawn, however, badly needed to be mowed. Earvin had said that he'd hired someone to cut the grass, but that was a few weeks ago. The property had been undisturbed since his father's death. The lawyer had paid the utility bills, in the meantime, and promised David that he only needed to bring his belongings, and move right in. "There's no telling what you might find in there," Earvin had said. "You father lived the last few months of his life in that house, may his soul rest in peace."

That's perfect, David had thought. *Maybe I can figure out what Dad was doing before the accident. . . .*

King clawed the glass, jarring David out of his reverie.

"All right, boy, we're getting out." David cut the engine. "We're here."

King looked at him as if to say, *It's about time, man. You've kept me cooped up in this thing forever. Let me outta here!*

David opened his door, and King, normally patient, didn't wait for David to walk around and open the passenger door. The dog scrambled over the seats and leaped outside. He roved across the yard, sniffing.

"Don't run off," David said. He raised his arms and stretched.

At a brick home across the street, a woman who might have been his grandmother tended a bed of flowers. She waved at him. He returned the greeting.

He could get used to having friendly neighbors. At his town house community in Atlanta, he and his neighbors had rarely spoken to one another.

He had a lot of unloading and unpacking to do, but he'd take care of it later.

The screen door was unlocked, and opened silently.

Thick waves of humid air churned in the porch. Three lawn chairs stood inside, ranked beside one another. A copy of *The Chester County Ledger* lay on an end table, beside a glass ashtray filled with a cigar butt. His father had loved cigars.

David picked up the newspaper. It was dated March 9. Two days before his father had vanished.

A chill zapped through him, like an electric shock. He dropped the paper.

There was something eerie about touching an item that had been last handled by a dead man. But he would have to get used to it, if he was going to live in this house.

King bolted inside the porch. Tongue wagging, the dog bumped against David, eager to go inside. David opened the door.

The first thing that struck David was the smell: a stale odor hung within, as though the house had been sealed for years and not only for a few months. He found the thermostat in the entry hall, and switched on the fan. He'd open windows, too, as he encountered them, then turn on the air conditioner later.

King set off down the hallway, sniffing eagerly.

As he stood in the foyer, David had the distinct feeling that he had walked into a dream. Like a place in a dream, the house felt familiar, yet foreign. The last time he had visited, he was fourteen. He'd spent two weeks there during the summer, entertained by his two cousins (whose names escaped him) and, less often, by his father. He'd left convinced that it was the most boring place in the world—they had none of the cool stuff they had in Atlanta—and vowing that he'd never visit again, no matter how badly he wanted to spend time with his dad.

Funny how time could change a person's mind.

A staircase twisted up to the second floor. Four doorways were in the first-floor hall. David slowly walked past each room. The living room was the first room he passed, a spacious area full of overstuffed furniture, a grandfather clock, framed family photos, a television, a fireplace, and a rocking chair. Next was the dining room: a large oak table stood in the center, circled by matching oak chairs. On his right, a bathroom. A familiar slurping sound came from within.

"King!" He opened the door. The dog had its snout in the toilet, lapping up water.

"I'll get some water for you." David went through the doorway at the end of the hall, into the kitchen. He found a large bowl in a cabinet, filled it with tap water, and set it on the tile floor. King drank greedily.

The kitchen was basic: it had a gas range, Formica countertops, a pine dinette table. A Polaroid photo was pinned against the refrigerator with a magnet: his father, clad in fishing gear and standing on the deck of a boat, showing off his catch of the day, a large, gleaming bass.

Dad died on a fishing trip like that . . .

David's breath caught in his throat. He left the kitchen to explore the rest of the house.

On the second level, there were five rooms: master bedroom, a guest room, another bedroom, another bathroom, and an office. One look inside the office confirmed that this was where Richard Hunter had spent most of his time, because the other rooms lacked any distinctive mark of his personality.

Two large windows, veiled with half-open venetian blinds, admitted afternoon sunshine. Oak bookcases lined the walls; the shelves were packed with tomes—his father's works, and many others. A large oak desk stood along the far wall, a black leather chair in front.

From his research, David learned that his father had written at least three of his novels while sitting at this desk. An IBM Selectric typewriter sat in the middle of the desk, like a museum relic. His father composed his work only on typewriters, never on computers. A jar full of sharp pencils stood to the left of the typewriter, and a rubber coaster lay on the right, marred with a coffee stain. His father would drink coffee continuously as he hammered out his prose.

At David's town house in Atlanta, he had arranged his desk similarly: writing implements on the left, a coaster on the right, and a computer, instead of a typewriter, in the center.

He settled into the chair. He was the same height as his father, six-foot-one, and he found the angle of the chair and desk comfortable. Perhaps he would set up his own computer in this room, right here.

"This is where the great man worked," David said. His voice seemed loud, and he laughed, uneasily. The office was so quiet and still that he might have been sealed inside an airtight cell.

He noticed that a framed photograph lay on the corner of the desk, facedown. He picked it up. It was an old picture of

David, at maybe three years old, his mother, and his father. All of them had afros, and wide grins.

He was shocked to find that his father had kept this family photo close at hand. This gave him something new to think about. Had his father missed the family life he had once had?

He looked around. No additional clues jumped out at him—yet.

David yawned. He'd driven over nine hours and needed to take a nap. Thinking about this stuff was tiring him out.

Before leaving, he opened the blinds of the window nearest the desk, to see what kind of view the office provided. He saw a vista of rolling green hills, deep forests, and, perched on a hilltop in the distance, a sprawling antebellum mansion, a remnant of the old South.

Coldness tapped the base of his spine.

He didn't understand why looking at the house made him feel cold. He could not remember ever seeing the mansion, though surely it had been there when he'd visited the town as a teenager.

Someone should tear down that place, he thought, suddenly and irrationally. *It should be demolished—*

The door burst open, and David almost screamed.

It was only King. The dog dashed inside and leapt onto David, tail wagging.

"Okay, okay, I know, your bladder is full now and you need to pee." David stoked the dog's neck. "Come on, let's go outside."

David looked out the window one last time. The chill returned, skipping along his spine like an icy finger.

Hurriedly, he left and shut the door.

Outside, while King cavorted across the yard, David began to unload the trailer. Although he was exhausted, he worried that if he dared to sleep he would not wake until late in the evening. He didn't want to leave his possessions in the trailer overnight. He likely had no need to fear thieves in this town, but years of city living had made him cautious.

He had opened the trailer door and gripped a cardboard box full of books when the grandmotherly woman who had waved at him earlier walked across the street. She was accompanied by a tall, lean man who appeared to be her husband.

"Good afternoon," the man said. He had a crisp, deep voice. "Are you our new neighbor?"

"That I am." David placed the box on the ground. "My name is David Hunter."

"A pleasure to meet you," the man said. "My name is Franklin Bennett. This is my wife, Ruby."

David and Franklin shook hands. Franklin had a strong, dry grip. David immediately had a good feeling about him. One of the few things his father had taught him was how a trustworthy man will always have a firm handshake.

Franklin and Ruby looked to be in their mid-sixties. Ruby was dark-skinned and petite, with large, clear eyes. She wore jeans, tennis shoes, a United Negro College Fund T-shirt, and a cap that covered a full head of salt-and-pepper hair. Franklin was bespectacled and balding, with a trimmed gray beard. He wore a white dress shirt, slacks, and suspenders. He had a scholarly demeanor. David was willing to wager that he was a teacher.

King came over and snuffled the Bennetts' legs. David introduced the dog, and the couple smiled and petted King. They were obviously dog lovers.

"So you're a Hunter?" Franklin said. "Was Richard Hunter your . . ."

"He was my father," David said.

"We're so sorry to hear about what happened," Ruby said. "What an awful accident."

"Your father was a good man," Franklin said.

"Thank you," David said. "I moved here from Atlanta. Someone has to take care of the house for a while. It's been in our family for a long time."

"That is most certainly true," Franklin said. "Since nineteen twenty-seven, in fact."

"Really?" David said. "I didn't know that."

Franklin chuckled. "I'm a bit of a history buff, David. One of my long-standing hobbies has been exploring the history of our fine town."

"Don't get Professor Bennett started." Ruby grinned. "Will you be living here permanently, David?"

"Maybe for a year. After that, we'll see. I've never lived in a small town, so I'll see how I like it."

"It's a markedly slower pace of life than what you're likely accustomed to," Franklin said. "But we love it. We grew up here, moved away to Washington, D.C., to have our careers and raise our family, then decided to come back here for our retirement."

"What's the age range of the people here?" David said.

"It's not a town full of old folks, sugar," Ruby said. She chuckled. "We've got returned folks, like us, stable, working families, then some kids your age, and younger. We've got our share of young, pretty women, too. Are you single?"

"Ruby, don't pry—" Franklin started.

"It's no problem." David laughed. "I'm single."

"Keep your eyes peeled, then," Ruby said. She winked. David laughed again.

"We could talk your ears off all day," Franklin said. "But I see that you were in the process of unloading this trailer. Why don't I assist you?"

"Thanks, but that's okay. I don't have that much to take inside."

"Franklin only wants an excuse to keep asking you questions," Ruby said. "David, please let him help you, or else he'll talk me to sleep wondering about you."

Franklin scowled. "Woman, you do not know my mind at all." Then he laughed.

"Since you put it that way, I could use a hand." David smiled. These were the nicest people he had met in ages. Although he could have unloaded the trailer on his own, he was interested in continuing his discussion with Franklin. The old man claimed to be a history buff, and he might know a great deal about David's own family history as it related to the town.

Most of all, David wanted to ask him about his father.

They chatted as they conveyed boxes inside. David learned that Franklin really was a retired history professor. He had taught at Howard University for over thirty years. In his life as a retiree, he spent his time pursing his lifelong passion—history—and had become the town's official historian. The historian position had never been formally conferred upon him by town authorities—they didn't have an official post for such a person. It was official, Franklin said, because everyone, including the mayor, approached him whenever a question about history arose.

"Are you a writer, like your father was?" Franklin said as they hefted boxes full of books into the house. "You've got quite a few titles here."

"I'm an avid reader. Outside of English classes in college, the only writing I've ever done is in computer code. I worked as a programmer for a consulting firm before I started my Web design business two years ago."

"Ah, so you're an entrepreneur!" Franklin set down the box he'd been carrying beside the staircase. Sweat glistened on his face. He pulled out a handkerchief and blotted his skin dry.

"Listen, you don't have to help me with all of this moving," David said. "I can finish the rest on my own."

"Nonsense. I need the exercise. Don't be concerned, I won't have a heart attack on you."

It took half an hour for them to finish lugging everything inside. Ruby returned to bring them tall, icy glasses of lemonade. David sipped the lemonade gratefully; King looked at him with sad eyes, as if expecting him to share. "None for you," David said, and stuck out his tongue at the dog. King barked.

Exhausted, David and Franklin took seats at the dinette table in the kitchen. David thanked Franklin again for his assistance, and Franklin waved it off.

"The only physical exercise I pursue these days is riding my bicycle around town," Franklin said. "I'm happy to do some weight lifting."

David nodded. "You know, since you live across the street, I was wondering: Did you know my father?"

Franklin pursued his lips. "Interesting question. Although I was Richard's neighbor for seven years, and though he was often present during that time, I'd have to say that we were acquaintances, not genuine friends. This is the first time I've set foot within this house."

"So my dad wasn't very friendly."

"He was friendly, but he was a private man—rightly so considering his public persona. I think when he was here, in his home, he wanted to be left alone, to enjoy life like an ordinary man. He was famous here, understand. Tourists came from hundreds of miles away to drive by this house and gawk, or they hoped to spy him as he made one of his brooding walks throughout the town.

"That said, I don't think Richard had many friends in Mason's Corner. But of course, absolutely everyone knew him."

"I didn't," David said. When he realized what he'd blurted out, he blushed.

Franklin arched his eyebrows.

"I might as well tell you," David said. "My father and I didn't exactly have a good relationship. He was a stranger to me, to be honest." He swept his arm across the kitchen. "Then, when he passed, he gave it all to me. Everything he'd owned."

"Which perplexes you, and understandably so," Franklin said. He shook his head. "I'm sorry, David. Richard Hunter was an enigma to me. I don't pretend to understand his motivations."

"Neither do I, and that's why I'm here. I want to piece everything together—as much as I can, anyway. I won't be satisfied until I get some answers."

David was surprised by how openly he spoke to Franklin. He'd told his mother, and no one else, about his purpose for moving to Mason's Corner. His family and friends believed that he was there because he wanted a temporary break from Atlanta.

"I wish you Godspeed in your mission," Franklin said. "I suspect you'll find life in Dark Corner to be an enjoyable change of pace."

"Dark Corner?"

"The locals call the town Dark Corner. Do you think you know why?"

"I've no clue."

"Because the town is over ninety percent African-American, and has been for generations. Dark Corner was originally a slanderous name, actually—think of the derogatory term, 'darkie'—but over time, it acquired a certain charm and became part of the shared language of the residents. I suspect Edward Mason would be aghast if he were alive today to see what had become of his lovely corner of the South. The Negroes have taken over the plantation!" Franklin laughed.

David laughed, too. "Was Edward Mason the town founder?"

"Correct. Around eighteen forty-one, Mason established an immense cotton plantation here. Have you seen his estate, Jubilee?"

David thought about the mansion he had spotted from the window, upstairs. The place that had given him a chill.

"Is it one of those antebellum houses, with columns out front?"

"That's the one, you can't miss it. It's perched on a hill at the eastern edge of town, like a castle. Edward Mason liked to stand on the veranda of Jubilee and survey his cotton kingdom, and glorify in his achievements."

"Does anyone live there today?"

"Certainly not. Jubilee is reputed to be haunted. Townsfolk won't go near it."

David's hand was curled around the cold glass of lemonade; the iciness in the glass traveled up the length of his arm, and spread throughout his body.

"Haunted?" David said. "Are you serious?"

Franklin shrugged. "That is what the stories claim. I've never seen evidence of it myself, but then, like other townspeople, I avoid Jubilee, too. It has an aura about it that . . . well, it disturbs me, to be frank."

"I felt the same thing when I saw the house earlier. A chill."

"Trust your instincts," Franklin said. "I'm a man of reason and logic, but the more I learn, the more I realize that there is much in our world that resists easy classification."

"I don't plan to visit the place anytime soon," David said.

"Wise choice." Franklin nodded. "One of these evenings, you must join Ruby and me for dinner. I'll share some of the tales with you. There are many. Mason's Corner is a small town, yet claims a colorful history."

"I'd like that," David said. A yawn escaped him.

Franklin hastily pushed away from the table.

"You need your rest, you've had a long day," Franklin said. He retrieved the empty glasses. "We'll talk more soon. And you're welcome to come over anytime."

"Thank you again for your help." David accompanied Franklin to the door. Franklin crossed the street, a bounce in his step.

David smiled. What a guy. He had made his first friend in Mason's Corner.

But he'd had enough activity for one day. Tomorrow, he'd finish getting settled in and would begin exploring the town.

He dragged himself upstairs. In the master bedroom, King lay across the bed, snoring loudly.

"King, I think that's my spot."

The dog raised its head, groggy.

"On the floor, buddy," David said. "The rules haven't changed."

Groaning, King hopped onto the floor, and slumped on the rug.

David lay on the mattress and sank into a deep sleep.

"Now David seems like a nice young man," Ruby said to Franklin. She was in the kitchen preparing dinner. "He's a spitting image of his daddy, too."

"That's the first thing I noticed." Franklin put the empty glasses in the sink. "For a moment, I thought I was seeing a ghost."

"I hope you invited him to dinner."

"I extended a dinner invitation for the near future, but I'll wait a few days before I mention it to him again," he said, thinking of David's purpose for moving to Mason's Corner. The boy was on a mission to learn about his father, and Franklin didn't want to hound him, though he would like to spend more time in the Hunter house, exploring.

"He's a friendly kid, quite open, not at all like his father," ranklin said. "We'll be spending more time together, chatng."

"Don't you go digging through his family's possessions," uby said.

"The Hunters have lived in Dark Corner for generations. hey must have books, photos, relics—"

"Like I said, Professor Bennett. Respect the young man's rivacy."

"Am I that intrusive, my dear?"

She smiled, "Sugar, when you've got something you want find out, only God Himself can hold you back."

Franklin leaned against the counter. He stroked his chin.

"Ruby, as much as I've learned about this town, I feel as I'm missing something. I know all about Edward Mason nd his vile plantation; I know sordid tales about many of e families here; I could draw a timeline of every major in-dent that's occurred in this town over the past one hundred nd sixty years. But my intuition tells me that I am missing n integral piece of the puzzle. The Hunters always have een a private clan. I believe there's a reason why."

Ruby clucked her tongue. She opened the oven and checked e progress of the roast beef.

"I'm not befriending David only because I want to dis-over his family's secrets," he said. "You know me much bet-r than that. I genuinely enjoyed speaking with him and ope to develop a friendship. However, if I can discreetly ncover a few historical gems in the process, that would lease me immensely."

"You know how I feel about digging into people's busi-ess," Ruby said. "But I know your ways. You won't be satis-ed until you find the dirt."

"It's not dirt. It's only data."

She smiled. "What do the kids say these days? Whatever, an."

He kissed her on the cheek. "I'm going to feed the hound."

"Dinner will be ready in ten minutes," she said.

A large bag of Purina dog food stood near the back door. Franklin took the big scoop that lay on top of the bag and dug it inside, filling the cup with the brownish nuggets.

The dog waited for him at the foot of the steps. It was a mutt, a mix of a collie and another breed he couldn't place. He's discovered the hound rooting through the garbage one day, and he had adopted it as his own. He never brought the canine inside the house or threw a leash around its neck. He let the dog roam throughout the town as it wished. It came to him when it was hungry and wanted to be petted, normally at the same time every day.

He'd named the mutt Malcolm, because on the day he found the dog he'd been rereading the autobiography of the famous civil rights leader.

"Hey, how're you doing, Malcolm?" Franklin scratched the dog behind the ears. It whined in pleasure. He poured the food into the large bowl that rested at the base of the steps. He refilled the water bowl, too.

As he watched Malcolm eat, he considered what he and Ruby had discussed. He had been honest with his wife— after being married for over forty years, he'd learned that it was simply easier to be honest. He was convinced that the Hunter family possessed information that could deepen his knowledge of the town's historical background. After living across the street from the notoriously taciturn Richard Hunter for seven years, Franklin had almost given up hope of learning what secrets the Hunters might be guarding. But David— now he was a nice young man. And Franklin suspected that David did not know his family's history himself. The two of them could, if David allowed it, learn together. Indeed, he might very well be a great help to David.

Life in Dark Corner, normally predictable and quiet, was going to become a lot more interesting, very soon.